BRING
THE HEAT

G.A. AIKEN

ZEBRA BOOKS
KENSINGTON PUBLISHING CORP.
http://www.kensingtonbooks.com

ZEBRA BOOKS are published by

Kensington Publishing Corp.
119 West 40th Street
New York, NY 10018

All Kensington titles, imprints, and distributed lines are available at special quantity discounts for bulk purchases for sales promotion, premiums, fund-raising, educational, or institutional use.

Special book excerpts or customized printings can also be created to fit specific needs. For details, write or phone the office of the Kensington Sales Manager: Attn.: Sales Department. Kensington Publishing Corp., 119 West 40th Street, New York, NY 10018. Phone: 1-800-221-2647.

Zebra and the Z logo Reg. U.S. Pat. & TM Off.

First Printing: September 2017
ISBN-13: 978-1-4201-3163-5
ISBN-10: 1-4201-3163-X

eISBN-13: 978-1-4201-3164-2
eISBN-10: 1-4201-3164-8

10 9 8 7 6 5 4 3 2 1

Printed in the United States of America

"STOP TALKING."
HE PULLED THE BLANKET OFF HIS HEAD,
PUSHING HIS GOLD HAIR OFF HIS FACE.
"ARE YOU JUST USING ME FOR SEX?"

"At the moment, yes. It's the easiest way to work out anxiety."

"I just read a good book," he suggested.

"That's what Annwyl does." She glanced off. "And me dad." She shrugged, dismissing his suggestion. "I'm not much of a reader. I'd rather have someone tell me a story than make me read a book. With words."

Aidan's eyes crossed and he fell back onto his bedding.

"I don't know why you're mad." She felt the need to argue when all he wanted her to do was stop talking. "It was a valid question."

"It was a valid question for a camp whore."

"Now you're being a baby."

Aidan propped himself up on his elbows. "Do you really think so little of me?" he asked.

"I have no idea how to answer that."

"Thank you very much."

"No, no. I mean, I don't know what you're asking me. Do I think so little of you . . . how?"

"That I am just good for sex?"

"O . . . . ust for sex. You'. . . . ."

The Dragon Kin series from G.A. Aiken

Dragon Actually

About a Dragon

What a Dragon Should Know

Last Dragon Standing

The Dragon Who Loved Me

How to Drive a Dragon Crazy

Light My Fire

Dragon on Top (eBook novella)

Feel the Burn

Bring the Heat

Published by Kensington Publishing Corporation

Prologue

"Your son." It swept through him. Cold. Brutal. The rage that had made his name for him. The rage that allowed him not to care. About anyone. Anything. Growling now, he said again, "Your *son*."

Vateria, not quite the last of the House of Atia Flominia, wrapped her forearm around her offspring's body. For the first time ever, Gaius Lucius Domitus, the Rebel King, saw fear in his cousin's eyes. True, absolute fear. Because for once, she cared about something other than herself.

"You wouldn't dare," Vateria told him.

But this Gaius would dare. This Gaius, who remembered his sister, trapped with Vateria, *tortured* by Vateria, *would* dare many things to right that wrong.

Gaius raised his blade over his head, his entire body shaking, his gaze locked with his cousin's, enjoying the pain he knew this blow would cause her.

Even understanding that this was wrong, he knew nothing would stop him. Nothing.

Gaius yanked his forearms back a bit more to get the most power behind his attack when he heard Kachka Shestakova scream at him from above, "*Gaius, no!*"

He fought against her voice. Fought against how right it sounded.

"Do not! He is just child!"

"Vateria's child," he reminded her.

"Would this make your sister proud? Or are you finally becoming Thracius himself? Do not do this."

Gaius's will began to wane. Kachka was right. Harming a child to get at its mother? That's what his uncle not only would do but *had* done.

And now he was about to do the same.

Don't, Gaius.

Aggie—

Please don't.

He'd let his sister into his mind and hadn't even realized it. So, if he did this, she would do it, too. It would be her memory as well as his.

That he couldn't do. She had enough bad memories to last her a lifetime. He wouldn't add the guilt of this sin.

Gaius lowered his weapon and, gripping her offspring tight, Vateria reached back and opened a doorway. She was in it and gone in seconds.

Vateria rolled out of the mystical doorway she'd opened and gripped her eldest son against her chest. He might *look* human—and mostly was—but he was her son. Her true son. Part human. Part dragon. All hers.

And, for what felt like an eternity, she'd thought she'd lose him to that bastard cousin of hers. He was ready to do it, but his sister . . . weak as always. Vateria could hear the bitch's words in her head even though she only spoke to her twin. "Don't, Gaius. Please don't."

Pathetic. If the situation had been reversed, Vateria would have cut down any offspring of Gaius's without delay. And she would have laughed as his child died.

But, like his sister, he too was weak.

Still, Vateria had her son and that was all that mattered.

"Mother?"

"Am I hurting you?" she asked, slightly panicked. "Are you hurt?"

"No . . . I . . . Father."

Shit.

She hadn't shifted back to human before going through that doorway. She hadn't shifted back to Duchess Ageltrude Salebiri. The very human wife of Duke Salebiri. A pretense she had been keeping up for years.

Slowly she lifted her head and saw her human husband and his elite guard across the enormous Main Hall, staring at her.

In horror.

She carefully placed her son on the ground, but didn't push him away. He was old enough now, at eleven, to learn what his role would be one day. And what that role would entail.

Vateria moved until she was sitting back on her hind legs. Then she thought of the spell that would shift her to human. In an instant she was covered in flames that also engulfed her son, but those flames would never harm him. They were part of him. When the flame was gone and she was in her human form, she smiled at her husband.

"My dearest . . ."

"*Kill it!*" the head of his elite guards screamed out.

Swords were pulled and men charged.

Vateria raised her hand and, with the power of Chramnesind, the eyeless god, she tossed them back with a flick of her fingers.

Still staring at her husband, she said, "Call them off or I'll kill them all."

The duke gazed at her, their eyes locked.

His voice low, he growled, "In the name of our mighty god . . . kill that bitch."

The men got to their feet and charged her again. This time, she folded her arms over her chest and unleashed another gift from her loyal god.

Multiple tentacles snaked out from between her legs and out her back, shooting across the room and impaling the guards in their chests—near their hearts but not through them.

With a shove, she pinned their screaming bodies against the stone walls.

Shaking, filled with rage and loathing, Salebiri unsheathed his sword.

Vateria watched him, her son moving behind her. Hiding behind his mother. If she died, all her offspring would die, and she would not allow that.

But as Salebiri neared her, he suddenly froze midstep. His eyes widened in shock; his head fell back; his breath came out harsh.

She saw it, too. The spirit of their god moving through the human, filling him up, empowering him with His blessing.

Still shaking, Salebiri lowered his head and looked straight at her.

"Now do you understand, my husband?" she asked. "Now do you see?"

He dropped his sword and came to her, standing in front of her. He slid his hands into her hair, looked deep into her eyes.

"I understand everything . . . my wife."

She turned her head and kissed his hand. "He's never broken a promise to us. He'll give us everything we've ever wanted. Blood. Revenge. And the unrelenting suffering of others. We just need to be loyal to Him. To bow before Him. To promise Him our souls. Can you do that, my love? Can you love me? *All* of me?" she asked, letting one of her tentacles stroke the back of Salebiri's neck. "Love me and commit to me as you do our god?"

"I can. I do. I see now that you are His blessing to me. That our children . . . a blessing to *me*."

Vateria rested her hands on his hips and another tentacle stroked his cock through his chain mail leggings.

"That is all I ask, husband. All I need."

Salebiri glanced at his men still pinned to the wall, still screaming.

"What about them?" he snarled, seeing them now as betrayers. "They can't be trusted."

Vateria reached down to his sword belt and pulled the dagger from its sheath. She held it in front of her husband.

"Don't worry, my love. We'll find you loyal guards who see only what our god chooses to show them."

She leaned in, kissed him softly on the lips . . . and handed her son the blade.

Benedetto Salebiri took the blade from his mother and, as his parents watched with immense pride, began the process of gutting the entire squad of elite guards because he couldn't yet reach their throats.

While the men screamed in death and begged for mercy from a child, Vateria rubbed her nose against her husband's jaw and said, "We will bring that bitch and her vile offspring to their knees."

"I'll bring Annwyl's head to you myself," he promised, speaking of the human queen of the Southlands.

"Not Annwyl," Vateria replied with a quick head shake. "She is meaningless. A mad whore who will find her true destiny soon enough."

Salebiri gazed down at her, confused. "Then . . . who?"

She kissed his cheek, licked his chin. "I talk of Rhiannon,

my dear heart. The Dragon Queen. The only one that has ever mattered in all this."

She gave him a wide grin, knowing that now he truly understood everything she wanted and that she no longer had to pretend. That he saw her just as she was and he was loyal to her.

"We take down Rhiannon the White—and this *world* will be ours."

Chapter One

Seven winters later . . .

The broken spear caught her on her right side, knocking her off her war horse. She landed hard on the blood-soaked ground but allowed herself no time to get her breath back. She forced herself to her feet and quickly blocked the damaged spear with her armor-covered forearm.

She swung at her attacker with her free hand, her fist slamming into his chest, sending him flying back into the wave of soldiers coming toward her.

She reached over her shoulder and grabbed her halberd. A long poleax that she liked using because the head was made up of an ax, a spear, and a steel point. To her it was like three weapons in one.

Impaling the first man she saw, she jerked her weapon to the side, tossing her victim off and readying herself for the next attack.

They surrounded her and she took a quick moment to size them all up. She crouched a little lower, adjusted her stance a bit more . . . then she struck.

She slashed the tip of her weapon across several throats, lowered it, turned it slightly, and then thrust the tip into the sockets where some of the Zealots had eyes, but she pushed it in far enough to tear through skull and brain.

The remaining soldiers moved in, and she dragged her weapon closer, lengthened her stance, and anchored the end of the staff against the inseam of her foot. Turning it, she thrust up with the ax head and into the groin of one soldier, sending his bowels pouring onto the ground. She yanked the weapon out and used the ax head to cut legs off at the knees.

She felt a breeze, a change of energy around her, and quickly lifted the staff while lowering the head. She blocked the oncoming blade attack and twisted her weapon to disarm her attacker before slamming the staff end against his head and knocking him out.

She then swung the weapon up and over, letting the momentum turn her around to face those behind her.

She moved in time to avoid a blade aimed for her head and thrust her weapon at her attacker's inner thigh, piercing flesh and tearing open an artery. With a twist of her hands, she brought the weapon over her left forearm, jabbed it forward, and impaled the man next to her before he could strike. Did the same in the opposite direction and impaled a soldier on her right.

She blocked another attack from the front and brought the man down to the ground, holding him there with her foot against his throat while she used her halberd to dispatch the last two of those who'd attacked. Once they were dead, she impaled the man under her foot and finished off the one who'd just started to come around from his bash on the head.

Letting out a breath, Branwen the Awful, Captain of the First and Fifteenth Companies of the Dragon Queen's Armies and Colonel of the Ninety-Eighth Regiment of the Southland Armies, slammed the end of her halberd against the blood-soaked ground and took a moment to look over the carnage she'd caused on this mountainside.

Her troops were in the valley below fighting the ones they now just called the Zealots—those who were loyal unto death to the eyeless god, Chramnesind.

As she stood there, staring, she instinctively knew someone was coming up behind her. Turning only at the waist, Brannie brought the weapon up and through the head of the blood-soaked priest who stood behind her. As her weapon tore through the top of the priest's head, she had to jerk her body slightly to the left to avoid the spear that came through the back of the priest's head, almost skewering her in the process.

"Sorry!" Aidan the Divine called out. The gold dragon winced a bit when he realized how close his spear had come to impaling her. "Just trying to help."

That's what he always said. "Just trying to help!" He should have that branded on his bloody forehead.

"Yes, I know," Brannie replied. "But I didn't need your help."

"Everyone needs a little help now and again."

"Not me."

Yanking her weapon from the priest's head, Brannie secretly enjoyed the way blood splattered across that pretty face and right into those bright gold eyes.

Aidan said nothing as he attempted to wipe the blood away, but then he gave her that wide smile again, showing Brannie those annoying dimples. Or, as her uncle Addolgar called them, "Pits in the face."

Turning away, she took a step, but then heard, "Aren't you going to thank me?"

"No."

"Not even a thank-you kiss?"

She faced the gold dragon. Like her, he was in his human form, shoulder-length gold hair perpetually falling in front of his gold eyes and nearly blocking the sight of those sharp cheekbones. Brannie stepped close to him and put her fist under his nose. She didn't hit him, just held her chain mail–covered fist there and asked, "What about a thank-you punch to the face?"

"Is that my only option?"

She chuckled, even though she didn't want to. *Bastard.*

Branwen didn't know when it had happened or why, but somehow she'd become friends with Aidan the Divine. An actual royal from the House of Foulkes de chuid Fennah. A far cry from Brannie's low-born Cadwaladr Clan roots.

But for these past long years as they'd been fighting against the Zealots, they'd become close despite his royal hatching and her lack of one.

It amazed her even more that she liked him despite his affiliation with the Mì-runach. Dragons loyal only to the queen, the Mì-runach were nothing more than a hit squad who killed on command.

Brannie didn't have the luxury of running around, killing randomly, and only listening to the queen. As an officer and a dragoness, she had to think about all sorts of things before *and* after her troops got neck-deep in battle.

She didn't respect the Mì-runach, but she had come to—grudgingly—respect Aidan the Divine. And, over the years and in their own way, they'd become somewhat close.

Which was why she knew something was really wrong by the sudden look on Aidan's face, his eyes widening in panic. His mouth opened like he wanted to say something. And all of that meant only one thing—Aidan's idiot brethren were up to something again. Something that would only make her angry. Before Brannie could figure out what, though, she heard a distinctive noise. A noise she had better *not* be hearing.

Mouth open, Brannie spun around and glared up at the dragon oaf eating her horse!

Human body shaking, teeth gritting, Brannie felt her rarely unleashed rage explode.

"*What have you done?*" she bellowed.

Caswyn the Butcher, in his enormous dragon form, gazed down at her as he kept chewing. The front half of her beautiful, loyal horse hanging from his snout.

"Wha?" he mumbled around his meal.

Her human hands tightened on the staff of her weapon and she raised it. She slammed the end of the weapon against the ground and it grew to its full height for use when she was in her dragon form. She was so angry right now, her human form wasn't even overwhelmed by the now-enormous weapon. She simply pressed the tip of her halberd against a main artery in the dragon's neck.

Caswyn stopped chewing, eyes wide, her poor horse's front hooves still sticking out of his maw. Still twitching.

They were still twitching!

But before she could embed her weapon into the idiot's neck and end him for such an affront, Aidan jumped between them. Protecting his idiot friend and getting in her way!

"Perhaps we should think about this?" Aidan gently suggested, as was his way. The only Mì-runach she knew who tried to use reason rather than brute force.

"No," she snapped. "Move."

"You're not thinking this through."

"Get out of my way before I kill you both."

"He didn't mean it!"

"*I don't care! I will have his head!*"

"He was dying anyway," Caswyn mumbled around the hooves.

"It's just a bloody horse," Uther noted, his blood-covered human form coming at her from the opposite side.

But he stopped when the tip of Brannie's sword now pressed against the artery in his neck. She'd pulled it from her scabbard without making a sound and so quickly, the males had no time to react. As Branwen well knew, it was her speed that had always kept her alive.

Of course, at the moment, she really wasn't in danger. These dragons, no matter their form, would never hurt her. Not because they fought on the same side. Not because she outranked them, no matter which army she represented. Not even because she was faster and a better fighter than any of them. But because she was the "baby cousin" of Éibhear the Despicable. Their brother in arms. As brethren of the Mì-runach, they protected each other's kin as they would their own. So she knew that none of these males would ever harm a hair on her head, which only meant she could kill them quickly and leave their bleeding corpses to the wild animals of these mountains.

It seemed fair enough for what Caswyn had done, and for Uther sticking up for the idiot.

Of course, Éibhear wouldn't be happy, but what did he expect when he allowed his Mì-runach brethren to roam around free, doing stupid, *stupid* things?

"Could you both do me a favor?" Aidan asked his friends. "And stop talking?"

When neither male responded, Aidan faced Brannie, and opened his mouth to speak . . . but the sound of crunching that came from Caswyn as he slowly began to chew on her precious horse's hooves made him stop, his head dropping forward in silent defeat.

Talwyn, only daughter of Fearghus the Destroyer and Annwyl the Bloody, buried her ax into a brawny chest and forced her enemy to the ground. Once she had him there, she yanked her weapon out and slammed the blade into the man's head, ignoring the spray of blood that splashed across her face.

She turned and looked through the battle raging around her until she locked eyes with her twin brother.

"What did you say?"

"I said get Mum!"

"Why is she *my* responsibility?" Talwyn wanted to know before cutting off the leg of a man standing next to her.

"She's our *mother.*"

"Then why don't you do it?"

Her brother, covered in blood, looked away from the corpse he was trying to raise. "I'm busy."

"Busy *failing.* You can't raise human dead. Accept it!"

"It takes practice!"

"Oy! You two!" General Brastias—or, as Talwyn used to call him when she was a little girl, Uncle Bra-Bra— motioned to both of them. "One of you idiots get your mother. No one watches her back!"

"Does anyone *need* to watch her back?"

Brastias grabbed one of their enemies by the neck and bent him over at the waist. He buried his sword into the back of the man's exposed neck, killing him instantly. And not once did he take his disapproving gaze off Talwyn.

Always her! Why not Talan? How come her mother's care always fell to her?

She cut the throat of another soldier coming at her and quickly looked over and through the battling crowd, trying to find her oh-so-precious mother.

One would think the ruler of the entire Southland regions could take care of her bloody self.

But after all these years of war, somehow Talwyn had become the overseer of all things that involved Queen Annwyl of the Garbhán Isle. Or, as she was more commonly known, Annwyl the Bloody, the Mad Bitch of the Southlands.

Talwyn just called her "Mum." Mostly.

Finally spotting the queen, Talwyn saw that her mother

was doing what she still did best. Killing anything near her
that did not wear her colors.

The queen brought one sword down on her opponent,
cutting into him from the shoulder through the torso at an
angle, until he was in two pieces. She turned and slashed her
sword again, taking a head. Turned once more and slashed.
Turned and slashed. Over and over, cutting a swath through
the battling men.

Her mother wasn't like most queens. She didn't stay in
the safety of her castle and get information relayed to her
from messengers on horseback. No. Talwyn's mother was
always knee-deep in the muck and blood and body parts.
She hated her nickname, but the woman had truly earned it.

Talwyn sneered. What were her brother and uncle so
worried about? If there was one being in this world who
could take care of herself, it was Annwyl the Bloody.

She was about to tell the worried males just that when
her mother suddenly stood tall, ignoring the enemies at her
feet, begging to be finished off so that they could go to their
god as a martyr.

That was usually something Talwyn's mother took great
joy in providing to her enemies, and Talwyn didn't think
she'd ever seen her stop in the middle of a bloodbath.

So why was she stopping now?

Annwyl lifted her head, gaze scanning above the heads
of the soldiers battling before her. What was she searching
for? It wasn't prey. They were all around her.

"Mum?" Talwyn called out. "Mum!"

Her mother either didn't hear her or ignored her completely, something she was known to do when she was in
one of her rage-fits. But when that was happening, Annwyl
the Bloody was usually hacking at anything that moved. Not
standing and staring.

Annwyl's head cocked to the side. Did she hear something? What could she hear that Talwyn couldn't?

"Talan," she called to her brother. "Something's wrong."

Talan finally left his now-rotting corpse—once dead, the Zealots seemed to decay faster than most humans, an annoyance to the queen, who really enjoyed planting the heads of her enemies on her castle walls—and moved to his sister's side.

"What's she doing?" he asked, using magicks to send a small passel of Zealots flying in the opposite direction with a quick twitch of his hands.

"I have no idea." Talwyn went up on her toes to get a better look.

What disturbed Talwyn more than anything? That none of the Zealots were trying to kill her mother. None attacked. Suddenly Annwyl the Bloody was invisible to them. The woman they wanted dead more than anything else in this world for bringing forth what they called the Abominations—Talwyn and Talan, specifically—was the one woman they were suddenly not paying any attention to.

"We better get her."

Talwyn agreed and followed her brother, briefly pausing once or twice to hack at a few attackers with her short sword. But as they neared Annwyl, the queen's head twitched to one side . . . then another. Like Talwyn's dog. She almost laughed until her mother suddenly charged off.

Talwyn and Talan ran after her, no longer bothering to fight the soldiers coming at them. They just pushed them aside and kept running, trying to catch up with their fast-moving mother.

If this was anyone else, Talwyn would be less concerned. But their mother was known for her "bouts of rage," as their father put it. He was just being kind, though. Saying their mother had bouts of rage was like saying that a typhoon was a "little storm."

The twins also knew that their mother's rage could be coming from her frustration. She'd expected this war would have ended long ago. She'd had more legions, more supplies, and more seasoned generals and soldiers than the enemy. But Talwyn's father had tried to warn her. Fighting Zealots was different. And all of Salebiri's loyalist troops were Zealots. So loyal to their eyeless god that many of them had purposely had their eyes removed during some ceremony. Yet, even without eyes, the Zealots still fought amazingly well and did constant damage to Annwyl's troops.

Then, in the last year, the Zealots tried a new tactic. Scorched earth.

They'd been destroying the Southland territories, burning down farms, towns, even cities. They'd done even more damage than the dragons when, several centuries ago, the dragons and humans had an all-out war.

Apparently Salebiri's Zealots told the people whose land and lives they were destroying not to worry, "our god will replace all that you have lost once the whore is dead."

Annwyl being that whore, of course.

The name-calling didn't bother Annwyl as much as the suffering of her people. Knowing they'd lost their homes and livelihoods tore at the queen more than she could say, but she kept pushing forward.

Annwyl knew the gods well enough to know that the eyeless god would never hold true to his word. With or without their land, her people would never be safe under the rule of Chramnesind. So she fought on.

And, now, they were nearing the City of Levenez. The seat of power of Salebiri and his female.

Talwyn still wondered if Duke Roland Salebiri knew the true identity of his wife. The one he called Ageltrude, but that the rest of them knew as Vateria Domitus. A cousin to the Rebel King of the Quintilian Provinces and most hated bitch of the free world.

Salebiri had at least one son by Vateria, which meant he had his own "Abomination," offspring of one human parent and one dragon. But despite the duke's vow to destroy the Abominations, as far as any of them knew, the child still lived.

At least for now. Who knew what Annwyl would do once they took the city?

Although, these days, some of the soldiers were beginning to say, "*if* they took the city." And no matter how quick Talwyn was to correct them . . . she was starting to think the same thing.

Then again, her mother might be right. Take this city the Zealots were fighting so hard to protect, kill Salebiri and Vateria . . . and all this might end.

Talwyn and Talan stopped. When they'd briefly lost sight of their mother in the crush of bodies, Talwyn had thought about using her mind to call out to nearby kin, but nearly a year ago all dragons—even the Dragon Queen—had to stop doing that to communicate. They'd discovered that the Zealot priests had somehow been listening in, learning about battle plans and their movements. It was a pain in the ass, though. Communicating with kin like normal humans. With parchment and ink and messengers.

Thankfully Talwyn finally caught sight of her mother . . . staring into a well.

Talwyn glanced at her brother. "What the battle-fuck is she doing?"

"I have no idea. But we better get her anyway."

They easily batted away the few soldiers that attacked and were only a dozen or so feet from their mother when Talwyn watched in horror as a claw reached up from deep inside the well, caught Annwyl around the face, and yanked her in.

"*Mum!*" both Talwyn and Talan screamed before charging over. But seconds before Talwyn could dive headfirst into the well after her mother . . . both the well and their mother vanished.

* * *

Aidan the Divine had spent most of his life doing what he was doing right at this moment—protecting his friends from sure death.

No. Not during battles. They were mighty fighters and didn't need his help there. Instead, it seemed to be Aidan's job to protect his brethren when they were *not* in battle. When they were *not* facing the enemy. And who knew such a task would be so gods-damn hard?

He slowly faced Caswyn and glared up at the dragon while the idiot continued to chew on that damn horse's hooves. It seemed to take forever, with the tip of Brannie's intimidating weapon pressed against Caswyn's throat.

Although, honestly, the tension of the moment had little to do with the weapon and more to do with the She-dragon wielding it. Branwen the Awful had been trained to use every weapon that Aidan knew about. And she not only used them, she mastered them. Swords, axes, war hammers, spears, pikes, bows . . . the list went on.

Her skills had even managed to impress her unimpressible mother, the great dragon army general, Ghleanna the Decimator.

And now, Branwen the Awful coldly stared up at Caswyn while he continued to chew.

Black smoke curled from Brannie's human nostrils and Aidan feared he'd have to sacrifice himself to save his friends. Not that he wanted to, but it might be his only choice. . . .

Aidan finally looked away from the imminent death before him and down at the ground. Then he lifted his head and looked out over the battlefield below.

Annwyl the Bloody and Iseabail the Dangerous had combined the legions under their direct command to take on Duke Salebiri's Zealot army in the territories between the

Quintilian Provinces and Annaig Valley. And, not surprisingly considering their number, their side was winning. Moving forward steadily. Easily gaining ground.

But from this vantage point, halfway up the mountain-side, Aidan could tell that something was terribly wrong. He could *hear it*.

"Brannie."

"Forget it. They're both dead. It's the least my horse deserves."

"No, Brannie. Listen. Do you hear it?"

She did, her head tilting slightly. Their eyes met and Brannie immediately began to lower her weapons.

Realizing they didn't have much time, Aidan began, "We better—"

The ground jerked hard, all of them stumbling back, almost falling.

That's when the sound became clear. Coming out over the morning air. A song. A prayer.

No. Aidan quickly understood he was wrong. Not a prayer. A powerful spell.

The ground shook again, but this time the quake was so strong that none of them kept their footing as the very mountain they stood upon broke apart.

"Shift!" Brannie ordered seconds before she disappeared beneath the earth. The rest of them followed her into the blackness.

Devastated. Panicked. The twins ran into the main camp looking for help from those who could give it.

The queen was gone and, unless they got assistance from those with powerful magicks like their own, she would be gone forever.

Like him, Talan knew his sister was not considering the option that their mother could already be dead. She'd been dead once and they'd gotten her back. So a simple trap could never kill her.

That's what they believed. That's what they had to believe.

And, for once, it wasn't just their selfish royal needs that made their mother indispensable. The Southland people needed her. The troops needed her. Legions of soldiers who counted on the Mad Queen of Garbhán Isle to lead them into battle. If she was willing to risk all for her people and her land, then so were they. But without Annwyl?

Of course, the human troops would still fight, but would they be willing to give all? Talan didn't know and he wasn't going to think about it now.

In this moment, all he and his sister were concerned about was getting Annwyl the Bloody back. No matter whom they had to sacrifice.

As they entered the camp, Talwyn's war horse and battle dog joined her. She'd left them behind this morning because the red eyes of the horse and the horns on both animals upset the human soldiers. The fact that they were gifts from the Kyvich—warrior witches from the Ice Lands—meant nothing when watching a red-eyed horse eating human flesh after stomping a soldier into the ground.

Without having to say a word, the twins headed toward the same place. General Iseabail the Dangerous's tent. They'd start there and work their way out, bringing in their cousin Rhianwen and their aunt Morfyd. Strong witches who could help them—

Talwyn stopped first and Talan stopped beside her.

"What?"

"You don't hear it?" his sister asked.

"Hear what?"

Then he did.

A beautiful voice, soft notes, coasting through the crisp morning air. A powerful spell sung to a god. Talwyn's hands curled into fists, her body vibrating on the spot where she stood.

"Talwyn? What is it that?"

A screech exploded from Izzy's tent and they watched their cousin Rhianwen, another powerful Abomination like them, stumble out, her hands over her eyes, blood pouring through her fingers.

Talan caught his cousin in his arms.

"Make it stop!" Rhian begged. "Make it stop!"

Talwyn pressed her fingers against their cousin's forehead and Rhian passed out. A protection spell also surrounded her. Talan could feel it encasing her body like a thin sheet made of iron.

"Put her on my horse," Talwyn ordered and Talan set Rhian on the beast's back, allowing her to slump forward so that her head pressed against the animal's neck.

"Protect her, Aghi," she told her horse.

"There," Talan said, pointing out the spell caster.

A beautiful, eyeless woman on one of the high hills.

"I'll—" Talwyn began but then everything changed.

The ground beneath their feet moved and cracked, jerking them hard, startling the soldiers around them.

Talan knew then there was no time for plans and plots. They had to move.

"Pull back!" Talwyn yelled at the soldiers. "*Pull back now! Go!*"

The pair took off toward the hill, both of them now screaming for the soldiers to get out.

"Go! Don't look back! Just go! Run!"

Thankfully her mother had trained the legions to listen to Talan's and Talwyn's orders as if they were coming from Annwyl directly.

So the soldiers ran. They ran fast and hard. Many grabbed the reins of their horses and made a break for it, few willing to leave their loyal mounts behind.

As Talan ran by an archer, he grabbed the woman's bow and yanked the quiver from another's back. When he was close enough, he knelt, knocked his arrow, and released.

His aim was true, and the arrow flew up the hill with great power and speed and—broke into pieces before ever reaching the eyeless Zealot priestess.

Something protected her as something now protected Rhian.

Even worse, though, she wasn't alone. There were other priestesses, on other hills. They began to sing the spell with her. Their beautiful voices uniting.

The twins glanced at each other and, with a nod, moved.

Talwyn crouched and placed her hands flat against the ground. A spell tumbled from her lips, too fast for Talan to understand. While his twin did that, he caught sight of two knights attempting to mount their skittish horses, the poor animals terrified by everything going on around them.

Talan ran up to the soldiers, pulled out the short sword at his side, and cut the throats of both horses.

The animals immediately dropped, one landing on his rider.

"*What have you done?*" one of the knights bellowed.

Talan never answered. Instead, he watched in horror as two mountains in the distance crumbled like tiny hills of dirt built by a small child.

He faced the knight. "Go!" he ordered and dropped to his knees beside the carcasses. Talan placed his hands on the neck of each animal, closed his eyes, and let the darkness that lay beneath the land flow into his body until it reached his hands. He unleashed the power into the dead horses and, in a few seconds, watched them struggle to their hooves. Their eyes were blood red now and he could see the inside of their throats from where he'd cut them open.

Talan pointed at the priestess and ordered the horses, "Kill her!"

The dead animals took off running and Talan turned in time to see the power of his sister's spell spreading through the ground, up through the hill under the priestess's protection, and out of the green earth.

Talan's dead horses had also made their way up the hill and the magicks used to protect the priestess were unable to stop the living dead, as vines and limbs burst through the ground and wrapped themselves around the priestess's legs.

Her beautiful voice was cut off abruptly as the vines began to wrap her from toe to blind face. She tried to fight and started singing again. But the vines, once they had hold of her, began to pull her down. Down into the dark. While Talan's dead horses attacked her with their hooves, battering her around the head and shoulders.

The twins turned from her but they knew their work wasn't done. There were now at least five blind priestesses, singing their spell. And more mountains were falling. Mountains that had been there since before the dragons.

Talwyn and her brother stared at each other. Again, no words were spoken between them. They already knew what had to be done. Their mother's troops had to be saved. Everyone had to be moved to safer ground. Rhian had to be retrieved and healed.

So . . . what about their mother?

They moved away from each other, neither willing to discuss that. They just knew what they had to do. What Annwyl the Bloody would expect them to do, leaving the queen—if she was still alive—to fight her own, terrible battles.

Chapter Two

Annwyl would wake up briefly. Pass out. Wake up. Pass out. Again and again. When she was awake, she knew she was being dragged. But to where or why, she didn't know.

The fall hadn't killed her but she also didn't know why. Because it felt as if she'd fallen for hours. Days. Like she would never stop falling.

But, eventually, she'd landed and lost consciousness. Whenever she would wake up, though, she'd realize that she was being dragged. By something that smelled *awful*.

Finally she woke up and was able to stay awake, quickly noting that she was in some kind of dungeon or jail. Something had hold of her right foot and was still dragging her along the ground, not taking care to avoid any bumps or holes in their path.

She lifted her head to get a look at her captor and saw . . . a tail. A green-scaled tail with a spiked end.

Annwyl sat up a little more and realized that yes, she was being dragged through a dungeon by a walking lizard. A big, walking lizard.

Before she could really analyze that, the lizard stopped in front of metal bars. He opened the door set in the middle of the bars and threw Annwyl inside by her leg. Her body flew across the room and rammed into the far wall.

She managed to protect her head from the impact but the wind was still knocked out of her by the time she hit the ground.

It took her a bit to get her senses back and by then, the door to her cell had been slammed shut and locked. She struggled up until she was sitting on her ass and could study the beings staring at her through the bars.

There were five of them now. All walking lizards. There was something human about them, though. Like the fact they were all wearing leather kilts to hide their groins and several had on earrings and decorative necklaces.

They spoke to each other in low guttural sounds, their bright yellow eyes locked on her.

Annwyl decided to try and speak to them.

"Where am I? And who are you?"

One of them barked at her—literally—and she knew he was telling her to shut up, even though she didn't understand his words.

"Piss off then!" Annwyl snapped back.

A lizard wearing a necklace made of animal fangs and human teeth, stepped forward and opened its mouth.

A forked tongue like a snake's shot out. But unlike a snake's tongue, it managed to reach across the entire room and flick over a bare spot on Annwyl's elbow.

She cried out from the searing pain, cupping her wounded elbow with her other hand.

"Bastard!"

He flicked her again.

"Ow! Stop it!"

The other lizard-men laughed as their friend did it again—so Annwyl caught his tongue with both her hands, ignoring the burning pain in her fingers and the palms of her hands. And she pulled.

Eyes wide in panic, he slapped at his friends with his clawed hands and several grabbed hold of him to keep him away from the bars while the others took hold of his tongue, trying to get it back. One or two even used their own tongues to hit her in the face and neck, trying to get her to release him. But Annwyl was angry now. She didn't really feel pain when she was angry.

So she held on and kept pulling.

Together, the lizard-men dragged Annwyl across the cell floor, using their friend's poor tongue. But when Annwyl neared the door, she raised her legs and planted her feet against the metal bars. Secure, she began to wind the lizard's tongue around one arm like a lengthy rope. She wound and wound until he was pressed up on the other side of the bars.

The other lizard-men growled and barked and bared their fangs at her. She still didn't understand their words, but she sensed they were telling her to let their friend go.

She didn't.

Instead, Annwyl dropped her legs to the ground and, taking one big step back, turned and yanked. She let out a triumphant scream when she knew she'd torn the tongue from the bastard's snout.

Slowly she faced her shocked captors and told them, "I. Said. Stop. *That*." She tossed the insanely long tongue into a corner on the far side of the room. "Now you know I meant it."

Blood pouring from his snout, the tongueless lizard grabbed at the bars of the door and Annwyl met him on the other side.

While she screamed and he roared, they reached through the bars and battered each other with punches until the lizard-man's friends pried him away from her cell.

Annwyl, still caught up in her anger, continued to scream and reach through the bars for her prey. She was so lost in what she was doing, she had no idea how long she kept it up and no idea how long the lizard-men had been gone.

Finally, though, her anger left her. That's when she yelled, *"And if I don't get any food, I'm going to eat his tongue!"*

No one replied, so she released her grip on the bars and dropped back down. She hadn't even realized she'd been a good three or four feet off the ground, but that's how it was when her anger got the best of her. It wasn't her fault. It was *their* fault for making her so angry. Those lizard-people.

She would not take responsibility for any of this. Just like always.

Letting out a breath, she put her hands on her hips and took a quick look around to see if there was a way out of here. That's when she noticed the captive men in cells across from her.

Silently they gawked, mouths open.

Annwyl shrugged her shoulders. *"What?"* she barked and they all quickly turned away or disappeared into the darkness at the back of their cells.

"Yeah," she muttered, still annoyed and her rage *still* pulsing through her, "that's what I thought."

Chapter Three

Branwen pushed her claws through dirt and trees and rock until she finally felt the heat of the two suns against her scales.

Desperate to be free, she continued to fight her way out. Unwilling to give up. She was a Cadwaladr, she kept reminding herself. *We never give up!*

So she fought on until her forearms and head cleared the pile of rubble. She grabbed on to anything she could, her claws groping. She shook her head, trying to get the dirt out of her eyes.

She found something sturdy, using it to help her drag herself out.

Once she was free, Brannie dropped her head against her forearm and took in deep gulps of sweet air.

Not a lot frightened her. Not even death. But being buried alive? The torture of dark suffocation before death? *That* she was officially terrified of.

Something grabbed Brannie's forearm and she jerked back until she saw gold glinting in the light of the two suns.

"Aidan," she gasped, quickly realizing she'd forgotten all about him.

She gripped his claw with her own so that he knew he

wasn't alone. That someone was here for him. Then she pulled the rest of her body out of the dirt. She didn't stop, though, to appreciate the fresh air this time. Instead, she began digging. Using her claws and the tip of her tail, going deep until she saw the top of Aidan's head.

She dug farther until she could grip his shoulders. She pulled him up, while Aidan did his best to get out on his own. Probably panicking as much as she had when she'd realized how easily she could die right there.

Aidan's claws reached up and gripped her upper arms, holding them tight as Brannie gritted her fangs and heaved.

She dragged him halfway out, until they both dropped to the ground, panting hard.

"Gods," he gasped. "Thank you."

"I couldn't leave you there."

He shook his head, dirt flying from his gold hair. Then he abruptly froze.

"Caswyn and Uther."

Together they scrambled over what was left of the mountain, digging through broken, ancient trees, boulders, anything that was in their way, desperately looking for signs of Aidan's two Mì-runach brothers.

Brannie had just thought she'd felt something on the tips of her claws when she heard the rustling of trees nearby.

She stood and turned, quickly realizing she no longer had any of her weapons.

A small troop of men came out of the woods. Scouts. Zealots.

"Aidan," she said softly.

He wanted to search for his friends, and had no time to negotiate with these men so willing to die for their one god. Some of them were maimed in the name of their god, missing one eye or both.

With a quick intake of breath, Aidan unleashed his

flame. But when the fire had settled down, the men still stood. Alive and well and not turned to ash.

The one in front—he was only missing one eye—raised his hands into the air and looked up at the sky. "Thank you, mighty Chramnesind!"

He laughed hysterically. "You cannot harm us, dragons! Our god has given us His protection. Your fire means nothing to us!"

The land shook and trees swayed as a battered, limping Uther pushed his way into the clearing. He cradled a damaged forearm within his opposite claw and his poor leg dragged uselessly behind him. One side of his face and snout were bloody and his left eye was swollen shut. But he was alive.

"Another!" the Zealot cheered. "It does not matter! Even now our legion is near, marching toward this clearing. They will destroy all of you and your weak flame will not harm us! For we are the mighty, fighting for the one, true—"

The Zealot's rant ended when Aidan slammed his black claw down on the group of scouts. His flame might not be effective, but he was still a dragon.

The few who weren't instantly crushed by Aidan's claw tried to make a run for it, but Brannie swiped at them, sending them flying into nearby trees. Their backs and heads breaking against hard trunks.

"Humans," Aidan muttered in disgust while scraping the blood and gore from the bottom of his foot.

"They were right, though," Uther said. "There are at least two legions minutes away and they've got siege weapons."

Siege weapons that could take down dragons with ease.

"It looks like we'll die on the field of battle this day after all, my friends," Uther announced with great pride.

Brannie, in no mood for such ridiculous sentiment, glanced at Aidan so that he could clearly see her eyes before she focused on finding trapped Caswyn, still buried under the mountainous rubble.

Understanding that look on Brannie's face, Aidan quickly picked up the remains of the fallen Zealots and tossed them in a direction away from the legions heading their way. Then he moved to deal with Uther, knowing Brannie would have no patience for Uther's need to "die with honor."

"No, Uther," Aidan said, keeping his voice stern. "We will not be dying this day."

"We have no choice." Uther pointed. "They're right there. Cutting through the tree line. They'll be here in—"

"Get it out of your head, idiot. We didn't survive all this so we could die five minutes later at the hands of Zealots. So get your shit together and shift to human!"

"But—"

"Now! Or I swear by all that's unholy—"

"Got him!" Brannie cheered, and Aidan rushed to her side.

He crouched and saw the top of Caswyn's head. They dug their claws deep into the dirt and, together, dragged his unconscious—but breathing!—friend from what had almost become his untimely crypt.

Once they had him free, they laid him out and Aidan lightly slapped both sides of his face, attempting to wake Caswyn.

"Hurry," Brannie urged as she shifted to human and helped a slow-moving Uther deep into the trees.

"I'm trying." He lightly slapped Caswyn's face again. When that didn't work, he punched him hard. Like he often did when his friend was drunk.

Caswyn's eyes opened slightly.

"Can you shift to human, brother?"

Unable to speak, Caswyn closed his eyes and, after a moment, weak flames surrounded him. It took longer than usual but with some effort, Caswyn managed to shift to his human form.

Staying dragon—and praying none of the Zealots caught sight of him as they crossed a nearby hill—Aidan carried his friend to the line of trees and, once there, shifted to human as well.

He hoisted Caswyn onto his shoulders and rushed into the forest after Brannie.

He found her and Uther sitting safely by an enormous boulder and placed Caswyn next to Uther.

"Keep him quiet," he told Uther, since Caswyn was known for the occasional night terror when he was passed-out drunk. No use believing it would be any different now simply because he was unconscious for other reasons besides drink.

Aidan crept up beside Branwen and crouched near her. Together they peeked around the boulder as the Zealot legions came into sight. They marched toward the clearing, not too far from where Aidan and Brannie were hidden.

As they marched, several of the soldiers, most of them completely blind, began singing songs in praise of their eyeless god. They all seemed happy, but Aidan didn't understand how anyone could be happy living like that.

Not being blind—as many of them were—because blindness could happen to anyone and several of the Mì-runach had gained their legendary status when they continued to fight for their queen without the gift of eyesight. They merely learned to rely on their other senses. It was, as one of Aidan's early trainers had told him, "only a tragedy if you make it one."

So, no. It wasn't the blindness. It was giving your soul over to a being who merely fed off hatred and bigotry. In

Aidan's estimation, life was entirely too short to be that gods-damn miserable.

But the Zealots happily wallowed in their hatred, singing about the destruction of beings who'd had no say about being placed in this universe. The Abominations.

Rather an Abomination, Aidan thought, *than a Zealot puppet for an undeserving god mired in shit, dirt, and rage.*

As soon as the first regiment made it to the other side of the clearing, the soldiers began to set up camp.

"We need to get out of here," Branwen whispered. "I'll take Caswyn."

"He's still unconscious. I should take him."

"I need you to keep Uther quiet until we get far enough away. If I stay with Uther, I'll give him the death he's so eager for."

She was right, of course. An injured Mì-runach could be dangerous because they were more than willing to sacrifice themselves for others, which was all well and good, but they rarely did that sort of thing *quietly*. And stealth was the only advantage their small, weaponless group had at the moment.

Brannie went to Caswyn's side and, with amazing ease, lifted the dragon in human form onto her shoulders. Aidan knew from vast experience that even in his human form, Caswyn was no "easy carry," but Brannie made it appear effortless.

Maybe for her it was.

Aidan had seen the great General Ghleanna carry two dragons at a time off a battlefield and not even appear winded. Why should it be any different for the daughter of Ghleanna?

As soon as Aidan came to Uther's side, the dragon began to argue about how he needed no help. Aidan quickly slapped his hand over his friend's face. Uther's voice was known to carry when he was drunk or badly wounded.

"Do me a favor, old friend," Aidan whispered. "Keep your mouth shut."

Uther began to argue behind Aidan's hand.

"Unless you want Brannie the Awful to come back here and finish you off herself, you'll stop talking and do what I say."

The one eye not swollen shut widened. Getting put down like an old horse held no allure to Uther, so he put his arm around Aidan's shoulder and together they silently followed the others.

Morfyd the White pried her niece's blood-covered hands from her blood-covered face.

"Let me see, Rhian," she begged.

"It hurts," Rhian whispered.

"I know, love. I know," she soothed.

Morfyd pressed her niece's hands into her lap and gently washed the blood from Rhian's eyes while all around them was chaos.

Ancient mountains had crumbled this day, the land split apart. All because someone had taught Zealots spells so ancient and powerful, the casters didn't realize that even if the twins hadn't destroyed them, the power of those spells would have completely drained them. Leaving nothing but burnt-out husks.

Of course, the twins hadn't let that happen. Combining Talwyn's power over nature with Talan's dominion over death—even if he still had no power over human dead yet—had created a mighty force. The damage done would have been quicker, though, had Rhian been with them. But the spells cast had wounded her, and Morfyd was still trying to find out how much.

While she worked slowly, sensitive to her niece's fear, anarchy reigned. The panic of horses, the screams of soldiers, the angry growls and snarls of war dogs as they all tried to move to safety.

And the one thing that could get control of them all, that could calm the men, the horses, and the dogs, and unite what was left of the legions . . .

That one thing was gone.

Annwyl. Gone.

And no one had any idea what had happened to her or where she was.

The blood removed, Morfyd was still unclear on how bad the damage to her niece was.

"I need you to open your eyes, Rhian."

"I'm afraid."

"I know, love." So was Morfyd. But she'd never say that to Rhian. Since birth, her precious niece had been more sensitive than anyone else among their kin. Not weak. She would never be weak. No, she was sensitive. She felt more deeply, lived more heartily, loved with her entire being. But she could also break more easily and all that lovely goodness curdle. That was something none of them wanted. Not only because they all loved their sweet, loving Rhian, but because she was the only thing that balanced out the twins and their power. Without her, Morfyd could easily see her niece and nephew heading down a path from which they might never return.

"Open your eyes. Please."

Frowning deeply, on the verge of fresh tears, Rhian blinked and blinked, then finally lifted her lids fully. More blood dripped out but—thank the gods!—her eyes were still there.

Morfyd had been afraid those Zealot spells had somehow removed sweet Rhian's eyes.

Perhaps the Zealots had tried but couldn't get past the strength of her magicks. Or she might have simply been less affected by their spell than they'd anticipated. Rhian's power and training came mostly from her witch mother. The Nolwenn witches of the Desert Lands were as powerful as the Kyvich witches in the north. But her Nolwenn blood wasn't all Rhian possessed. She was the third-born Abomination and the blood of dragons flowed through her veins along with her mother's human blood. And nestled in that dragon's blood was the power of her grandmother, Rhiannon the White. Like Morfyd, a white She-dragon—and the most powerful of Dragonwitches among their kind.

Although Rhian had been born with the brown skin and hair of her Desert Land people, a shock of white on her scalp now fell down her back along with all that curly brown hair. It had developed over the last year and she kept it in a long braid so that it was almost lost among her mane of thick brown curls.

But it was there and Morfyd knew what that white hair meant. That Rhian's powers were only beginning to develop. At some point, she would outshine her cousins and, perhaps, Rhiannon herself.

But until then, until Rhian finally discovered the extent of the power buried deep inside, she would need more protection than the twins. And Morfyd had taken it upon herself to be that protection for now.

"Can you see, Rhian?"

She turned her head, violet, bloodshot eyes searching.

"Yes," she said on a deep sigh. "A little blurry, but I can see." She tried to wipe her eyes with her fists but Morfyd stopped her, pushing her hands back into her lap. "What happened?" she asked.

"An ancient spell. One long buried. Used to destroy this land."

"And Auntie Annwyl's legions?"

"Damaged but many survived because of the twins."

Rhian blinked, frowned again. "Uncle Brastias."

Morfyd dropped her gaze. She'd been afraid to think

of her mate. Afraid she'd break down and be of no use to anyone. But she wouldn't lie to Rhian, who would see through that with little effort.

"I don't know where he is, love. I can only hope—"

"I wasn't asking," Rhian said plainly. "Because I see him right there."

Still crouching, Morfyd spun and saw her mate standing among the troops. He was covered in dirt and blood and bruises, spouting off angry orders, lashing into anyone not moving fast enough or still too dazed by all that had happened to function, but he was alive.

Alive.

"I'm not dying," Rhian pointed out. "You can go to—"

Morfyd didn't bother to let her niece finish. She simply ran to Brastias and threw herself into his arms.

He hugged her tight. "I'm fine," he told her. "I'm fine. I'm just glad you are. I didn't know where you were, but I had to take care of the troops or—"

"It's all right." She reminded him, "I can take care of myself. I may not handle a sword like my cousins, but I'm still a Battle Witch."

Brastias's name was called; his officers needed his assistance. But she could feel that he didn't want to let her go, which was all she really needed to get her through the next few hours.

"Go," she said, forcing herself to pull away. "Go and know that I love you."

He still gripped her hand and kissed the back of it before finally releasing her.

When Morfyd returned to her niece, crouching in front of her, Rhian placed her hand on Morfyd's shoulder and leaned in.

"This is bad," she whispered, her eyes no longer bleeding, her sight perfectly clear.

"I know."

G.A. Aiken

"And Auntie Annwyl—"

"Yes." Morfyd cut Rhian off, not wanting the troops to hear about their queen until the chaos had calmed down and Brastias had better control of the situation.

"Auntie Morfyd . . . there's only one thing to do. You know that."

"We can't. They will hear."

"It's not like we have much of a choice."

Rhian, as always, was right.

Morfyd closed her eyes and, using her mind, she called out. *Mother . . .*

Chapter Four

Without wings or clothes and on their human feet, the small group made it several miles from their enemies. It was at times like this that Branwen wondered how humans did it. How did they go on, day to day, without wings, practically hobbled by their tiny feet? It wasn't that she had to use her wings all the time—it was knowing that she *could* that made all the difference.

But now, in order to avoid alerting any of the Zealots lurking in the trees—probably on the lookout for enemy dragons—they had to stay on the ground. They had to move silently. On their tiny human feet.

She wouldn't call all this hell, exactly, but it was close.

Thankfully Caswyn eventually woke up and was able to at least drag his feet along, his arm over Brannie's shoulders. She was grateful for that bit of help. After two, three hours, the big bastard had gotten heavy.

Five hours in, the enemy legions behind them, Brannie stopped.

"What are we doing?" Aidan asked, Uther limping not far behind. He'd quickly gotten fed up with being "made to feel weak!" But Aidan had kept close, helping when needed to keep his friend moving on their long, wingless journey.

"I think this is a good place to turn around and head back."

"Head back?" Aidan frowned. "Head back to where?"

"To our troops. To Izzy and Éibhear. To everyone."

"That does not sound like a good idea, Branwen."

Brannie focused on Aidan, her gaze narrowing. "You want to run away?"

"We already ran away. But if we're going back, I want to take a more logical course than the one that will lead us directly into the arms of our enemies."

"Which is what way?"

He took a moment to look around, examining the area, before pointing. "That way. We go down to—"

"That'll take us completely off course."

"If you'd let me finish . . ." When Brannie folded her arms over her chest and began tapping her foot, Aidan went on. "We go down that way through the next few towns. Then we turn back and follow *around* the Big Lakes of Rhionganedd. That will allow us to—"

"Lose *days,*" Brannie cut in. "Absolute days, if not more than a week. I won't do it. We'll go this way."

"No. We won't."

Brannie didn't know how it happened. How she and Aidan found themselves almost nose to nose, their anger palpable. Logically she knew they were both exhausted and feared greatly for their comrades. But that didn't seem to matter at the moment as the pair squared off against each other.

"We are not about to sacrifice ourselves on the altar of your guilt."

"*What the battle-fuck does that even mean?*" Brannie exploded.

"It means you need to stop blaming yourself for what happened. You had nothing to do with this."

"I never said—"

"And we're not about to run into a battle we can't possible win because you feel guilty!"

"I do not feel guilty!"

"Liar!"

"Oy!" Brannie thought she heard the sound coming from behind her, but chose to ignore it.

"Don't you dare call me a liar," Brannie warned.

Aidan leaned in even closer, their noses now touching, and snarled, "*Liar.*"

"*Oy!*"

Startled, the pair parted and looked at Uther, who may have been trying to insert himself into their conversation for quite some time.

"*What?*" Aidan barked.

Uther pointed with his good arm. "That."

Brannie looked down the opposite side of the road and watched four horses pulling a carriage, happily trotting along.

The animals began walking toward them until the horses reached them and stopped.

Brannie immediately began petting one. "They don't seem hurt," she noted. "Or frightened. Anyone in the carriage?"

Aidan opened the door of the elaborately designed vehicle and leaned in. "No. It's empty."

Brannie stepped away from the horse and walked past the carriage. She gazed down the road, trying to see if someone was running after the animals. But she saw no one and she didn't have the time to look.

An expensive carriage like this . . . "Is there blood?" she asked Aidan.

"No."

Brannie waited a bit longer, but when she still saw no one looking for the carriage, she announced, "We'll take the horses." But when she turned she saw that Aidan had already unhooked the horses and was handing the leather straps off to Uther and Caswyn so the horses could be easily led around.

When he handed her the straps of the horse she'd petted, he asked, "What?"

"I hadn't said yet that we were taking the horses."

"You just did."

"But you were already unhooking the horses from the carriage before I said anything."

"Because I knew you'd be logical about this."

"I hadn't given the order."

"Oh. I understand. You seem to think of me as someone who actually reports to you. I *don't*."

"You two," Caswyn gasped out as Uther somehow managed to help him mount one of the bigger horses. "Before you start again with all the arguing, think I can get a drink of water before I die a long and painful death?"

"No," Brannie immediately replied.

"Of course," Aidan said at the same time.

They glared at each other.

"Please," Caswyn practically begged. "I'm thirsty and I'm almost positive I'm bleeding internally."

Deciding that arguing with Aidan at this moment wouldn't be in anyone's best interest, Brannie easily mounted her un-saddled horse and wrapped the thick leather straps around her hands. She turned her horse and headed back from where the animal came from, assuming water would be that way if someone had been traveling from that direction. She didn't know this area well and didn't want to end up taking them to waterless territory.

After a solid fifteen minutes, Uther called a halt and pointed into the trees next to the road. "I hear running water. That way."

"Uther, stay with Caswyn. Aidan and I will bring water back for you."

Thinking the horses might need water too, she and Aidan

brought them along. Brannie dismounted and led the horses in carefully. As they moved, she realized how much sound the animals made even on this mossy ground and thought about finding material that they could wrap around the horses' hooves to silence them. The Daughters of the Steppes were known for doing that when they wanted to sneak up on an enemy, and Brannie was more than happy to try their tricks when necessary.

After a short walk, they reached what turned out to be a pond. What Uther had heard, though, was the small waterfall that fed it.

Brannie released the horses, assuming the animals would follow on their own, and went the last few steps to the pond. She dropped on her knees and scooped up the water with her hands. As she brought the clear liquid to her lips, she noticed that the horses not only didn't follow her, but they were backing up.

She was watching them, baffled, when she heard a familiar female voice suggest, "I wouldn't drink that if I were you."

Brannie quickly looked across the pond and with a gasp, quickly slapped Aidan's hands, knocking the water he'd just scooped up away from his mouth.

"Hey!" Aidan complained. "What was that for?"

Brannie pointed. "Her."

Aidan stared in confusion at Keita the Viper in her human form. Actually, her full name was Keita the Red Viper Dragon of Despair and Death, Princess of the House of Gwalchmai fab Gwyar, Second Born Daughter and Fourth Born Offspring of Queen Rhiannon and Bercelak the Great.

But most just called her Keita the Viper. It was easier.

She stood on the other side of the pond, looking beautiful and very royal in a purple silk gown covered in a darker purple cape, the hood pulled up so that it *almost* covered her long red hair, but not really. There was enough there to tantalize any dragon or man who might want to see more.

"I don't know why you are using that accusing tone, cousin. I don't appreciate it."

"What have you done?" Brannie demanded, standing tall.

"There it is again. Still don't like it."

"Answer me, Keita. What have you done?"

With a dramatic sigh—although Keita always seemed dramatic to Aidan—she lifted her skirts, turned, and flounced off.

With a growl, Brannie followed and Aidan went after both She-dragons.

He quickly caught up with Keita as she reached a small group of royals. She faced them and with a majestic wave of her hand announced, "I did this."

They were all dead. Every last one of them. After they'd had a drink of water from the nearby pond, he was guessing.

"Oh, Keita," Brannie sighed, shaking her head.

"What? What is that tone?"

"Why did you kill them? Are you just bored?"

"Of course I'm not!"

"If you're that bored, there's a whole battlefront you can go to where you can kill to your heart's desire."

"Oh stop, Branwen. I killed these people because they had to die."

"Because you were bored? Or do voices tell you things? *Evil* things?"

Keita rolled her eyes . . . again, dramatically.

"For the love of the gods," Keita sighed. "They were transporting gold that would then be shipped to Duke Salebiri so he could hire more troops."

"He hires troops?"

"They're not all Zealots, cousin. Anyway, I was traveling

with them, to see if my information was correct, and it was. So I poisoned the pond water and there you go."

"And there you go?" Brannie barked. "What if someone else drinks it? *We* almost drank it! We were going to give the water to Caswyn and Uther, too!"

"Who knew you idiots were roaming around here?"

"That's not the point."

"The poison I used has a very short lifespan and with the fresh water coming in from that waterfall, everything should be fine in a . . . week or two."

"*Week or two?*"

"I had to make sure they were dead."

Brannie briefly closed her eyes and Aidan winced. He knew she was getting angrier by the second.

Finally she asked, "Why aren't you safe back in Devenallt Mountain, cousin? Or, even better, with your bloody mate in the Northlands?"

Keita raised a finger. "First, I see I need to remind you, *again,* that I am unmarked by any male. I have no mate."

"You've had twelve of his offspring. Twelve! How can you *not* be Ragnar the Cunning's mate?"

"I don't have to explain myself to *you,* child."

"I am not a child anymore, Keita."

"Well, you never were," Aidan pointed out.

Brannie glared at him.

"Because you're *dragon,*" he explained, which got him one of Brannie's rare eye-crossings.

"You know . . ." Keita suddenly studied them both and Aidan was dragon enough to admit . . . that made him very nervous.

"We know what?" Brannie asked, also sounding a little terrified.

Keita's head tipped to the side and one long finger tapped the side of her mouth as she studied them.

And, for the first time ever, Aidan saw what Éibhear had

always said. "If you look closely, you realize Keita resembles my mother more than Morfyd ever could."

Aidan had dismissed Éibhear's statement, believing that Morfyd, with her white hair and crystal-blue eyes, was like a twin to the queen. But Éibhear had been right all along, hadn't he?

Aidan knew that now as he watched the princess coldly size them up like cattle she'd found at an open market.

"Plus you also have Uther and Caswyn with you?"

"They're wounded."

"I'm sure that can be fixed." She nodded. "This could work out perfectly," Keita announced. "Yes. Perfect. I can definitely use you all."

Aidan just bet she could.

"Use us for what?" Brannie asked.

"To help me—"

"No," Brannie stated quickly, with no room for argument. But Keita found room. She always found room.

"If you'd only listen—"

"No."

"It's import—"

"No."

Keita put her hands on her hips, her expression now truly annoyed. "I am a *princess*. I *order you,* Branwen the Awful."

And when Brannie bent over at the waist, her hands on her knees, her hysterical laughter ringing out over the entire forest—Aidan wasn't exactly surprised.

Then Brannie looked at him. She looked at him in that way she had.

And that's when he started laughing, too.

"Oh, thank you, Keita," Brannie stated with all honesty. She wiped tears from her eyes. "Poor Aidan and I had been sniping at each other the last hour or so, but you made us feel so much better. Didn't she, Aidan?"

He nodded since he was unable to reply verbally. What with the hysterical laughter and all.

"I'm *not* joking, Branwen. I'm ordering you *all* to accompany me on my journey."

"Stop! Stop!" Brannie begged, now leaning against Aidan's shoulder, unable to keep herself standing. "You're killing us!"

Keita's dark brown eyes narrowed on Brannie, but what did her ridiculous cousin expect? That she actually had any control of this situation? Yes. She was a princess. Yes. She was royal born. But during a war the only ones with true power over troops were the queen and those given military titles. Like Branwen. Like her mother. Like all her uncles and aunts. Not like Keita. Never Keita.

She loved her cousin, she really did, but she'd never taken her seriously. Not unless it involved juicy gossip about the family or other useless royals like herself.

Still . . . no point in hurting Keita's feelings—assuming she had any feelings—so Brannie choked back her laughter and reached over to slap Aidan's shoulder to get him to stop laughing as well.

"I'm sorry. I'm sorry." He stood tall, his laughter under control.

Until they made the mistake of locking eyes. Then they both burst out laughing once more, Brannie bending over at the waist, Aidan forced to lean against Brannie this time in order to continue standing.

"We're sorry, Keita," Brannie gasped out, seeing through her tears that her cousin had closed her eyes. She assumed in frustration. "It's just—"

"Finding amusement at my daughter's expense?" Brannie heard a voice ask. A voice she recognized better than her own.

Brannie wiped the tears from her eyes with the back of her hands, and she gawked at her Aunt Rhiannon, who was standing not too far from her. She was in her human form, completely naked, and eating plums from a nearby tree.

Plum trees? There were no plum trees in this forest.

"Auntie . . . Rhiannon?" Brannie shook her head, glanced around, confused. "How did you . . . ?"

Aidan was still laughing so she punched his shoulder and pointed. When he saw Rhiannon, the Mì-runach immediately dropped to one knee, head bowed.

Brannie fought her desire to sneer and roll her eyes. Her aunt wouldn't appreciate that one bit.

To avoid doing any of that, Brannie looked around again and now understood what was confusing her. They were no longer in the forest with the poisoned pond. They were somewhere else.

"My sacred space, dear," Rhiannon replied, even though Brannie hadn't asked the question. "Much easier than sending messages back and forth through Keita since she can never seem to get that right."

"I didn't do anything wrong," Keita complained while reaching for one of the plums hanging near her. She had one in her hand but her mother slapped it away.

"Mum!"

"My plums!" Rhiannon snarled before smiling sweetly at Brannie and Aidan. "Stand, my dear Aidan the Divine. Stand."

He did but, to Brannie's growing disgust, she immediately noticed he still didn't make eye contact with the queen.

Oy. The Mì-runach. They took their kowtowing to the queen *so* seriously.

"Now, my sweets, what is going on?"

Before Keita could answer, Brannie explained, "Your daughter's murdering people again."

"It wasn't murder, you peasant," Keita argued. "It was necessary action."

"That's what all murderers say."

Rhiannon held up her hand with a half-eaten plum in it. "Wait. Who are we talking about?"

"Duke Abernathy, his wife, his two eldest sons, and their guards," Keita blandly explained. As if she was talking about inviting them to some stuffy tea rather than confessing she'd just killed *all of them*.

"Oh, yes." Rhiannon shrugged. "Keita's right. They had to go. They were giving gold and supplies to that idiot Salebiri. You must know, Branwen, that Abernathy has never been a fan of our Annwyl."

"So his whole family had to die?"

"Yes," mother and daughter said simultaneously.

"And Annwyl's all right with that? Since they were human and under her reign."

Staring at Brannie coldly, Rhiannon's lips twisted to the side and, to her amazement, Brannie's view was suddenly blocked by Aidan's back.

"My queen," he said in his best soothing voice, "Branwen's been through much today and I'm sure—"

"I can talk for my—" Brannie began, but Aidan abruptly caught hold of her wrist and pulled her around until she was in front of him. Then he wrapped his arms around her as if he was hugging her from behind, except that his hand covered her mouth.

"—you can easily understand," he went on, "how she is feeling. We were buried under a mountain. Poor Uther and Caswyn are injured."

"My Mì-runach babies!" the queen gasped. "Perhaps I should go to them."

"Mum!" Keita snapped. "We have a problem here. *Now!* Your pets can wait."

"Can they travel?" Rhiannon asked Aidan.

"With a healer and a good night's sleep, I don't see why not."

"Take care of that, Keita."

"Mum—"

"Do as I say. You have a stop tonight anyway."

"Which is what I need them for."

"Then it should all work out, shouldn't it?" Rhiannon snapped.

Brannie finally yanked Aidan's hand away from her mouth. "I never said that I would—"

Now Aidan's forearm covered her face so that she could again *not* speak.

Bastard!

Aidan was having the hardest time keeping Brannie quiet. As human, they were nearly the same tall height, which made putting his arms around her easier, but also made her his equal in a fight. And she was fighting.

He didn't understand. Why didn't she see that he was simply trying to protect her from her own Cadwaladr stupidity? No matter who she was, whom she was related to, or what rank she held, at the end of the day . . . Rhiannon was queen and she had only so much patience with those who questioned her orders.

How could Brannie not see it? How could she not see how much power the queen wielded? Not just as queen but as a witch. They were standing in what Rhiannon called her "sacred space." A place with trees that had fresh fruit that could be eaten, one sun, and squirrels. There was one right there, climbing up a tree behind the queen. That was power. That was a She-dragon who could eat the world if she so chose. So what made Brannie think that she could get away with questioning Rhiannon's orders?

Brannie managed to pull away by slamming her foot

against his instep. Aidan stumbled back as she swung her arms wide to force him farther away.

"Get off! Get off! Get off!" she barked.

"He's merely protecting you, Branwen."

"Protecting me from what?"

Rhiannon smirked. "Me, silly girl."

"I take my orders from your generals, Your Majesty. And until I hear from one of them, I will be heading back to my troops." She turned to make a strong exit, but quickly realized they didn't know how to exit Rhiannon's world.

"You want orders?" Rhiannon asked.

"Actually, I want to get out of here."

"Then orders you shall have." Rhiannon raised her left hand and snapped her fingers.

Ghleanna the Decimator suddenly appeared. Wherever she'd been, she'd been leaning over. Perhaps at a desk. Probably going over battle plans. But the desk was no longer there and Ghleanna hit the ground hard.

She came up cursing. "*What the unholy fuck—?*" she bellowed, stopping short when she got to her feet, her eyes taking in the one sun above.

"Rhiannon," she growled, "I hate when you do this."

"Sorry, sister, but I need your assistance"—she swept her hand in Brannie's direction—"with her."

Ghleanna turned, her eyes widening at the sight of her daughter. "Branwen?"

"Hi, Mum."

Suddenly Ghleanna stalked over to Brannie and grabbed her in a long hug.

"Uh . . . Mum?"

"We thought you were dead, Branwen," Rhiannon explained.

Brannie blinked in surprise, her gaze flicking to Aidan's over her mother's shoulder. Then her arms were right around her mother, the pair hugging like they hadn't seen each other in a century rather than a few months.

"I'm fine, Mum. Really."

"What happened?" Ghleanna asked.

"Mountain went down."

The general pulled back and gawked at her daughter. "The *mountain* went down?"

"Yeah. Mountain went down."

"How is that even possible?" Ghleanna asked the queen.

Fearghus landed hard, Briec and Gwenvael right behind him. Taking a few more tentative steps, he leaned over and studied the long, wide schism that had opened up in what had once been the most recent battlefield of this war.

"What the battle-fuck *is* this?" Briec asked, leaning over Fearghus's shoulder.

Without an answer for his brother, Fearghus instead examined the area. "Weren't there mountains? Like . . . lots of mountains. All around here?"

"Aye. There *were*."

Fearghus had been leading his troops here to attack from the skies when the very air around him turned violent, tossing him and the troops around for several seconds before they were able to right themselves again and proceed. He'd decided to keep his troops back until he investigated what the hell had happened. He still didn't know, but he was sure that whatever had happened was not good. For anyone.

Gwenvael pushed past his brothers and leaned far over the pit to stare into the blackness. "Do you think they all fell down there?" he asked.

Briec glanced at Fearghus.

"Maybe you should find out," Fearghus suggested, seconds before Briec shoved their younger brother in.

They ignored the screaming as Fearghus told Briec, "Let's find the children."

"They took out all the mountains in that region," Rhiannon explained, her hands clasped together. "They used spells centuries old. From before even my mother's time."

"Destroying eons of work by gods and dragons." Ghleanna shook her head. "Bastards."

"Now my dragons have nowhere to safely hide from man or enemy. All in that region will be trapped out in the open."

"So we're pulling out?" Brannie asked, her rage seemingly gone now that her mother was here.

Aidan was relieved. He wasn't sure that Brannie knew Rhiannon as well as she thought she did. She saw her as an aunt, but the queen didn't let the love she had for her mate's kin get in the way of her reign. Brannie hadn't seen that side of her "dear auntie Rhiannon."

Glances passed between Rhiannon and Ghleanna at Brannie's question.

"What?" Brannie asked.

"We've pulled back, but we're not pulling out," Ghleanna told her daughter. "Instead, we're planning a full strike— led by your uncle Bercelak."

Aidan immediately turned to the queen. "Lord Bercelak is leaving your side?"

"I want this done, Aidan. They've been destroying my lands, now our mountains. Burning the forests, salting the earth. And next they'll go for our water supplies. We can no longer afford to go back and forth with them. Another year of this and we'll have nothing left for all of you to come home to."

"At this moment," Ghleanna explained, "King Gaius is using his legions to push Salebiri's troops back to their soil.

Then we close ranks around them—and crush them. Once we're done there, we take out Salebiri at his home front, leaving nothing behind."

Brannie nodded at her mother's words. "Good." She glanced at Aidan and said, "We need to get back and—"

"No," Ghleanna cut in. She jerked her thumb at a surprisingly quiet Keita. "You go with your cousin."

Brannie reared back as if she'd been slapped.

"I'll do no such thing."

Black eyes locked on black eyes. "You'll do as I order you to."

"No. Not on this. I will not risk *my* troops—Mum! *Ow! Stop it!*"

Aidan cringed watching Ghleanna the Decimator grab her daughter by the hair and walk off with her.

"Excuse us a minute," she growled at Rhiannon.

"Take your time."

Once the two She-dragons were a bit away from them for privacy, Rhiannon smirked at Aidan and asked, "Do you plan to disobey any orders, dearest Aidan?"

"Who? Me?" He snorted. "I like my hair just where it is, my queen. On my head."

"It does look lovely there."

He smiled. "Doesn't it?"

Brannie tried to pull away from her mother without hurting her, but Ghleanna gripped her the same way she used to when she had to separate Brannie from her brother Celyn.

"Mum!" she barked again. "Let me go!"

Her mother abruptly released her, sending Brannie back-first into the trunk of a very large oak.

"What do you think you're doing?" her mother demanded.

"What am *I* doing? Trying not to get in a brawl with me own mum. That's what!"

"When you're given an order—"

"But, Mum—"

Her mother held up one blunt, angry finger. And it was *so* angry.

"When you're given an order by a *superior*," she said again, "you bloody well follow it."

"Even when I know it's wrong? Even when I know it's a waste of my bloody time?"

"Who are you to say it's wrong?"

"You want me to follow *Keita*. I love my cousin, but—"

"Ren has disappeared."

"Ren? Ren who?" Ghleanna raised a brow, and Brannie guessed, "Ren of the Chosen?"

Ren of the Chosen was the youngest offspring of Empress Xinyi, the dragon ruler of the Eastland Empires far across the seas. When he was much younger, he'd been sent to Devenallt Mountain by his then-ruling father. From what Brannie had heard, no one had known what to expect from any Eastland royal, much less one related by direct bloodline to the Chosen Dynasty.

But Ren had surprised everyone by fitting in. Not only with the royals, but even the Cadwaladrs. Bercelak had nothing but good things to say about him, and Brannie's uncle had nothing good to say about anyone.

It was Keita, though, who became Ren's closest ally, the pair heading off on their own adventures when they'd become old enough.

And their friendship over all these years had never waned.

"I'm sorry for Keita, Mum, but . . . so?"

"He was heading back to the Eastlands to see if the Empress would join us in our fight against the Zealots."

Brannie let out a frustrated breath. "Well . . . again, that's unfortunate, but—"

"And somewhere between Annwyl's castle and the Port Cities Ren vanished. An event that has put us in a very bad situation."

"Why?"

"Because Ren was under *our* protection when he vanished and has been since the day he'd stepped on our territories."

"What did his guards say?"

"They're dead."

"Oh." Brannie glanced off. "Well . . . that's not good."

Talwyn saw her father land in the midst of the chaos as their troops worked to get their new camp set up. And by the time she'd pushed past all those in the way, her father was in his human form and had on his leggings and boots.

She ran into her father's open arms.

"Daddy!"

He lifted her off the ground and hugged her tight. "Are you all right?"

"I'm fine."

"Of course she is. She's pure evil."

Talwyn smiled. "Good to see you too, Uncle Briec."

"Demon offspring," Briec greeted back. "Now where is my perfect daughter? You kept her safe, didn't you?"

"She's fine." Talwyn tapped her father's shoulders and he placed her back on the ground. "She didn't react well, though, when the spells began to fly."

"What do you mean?"

"She started bleeding from the eyes, but—"

"*My baby!*" Briec barked, tearing off into the camp.

Talwyn shrugged and focused on her father. "She'll live." She glanced around. "Where's Uncle Gwenvael?"

"I'm sure he's fine," her father said dismissively.

"Why are you here, Daddy?" Talwyn asked, not in the mood to delve further about the missing Gwenvael.

"These recent attacks have changed our plans. Even before this nightmare . . . the queen had a new move."

Talwyn cringed. "That sounds ominous, Da."

"When it involves your grandmother—it usually is."

"We need Ren found."

"And if he's dead or if we can't find him?" Brannie asked her mother. "What then?"

"Then you accompany Keita to the Eastlands and protect her while she kills the Empress and most likely all of Ren's siblings."

Brannie's eyes grew wide as her mother tried to walk off. She grabbed her arm and yanked the She-dragon back.

"Have you two lost your minds?"

"If that dragoness thinks we're responsible for the death of her son, she'll call for war anyway. And that we can't afford. A new emperor may be more reasonable."

Ghleanna tried to walk away once more but Brannie still had hold of her and yanked her back.

"I'm not going to allow Keita the Viper to kill an entire ruling family. There has to be something else we can do."

"Do *you* plan to negotiate with royals?"

"That's not really my strength, Mum."

"All right then."

"But Keita can negotiate with anyone. Between her smile and her cock-sucking skills, it shouldn't be a problem."

"She has a mate now, so she doesn't do that sort of thing anymore. Except to him, I'm assuming. But if you think the Empress can be stopped from either joining Salebiri or just destroying us for the fun of it, then I strongly suggest you go with Keita. Because her plan is to wipe out the entire family, if necessary. And although she may never raise a sword or have her own battle cry . . . if she wants them dead, she'll make sure they're dead. Unless *you* can convince her otherwise."

"This isn't fair, Mum."

"You didn't want to listen to orders—from your queen, no less—but now you have one of your precious *moral* obligations to motivate you. That should make you feel better."

"It doesn't."

"Too bad. As I've told you since hatching, Branwen . . . life's rough for a Cadwaladr."

"Daddy always said life doesn't have to be that rough."

"Your daddy lied."

"*Mum!*"

"So what do you think, dear Aidan?" the queen asked about her sacred space, arms spread wide, her grin wider.

"It's lovely, my lady. Very relaxing."

"That's what I wanted. A place I can come simply to relax. To think, to strategize without all the distractions I have to deal with in my court."

"It seems perfect."

"It *is* perfect," she said, squeezing Aidan's forearm. "Perfect and private. It's the only place I can go and be assured the Zealot clergy can't listen in or even hope to invade my sanctuary." Arms raised again, the queen slowly turned. She was just so proud! Aidan couldn't help but smile along with her.

"Only those I've chosen may come here, dear Aidan. And you are one of the . . . one of . . ."

Now scowling, the queen's words trailed off, her angry crystal-blue eyes locked on what now walked toward them.

Her name was Brigida the Most Foul. It was once just Brigida the Foul, but the royal twins had renamed her some time ago and it had stuck.

The ancient She-dragon—who many felt should have died long ago merely from old age—was a Cadwaladr and, like Rhiannon, one of the rare white Dragonwitches.

She wore dark gray robes, the hood pulled onto her head but not quite covering her face. And that face! Aidan knew that old age was hard on everyone, but Brigida had clearly given up much more than most to maintain her life in this world and the mighty powers she possessed.

There were scars on top of scars on her face and neck. Even some gouges. What, exactly, had the dragoness fought in her search for power?

And then there were her eyes. One was a bright blue, seemingly untouched by age. But the other . . . a milky white and gray that seemed to possess a life of its own.

As Brigida limped past them, her walking staff slamming into the ground again and again as she moved, her blue eye stayed focused right in front of her, locked on exactly where she was headed. But the other eye . . . that one moved to each of them. Examining every being in Rhiannon's sacred space.

Studying each—it seemed—for risk and threat. Were any a danger to her? And, if not, did they have a soul worth taking?

At least that's how Aidan felt when that eye swiveled his way.

"Don't mind me," Brigida announced as she walked past a livid Rhiannon. "I needed to get somewhere fast, is all, and this was the quickest way."

The queen suddenly jumped as Brigida passed behind her; blue eyes growing impossibly wide, she looked stunned, and he realized that Brigida had pinched Rhiannon's ass.

"Good day to you all!" the old witch called out before opening another mystical doorway and disappearing through it.

"Locked up like a right fort, Mum," Keita ruthlessly teased. Not even her mother's glower stopped her from giggling in the angry She-dragon's face.

"I should have smothered you at hatching," the queen lashed back at her youngest daughter.

That's when Aidan decided it was time to check on Branwen and her mother. Anything was better than getting caught in a fight between two royal females.

But before Aidan could make his escape, Keita was standing in front of him, blocking his way.

Flipping back her red hair, Keita sized him up like a side of meat, and nodded. "You'll do."

"I'll do for what?"

"Aye," the queen echoed. "He'll do for what?"

"I need a bit of a favor, Mì-runach."

"I don't do favors."

"Fine. It's an order then. I need you to fuck my cousin."

Aidan gawked at the princess for a moment before turning to his queen. That's when they both laughed, and Rhiannon put her hand on Aidan's shoulder.

"What's so funny?" Keita snapped.

"Hard to say," the queen replied. "There's so much to choose from!"

"First off," Aidan explained, "I don't take orders from you. Only my queen. And second, it's funny that you'd think I'd put my friendship with Branwen the Awful in jeopardy for *you.*"

"Don't make me poison your food, Mì-runach."

"You will do no such thing!" the queen warned. "You will not harm a hair on his golden, perfect head.

"Besides," the queen went on, "why would you want

someone—anyone—to do such a horrible thing to your own cousin?"

"I expect him to make it good for her!" As if that excused everything. "But I need her distracted." Keita stepped closer to them, glancing back to make sure Brannie and Ghleanna were still caught up in their own conversation. "You know how Brannie is with her ridiculous moral ground."

Aidan couldn't help but roll his eyes. "Aye, such evil."

"Shut up," the princess growled at him, before returning her focus to her mother. "I'm merely trying to keep Brannie from getting in my way."

"Then figure out another way," the queen told Keita. "I will not have my dear Aidan's heart broken because you can't find another non-sexual or non-poisonous way to distract your cousin."

Aidan blinked. "My heart?"

The queen patted his shoulder. "I'm saving you." She leaned in and whispered, "She's just like her mother, our Brannie is, and I don't think you'd enjoy being one of many."

"Wait . . . what?"

But before the queen could say more, Ghleanna returned with a clearly despondent but resigned Branwen behind her.

"It's settled," the general informed the queen.

"Good." The queen stepped close to her niece. She raised her hand and gently pushed strands of black hair behind Brannie's ear. "What you're doing is more important than you realize, Branwen. And greatly appreciated."

Brannie nodded, her gaze down. "We'll take care of it"— Brannie lifted her head, dark eyes locking with Rhiannon's— "my *queen*."

Without another word, she walked off. But where she might be going, Aidan didn't know. The queen still had to release them.

Brannie seemed to realize that after a minute. She stopped, swung her arm wildly at the air, and bellowed, *"Would some-one mind letting me the battle-fuck out of here?"*

The queen leaned over and loudly whispered, "She's also moody like her mother. . . ."

Chapter Five

"Why isn't Uncle Gwenvael back yet?" Talwyn asked her father.

"He'll be along."

She didn't trust her father's glib reply but she was just so glad to see him, she decided not to argue. Instead she hugged him again and desperately attempted to ignore the ridiculous drama going on several feet from her.

"Oh, Daddy!" Rhi cried. "It was horrible! Horrible!"

"My poor, perfect, *perfect* daughter!" Uncle Briec glared over Rhi's shoulder at Talwyn. "I thought I told you to protect my perfect offspring, demon child!"

"She's breathing, isn't she?" Talwyn told him, one eyebrow purposely raised to antagonize him. Because, honestly, was all this necessary?

Had her cousin been through a lot? Yes. Of course. Talwyn would never deny that. But she was still alive and breathing so all the sobbing and accusations were more than Talwyn would ever be willing to tolerate.

"Of course," she felt the need to add, "if you want your perfect, *perfect* daughter not to suffer, I can always put a pillow over her head when she's asleep. And all her troubles will be gone"—she snapped her fingers—"like that."

Now she had father and daughter glaring at her.

"Why do you have to be so horrible?" Rhi demanded, her arms still around her father's big neck, her tiny feet miles from the ground because he was *still* holding her up like she was a fragile doll.

The kind Talwyn had used for archery practice when she was a five-year-old.

"Because my daddy loves me whether I'm perfect or not," Talwyn replied. "So, I can be as horrible as I want."

Laughing, her father kissed the top of her head. "I adore you."

She shrugged at her cousin. "See?"

Lips a thin, angry line, Rhi patted her father's shoulder, telling him to let her down.

He lowered her carefully—again, as if she were fragile glass. She smoothed the skirt she insisted on wearing over leather leggings and nodded at Talwyn's father. "Uncle Fearghus."

He put his arm around his niece's shoulders and hugged her close. "My little Rhi. I'm sorry you were hurt."

"I'm fine, Uncle. And thank you for *caring*," she added, her eyes widening at Talwyn.

"What did you want me to do while you were bleeding from the eyes? Lick it off?"

"Och! You're disgusting."

"And you're a spoiled brat!"

"*I'm* spoiled?"

"Daddy!" Talan called out, barreling through the tent flap, arms spread wide, his trajectory straight for their father.

But her father was fast as well and he held out his arm, palm up, his expression cautionary.

"No," Fearghus told Talan.

"Just a hug."

"*No.*"

"I bet you hugged Talwyn," Talan accused.

"I love her."

Talwyn laughed at that as Rhi quickly stepped between father and son. Although she didn't really have to. Talan enjoyed tormenting their father with forced affection. It made Fearghus the Destroyer incredibly uncomfortable, and anything that made their stoic father uncomfortable entertained her brother endlessly.

"We don't have time for this," Rhi announced. "We are in grave trouble here, and we need a plan. Yes?"

Fearghus nodded. "There already is a plan."

Talan immediately looked at her, but all Talwyn could do was shrug at his unasked question.

"What plan is that?" Talan asked.

"We weren't given full details. Not yet," Briec admitted. "But it will involve our father. Bercelak the Great will be joining the battle."

There was a long moment of silence as the youngest of the family let the information their fathers had imparted to them sink in. Then they each had their own reaction.

Talwyn swung her fist, gritted her teeth, and growled, "Yesssssss!"

Talan cringed like he'd been kicked in the balls.

And Rhi burst into copious tears, wailing, "Father, *nooooooo!*"

"They left us here to die," Uther said again. "Where's the loyalty?"

"They left the horses. I'm sure they'll be back." Caswyn let his friend use his working arm to lift him up enough to get a drink of the stream water he so desperately needed.

He was just about to take a sip when small hands slapped the metal cup from Uther's hands.

"Oy!" Uther barked, until he saw who stood before them. "Princess Keita?"

"Don't drink from the stream." She held out her hand and snapped at Brannie and Aidan, who were walking toward them all—from where? Uther had no idea, but Aidan carried chain mail armor and boots. "Give me one of your canteens, Branwen."

Handing the canteen to Aidan, Brannie motioned for him to help Uther while she kept walking.

And she continued walking until she reached the princess. That's when she spun Keita around, slipped her hands under her arms, and lifted the princess off the ground until they were at eye level.

"Don't think for a moment, *cousin,* that you are in charge. Because you're not."

"I'm a princess! And put me down, you giantess!"

Brannie shook Keita hard, shocking the royal into near-silence.

"Why, you—"

"Listen well, cousin, this little adventure that is pulling me away from my troops, from my friends, and kin, will be run by me. The Mì-runach report to me. *You* report to me. That is the only way this is happening. If you fight me on this . . . if you get lippy, complain, try to poison us—"

"I just saved them from poisoning!"

"—or get on my nerves in any way—"

"What?" Keita boldly demanded. "What will you do to me? Kill me? Scar me? Do you think there's really anything that you, peasant, can do to me? A daughter of the House of Gwalchmai fab Gwyar!"

"I'll tell your father . . . everything."

The princess, dangling from her much larger cousin's hands, snorted a laugh.

"Tell him what? My father has no delusions about me. He already knows everything about—"

"He knows you poisoned him?"

Keita's eyes widened, her mouth hanging open. "Wha-what?"

"Oh, yes. I know about that. All those days poor Uncle Bercelak was sick . . . after eating one of *your* victims."

"That was an accident."

"And poisoning a horse in the first place? What is wrong with you?"

"I needed a test subject! It never occurred to me Daddy would eat it."

"You didn't even tell him why he was sick." She "tsk'd" her cousin. "How many elders did Uncle Bercelak kill thinking they were the ones who had him poisoned?"

Keita's eyes narrowed into slits. "I don't remember."

Brannie smiled. "I do. So let's not forget our place, shall we? This is a military operation and royals don't run those unless they are warriors like your brothers. Or a Battle Witch like your sister. So you, cousin, will do what I tell you to do, when I tell you to do it. Or Uncle Bercelak will find out what a bitch of a daughter he truly has. Understand?"

"Perfectly."

Brannie pulled her hands back and the princess fell to the ground hard and on her ass.

Glaring up at Brannie, Keita snarled, "*Cow!*"

"Viper."

"Brannie," Aidan said. "We need to get somewhere safe . . . and with untainted water. Caswyn needs a healer, I'm afraid."

"No, no, my brother," Caswyn choked out. "My ancestors are waiting for me on the other side. Just let me—"

"Oh, shut up!" Brannie snapped, grabbing some of the chain mail armor and yanking it on. "If you think, for a second, Caswyn the Butcher, that you'll be getting out of this shitty little assignment except on the end of my spear, you're gravely mistaken. *Die on your own time!* Now let's move out!"

They took what they needed from the original traveling party, although Brannie was quite disappointed in the weapons. The guards only had swords and eating knives, and the workmanship on all did not meet the Cadwaladr's very high standard.

"I could probably wipe me ass with these and not even scratch this frail human skin," she muttered . . . more than once.

But Aidan was just glad they had something to protect themselves with. He hated walking around without weapons. Two of his best mates were weak and vulnerable, and now they had a royal to protect.

Aidan was grateful, though, that it was Branwen the Awful who was traveling with him on this mission. She was, truly, the best warrior he knew, and if anyone could help him get his mates and Keita the Viper out of this alive, it was Branwen.

But she was miserable and he hated that. She was ruthlessly loyal to her troops and he knew that leaving them during what would likely turn into a monumental battle would eat her up inside. There was nothing to do about it, though. The queen had given her orders and it was their duty to obey.

Unfortunately that didn't mean Brannie wouldn't complain every step of the way. . . .

"I couldn't even be stuck with a useful royal." Brannie fixed the saddle on the carriage horse she'd claimed as her own. "No, no. Gods forbid I'd get a Fearghus or Briec or even a Gwenvael. Instead I get the most useless of the lot. Keita the Do Nothing."

Keita's eyes narrowed on Brannie's vulnerable back and Aidan quickly stepped to the royal's side, afraid she was moments from shoving some vicious poison down her cousin's throat.

"Why don't you ride with me, Princess Keita?" he asked, even while he pushed her toward his horse. "There are only four horses and Branwen will have her hands full managing my two wounded mates."

"Fine." Keita lifted her skirts and moved toward the horse.

"So sorry, Aidan," Brannie scoffed, "that you have to be bothered with such a useless She-dragon."

"Oh!" Keita gasped seconds before she turned and started stalking back toward her cousin.

"No, no, no," Aidan said quickly, stepping between the two before they could get near each other. "Both of you stop it," he ordered. "We don't have time for this. Look at poor Caswyn. He's practically falling off his horse. He's weakening by the second and you two want to keep this ridiculous fight going? We have our orders—let's just get them over with."

Brannie closed her eyes, taking a moment to get control of her intense anger. She knew he was right, but Aidan also knew that she'd hate admitting it.

Which meant, of course, that she wouldn't.

"Let's go," she muttered. But she just as quickly stopped and pointed her finger at Keita. "But if any of my troops suffer because of you—"

"Oh, for the love of the gods, let it go!" Keita nearly screamed at her. "Your troops! Your troops! You and your troops have one purpose in this world! Protect the throne! *Do your job, Branwen the Awful!*"

Brannie was reaching for Keita's throat when Aidan slapped her arm down and stepped into her.

"Stand by the horse, Princess," he ordered. "I'll be right there."

With much flouncing, the princess stomped off and Aidan said to Branwen, "I need your help. I can't do this alone. Do you understand that?"

"I'm just so *frustrated*," she bit out between brutally clenched teeth.

"I know. But let's get Caswyn and Uther someplace safe, where they can heal. Food and a good night's sleep is probably all you need. I won't say tomorrow will be a better day, but it will be a new one. We'll start again, and we'll get it right."

"But I want to kill her," she admitted in a whisper.

"You can't. Otherwise, most of my kin would have been dead a long time ago instead of irritating Rhiannon with their needy presence at Devenallt Mountain."

A small smile managed to turn up the corners of her mouth. "Your mother will annoy our queen, won't she?"

"Greatly. She will *greatly* annoy our queen. And, to be honest, probably already *has* annoyed her. My mother doesn't usually waste time with that sort of thing."

Brannie nodded. "Knowing that does help."

Without another word, Brannie returned to her horse and mounted him. Once she was comfortable in the saddle, she took in a deep, cleansing breath, and let it out.

Closing her eyes, she finally said with obvious great pain, "Where to first, Keita?"

Keita, sitting sidesaddle behind Aidan, pointed down the road. "That way. There are friends of mine where we can stay with for the night. But remember, we're not kin, you and I, and we're definitely not dragons. All of you are my guards. Keep that in mind, and we'll be able to get much from them without any trouble."

Shaking her head, Brannie said, "You and I have vastly different definitions of the word *friends*."

Keita shrugged. "That's why I have so few. But who needs them," she asked, flashing that brutally bitchy smile, "when you have kin?"

Brannie, with some great force of will, choked back her next words, and headed off down the road. The rest of them followed.

Briec the Mighty, Shield Hero of the Dragon Wars, Lord Defender of the Dragon Queen's Throne, and extremely proud father of two of the most amazing and perfect, *perfect* daughters in the known universe, watched his first daughter, Iseabail the Dangerous, General of the Eighth, Fourteenth, and Twenty-Sixth Legions, help her men make quick work of a gigantic, burned tree stump.

Izzy didn't have to help her troops do this sort of grunt work. Briec definitely wouldn't. But she wasn't just a royal with a title. She loved the world of the soldier. From the most mundane guard duty to creating elaborate battle plans, she could do it all. And do it all well.

Briec hadn't been happy when his daughter had made it clear to one and all that she wanted to join Annwyl the Bloody's army. She'd only been sixteen. A baby, even for a human. But he'd foolishly assumed that a few months of living in the muck and mire as an army private would change her opinion and she'd be back, safe, with him and her mother at Garbhán Isle.

He'd been so wrong. She came home, of course, for leave, but always with her eye on getting back out there. Back to the muck and the mire and the blood and the danger and the harsh world of being a soldier in an active army. There were those who felt Izzy had only gotten her rank because of her family connection to Annwyl the Bloody.

As fast as Izzy moved up those ranks, this attitude wasn't exactly shocking. But the troops quickly learned that Izzy wasn't just some daft royal who thought it would be fun to play with true warriors.

And those who pushed her, those who really didn't want her as part of *their* army, soon learned she was not a girl— now a woman—to be pushed.

Briec never asked her for specifics of what her life in the military was like. He honestly didn't want to know. But as long as she came home with her usual smile and happy attitude, he didn't really worry about it.

Of course, if someone had hurt her, if someone had crossed those lines that Annwyl the Bloody insisted her troops respect, Briec wouldn't have stopped until he'd caught the bastard and had him on a spit for the entire Cadwaladr Clan to feast upon . . . as was their way.

But Izzy had never needed his protection. Over time, she'd even earned respect from the most bigoted and hardened human soldiers who thought royals shouldn't do anything but get out of their way.

Now she had control of three legions and was the right-hand woman of the queen and the queen's second in command, Brastias.

Once the stump was pulled out of the ground, she ordered it to be taken off and broken into kindling.

Hands on her hips, she looked around the growing camp and tried to figure out what issue would next need to be tackled. That's when she saw him.

Briec loved how her face lit up, her smile wide.

"Daddy!"

She ran to him, jumped up, threw her arms around his neck, and hugged him tight.

It was true. Izzy was not blood; her father had been her mother's first love. But she was still Briec's first daughter, as far as he was concerned.

"You're here!" she said when he'd placed her back on the ground.

"We're here."

She suddenly took his hand and pulled him toward the general's tent. Once inside, she faced him. "Where's Fearghus?"

"With the twins. They said they need to talk to him alone. But why is that?"

An answer came from a dark corner. "The mad queen is missing."

Father and daughter turned and watched the ancient Cadwaladr witch limp out of the shadows.

"Where did you come from?" Izzy demanded.

"Don't whine so."

"I wasn't *whining*, Brigida. What do you want?"

"I'm here to help." She made an expression that some might consider a smile but both Briec and Izzy stepped back from her.

She rolled her eyes. "I don't know why I bother with you idiots."

"Perhaps you shouldn't then," Briec replied. "Bother, I mean."

"Can you get Annwyl back?" Izzy asked.

"I have no idea where she is."

"Then what can you help with?"

"Preparing for what's coming our way." She rested against her walking stick and Briec noticed that the old She-dragon was having trouble breathing. She was as worn down as he'd ever seen her. But he wouldn't count Brigida the Most Foul out yet. No. Not her.

Only a fool would do that. And Briec was no fool.

At first, he'd traveled down the road of the Battle Mage, learning about magicks and the spells that controlled them. But his interest hadn't lasted and he had ended up becoming a Dragonwarrior instead, much to his mother's disappointment and his father's surprise.

Briec still remembered enough about the world of magicks and mystics, though, to know and *see* real power when it was staring him in the face. Even when that face was a little hard to look at.

"With the human queen gone," Brigida went on, "you risk that human army of yours losing its focus. Or making a run for it."

"Won't happen," Izzy quickly said. "We're not just fighting for Annwyl; we're fighting for our country. Our people—"

"Blah, blah, blah. No one cares."

Izzy shook her head and paced away.

"One queen is gone, most likely never to return—"

"I wouldn't say that around Fearghus," Briec muttered.

"—and the Dragon Queen is about to release her deadliest weapon. Your father, Bercelak the Great."

"He is unpleasant. Some see that as deadly."

"We either win here or we die trying. I'm here to help you win."

Briec stared at his ancient relative. "And what do you get out of us winning, Brigida the Most Foul? Until the twins and my Rhi were born, none of our kin had seen you in centuries. Now you're here, fighting by our side." He looked her over once. "*Why?*"

"Smarter than your brothers, ain't ya?"

"Not smarter. More cynical."

Brigida's true smile lifted one corner of her face. The part of her face without the vicious scars from lip to just below her eye. Like she'd been swiped by a clawed animal. Except there was no clawed animal in the natural world that could harm a dragon in that way. And he doubted a fellow dragon would even try something like that with Brigida.

"We don't have much time," she told them. "We need to get everybody together and get this moving. Once your father's here . . ."

"What about Annwyl?" Izzy demanded as Brigida headed toward the tent flap.

"What about her?"

"We have to get her back."

Brigida stopped and looked over her shoulder at Izzy, her sneer vicious.

"It's too late for all that."

"Yeah," Briec felt the need to point out once more, "I *really* would not say that to Fearghus."

Chapter Six

It took four hours, but they eventually reached Keita's "friends'" castle. Human royals who said they were loyal to Queen Annwyl.

Brannie didn't know them but that was a good thing. Annwyl talked often of those she hated and the names became memorable.

The name here was Breeton-Holmes and the family had a small castle well inside the Southland-Outerplains border. They weren't a powerful family, but they were well situated, and had access to a lot of gossip, making them important to not only Keita but Dagmar Reinholdt, the Northland woman who ran Queen Annwyl's lands in her absence and had bravely taken on Gwenvael the Handsome as her mate.

As soon as they were in range of the Breeton-Holmeses' castle, Keita went into full royal mode, her back straightening, her expression unbelievably haughty.

It made Brannie want to hit her, but she wouldn't.

Unless, of course, she had to.

The gates were immediately opened for them and the few guards that were around didn't even question them. Aidan had just helped Keita to dismount when Lord Breeton-Holmes appeared.

That's when the real performance began.

As soon as she saw her fellow royal, Keita burst into hysterical tears, throwing herself into the man's arms as his wife and adult children instantly surrounded her.

Brannie didn't even realize she'd started to roll her eyes until Aidan bumped into her, pushing her forward. That's when she remembered that a good royal guard doesn't roll his eyes at the idiot royals he was sworn to protect.

Everyone saw Brannie move forward, and the new royals were watching her closely, so she patted Keita's shoulder and mumbled, "Now, now, my lady, we're safe now."

She heard Aidan snort behind her—which he quickly turned into a cough—and even she had to admit, she sounded less than concerned over the royal in her care.

It didn't matter, though. Keita had an audience, and Brannie and her cohorts were soon forgotten.

Sobbing hysterically, Keita was helped toward the castle doors. Brannie followed but Keita abruptly stopped—walking and crying—and looked at her cousin over her shoulder.

"You'll stay in the stables. A healer will be sent for your men."

"The *stables?*" Brannie demanded.

Aidan's hand landed on her shoulder. "Of course, my lady. Please let us know if you need anything else."

"But—"

"Come on, Sarge. The lads need us."

Sarge? Had he called her "sarge"?

Turning to remind Aidan of her hard-earned rank, she saw his eyes widen in warning.

With human royal guards, no rank higher than a sergeant would lead a royal protection detail. A captain would never leave the castle unless it was the captain to a queen.

Realizing Caswyn and Uther needed her more than Keita ever would, she grabbed the reins of two horses—one carrying Caswyn—and made her way to the stables. Aidan right behind her with Uther and his horse.

As they walked, Brannie quickly understood that these royals weren't like the very wealthy ones that used to come see Annwyl. Of course, most of those royals never got past Dagmar Reinholdt. She spoke for the queen as her battle mage and vassal. Many thought Annwyl was harder to talk to, but they were wrong. Dagmar was tougher than many dragons Branwen knew. She was plotting and devious and dangerous despite her lack of battle skill and magicks.

Brannie adored her.

But clearly not all royals were rolling in gold. The Beeton-Holmes castle was on the small side. The castle grounds damn near tiny, with just a few guards protecting them. But despite the sparseness of everything else, the stables were glorious and the few horses they had were shiny and beautiful. Like they were groomed every day, which seemed strange.

"Show horses," Aidan remarked once they were inside.

"Show them to whom?"

"Before the war, there were show events where royals from around the land would bring their prized horses to be judged for strength, beauty, and breeding. And you don't keep amazing show horses in shitty stables, even if it means you live in a tiny castle with few servants."

"Shouldn't they have more horses? These stables are huge."

"Perhaps they gave the horses to the army for battle."

Brannie walked past the few animals in residence. "But . . . they're not big enough to be used in battle. Look at this one. Her legs are so . . . thin."

"Elegant."

"What?"

"Her legs are elegant, not thin."

"Elegant . . . and breakable. I wouldn't even eat her. Like gnawing on a chicken bone."

Aidan, chuckling, led their two riderless horses to their own stalls before he came back for his friends.

Taking a quick look around, Aidan pointed at a roomy stall by the doors. "Let's put them here."

"No," an old woman said, coming into the stable. She carried a weighted-down bag and had on a gray wool shawl. She was the healer.

"Put them in the back stalls, past the double doors," she ordered. "That's where I treat injured men and it'll allow them to get some quiet. She glanced over Uther and Caswyn, who was being held up by Brannie and Aidan. "They'll need the sleep."

"We need them ready to go by tomorrow," Brannie told her.

"Maybe this one." She gestured at Uther. "He probably just needs a splint." She leaned in closer, trying to look into Caswyn's face; his head was down, his eyes closed. He was, thankfully, still breathing, but that was it. "This one . . . this one will need more."

She touched Caswyn's face to lift his chin, but quickly pulled her hand back, her eyes widening and locking on Brannie and Aidan.

This woman wasn't just a healer . . . she was a witch. Her power had told her what they were as soon as she'd touched Caswyn.

When she took a step back, Brannie lifted her hands, palms out, and said softly, "We're not here to hurt anyone. We just need a safe place to stay so we can heal."

The witch continued to gaze at them, eyes narrowed in obvious distrust. But then Caswyn could no longer hold himself up, and Aidan nearly went down with him.

"To the back," the witch ordered. "Quickly."

* * *

Brannie helped him carry Caswyn to the back and, together, they carefully laid him out in a stall on top of a nice pile of straw.

"You over there," the witch said to Uther. He went and sat down in his own stall and the witch kneeled beside Caswyn.

"He's lost blood."

Aidan crouched across from her. "What do you need from us?"

"Fresh water, clean cloth, and privacy. Having you two hovering over me makes me uncomfortable."

Aidan could understand that. Especially the way Brannie was glowering.

"Understood." He nodded at her. "Name's Aidan. This is Branwen."

"I'm Esmerelda."

"Can we call you Ezzie?" Brannie asked.

"No."

"We'll get the water and cloth for you," Aidan said quickly, rising.

He walked out, pushing Brannie in front, closing the double doors behind them.

"Why are you acting like I did something wrong?" Brannie asked.

"You were glaring at her."

"I glare at everyone."

"No, you don't. But when you're worried . . ." He smiled. "I'll be right back."

Aidan tracked down a helpful servant and asked for what he needed. While he waited, he peeked inside the castle to make sure Keita was doing all right. She was talking to the family, regaling them with stories of the supposed "attack" they'd suffered. There were tears, dramatic reenactments. It was quite . . . entertaining.

Aidan returned to the stables with the servant and all that Esmerelda needed. Once the supplies were delivered, he and the servant went to Brannie. The servant proceeded to lay out food for them. Bread and cheese, meat and ale.

As soon as they were alone, Aidan dropped onto the straw. "I'm exhausted," he complained.

"Going down with a mountain takes a lot out of a dragon." Brannie sat down across from him and grabbed a loaf of bread.

"That didn't happen today, did it?"

"It does feel like it happened days ago, but no. The quake happened just this morning." She tore off a piece of the loaf and handed him the other half. "You think Iz and Éibhear are all right?"

"You mother would have told you if they weren't."

"Maybe. Unless she was worried I would have fought even harder to go back." She sighed, took another bite of her bread. "Too late now, though, huh?"

"Too late."

"Do you think Ren is dead?"

"I hope not. The Eastlanders are not exactly a forgiving people. If he died on Rhiannon's territory . . ."

"Yes. I know. My mother made that clear."

She was quiet after that and they ate mostly in silence. Although not an uncomfortable one. They were both exhausted.

When they'd just finished their food, Esmerelda appeared at the stall opening.

"They'll sleep. Both of them. The one with the arm—"

"Uther."

"Yeah. His arm and leg are already starting to heal. His leg wasn't even that bad. But he should protect that arm for the next day or two, depending on how fast you . . . people heal."

"And Caswyn?"

"I stopped the bleeding and gave him something to get his strength back. And a few spells to speed up the healing." She shrugged narrow shoulders. "I've done me best."

"Thank you," Aidan told her, meaning every word. "They're both like brothers to me. Your helping them means much."

"Keep your word to me and no need for thanks."

"As promised. We don't intend to hurt anyone. Just need a safe place to stay tonight."

She glanced around. "This is as safe as any. If there are any problems with your friends, the servants know where to find me."

With a nod, she left and Aidan looked at Brannie. "Why didn't you say anything?"

"I was trying not to glare. That requires concentration."

"You had to concentrate on *not* glaring?"

"Because I didn't know I was glaring! So I kept thinking, 'Am I glaring now? What about now? I feel like I'm glaring now.' It was endless."

Aidan shook his head. "Do you realize that you make things—outside of battle, I mean—very complicated?"

"No, I don't."

"You do. Constantly. If a sword is in your hand and some-one is screaming bloody murder as they charge you . . . you are direct and ready. But you and Izzy trying to figure out what to eat for dinner . . . I think we're still waiting for you to make up your mind."

"Oh, it's not that bad."

"If that's what you need to believe," Aidan said.

He picked up the bones and any remnants of food and

tossed everything outside so the castle dogs could have it. Then he found blankets that, sadly, smelled like horses, but would be much more comfortable to lie on than plain straw.

Once he had the blankets laid out, he dropped facedown on one.

"What were you talking about with Keita and Rhiannon when I was with my mother?" Brannie asked.

Aidan turned his head so he could comfortably stare at her for several seconds.

"When?"

"Earlier today. When we were in Rhiannon's special place."

He snorted. "I think you mean *sacred* space."

"So . . . what did they want?"

Aidan had been hoping that Brannie would forget her question when he corrected her—as she often did—but she was too annoyed by her cousin to let it go. And if Aidan wanted to annoy her more, he'd tell her everything. That, however, would not help the journey they were about to make.

So, instead, Aidan told Brannie enough to get her off his back.

"The queen was bragging about how safe her sacred space is, which was fine . . . until your great-aunt Brigida casually strolled through."

"I *did* see her, then?"

"Yes. You did. And so did Rhiannon, who was none too happy about it. Especially when Keita began the mocking."

Brannie shook her head. "Keita is such a crazy, murdering sow. Pissing off her mother like that? Stupid."

Aidan rolled to his side and propped himself up on his elbow. "You do know that your cousin is not really a murderer, Branwen, right?"

"Oh, come now. You can't be fooled by her as well."

"I'm not. But she didn't kill those people earlier today because she was bored. She's a Protector of the Throne. That's what they do."

Brannie gawked at him a long while, her head cocked to one side, before she asked, "*Who* is a Protector of the Throne?"

"Keita."

"Keita who?"

"Keita the Viper. Your cousin."

Again, Brannie gawked at him before asking, "Why are you lying to me?"

"I'm not. Your cousin is a Protector of the Throne. Has been for"—he shrugged—"at least a century."

"Keita?" she asked again. "*My* Keita?"

"Yes." He sat up. "How could you not know? Everyone in your family has known since that cousin of yours—the green one—tried to have her killed for betraying her mother. Didn't any of them tell you?"

"They did, but . . . *I thought they were joking!*"

Brannie couldn't believe this.

Keita, a Protector of the Throne? Keita?

The same vapid female who'd once asked Brannie, "Are there any spells that would stop you from growing? What dragon is going to want a female the same size as him?"

That Keita was a Protector of the Throne?

"How is this possible?" she finally asked Aidan. "I'm shocked."

"I can tell. Éibhear never told you? Briec? Gwenvael? Who can't keep his mouth shut about anything?"

"No, no. I . . . think they did. But . . . again . . . *I thought they were joking!*"

She threw up her hands. "Even Izzy thought they were joking."

Aidan laughed.

"What's so funny?"

"You and Izzy. The pair of you. On a battlefield, no one wants to face you. But *off* the battlefield, you two are like little girls. Gossiping. Getting in trouble. And, like true Cadwaladrs, drinking too much."

"That's always my cousins' fault."

"You're actually blaming your cousins?"

"Of course."

Brannie stretched out beside Aidan. "I still can't believe it. Keita? A Protector of the Throne."

"You underestimated her all these years. Now, don't you feel bad?"

"*No.*"

Rolling onto his stomach again, Aidan covered his face with another, smaller blanket.

"Are you actually about to go to sleep?" she asked, flabbergasted.

He lifted the blanket a bit so she could hear him clearly. "I am not about to sit up all night listening to you analyze the truth about your cousin simply because Izzy isn't here to do it with you."

"But so much happened today. The battle. The mountain. Uncle Bercelak being released like a horrifying bird of prey. *And,* to top it off, Keita's a Protector of the Throne. How do you just go to sleep after all that?"

"By closing my eyes. Try it."

"I'll be up all night."

"Please don't be. I know you, Branwen. If you're up all night, you'll keep me up all night."

"I will?"

"We both know you won't shut up."

She shrugged, nodded her head. "True. If Izzy were here, I'd just talk to her. But she's not."

"I'm not nearly as chatty as the Great Iseabail the Dangerous."

"No. You're what we call a listener, which is of no use to me at the moment."

"Perhaps a servant can get you some warm wine. That helps some to sleep."

"Or we could just fuck."

Aidan sat straight up, the blanket still covering his head. "What?" he barked.

"I said—"

"I heard what you said."

"Then why did you ask?"

"Why are you asking me to fuck? Is this because of Keita?"

"Ew! What does *that* mean?"

"Nothing," he said quickly.

"I'm just suggesting it because a distraction would do us both good. Don't you think?"

"No."

"But you're not chatty and I need to get some rest before tomorrow. Fucking usually helps. If we were still with the army, I'd grab Sergeant—"

"Stop talking." He pulled the blanket off his head, pushing his gold hair off his face. "Are you just using me for sex?"

"At the moment, yes. It's the easiest way to work out anxiety."

"I just read a good book," he suggested.

"That's what Annwyl does." She glanced off. "And me dad." She shrugged, dismissing his suggestion. "I'm not much of a reader. I'd rather have someone tell me a story than make me read a book. With words."

Aidan's eyes crossed and he fell back onto his bedding.

* * *

"I don't know why you're mad." She felt the need to argue when all he wanted her to do was stop talking. "It was a valid question."

"It was a valid question for a camp whore."

"Now you're being a baby."

Aidan propped himself up on his elbows. "Do you really think so little of me?" he asked.

"I have no idea how to answer that."

"Thank you very much."

"No, no. I mean, I don't know what you're asking me. Do I think so little of you . . . how?"

"That I am just good for sex?"

"Of course, I don't think that. You're not good just for sex. You're good for lots of things, *as well as* sex." She grinned as if she'd made some brilliant observation that he should appreciate.

Aidan tossed one of the blankets at Brannie, hitting her directly in the head. It hung over her face and she didn't bother to remove it. But she did keep talking.

"You're being ridiculous," she told him . . . through the blanket.

"I have honor. I may be a murdering, torturing, son-of-a-bastard Mì-runach, but I'm *not* a whore, Branwen the Awful."

With a sigh, she pulled the blanket off and tossed it down beside him. She stretched out, their arms nearly touching.

"Well, don't ever say I didn't offer you anything," she muttered.

He turned his head to look at her. "Are you saying you offered me your pussy?"

"*No*," Brannie said immediately, but then she started giggling. "I guess I am."

Now they were both laughing. And after the day they'd had, it felt really good.

Not no-strings-attached sex good, but . . . good.

Chapter Seven

A hand over her mouth woke Brannie up. She had her blade out and pressed against Aidan's throat before she realized who he was.

He was on top of her, his weight holding her down. And strangely, she didn't mind. It felt kind of nice, but she didn't have time to think about that too much. Because Aidan's expression told her something was very wrong.

It was morning. The two suns up outside the stables. The nearby horses in the other stalls restless.

Brannie listened beyond that, ignoring the sounds she recognized to focus on what was more strange to her.

She heard it. Muffled sounds coming into the small courtyard. She closed her eyes and listened harder. Yes.

Muffled hooves. The Daughters of the Steppes muffled their horses when they were planning a late-night attack.

She motioned to Aidan, her index and middle finger together, waving forward twice.

He nodded and slipped off her. She grabbed the unimpressive sword of the guards Keita had killed the day before and got to her feet.

Aidan was already gone, disappearing into the stables to make his own way out. He didn't make a sound, but that was his way. Unlike the Mì-runach that she'd known over the years—her cousin Éibhear included—Aidan didn't go screaming into battle, covered in dirt and blood and cutting down all those in his way. He didn't choose a time to move like a jungle cat as his brethren did. Instead he moved like that at all times, whether in battle or merely walking down the road toward town. Often striking the killing blow before his enemies knew they were under attack.

Standing outside the stall she'd slept in, Brannie briefly thought about the two other Mì-runach down at the end of the large building. She decided against waking them. No matter how injured they still were, they would go out of their way to join the fight, if there was one.

Then again, how often *wasn't* there a fight when someone muffled their horse's hooves?

Brannie walked to the doors and eased one side open just enough to be able to look out. Her lip curled.

They were Zealots. One of the squads Salebiri had been sending out to scorch the land, Brannie guessed, based on the way their cloaks were singed at the edges. Some even had burn scars on their hands and faces, as if they hadn't moved away from the flames they'd begun fast enough.

There were about twenty, all human from what she could tell.

It still shocked Brannie to no end that there were dragons who'd involved themselves in this foolishness. Insane. Why devote one's self to a single mad god when there were so many nicer ones to choose from?

Five more Zealots came from inside the castle, pushing the royal family out into the courtyard. Keita was not among them, so Brannie could only hope that her cousin's skill at survival had kicked in and she was hiding somewhere safe.

A priest was helped down from his horse and, with a beautiful smile and missing eyes, he spread his arms wide and cheerily called out, "May your sight shine bright, Lord Breeton-Holmes! Salutations and great joy to you!"

Lord Breeton-Holmes didn't answer. The poor man was so terrified, all he could do was stare blankly at those who'd invaded his tiny home.

It wasn't like Breeton-Holmes was a danger to anyone. He had no army. Showed no sign he wanted to be anything more than a royal with a small castle and shiny horses that were basically useless for any kind of real work. But for the last few months the Zealots had been attacking these small royal estates and forcing the inhabitants to either join their cause—usually by sacrificing at least one eye—or suffering greatly for choosing to stay loyal to their own gods and to Annwyl.

But Brannie wasn't about to let that happen to anyone on Annwyl's lands and definitely not to humans who had offered them food, protection, and healing.

She cracked her neck and lifted her weapon, ready to attack, when she saw Keita step out of the safety of the castle.

"Greetings, my one-god-loving friends!" the little idiot called.

Brannie gritted her teeth. "What is *wrong* with her?"

"What is she doing out there?"

Jerking at Uther's voice behind her, Brannie ended up gritting her teeth again. Damn Mì-runach. She hated when they snuck up on her.

"Don't do that," she growled at him.

"Learn to hear better," Uther chastised. And she briefly thought about slapping him. Not hitting, just slapping. Until he cried like a babe.

"What's going on?" Caswyn asked, coming up behind Uther.

"Why are you up?" she asked. He still looked weak but much better than he had the night before.

"You can't expect me to lie around when danger is near."

"I expect you to not undo what the healer has accomplished, idiot."

"You must be better," Uther joked. "She's back to abusing you."

"You both make it so easy," she muttered, looking back. That's when she caught the horrifying sight of Keita . . . *gesturing* to Brannie to come out.

"What is she doing?" Brannie demanded.

"I think she just . . . revealed our location to the enemy." Uther shook his head. "Would she really do that?"

Brannie sighed. "Probably."

"Why would she do that?"

"We're dragons," Brannie explained, pushing the doors all the way open. "She probably thinks we could just burn them all to death. So why hide?"

"If we shift now or unleash our flame, *all* the humans die. Including her precious royal friends."

Brannie glanced at Uther. "You have no idea how sad it is to me as a Cadwaladr to know that my cousin is even more stupid than you two."

Aidan stayed hidden on the roof of the stables until Keita looked right at him and, with a smile, told him to come down.

Now he had no chance. Zealots with bows aimed arrows at him until he jumped down to the ground.

He'd never thought Keita could be so stupid . . . but she was. She *was* that stupid.

Aidan stood by a seething Brannie. He thought it was best if he stayed close to her to prevent her from killing her cousin. Because he only had to look at her face to see that's exactly what she was planning to do.

"Now see?" Keita said to the priest. "We're all friends here. No need to lie or hide things. Yes?"

"Your honesty is a true blessing, my lady. My god will be happy to have you on our side."

"Oh, I'm sure he will. I am absolutely *delightful.*" Keita pressed her hands to her face. "But the eye thing . . . I can't do that. My eyes are just too beautiful. As is my face. Actually, everything about me is beautiful. To destroy that for some god I could not care less about seems absolutely ridiculous, don't you think?"

The priest's handsome smile never wavered. "Trust me, my lady, your other choice is even less attractive."

"Is it?" Keita asked, her head tipped to one side, her hand abruptly pointing at one of the Zealot guards standing near her.

The guard coughed and blood shot out of his mouth and down his chin. Seconds later, blood flowed from his eyes— he still had both—and his nose.

The priest, although physically missing his eyes, still had a sight provided to him by his god.

"What have you done, witch?"

"Me? A witch?" Keita smiled at that. "No, no. I am lacking that skill. But tell me . . . did you enjoy the water from the stream you rested by last night?"

Brannie stomped her foot. "Keita!"

"What? It will wash away soon enough."

"You hope!"

"Can your chastising wait, O' flawless one?" When Brannie looked away from her cousin's gaze, Keita went on. "Now . . . where were we? Oh, yes! The death of your guards." With a flip of her wrist and a flourish of her arm, she gestured to the guards once more, who began dropping like dead trees. Some fell right over. Others dropped to their knees first and then landed facedown. Blood poured from every orifice and the royals backed away.

"You shouldn't be here for this," Keita told the royals. She handed Lord Breeton-Holmes a sealed parchment. "Take this directly to Dagmar Reinholdt. She will take good care of you. And thank you, my lord."

"Of course, my lady." He rushed his family back into the castle and Keita sent their few guards to saddle the horses from the stables so they could get on the road right away.

"Now," Keita said once she had the Breeton-Holmeses on the move, "back to you, priest."

"I drank that water . . . why am I—"

"Still alive? Because I know from my studies that all your priests and priestesses partake of the Sinnoch root. It helps with your mystical sight. It also is a natural protection from the poison I used. It stops the toxin from killing you. So while your guards may be dead, you have as long as I allow you to live."

No longer in good humor, the priest snapped, "What do you want, woman?"

"Information, of course. What else do you think I want?"

The priest suddenly looked around. "You brought us here on purpose."

"Of course, I did. You're all so fucking predictable with your shit-loving god, it wasn't really hard."

"I'll die before I—"

"You came in contact with an Eastlander not too long ago," she cut in to the priest's declaration. "Three weeks ago specifically. You met him in a pub and followed him out later that night. What happened after you followed him?"

The priest smirked. "I'll tell you nothing. Have your"— he glanced at Brannie—"manly thugs—"

"Hey!"

"—do their most evil. I can withstand anything."

"Can you?" Keita asked. She winced a bit. "I guess I should have mentioned. The root you eat nightly for your

sight. It will keep you from dying. It will not, however, keep
you from the brutal *pain*."

Once the Breeton-Holmeses made their hasty exit, Keita
had Aidan drag the priest into the castle and leave him in the
middle of the floor, far from weapons or anything he could
use to kill himself. While the man screamed and writhed in
utter, devastating pain, Keita sat at the main hall table, her
feet up on the wood, a chalice of wine held in one hand.

When the priest wasn't screaming and begging for an end
to his misery, Keita yawned and sipped from her chalice.

It became so bad and went on for so long that Brannie
had to leave for a bit so she could hunt down some fresh
meat. It—thankfully—took a while before she found game
worth the effort.

She had the animals skinned and put on the spit by the
time the priest finally reached his breaking point.

Standing close enough to stare down at him but not close
enough to be grabbed, Keita asked the same question she'd
been asking for hours. "What happened to the Eastlander
you followed out of that pub?"

"We . . . we tried to take him," the priest, covered in sweat
and his own blood, vomit, and excrement, panted out. "But
he fought off my guards . . . and disappeared . . . into the
forests." He reached out for her but even her bare feet were
too far from his fingers. "Now please. Please . . . end it."

"Don't evade, priest. You followed him *out* of that forest.
To where?" He shook his head, trying to fight, but there was
nothing left but his suffering. "Answer me, priest," Keita
said, her voice almost soothing. "Answer me or I will enjoy
watching you suffer for days."

He curled into a ball. "We followed . . . followed him to

about ten leagues . . . leagues . . . northeast of . . . Port . . . Cities."

"And?"

"And . . . he suddenly . . . disappeared just when . . . we got . . . got close."

Keita smiled. "That was very good."

She turned from him and walked back to the table. Once she was again situated in the chair, her feet up on the table, a chalice of wine in her hand, Brannie asked, "Well . . . ?"

"Well what?"

"He told you what you wanted. Aren't you going to finish him?"

"No." Brannie, disgusted, stood, but her cousin snapped, "Sit down, Branwen."

Without really thinking about it, she did. "Keita—"

"I don't want to hear it, Branwen. Unless you've actually seen their idea of a cleansing . . . I don't want to hear anything."

"I've seen their cleansings," Brannie told her, clearly remembering finding rows of those who refused to take Chramnesind as their one and only god. Staked to the ground in the kneeling position, molten silver poured into their eyes so they were frozen in sparkly horror. It had been one of the most appalling sights Brannie had ever been forced to witness and the first time during a nighttime battle break that her and Izzy had ended up so drunk they couldn't even stand.

"Then I don't know what we're arguing about, cousin."

"Just because they're bastards, doesn't mean we have to be."

Keita's eyes rolled all the way to the back of her head. "You are such a goody two-claws."

"Can we eat outside?" Uther asked. "Or in the stables? I just don't think I can eat with the sound of his screaming."

Keita gawked at the Mì-runach. "What kind of dragon are you?" she asked.

Uther shrugged. "A nice one."

She let out a sigh. "Fine. If your fragile sensibilities can't handle a little screaming—"

Before she could finish, Caswyn was up and across the room. He cut off the priest's head midscream and the silence was . . . amazing.

Pointing the sword at Keita, Caswyn accused, "I thought you were some prissy little royal princess. But you are—"

"Lovely? Divine? Bold and sassy?"

"Vile."

Keita shrugged, sipped her wine. "That, too."

Chapter Eight

Aidan sat in silence with his Mì-runach brothers for at least an hour in one of the castle bedrooms until he heard a faint knock at the door.

He opened it and Brannie stood on the other side. Her black hair was wet from a recent bath and combed off her face. She had a long, plain cotton shirt on and a map in her hand.

"We need to discuss tomorrow's plans," she said evenly.

"Yes. Of course." He stepped back and allowed her in.

But once Aidan closed the door, Brannie suddenly spun to face him, her eyes wild. The map went flying as she hysterically asked him in a desperate whisper, *"Who is that she-demon?"*

"Your cousin!" Aidan whispered back.

"That's not the Keita I know!" she continued to whisper. "We can't go traipsing around with her! She'll kill us all in our sleep!"

"No," Uther corrected, also whispering, "we'll probably all be awake when she does it. She'll want to stare us in the eye as we're bleeding out of every orifice!"

"But—" Caswyn said in his normal voice and they all immediately hushed him.

Poor Caswyn reared back and refused to speak again. Probably for the best. At the moment, they were all panicked and easily startled.

Brannie began to pace around the room. "Now I see what my mother was worried about."

"What are you talking about?"

"If it turns out that Ren died on our queen's territory, while under our protection, the Empress will declare war on Rhiannon and strike."

"Well, that's bad but—"

"Mum's worried Keita will try and stop her by killing the *entire* royal family. From the Empress on down."

Aidan had a hard time believing that. "You don't think she would, do you?"

"If you'd asked me this yesterday, no. I wouldn't have believed it. But after this . . ." Brannie shook her head. "She *lured* that priest here. But before that, she studied the habits of the Chramnesind priests and priestesses so she knew what poison to use to kill the guards and keep him alive but in torturous pain. That goes beyond mere dragon mayhem."

"She *is* a Protector of the Throne."

"I don't want to hear that anymore, Aidan!"

Since they'd still been whispering all during their conversation, the strong knock at the door had all four of them screaming in panic.

The door opened and Keita stepped in. She'd also had a bath and was now sheathed in a soft red robe.

"Everything all right?" she asked, gazing at them.

Brannie cleared her throat. "Yes. Of course. You just . . . uh . . . startled us."

"Don't worry. I wouldn't expect any more of the Zealots anytime soon. Last I heard, their attack squadrons were heading north."

"Great," Brannie muttered.

"So, tomorrow . . ."

"Yes. We were just discussing that."

"We'll be heading to the Port Cities. See if we can pick up Ren's tracks. If we're lucky, he's already caught a boat back to the Eastlands."

"I don't understand, Keita. I know Ren's skills. Why wouldn't he just open a doorway and . . . you know . . . *go home?*"

"Unless you're at my mother's or Brigida's level of skill, the Zealot priests can disrupt open doorways. Snatch witches right out of them. If Ren had tried, he'd have definitely been caught. We tried to get him to my mother, but we had to separate when we ran into a few . . . legions. I haven't seen him since."

"I'm sure he's fine, Keita."

"I hope so," she said softly, her expression—for once—sad. But just as quickly she went back to the old Keita. "Anyway, we head out tomorrow morning?"

"We'll be ready."

"Excellent! See you all in the morning then." She smiled and waved before walking out, closing the door behind her.

Once Aidan heard another door close somewhere in the castle, he went back to whispering. "If we're going to survive this, we're all going to have to calm down!"

"You calm down!" Brannie snapped back in a desperate whisper. "She likes you! I'm just the cousin with the high moral ground!"

"Aye, Branwen," Uther muttered. "I do not envy you that."

Brannie spun, one finger pointed in Uther's poor face. "*Is this you helping?*"

"Oh, no," Uther answered honestly. "Not at all."

The next morning, Brannie rose before the two suns. She put on her chain mail and boots and went down the stairs and outside to the guards' quarters. There she found only a few, very battered old weapons—not much better than the ones they'd taken off the dead guards—but an ample supply of surcoats. Some that might actually fit the Mì-runach, big bastards that they were.

She slipped one of the surcoats on over her head and wrapped a belt around her waist. The guard's weak sword and dagger hung from it. Better than nothing she supposed, but she'd give anything for a real weapon. Perhaps they could find a solid blacksmith along the way. Even weapons made only for humans that never changed their size would be better than these.

"I'm coming into the room," Aidan called out seconds before he did just as he said.

Brannie frowned at him. "What was that?"

"When I don't announce, you yell at me that I snuck up on you."

Brannie was going to argue that point until she realized Aidan was right.

Shrugging, she turned back to a small box filled with axes, most likely used for chopping wood rather than anything war-related. She grabbed one, figuring it was, again, better than nothing.

"It's not my fault all of you move like jungle cats. Perhaps if you stomped a bit."

"Unlike my brothers, I don't know how. I learned to be stealthy very early in life. It helped me survive my kins' form of familial kindness."

He grabbed one of the surcoats and put it on. It pulled tight over his chain mail–covered chest but there was nothing they could do about that. There were only a few other surcoats that were bigger and those would have to go to Uther and Caswyn since they were much larger than Aidan.

Good thing Éibhear wasn't here. They had enough trouble finding leggings to fit that body. And his chain mail shirts took twice as long to make as everyone else's.

"He's so ridiculously big!" she exclaimed to the air.

Aidan looked around. "What are you talking about? And to whom?"

"I'm talking about Éibhear and his chain mail shirts."

Aidan gave a small smile. "Your mind just . . . wanders away, doesn't it?"

"All the time. Got me in so much trouble during my training." She picked up the rest of the surcoats and started walking back to the castle. "The Warrior Trials were a nightmare. For a whole year I at least had to *pretend* that I was listening . . . when I really wasn't."

Aidan stopped, gazed at her a moment. "It took you a year to become a Dragonwarrior? A *year?*" He threw up his hands. "I never heard less than a decade. Minimum."

Brannie rolled her eyes. "Me mum took six months, and to this day I haven't heard the end of that shit."

Aidan nodded and admitted, "Your mother frightens me."

Brannie patted his shoulder before she walked on. "She should."

By the time they reached the castle doors, Uther and Caswyn were awake. Uther's arm was still in a sling made of cloth but his fingers could now move a bit. And Caswyn was grinning ear to ear, his human color back to normal.

"What a great healer!" he announced loudly, taking the surcoat from Brannie. "I haven't felt this wonderful in years! I could take on a . . . take on a . . ." Words faded away as he struggled to pull the surcoat down over his chest.

He stopped when it wouldn't go past where his nipples would be under the chain mail.

Cringing, Brannie dropped the surcoats to the ground and sorted through them, tossing the obviously too-small ones aside until she found a few that looked—hopefully—big enough.

She handed one to Caswyn and he again struggled to get the garment on.

Brannie and Aidan joined in to yank the surcoat down the dragon's human chest. It took some time and a lot more energy than they'd thought it would. But once it was done, he was tucked in there.

"Can you breathe?" she asked.

"Enough."

Uther's took a bit less time and Caswyn accused him of having a bigger surcoat than his and for his mate to give it to him. "You stingy bastard."

As the two bickered, a happy and vibrant Keita swept out onto the steps.

Wearing a red velvet dress covered with a red velvet robe, she spun in a circle, and asked, "Isn't this beautiful?"

"Compared to what?" Brannie asked. It was a nice dress, but she felt the need to be difficult.

But, as usual, Keita ignored her, taking another spin. "Breeton-Holmes's adult daughters left me a divine wardrobe to choose from."

"Good thing they had to run for their lives and leave their family home and all their belongings."

Keita stopped posing in her finery and stomped her bare foot. "Are you blaming me for this?"

"You drew the Zealots here, Keita. What if you hadn't made it here in time to do what you were planning?"

"But I did make it on time. I'm very good about timing."

"Since when? You'd be late to your own funeral pyre if we weren't the ones forced to carry you there when your time comes."

"Already planning for my death, cousin?"

"Have been for quite a while now."

"All right," Aidan said, quickly stepping in between them. "Perhaps we should get on our way. The Port Cities aren't around the corner, you know."

Keita lifted her skirts and, with a toss of her royal head,

walked around her cousin, making sure to brush up against her as she did.

Brannie had her fist pulled back when Aidan caught her hand and held it in both of his.

"Why are you torturing us?" he asked Brannie. A question that confused her so much, she was distracted from Keita being a bitch.

"What?" she asked Aidan.

"Why are you torturing us?"

"How am I torturing you?"

"You'll get yourself killed—"

"By your own cousin," Uther tossed in.

"—which means we'll be alone with her—"

"Eventually she'll decide to kill us, too," Caswyn added.

"—and you won't be here to protect us." Aidan shook his head. "Is that what you want for us?"

Brannie thought on that a moment before answering with a firm "Yes. It is." And she walked off, hiding her smile until she was sure they couldn't see her face.

When Aidan first marched out with Her Majesty's armies at the beginning of this war, he'd known that his whole goal in life was to keep his Mì-runach brethren alive by not letting them get into too much trouble with the rank and file of the regular army. A general who was used to having his or her orders followed without question never appreciated the disdain with which most of the Mì-runach took those orders.

At first, trying to watch out for all those Mì-runach had been troublesome but, as time moved on, he'd been able to focus on just two. Sometimes three. Uther, Caswyn, and occasionally Éibhear.

He hadn't worried too much about Éibhear, though. He was, at the end of the day, still a prince and, more important, the favorite youngest son of the queen. He could only get into so much trouble. And Éibhear's mate, Iseabail, had calmed his now-famous temper. She knew how to keep him busy when he got in a mood simply by having him deal with entire forests. Aidan didn't know what it was, but that dragon loved to take down trees. And he was damn good at it, too.

Uther and Caswyn, however, seemed to make it their goal to irritate the higher ranks of the queen's army until Aidan had feared they would end up ass first on a standing pike. Eventually, though, it seemed that Branwen had made it her personal business to deal with the pair. And she was much easier to distract from their foolishness than some of the harder generals.

Still, on his worst day interceding between a pissed-off general and the unruly idiots he loved as brothers, Aidan had never been so overwhelmed, so terrified of the outcome, as he was trying to keep two She-dragons from killing each other.

He'd admit, his mother and older sisters were . . . well, horrible beings. Plotting, deceitful, and terribly, unbelievably, bigoted. If one was not of equal royal stature or greater, one was not to be spoken to with even a modicum of respect. And yet . . . he'd rather stand between them and the unwashed masses asking for bread than deal with Keita the Viper and Branwen the Awful when they didn't get along.

What made it worse? Unlike true enemies, they had no intention of fighting. Instead they kept slapping at each other like two human girls fighting over the last piece of dessert at a family meal.

Which meant that, with Aidan attempting to keep them apart by staying between them, he was getting hit. Constantly. And their human hands hurt his frail human skin.

He'd rather face the claws of a bear than the punches and slaps of these two angry She-dragons.

At the fifth hour, when he finally could stand no more, he bellowed, *"That is enough!"*

Their small party stopped and the two females glared at him in surprise.

"I am covered in bruises and scrapes because you two can't put your differences aside for five minutes! I'm sick of it!"

"She—"

"It was her—"

"I don't care!" he barked. "Now I'm going to say this once and never again. If you two bitches don't settle down—"

"Settle down?"

"Bitches?"

"—and act like you have some common sense, I'm going to—"

Aidan's words ended abruptly when both Keita and Brannie put their hands over his mouth. At first, he assumed they were both going to kill him. Poison from Keita. A quick blade across the throat from Brannie. But, he realized, they weren't focused on him. They were looking off into the nearby trees.

"Someone's coming," Keita said.

"From the east." Brannie motioned to Uther and Caswyn. "Get Keita out of here."

Aidan pulled the females' hands away from his face. "What about you?"

"They know we're here." Her head tilted to the side a bit. "They've sent riders ahead. I'll deal with them."

"Bran—"

"It's all right. Just go."

"I'm not leaving you."

"Your orders are to protect Keita. Do it."

Reluctant, but unable to argue—his orders from the

queen had been very clear—Aidan pulled his horse back and rode off to the trees. Keita right behind him, with Uther and Caswyn protecting her flank.

Brannie dismounted her horse and pulled out her sword. Not knowing the horse as well as she'd known her brave old steed—gods, how she missed him—she didn't want to risk fighting on his back. So she slapped his ass and sent him to the side of the road.

She stood her ground and waited . . . but after a few minutes she saw nothing. No one coming her way. All sound of advancement had stopped. Some would feel relief, but she didn't. Instead, she was only more concerned. Because that could mean—

Something small, human, and powerful landed on her back, arms around her neck.

Choking, Brannie grabbed the arm, and yanked. She flung the body away from her but another small and powerful body hit her from the right, pinning her sword arm to her side.

Standing her ground, not allowing herself to be dragged to the ground, Brannie used her free hand to grab hold of a good amount of hair and pull.

There was a screech and she sent the body flying. But before she could raise her arm, yet *another* body attacked her. Hands over Brannie's face, legs around her waist.

Fed up, Brannie reached back and grabbed an arm. She lifted the body up and over her head, slamming it to the ground. She used her foot to pin it in place and raised her sword. That's when she realized that the weak blade had broken in the middle.

"I *knew* this thing was a piece of—"

A strong, *sturdy* blade slid under her chin. "Such shitty

weaponry, Cadwaladr. You should be ashamed. For that affront alone, you should die. . . ."

Aidan heard screams. He would have ignored them, but one of those screams was definitely Branwen's.

Still, his orders from the queen—

"What are you waiting for?" Keita practically bellowed at him. "Go to my cousin. *Now!*"

Aidan immediately turned his horse around and rode back.

As he cleared the trees, he dismounted his horse in mid-gallop and pulled his weapon.

Three vicious she-demons had wrapped themselves around Branwen, pummeling her with fists and assaulting her with their screams. Aidan stormed up to them, grabbing the first one by the neck and yanking her off. He threw her to her back and was about to impale her with his blade when his hand was caught and held.

Smelling the flame of dragons, he froze and looked down at the female holding him. He blinked twice, shocked.

"Rhona?"

Rhona the Fearless of the Cadwaladr Clan smiled at him. "Aidan the Divine? What are *you* doing here?"

"Trying to—"

"Rhona?" Keita the Viper called out from the side of the road, both Caswyn and Uther wincing behind her. "My dear, sweet cousin! Is that you?"

Rhona briefly closed her eyes and said softly to Aidan, "Oh . . . you poor dragon."

Aidan sighed. "Rhona, my old friend, you have no idea."

* * *

Brannie tossed off the last of her cousins and gazed down at them on the ground while the triplets moaned.

"Is that the best you lot can do?"

"I tell them they need more training," Rhona said about her sisters. "But they never believe me."

Nesta, Breena, and Edana slowly got to their feet and brushed their asses off as a caravan came onto the road about a half a mile away.

"What's that?" Brannie asked, pointing.

"That's why we're out here and not fighting with the queen's armies at the moment. We were heading back, but many of the roads were inundated with the bloody Zealots. We had to take tunnels to get here. Word is these roads aren't bad."

"No. They're not. But be careful what you drink and eat," she warned.

Rhona looked over at Keita being helped down from her horse by Caswyn. "Gods, how many has she poisoned now?"

"I've lost track."

"Now wait one minute!" Keita snarled, slapping Caswyn's hands away so she could stomp her way over. "I'll have you know that everything I've done has been for the protection of the throne."

"Stop looking so smug, Keita," Rhona told her flatly.

Keita's arms dropped to her sides and her bottom lip poked out. "But she's being so mean to me, Rhona," she now whined. "Beat her for me, would you? Teach her where she stands in the hierarchy of this family."

"In this family?" Rhona asked. "She's *way* over you."

"How could you say that to me?"

"Everyone knows it. You're a sneaky spy who kills without honor. The only thing that stopped any of us from killing you decades ago was that Uncle Bercelak adores you and Protectors of the Throne are important during wartime. As for Brannie, she roars into battle, fighting with skill and force, and bringing nothing but honor and respect to the Cadwaladr name." Rhona stepped close to Keita, looking down at her. "Do you think for a second that you could ever live up to her in our eyes?"

"You know what, cousin? I never liked you." Keita put her hands on her hips and turned to Brannie. "And you're just lucky I haven't given you something to make you lose all your scales. Ask Gwenvael how well that went for him and how long it took to grow his scales back. Then give me that tone."

Rhona the Fearless really did love her kin. She did. Really. Honestly!

But sometimes they were a lot of work. Especially when a few of them weren't getting along.

First Keita, with her inability to simply tell those working with her exactly what was going on so everyone was clear and involved. True, she'd probably been trained that way by those who'd brought her into the Protectors of the Throne because secrecy was what kept them alive. But if Rhona was to be honest—and when wasn't she?—Keita enjoyed tormenting others just for the hell of it. Like her brother Gwenvael, nothing entertained her more than confusing and ridiculing everyone around her.

Then there was wonderful Branwen, whose biggest issue was her lack of focus. In battle, there was no question that Branwen was the cousin Rhona wanted at her side. Like her mother, Brannie was a true warrior. But when she wasn't in battle . . .

Gods! It was like talking to a human who'd been hit on the head one too many times.

"Why doesn't someone explain to me what's going on. And why you are here, Branwen, and not with your troops?"

Brannie's eyes narrowed dangerously and she opened her mouth, but Aidan suddenly stepped between them.

"No, no," he said to Branwen. "We don't have time for you to start yelling again. And, to be truthful, I just can't listen to that anymore."

"But she—"

"Caswyn killed your horse," he suddenly announced to Branwen, causing his dragon friend to turn to him in horror.

"You treacherous bastard!" Caswyn cried.

Rhona leaned to the side to look at her cousin. "Awwwww. Not Puddles."

"He was injured in battle and *I* was going to put him down with honor!" Brannie yelled, still upset. "And that dozy bastard *ate him!*"

"*He was dying anyway!*"

"*I still don't care!*" Brannie snarled at Caswyn before she turned to Keita and barked, "And what are you laughing about?"

Standing a few feet away and giggling, Keita replied, "The Mì-runach killed your horse. That's the funniest thing I've heard all *century.*"

Branwen gazed at her cousin for long seconds before announcing, "You have wide hips like your mother."

With a roar, eyes wild with rage, Keita shifted to a roaring She-dragon, uncaring that everyone else had to dash out of her way or be crushed in their human forms.

Rhona grabbed Aidan's arm and pulled him farther off. She used her free hand to motion to the triplets. They could handle Keita and Brannie and keep them from killing each other.

"All right, Aidan the Divine . . . tell me what the battle-fuck is going on."

* * *

Uther moved the horses off to the side and stood beside them with Caswyn. They ate dried meat from their travel packs and watched as Keita and Brannie rolled across the land. Knocking down trees. Crushing boulders. Sending wildlife running for safety.

And running after them? The triplets, now in their dragon forms, desperately trying to stop them.

"That Rhona," Caswyn said around his snack, "she's—"

"Taken," Uther reminded him.

"Yeah, but to a Lightning. Like there aren't enough worthy Fire dragons for her to find a mate."

"She must like him. And I hear that's what counts when ya choose a mate. Liking them."

"Eh." Caswyn took another bite. "What about them triplets?"

"Little young, aren't they?"

"Does that matter to us?"

"Yes," Uther said quickly, thinking of his own younger sisters. "That matters."

"All right. No need to get testy."

Keita and Brannie rolled back the other way with the triplets still behind them. Uther and Caswyn managed to duck just in time to avoid a slashing tail. Sadly, one of the horses wasn't fast enough and he lost his head, his body dropping to the ground, spasms shaking it.

Caswyn stared at the horse's body and licked his lips.

That's when Uther had to say it.

"By the gods, brother! You never learn!"

"I'm glad you told me everything. Now I know what needs to be done."

Aidan smiled at his one-time trainer, who had told him

in no uncertain terms that "You are a mighty killer, Aidan the Gold, but a soldier of this queen's army? Never."

"You can get me out of this?" Aidan teased.

Rhona laughed. "If only I could. But the orders came from Rhiannon *and* Ghleanna. You're stuck." She looked over at her cousins. Now they were trying to choke the life from each other while Rhona's youngest sisters desperately attempted to tear them apart. "But I do think I know what to do with those two."

"I've already got Uther and Caswyn to deal with. So anything you can do to help me . . ."

The back of Brannie's neck was grabbed and she was yanked off Keita. Keita jumped up, claws aiming for her eyes, but Rhona caught a handful of all that red hair and yanked her until she lowered her forearms.

"*That is enough!*" their cousin bellowed, stopping them both in mid-attack.

Brannie might outrank Rhona the Fearless because she was only a sergeant. And Keita might be a princess. But among the Cadwaladr, Rhona had the highest rank of all the cousins who were the offspring of the offspring of Ailean the Wicked and Shalin the Innocent.

For good reason, too.

Rhona, since hatching, was the most dependable, loyal, and rational of all the Cadwaladr cousins. Often more rational than the elders. She kept them all from doing immensely stupid things with nothing more than sound reason. She didn't hit unless necessary and didn't throw anyone into volcanoes unless they really deserved it.

Even Branwen couldn't say that.

So when she spoke . . . they all listened. Even Keita, queen of the difficult!

"My hair! My precious hair!" Keita screeched, desperately

trying to untangle Rhona's claw from her long tresses. "Let me go, you evil female!"

Brannie, who was being completely calm and had stopped attacking Keita as soon as Rhona had told her to, hysterically laughed at her cousin until Rhona said, "I have weapons."

Standing straight, her laughter dying in her throat, Brannie asked, "Weapons? Where?" she asked, looking around. "Where are the weapons?"

"In the caravan crates."

Excited beyond anything, Brannie ran over and quickly shifted back to her human self. Naked—her crappy chain mail and surcoat ruined when she'd become dragon—she climbed into the back of one of the carts and tore open the first crate she saw.

"You are so easily distracted," Aidan remarked, leaning over the cart wall and smiling.

"Personally," Uther added, "I like seeing you naked when we're not running from Zealots and Caswyn isn't dying. You should be naked more."

Brannie pulled out a two-handed sword nearly the length of her body and easily held it in front of her.

Uther stepped back, hands up, and added, "I was just joking. You don't have to get naked for me. I like you dressed. You should be covered from head to toe in full armor at all times."

Using a finger to pick something out of his teeth, Caswyn said, "I like naked Branwen."

Branwen stared down at Caswyn. "Why do you have blood on your face?"

"*I don't believe you!*" Uther suddenly yelled at his friend before stomping off.

Branwen looked at Aidan. "What was that about?"

"Your beauty confuses them."

"Oh, shut up."

Rhona walked up to the cart with a red-faced Keita.

Brannie placed the point of the weapon into the cart floor, hand on the pummel, legs braced apart, and she knew she was smirking. She couldn't help it.

Aidan cleared his throat. "You do know you're still naked, don't you?"

"Oh, I *know.*"

He dropped his head but she could still hear his laughter.

Standing in front of her, Rhona bumped Keita's arm. "Do it," she ordered their royal cousin.

"Sorry," Keita muttered.

"Couldn't hear you," Brannie taunted. "What was that?"

Now glaring at her, Keita snarled, "Sorry I was being such a right prat."

Smiling, her back straight, her human tits out and proud, Brannie nodded. "Apology accepted."

"Now you," Rhona said.

Brannie pointed at herself. "Me?"

"Aye. You."

"I didn't do anything! It was the prat," Brannie accused.

"You can apologize," Rhona said smoothly, "and the two of you can act like the mighty warrior and deceitful spy—"

"Oy!" Keita snapped.

"—that you are. Or you can *not* apologize and I can take all my wonderful weapons and go."

Brannie snorted. "You would never leave me without weapons. Defenseless."

"True. But, my cousin, there are weapons"—Rhona's grin was slow and wide—"and there are *weapons.*"

Brannie took in a sudden breath, pointed at Rhona. "You . . . you made weapons with your father, didn't you?"

Rhona and her father were brilliant blacksmiths. Her father, Sulien, was a Volcano dragon who'd taught his daughter the art of alchemy and creating weapons and armor that could change with a mere thought. He'd been sent away when the war started to work in a safe location where the Zealots could not get to him. Rhona had been working with him off and on over the years—she loved being a blacksmith much more than being a soldier, but she was great at both—and would bring newly created weapons back and forth to the front as needed.

Still grinning, Rhona tilted her head and said, "Maybe."

Brannie tossed the two-handed sword away—barely noticing that the only thing that prevented Aidan from getting his head cut off was his speed at ducking—and jumped off the cart in front of Keita.

"O' Keita!" she loudly intoned. "Much loved cousin—"

Keita glanced at Rhona. "What's happening?"

"—I am sorry for ever doubting you." She grabbed Keita's hand and the She-dragon desperately tried to pull it away. "You *are* a Protector of the Throne and our throne and queen could not be in better claws than yours. I pray to the gods I never again offend you and that our familial love and adoration spans the centuries—"

"All right! All right!" Keita yelled, finally yanking her hand away. "I get it. You're sorry. But whatever you're doing is making me nauseous. So stop it." She turned, but tossed at her, "And put some clothes on. Those giant tits of yours are making Aidan the Divine drool."

"Actually," Aidan said softly, "I think that was simply a reaction to my near-death experience."

"I missed your head, didn't I?" Brannie demanded.

"Barely!"

She dismissed the whining dragon with a wave of her hand and turned back to her cousin. "Tell me what you have, dear Rhona. Tell me. *Show* me what you have." She made a little squealing sound in her excitement. "I must see!"

Laughing, Rhona put her arm around Brannie's shoulders and led her to another cart. "That apology was so epic . . . let's see what we can find for you, my dearest cousin."

Aidan watched Brannie and Rhona walk away. He was laughing because he couldn't believe how excited the army captain was. Who got that happy over weaponry but a Cadwaladr? No one, that's who.

To the rest of them, weapons were merely tools to perform their jobs in the best and quickest way they could. But to a Cadwaladr, and especially to Branwen the Awful . . . they were like the finest jewels.

It was rumored that Cadwaladr didn't stock their caves with jewels and gold like most dragons. Instead, they used their spoils to purchase new weapons, and that's what one would find piled high in their caverns.

And after seeing this . . . Aidan now believed that rumor.

Aidan watched the two She-dragons open a crate and begin to dig through it. He didn't know what they were going to get, and he became completely distracted when he realized he was surrounded by three females.

Slowly turning, he nodded and greeted them. "Triplets."

One of them frowned. "We have names."

"Yes. But you all look alike and I can't tell you apart." He shrugged. "So I never bother to learn your names. It's easier for me that way."

"You're very honest," another said.

"I am. Much to my mother's great annoyance."

"We met your mother when we visited Devenallt Mountain. She's very . . . um . . ."

"She's a horrible female. Don't spend time with her. She'll sap your will to live."

"That could explain why Auntie Rhiannon sent her and

her daughters—your sisters—to Garbhán Isle and ordered Dagmar Reinholdt to manage them."

"That was the word she used," the first added. "*Manage*."

Aidan couldn't help but smile at that. If his mother thought she could run roughshod over the human Dagmar Reinholdt, who was known in the harsh Northlands as The Beast . . . well . . . *heh*.

"You were staring at our Brannie's ass," noted the third.

"She has a very nice ass. Very firm."

"Do you like her?" asked the second.

"I don't dislike her."

"You should like her," said the third.

"Your cousin's a heartbreaker. And I'm very sensitive and beautiful."

"She could use a sensitive male in her life."

"And beautiful. Don't forget beautiful."

The first shook her head. "He thinks we're joking, Nesta."

"He'll learn, Breena." She patted his shoulder. "Because when it comes to our favorite cousins—"

"And few are our favorites."

"—we are very serious."

"Favorite cousin?" Aidan asked. "You were just trying to throttle her not fifteen minutes ago."

"Not throttling. Showing her how far we've come since she used to train us how to throw knives when we were just little hatchlings."

"I do love Cadwaladr family stories," Aidan noted wistfully. "And how far you've come? It was like she was being attacked by screeching fleas."

"Hmmm," the first one said before turning and walking off.

"Huh," the second said before following her sister.

And the third just sort of wandered away after staring at him for several silent seconds.

Caswyn joined him, punching his arm. "That whole clan is a bit . . . touched, yeah?" he asked.

Aidan glanced at his friend and pointed out, "You still have headless horse stuck between your teeth."

"Damn." Caswyn covered his mouth and quickly walked off before Brannie could see him and start threatening him again.

Chapter Nine

The sorting of weapons and armor took longer than Brannie thought it would. Took so long, in fact, it was decided they would camp in the nearby forest for the night. As soon as a fire was started, Brannie dove headfirst into all the wonderful weapons and armor her cousin and uncle had created. Eventually, though, she had to borrow Aidan's surcoat to cover her nakedness so that Uther and Caswyn would stop staring.

Idiots.

Like she didn't know how those two really felt about her as a dragoness. Apparently her tail was "too short." Uther used to call her "Stubby" behind her back. And if they didn't enjoy looking at her true form, what did she care if they lusted for her human one? They both went together and she loved every part of herself.

Why shouldn't she? As she always told her brother Celyn . . . she was adorable!

What Brannie didn't know . . . ? How Aidan felt about her. She'd never heard that Aidan had said anything about her one way or another. But when she'd suggested they'd have sex for a little stress relief, he hadn't been remotely interested.

Strange. She'd always thought he kind of liked her. Not seriously, but enough to fuck a time or two. She wasn't asking for a lifetime mating. She had no doubts she'd find her mate one day, but she was sure it would be another warrior like her. Loyal to the army and the troops. Another captain perhaps. Or even a general. That would be nice.

But until that happened—and she knew it was a long way off—she still had "needs" as her mother liked to call it when her youngest daughter had volunteered for Her Majesty's Army.

"You'll have needs," Ghleanna had said, picking a quiet time when everyone, even Brannie's father, was out somewhere else. "And there's no shame in that. You just have to be careful who you choose. Don't be like your grandfather or cousin Gwenvael and choose whatever piece of ass crosses your path. Pick someone kind, who won't call you a beauty to your face and a whore behind your back."

It seemed a strange conversation with her mum. Especially when Brannie found out Ghleanna's conversation with Celyn was "Treat females like trash, and I'll hunt you down and cut your prick off. Understand?"

But as Brannie advanced through the ranks, she'd kept her mother's words in mind and found she was right. Those she'd chosen to share her bedroll with had been fun, nice, and discreet. Only one had decided to get drunk in a pub and expound on what a "great lay" Brannie was. Too bad for him, her cousin Éibhear had been standing behind him. It was before he'd become Mì-runach but he was already becoming known for his temper.

But you know . . . some dragons don't need their wings. Or tail. Or right front claw.

Rhona walked up to Brannie, pulling her out of her thoughts. "I have something special for you, cousin."

Brannie sat up straight and didn't bother to hide her grin. "A halberd? To replace the one I lost."

Rhona held out her hand and Brannie stared at it. "Oh . . . how nice," she lied. "A stick."

Rhona glared at her. "It's not a stick."

"Really? Because it looks like a stick." The glare became worse, so Brannie took the metal stick from her cousin and held it under her cousin's nose and demanded. "What do you see, Rhona? Because all I see is a bloody stick!"

"Perhaps," Aidan decided to interject, "it's a stick that turns into an actual weapon with a thought. I believe you have a spear like that, Rhona. Yes?"

"It's a spear?"

Rhona grinned. "It's whatever you want."

"Gold?"

Her cousin's glare instantly returned.

"Bread?" Brannie tried again. Of course, now she was just being an ass. "Wine!"

"No, ya irritating cow!" Rhona let out a frustrated breath. She used to make that same sound whenever she had to train Brannie and Izzy back in those early days. When they were just privates with dreams of being more. It was, as Rhona had told them more than once at the time, one of her *least* favorite things to do in the "universe."

She'd actually said "universe" not just "the world."

"Think of your favorite weapon and see what happens," she finally told Brannie.

Of course, Brannie liked lots of weapons. But her favorite? Well . . . that would be the halberd, wouldn't it? But she did love swords. Short swords. And she did love axes . . . and hammers! Gods, she adored hammers!

"You are overthinking this, Branwen the Awful!" Rhona yelled in the same voice she'd used when she'd been training Brannie. "*Make a decision!*"

Startled, Brannie thought *halberd!* because she wanted to use it to strike down her bellowing cousin.

And the metal stick in her hand immediately began to

grow. It lengthened and thickened right in her palm. The tip turned into a spearhead and from the right side of the tip grew an ax head.

Brannie immediately stood, her mouth open. She'd never seen anything so beautiful before.

"It automatically knows if you're in human form or dragon and will adjust accordingly," she heard her cousin explain, but Brannie was barely paying attention anymore.

She thought about a hammer and watched her halberd turn into a war hammer with an oversized head. Then it turned into a gladius. Then a spear. Then a bow. Then a long sword. Then back into a halberd.

That's when she squealed.

It was that smile. He watched it spread across Brannie's face. So wide, it almost made her eyes disappear entirely, her poor nose forced into a scrunched-up position, her shoulders coming up until they practically covered her ears.

Her glee exploded from every pore on her body and she went up on her toes as she began to sort of . . . dance around with her newly formed halberd in her hands. Yes. She danced.

Over a weapon.

And then there was the squealing. Aidan was sure he could hear nearby wolves howling in response, and Uther and Caswyn moved as far away as they could without leaving the fresh roasting meat the triplets had hunted down and put on the fire. But Aidan wasn't annoyed at all. How could he be when he'd never seen Branwen the Awful this happy or excited before?

She was so busy hugging her new weapon to her chest and grinning that Brannie didn't notice that her triplet cousins were walking up behind her, their own weapons at the ready. Triplet one had a hammer. Triplet two had a double-headed lance. Triplet three had a long sword.

Triplet one brought her hammer up and over, aiming toward Branwen's head. The second swung the sharp end of her lance at Brannie's legs. The third went straight for her gut.

No one said a word to Brannie. Not one word of warning. Not even a grunt from her cousins. They did nothing but attack. With full force.

Yet she must have sensed them. She must have known they were there. How else could she move so quickly, using the blunt end of the halberd to block the blades of the lance so they never reached her legs? At the same time, she used the curved spike on the opposite side of the halberd's ax-head to catch hold of the wood handle of the hammer.

But Triplet three was still coming with her sword. So Brannie, gripping her weapon tight, jerked just her torso far enough over that the blade missed her and sent her cousin falling forward. She would have landed on Brannie, but the army captain stepped back and her kin hit the ground hard. Then Brannie twisted her weapon and body, sending the other two flipping up and over in different directions.

Her cousins immediately tried to get back up but Brannie brought the blunt end of her weapon down against Triplet one's head. As she roared in pain, Brannie flipped backward, away from the hammer Triplet two was swinging at Brannie's legs while she was still on the ground.

When Brannie landed, she brought the ax-head of her weapon down on the wood part of the hammer, breaking the handle into two pieces.

Without a word and with absolutely no anger, she slammed her foot down on the back of Triplet three's back, pinning her to the ground. And the halberd she held in her hands stretched and lengthened until it could reach the other two. Metal spear tips grew out of both ends and she pressed each against her cousins' throats, quietly waiting until they both raised their hands in defeat.

Brannie stepped back and, with a quick twist of her hands, she spun the weapon up and back until she held it behind her body. By now it had changed once again so that it was a six-foot metal staff.

And she'd done all that while wearing only his surcoat and a belt around her waist.

Uther and Caswyn gaped as well until Caswyn demanded, "I want one."

Rhona rubbed her hands together and shook her head. "No. That is not a weapon for you."

"Why not? I can handle anything. I'll pay if that's what you want."

"It's not about money," Rhona explained calmly, quickly organizing the chain mail and armor they would wear for the rest of their trip. "You're simply too stupid."

Aidan snorted out a surprised laugh and Brannie's eyes widened in shock at her cousin's words.

"Rhona!" Brannie chastised. "What a horrible thing to say to someone!" She jerked her thumb at a stunned Caswyn. "And I say this as someone who doesn't even like him."

"Did you have to add that last bit?" Caswyn asked.

"Puddles!" she reminded him.

"It's nothing personal really." Rhona tossed each of them chain mail shirts. "He just doesn't think fast enough. You do. Where's the shame in that?"

"You didn't have to call him stupid!"

"Dumb?"

"Rhona!"

Now she tossed metal sword belts at them. Their sword belts were usually leather but these were different. Aidan examined his. It was made of chain mail, was flexible, and had a clasp at the front to secure it rather than tying it into a knot.

"All I'm saying," Rhona explained to Brannie, "is that your weapon is the kind that can help some warriors or get others killed. I trained you, Branwen the Awful, when you were just Branwen the Black. I know exactly how you work and how fast you think on the battlefield. I also know your mother started training you long before that. And what every Cadwaladr knows is how to make anything a weapon. Your battle-mind is"—she snapped her fingers several times—"fast. We all just witnessed that. But that weapon is only as fast as the one who wields it."

Rhona looked Caswyn, Uther and, finally, Aidan over before announcing, "These dragons are Mì-runach. Slow. Lumbering. Like bears." She shrugged. "They run naked and screaming into battle to terrify the weak and startle the strong. So I will give them very good weapons that fit their"—she thought a moment—"skills. That fit their skills better than your weapon. Okay?"

Brannie opened her mouth, but Rhona quickly cut her off with "Good."

Not bothering to argue any of this with Rhona the Fearless—she'd always made her feelings on the Mì-runach abundantly clear—Aidan held up the new equipment she'd provided and asked, "Anything we need to know about this?"

"Chain mail shirt and leggings, sword belt, and weapons will shift with you. Chain mail boots are for when you are human, but when you shift to dragon, they will turn into greaves to protect your lower legs and cover your heel tendons." She handed each a dark red cape and stated, "These are bewitched. They'll shift when you do and the color will change as needed. Shadows will be your friends in these."

"Will we be invisible?" Uther asked.

And the look Rhona gave him . . . no wonder she didn't trust him with Brannie's weapon. "No."

Uther recoiled a bit. "I was just asking."

"These surcoats are like the capes and have the crest o
a royal family that hasn't chosen sides one way or the other
It should keep you safe enough on these roads."

After the clothes, Rhona handed out swords and shor
daggers for eating, expertly crafted by her and her father
Once done, she gave Uther a big ax, Caswyn a medium-
sized hammer. And Aidan she gave a long-bladed dagger
All these weapons would change size when the wielder did

Aidan held up his long-bladed dagger. "What am I to do
with this, Rhona the Fearless?"

"What you do best," she replied with a wink.

Then she handed Brannie an ax, a war hammer, and a
gladius. All for her and her alone.

"But me stick?" Brannie asked.

"Looks like a stick. Use it when they least expect it."

With a yawn, Rhona pointed at the meat over the fire. "Is
that done? I'm starving and we need to get some sleep. We
start early tomorrow."

Uther and Caswyn pushed past Rhona, the triplets, and
the dragon protectors traveling with them to be first in line
for food. Then Rhona had to pry a hammer from one of the
triplets, who tried to use it to crush the pair's heads in.

Chuckling, Aidan slipped the dagger into its sheath.

"What did Rhona mean?" Brannie asked. "What do you
do best?"

"When I first came for training, I was known for my skill
of sneaking up on the other trainees and slamming their
heads against walls."

Brannie smirked. "Give you a hard time, did they?"

"I was the only royal in that class. They thought I was
easy prey. I enjoyed pointing out how wrong they were.
Sadly, my trainers didn't appreciate my . . . reluctance to
stop my reign of terror against my enemies."

"That's how you ended up in the Mì-runach?"

"The queen thought I'd be better suited in small groups of dragons who enjoyed sneaking up on others and smashing their heads into walls." He held up the sheathed weapon. "Eventually I moved from smashing heads to a quick flick against the throat. A little messier but faster. Unlike you, I don't need to revel in the destruction of others."

"I don't revel," she lied, walking away in hopes of getting food from the cold, dead hands of Uther and Caswyn. "I just like to make sure they're really dead. Nothing worse than when they pop up behind you. Still breathing."

They ate their meal on large stumps, no one saying much.

When a large burp filled the silence, they all jumped a bit and everyone looked over at little Breena.

Picking venison out of her teeth with the tip of her finger, she stopped when she realized she was being stared at. "Wha'?"

"A little class, sister," Nesta chastised.

Breena leaned in close, her nose against her sister's cheek, and unleashed a burp that went on for a good two minutes.

Brannie saw Uther's and Caswyn's mouths drop, stunned as they gawked at the triplets. It wasn't merely that Breena was still midway in her burp display or that Nesta, her jaw tight, was sitting there, silently raging. But that Edana had continued to shovel food into her mouth as if it was her last meal, completely ignoring or oblivious to her sisters' antics.

As Brannie glanced over at Aidan, their gazes caught, held, and both ended up turning away, their stifled laughter shaking their bodies and causing tears.

When Breena finally finished, she kissed her sister on

her cheek and went back to putting food in her mouth. Nesta's brutal glare should have engulfed her sister in flames but, sadly, life didn't work that way and she, too, eventually went back to eating her meal.

Once everyone had finished eating, it was Edana who pulled out a flask of Cadwaladr ale. She had the stopper pulled and the flask to her lips when Rhona snatched it from her hands and tossed the entire thing into the fire.

"*You mad cow!*" Nesta and Breena screeched in unison, the pair united in their need for ale. Edana just kept looking at her empty hand as if she expected the flask to reappear.

"We were drinking that," Nesta barked at a steely-eyed Rhona.

"No. You weren't." Rhona looked over all of them. A sergeant in Her Majesty's Army. But a general in the Cadwaladr Clan. "We are *not* on holiday. We have duties. Important duties that need to be accomplished quickly and efficiently. Can't do that if you lot are drunk off your asses, now can we, Branwen the Awful?"

Blinking, Brannie looked up at her cousin. "What the battle-fuck did *I* do?"

"How many times have you gotten drunk one night, only to wake up the next day someplace else, with no idea how you got there?"

Brannie opened her mouth to argue that, but Aidan leaned in and whispered, "Let it go."

He was right. Nothing Brannie said would convince Rhona that she was wrong on this point. She was a firm believer that the Cadwaladrs, as a whole, drank too much. And it was one thing to drink when you just had to get up the next morning to perform some basic army duties or handle guard duty. But when on a mission . . . there was no excuse for "that," as she liked to call the Cadwaladr

Clan's love of heading out to a local pub and indulging in a few pints.

"You lot going off to do *that* again?" she'd ask with that tone.

Not that Rhona didn't drink. She did and she did it well, but it'd better be the right time. And traveling on an important mission for the queens was not, in her mind, the right time.

"Now"—Rhona pointed at the triplets—"you three take first watch."

That was met with eye rolls that had Rhona walking over to them, but the She-dragons were off the log and disappearing into the surrounding trees before their older sister could launch into one of her famous tirades.

"The rest of you get some sleep," Rhona ordered. "I'll wake you up when it's time for your watch."

"Are you going to get some sleep?" Brannie asked her.

"I will. But you know me."

Brannie did. Her cousin slept like a house cat. Waking up the instant she heard a sound that she knew wasn't normal. And as soon as she woke up, the dragoness was ready for battle.

Although Brannie often woke up swinging, she wouldn't say she was necessarily ready for battle or even really awake. One time she was halfway through a battle before she realized that she hadn't been dreaming but had actually been knee-deep among the enemy.

Brannie tossed the bones from her meal out into the woods so that the local animals could eat and gratefully took one of the bedrolls that Rhona provided her and the others. Sleeping on hard ground was not one of her favorite things. Unless, of course, she'd been drinking with her kin. Then, wherever Brannie landed would be her bed for the night.

As Brannie yawned and dropped her bedroll on the ground, she noticed Keita standing off to the side, staring up at the sky.

Brannie would never call her cousin pensive. Far from it. This was usually Keita's time to shine. Flirting with the males and joking with the cousins. But she'd been of few words for hours now.

At first, Brannie was just going to get some sleep and leave her cousin to whatever her problems were, but . . . that simply didn't feel right. She didn't dislike Keita. She was annoyed by her. And some days she wanted to punch the little twat in the throat, but they were still kin.

Leaving her bedding, Brannie walked over to Keita, standing next to her.

"You all right, cousin?" she asked when Keita didn't acknowledge her.

"I'm fine."

"You're worried about Ren," Brannie guessed.

"Concerned."

"We'll do our best . . . to find him, I mean. Promise."

Keita glanced at her, forced a smile. "I know."

Keita headed to her own bedroll, which was placed near Uther and Caswyn because Brannie knew that pair would destroy anyone or thing that came too close to her cousin.

Brannie returned to her own bed and as she snuggled down, she saw that the always observant Aidan was watching her, his brows raised in question.

She only had to tilt her head a bit, shoulders giving a tiny shrug for him to understand her perfectly. Of course, they'd been in battle together for years now and Aidan had been protecting his Mì-runach brethren from her since the beginning. The dragon knew how to read her.

With a sweet, understanding smile, he stretched out on

his own bedroll. Brannie followed suit, her hands behind her head, her gaze focused on the sky above.

Except for Caswyn's intolerable snoring, it was a nice evening.

And probably the last one they'd have for a very long time.

Chapter Ten

It was late when Rhi tracked her great-aunt down, with her twin cousins following right behind.

They didn't like to let her "go off by yourself. Who knows what trouble you'll get into?"

Talan and Talwyn still acted as if she were five winters old. It was irritating. She could take care of herself, thank you very much!

But that said . . . she didn't mind them attaching themselves to her when she had to face Brigida the Most Foul. That she'd rather not do on her own.

Brigida stood in a burnt-out clearing where giant trees used to live and thrive. She was in her dragon form, and a wounded horse was screaming as it tried to get away from the beast looming over it.

The She-dragon stared down at the poor animal, fighting to get back on its feet, but she didn't attack right off. She stared first. And Rhi got the distinct feeling the old Dragonwitch was enjoying the animal's suffering.

Rhi looked away as the twins stood on either side of her.

"Do it, Rhi," Talan urged.

With a nod, Rhi crouched low and touched the burnt

ground. She buried her fingers deep and closed her eyes. Power slipped from her fingers, cutting through the earth until it reached the horse. Its entire body tensed and it screamed out one last time before mercifully dying.

Talan crouched down beside Rhi and he also dug his fingers into the soil as she pulled hers free. His power, dark and uncompromising, flew from his hand, through the dirt, and into the horse. Its eyes turned red and the animal scrambled to its feet. It still bled from its many wounds and was no longer alive, but now undead.

Sucking her tongue against her fangs, Brigida glanced back at the three of them.

"Always ruining my fun, ain'tcha?"

"You don't toy with an animal like that," Rhi chastised. "It's wrong and you know it."

"Depends on who you pull your power from, little girl." Sitting back on her hind legs, she used her forearm to grab her walking stick. It lengthened and grew until she had to use both front claws to handle it. "My masters don't care what I do, as long as I make me sacrifices."

Rhi had long ago stopped asking her great-aunt what sacrifices those were. She honestly didn't want to know.

Walking away from Rhi and Talan, Talwyn moved closer to Brigida, crossing her arms over her chest. "Why are you here, Brigida?" she demanded.

"To help me kin," Brigida replied before she slammed the end of her staff into the undead horse. She beat its head until it stopped moving.

"Don't give us that centaur shit, old bitch," Talwyn snapped. "We know you. Why are you really here? What do you hope to gain?"

Brigida didn't answer right away. She was too busy picking up the horse's undead remains and shoving it into her maw.

Rhi glanced at Talan, her face—she was sure—showing her full disgust. Everyone knew that the remains of a re-animated animal or human were not for eating. As soon as Talan's magicks touched one of his victims, the soul was immediately forced out and the insides turned fetid.

But there Brigida was, gulping down that horse with ease. After a few minutes, she burped and happily stretched. As though she'd just dined on tea and cakes.

Flames exploded around the old She-dragon and she was in her human form again. She slipped on her wool dress and pulled on her gray cloak. Then, leaning heavily on her walking stick, she slowly limped her way over to them.

"Your grandfather will be here soon enough," Brigida said as she moved. "I want to make sure we're ready for him when the time comes."

"If Grandfather comes here," Rhi reminded her, "you know what he will do."

"He'll tear this land apart and rip the castle down around that fancy Lord Salebiri and his whore-wife Ageltrude."

Brigida had been cutting past them when she said that last part and Talwyn quickly stepped in front of her, stopping Brigida in her tracks.

"You know who Ageltrude really is—why are you acting like you don't? What are you up to?"

It was a sound question Rhi's cousin asked. They'd known for years now that Salebiri's wife Ageltrude was actually Vateria, last of the House of Atia Flominia and hated cousin of the Rebel King. Gaius had discovered her involvement with the Zealots and warned Rhiannon and Annwyl, because there was no way that Vateria was a true believer. She only loved herself.

Not only had she convinced her husband she was human and a loyal follower of Chramnesind, but they'd had children together. Offspring like Rhi and Talan and Talwyn, Abominations.

Brigida stepped into Talwyn, her face close. "What if I am up to something?" she asked, her voice low. "What will *you* do about it?"

Rhi and Talan were about to spring to Talwyn's side, but just as they were both going to move, Brigida's damaged eye, all milky white and painful looking, suddenly swiveled over in its eye socket and locked on the pair.

"That thing has a life of its own!" Talwyn had screamed more than once at them. And Rhi feared her cousin might be right.

"You three got much work to do," Brigida said, now moving around Talwyn to go her own way. "Better get to it. There won't be much time left once your grandfather gets here."

They silently watched her walk away until Talwyn asked Brigida, "Where's my mother?"

"How should I know?" was the reply they got back.

"Is she dead?"

"Maybe," Brigida said with a shrug. "Then again . . . maybe not. Who knows with that woman?"

The three cousins returned to the tent and Fearghus felt his heart drop when they told him what had been said. Sadly, though, he wasn't surprised. He knew that Brigida would never tell any of them what she might or might not know about Annwyl's disappearance, but they'd all needed to try.

He refused to believe his mate was dead. That somehow, Zealots had gotten hold of her. He refused to believe it because if he did, he'd never get through this. And he knew Annwyl would want him to lead this fight in her absence because she'd told him that more than once.

So he put his heartache away and focused on the more important matters at hand.

"We need to be ready *before* your grandfather gets here. There's always a chance Salebiri could be planning something. Has already moved on it."

"We have legions heading to his castle to surround it," Izzy told them, sitting on the big table with all the maps. Éibhear sat on the ground, his head resting against the side of her leg. He hadn't been himself since word came down that Branwen and his three Mì-runach brothers were missing, last seen heading to one of the mountains to take on a small group of Zealots. Most believed them already dead but bodies had yet to be found.

Then again, the debris from the fallen mountains went on for miles. They might never know what had happened to their kin and friends when everything was said and done. But Fearghus was sure that if Branwen could, she'd return to her soldiers.

Talwyn sat down on the armrest of Fearghus's chair and rested her head against the top of his. She didn't say anything, but she knew how he felt. Father and daughter had always understood each other.

Fearghus worried about the boy, though. He was as close to his mother as Talwyn was close to Fearghus. If something happened to her at the hands of the Zealots . . .

No. Best not to think of that, either. Not now. Not when they had plans to make, Zealots to kill. The idea of his only son becoming an evil necromancer kept him up some nights, but he hadn't worried too much because Annwyl's love had always kept their son from falling too far. But without her during his formative years . . .

They sat with their own thoughts for a long while until Rhi abruptly asked the room, "Anyone else worried about what Grandda is going to do once he gets here?"

"Gods, yes."

"Blood will soak the lands for centuries."

"The world is doomed."

"I've given up hope. Just seems saner."

She nodded. "Okay. Just wanted to make sure it wasn't only me."

The tent flap pulled back and a dirty and bruised Gwenvael stormed in.

"*Bastards!*" he roared. "They threw me into an endless pit!"

Rhi shook her pretty head at Briec. "Oh, Daddy."

"It wasn't just me," Briec insisted. "It was Fearghus's idea."

Fearghus shrugged. "He asked for it."

Dagmar Reinholdt stood on the top step of the stairs leading into the queen's castle. Even though it was late, she gazed out over the courtyard and wracked her brain, once again, about ways she could protect Garbhán Isle and the family she had inside.

As things spiraled out of control around them, Dagmar had been determined to not only keep Garbhán Isle as safe as possible for all those within but to keep it as much the place she'd always known so that when Annwyl and the others returned, they'd have something to return to.

On Dagmar's left stood her only son, Unnvar. On her right, her loyal nephew Frederick.

Together, the most reasonable beings Dagmar knew stood and studied the territory they had all committed to protecting.

They'd been doing this every morning and every night. Coming out here, staring, and wondering if they'd missed anything.

"The tunnels," Var prompted.

The tunnels that the minotaurs had used to invade their territory from the Ice Lands. An attempt to end Annwyl's life before she gave birth to the twins.

Turned out those minotaurs had been unnecessary. Annwyl's twins eventually killed her themselves. Their births had been too much for the queen's human body. But a god had brought Annwyl back and the queen had made it her business to fight anyone who had a problem with the presence of her babies. Then the presence of Talaith and Briec's child, Rhi. Then all the others. The children of humans and dragons, which included Dagmar's own offspring. Unnvar. Her eldest daughter Arlais. And the five younger ones that everyone called "Gwenvael's Five."

Offspring who'd had no choice in the games of gods. And that's what all this was.

The games of gods.

But unlike the witches and priests who worshipped the gods, Dagmar didn't. She believed in them. Knew they existed. But she did not make sacrifices or call on them in times of trouble. Especially since she believed that most often the cause of the "trouble" was the gods themselves.

Instead, Dagmar relied on reason to guide her decisions and life. Nice, sound, logical *reason.*

"Eh," she heard from behind her. "Reason is overrated."

Dagmar let out a sigh, not bothering to turn around and look at the god standing at her back.

Eirianwen. Goddess of war and death. The one who had given Annwyl her life back all those years ago, but not the one who had given humans the ability to mate with dragons. That had been her longtime mate, Rhydderch Hael, father of all dragons.

Frederick, oblivious to the god's presence, continued to stare out over the courtyard, looking for any signs of weakness. Var, however, glanced back at the god, eyed her once, before ignoring her completely.

"Just like your mother," Eir laughed. "He has more contempt than you, though."

"Perhaps he has more reason."

Frederick looked at Dagmar, frowned, but then his expression cleared. "Ah. Visitors."

Then he too ignored the ongoing conversation. Frederick still had a god or two he insisted on worshipping. Otherwise reason would make the gods easy to see. Although Dagmar had begun to believe that her nephew continued to worship those gods only because he had no desire to see any in the flesh. He had no desire to talk to them when they were bored. No desire to find them sitting on his bed late at night, wanting "a bit of a chat."

The boy had always been smart.

"Your son has grown, I see. Looks more like his father every day." Eir's grin was wide. "Gwenvael's going to *loathe* him."

"Why are you here?" Dagmar asked, facing her.

"Can't a girl come see her friend for a bit of a—"

"If you say 'bit of a chat,' I'm going to scream."

Eir laughed. "Sorry. Sorry."

"Where is she?"

The god gave a very convincing frown. "Where is who?"

"You know who. Annwyl. Rhiannon knows she's disappeared. Where did you take her? Or was it Chramnesind? Maybe his Zealots."

"None of us have Annwyl."

"And you'd know?"

"Of course I'd know. I've been connected to that woman since our bargain was paid in full. And right now, she is no longer in my sight."

"And Chramnesind—"

"He can hide nothing from me. So, no. I don't think he has her."

"But you're not sure."

"Nothing in this world is sure. You should have figured that out by now."

"Then why are you here?" Var abruptly asked, facing the

god. He showed no fear, gazing directly into Eir's brown eyes. "Why are you bothering my mother?"

"I didn't see it as bothering, but if you—"

With an annoyed sigh, her son turned his back on the god. Dagmar had to fight hard not to react to the look of shock on the god's face.

"Did . . . did he just dismiss me?" she asked.

"He did. Wouldn't take it personally, though," Dagmar explained. "He does that to everyone who bores him or can't give him what he wants."

"Can't? Don't you mean won't?"

"No. I meant can't."

The god raised a finger. Not to strike Dagmar and her precious son down, but to argue, as she always seemed to enjoy doing. But before Eir could speak a word . . .

"Good evening, small Northland female and the males she will not give us for our strong daughters!"

Dagmar rolled her eyes and gritted her teeth. Eir cringed and disappeared. Not even a god wanted to face the Kolesova sisters. They were Daughters of the Steppes and, as Var had pointed out more than once, "pains in our collective asses."

"Talking to yourself again, tiny Northlander?"

Dagmar slowly turned to face the two females that Annwyl had sent to "protect such a weak, insignificant woman."

She wanted to think that Annwyl really had been worried about Dagmar and her nieces and nephew by mating. But Dagmar knew better. The treacherous heifer had simply been tired of dealing with the three sisters. They'd committed themselves to fighting by Annwyl's side in the hopes of a glorious death so they could go to their horse gods with honor. It seemed like a good idea at the time.

But from what Dagmar had heard when information still flowed freely, they kept getting between Annwyl and those she wanted to kill. They thought they were protecting her. Annwyl saw it as plain rude.

The tribe the Kolesovas came from were considered annoying by their own people. Large, hearty females who didn't know how to lower their voices or keep from insulting people. They found men to be weak and stupid and only good for breeding. More than once Dagmar had had to step in when they'd get drunk and round up men too young to fight to send to their multitude of daughters left back in the Steppes.

Six months ago, when Annwyl had sent them back with orders to "protect all those I love at Garbhán Isle," there had been three sisters.

On their trip back, though, the three women fell into the hands of a battalion of Zealots. At least four hundred strong. All human. All loyal to Chramnesind.

Two days later, when the dust finally settled, only two of the sisters were left. But the battalion had been wiped out completely. The remaining pair brought back the body of their younger sister Inessa so they could have a proper funeral pyre and several days of mourning without worrying that more Zealots would come for them.

Those were the longest ten days of Dagmar's life. It wasn't the funeral pyre. The Southlanders and dragons did the same. And her people, the Northlanders, also burned their dead, putting them on wooden boats and setting them out to sea in flames.

So, no, it wasn't the pyre that had bothered her. But the singing. For five days, the two women stood in the middle of the courtyard with their sister's rotting corpse and sang songs of mourning to her "trapped" spirit.

Finally, on the fifth day, they'd built a funeral pyre and put their sister upon it and set her aflame.

Dagmar had let out a sigh of relief, thinking it was all over.

It wasn't.

What came next was five more days of singing songs of celebration for their sister's "freed" spirit.

And despite ten days of continuous singing, their horrid voices not only didn't fade, but they bloody traveled. For *miles,* their voices traveled.

Once the mourning and celebration were over, the two Riders had gone on to obey Annwyl's orders . . . by following Dagmar around. As if they were her dogs. But, unlike her dogs, they couldn't follow orders. At least not from *her.* The Daughters of the Steppes had no respect for the "North-women" as they called Dagmar's womenfolk. They thought them weak and unworthy of the respect they offered warrior women like Annwyl and Izzy.

Lately she'd been finding them camped outside her room inside the castle, like two stray dogs that had latched on to her for some reason. Except Dagmar's dogs smelled better.

"Where have you two been?" Dagmar asked the women, since they rarely left her side these days.

"We do not trust these lizards the Dragon Queen has put in charge of your lands. So we went around to make sure all is well."

"Those *lizards,*" Var informed them, "are my kin. I'd strongly suggest you remember that."

"Does it not bother you, boy," Nika, the eldest sister asked, "to be half of one thing and half of another? Would you not rather be all human, like me and my sister?"

Var laughed until he noticed the sisters did not join him. "Oh. You're serious?"

"Come, Oksana," Nika ordered her sister. "Let us go feed."

They came up the steps, Oksana pausing to glare at Var.

"I think our amazing daughters deserve better than this . . . strange boy."

Var smirked, looking more like his father than Dagmar wanted to think about.

Leaning in, he said to the Rider, "I can unhinge my jaw and swallow your soul whole . . . or you can get out of my sight, Oksana Kolesova of the Mountain Movers of the Lands of Pain in the Far Reaches of the Steppes of the Outerplains."

Lifting her chin, trying to at least pretend she wasn't terrified at the threat of her soul ending up inside Dagmar's son, Oksana sniffed and followed her sister into the Main Hall.

"Can you really do that?" Frederick asked Var.

"Do what?"

"Swallow her soul whole?"

Var snorted. "Of course not . . . but I can unhinge my jaw." He shrugged at Frederick's concerned expression. "At least I don't have a tail. Some of my fellow Abominations have tails."

Elina Shestakova of the Black Bear Riders of the Midnight Mountains of Despair in the Far Reaches of the Steppes of the Outerplains came out of her room, tying the black patch she often wore to cover her missing eye, only to immediately stop when she found the Kolesova sisters waiting for her.

She hated dealing with the Kolesova sisters. They were nice enough, usually. But they were such—such!—pains in the ass.

But they were here to protect Dagmar Reinholdt who Elina had become quite fond of over the last few years.

"Do you want something, Kolesovas?" she asked in the

language of their people as her stomach grumbled. "You are denying me food."

"You have become soft, Elina Shestakova, living among these decadent people who give you everything."

"Yes. I know. My sister informed me of that last time she was here. I've just learned to accept it. Is there anything else?"

"That boy," Nika said.

"You'll have to be much more specific."

"Dagmar Reinholdt's son. Is he a demon who can eat souls?"

"Are you talking about Var?"

"Yes."

Talaith, mate of Briec the Mighty, and mother of her own Abomination, was heading toward the Main Hall. She smiled at Elina as she walked by.

She caught Talaith's arm and pulled her close. "Nika and Oksana want to know if our Var is a demon who eats souls."

The two women stared at each other for a long moment before they faced the Kolesova sisters and said together, "Yes. Yes, he is."

"Thank you, Elina Shestakova; Talaith, the brown one—"

"I wish you'd stop calling me that."

"—we now know to avoid the boy. But I think the North-woman is safe with him. He seems to like her. As much as a demon can like anyone."

Talaith nodded. "Excellent point."

The Kolesova sisters walked off and Elina let out a breath. "Thank you, Talaith."

"Let me ask you, Elina . . ." Talaith put her hand on Elina's shoulder and leaned in close. ". . . can *we* kill them with honor? You know, give them that glorious death they're so desperate for? So we can stop having these bizarre conversations in the hallway."

"Sadly, Kolesovas are very hard to kill. I know this

because many have tried." The two women made their way to the Main Hall and dinner. "But I am sure that if anyone can figure out how to kill them . . . it will be Dagmar Reinholdt."

"And she is so close, my friend." Talaith sighed out. "So close."

Chapter Eleven

Aidan awoke before the two suns rose. He sat up and ran his hands through his hair, immediately noticing that Brannie was gone.

Getting up, he glanced over at the only other one who was awake. Rhona. Her hair was wet and she was already dressed to face the hard travels ahead.

Aidan motioned to Brannie's empty bedroll and Rhona jerked her thumb west, through the trees.

Yawning, he eased his way out of the camp so he didn't wake the others and headed west. Eventually he heard running water. He came through the trees just as Brannie broke the surface of the water, heading straight up into the still-dark sky. Her dragon form spun several times, hovering over that lake—and Aidan couldn't look away.

What short tail? Her tail was . . . perfection.

Brannie spun one more time, turned over, and shot back down until she hit the lake.

Aidan jerked back but not fast enough, and he ended up drenched from head to foot.

With his arms spread out from his body, Aidan watched Brannie step from the lake in human form. She dug her fingers into her medium-length hair and shook the black strands out. It wasn't until she flipped her head back that she saw Aidan standing there. And laughed.

"Yes, yes. Very funny," he said with a smile.

"Just shift," she told him around her laughter. "That'll dry you off quick enough."

Aidan did as Brannie suggested and she was right. When he went back to human, he and his new chain mail were completely dry.

"Anyone else up?" she asked, combing her hair off her face with her fingers.

"Just Rhona."

"Of course."

Aidan went to the lake's edge and crouched down. He scooped water into his hand and brought it to his mouth, drinking deeply. He took several more scoops before standing and turning. . . .

Brannie's ass was right there. She'd bent over at the waist to shake her hair out once again. Was she doing this on purpose? Because he didn't appreciate it one bit.

He leaned down and grabbed the robe that went with their surcoat and placed it over Brannie's shoulders when she stood up.

She looked down at the robe, then up at Aidan.

"Uh . . . why?" she asked, appearing confused.

Stepping away from Brannie and facing her, he didn't answer her question. "What's our plan for today?"

Brannie frowned, black eyes watching him closely. After a few seconds, she replied, "Believe it or not, I'm leaving that up to Keita." Without warning, she suddenly tossed the robe off her shoulders. Hands on her hips, she stood there. "This is really her mission. So, wherever we go, it will be up to her."

"You have a point," he said, moving closer so he could snatch up her robe and put it back over her shoulders. He briefly held the robe closed in front of her. But as soon as

Aidan released the wool material, Brannie tossed it off her shoulders again.

Growling, Aidan picked it up again and put it around her shoulders. There was a struggle between them. Aidan trying to keep the robe on her. Brannie trying to take it off.

Brannie yanked the robe from Aidan's grip. "What is wrong with you?" she asked, still laughing.

"Nothing," he lied, stepping away from her. "Nothing. I . . . just don't want you to get sick. It's cold out here . . . and you're"—he swallowed—"wet."

"I'm a *dragon*."

"Yes, I know," Aidan snapped. "I saw your tail." He glanced off. "It's perfect, by the way."

"Really? I've heard it's stubby."

"It's not stubby."

"Huh."

Aidan heard that tone and immediately got defensive on her behalf. "Tell me you're not listening to those two idiots."

"Caswyn and Uther? Hardly."

"That's good because their 'stubby' opinion may be my fault."

"Oh?"

"It was when we met with you and Izzy that first time and Uther and Caswyn were practically drowning in their own drool while they watched you bathe, so I may have said something about your tail—"

"Being stubby?"

"I *never* said stubby. I said 'a little short,' assuming they would lose interest since they are definitely dragons who do like a good tail."

"They're that easily manipulated by you?"

"Yes. Yes, they are."

"I see. But you didn't mean it?"

"Absolutely not. I just didn't want Éibhear tearing off their wings for lusting after his favorite cousin."

"But *you* like my tail."

"Of course I do . . ." Aidan cleared his throat. "In a . . . non-lusty, just as friends way."

"I see. Well that's good. I'm glad you cleared that up for me."

"Me too."

He peered up at the sky—not hard since Brannie had tossed off that damn robe again—and still saw no signs of the two suns yet. "Still dark, but I know Rhona. She'll be getting everyone up in a bit."

Without looking at Brannie, Aidan headed back toward the trees. He'd just reached the line when Brannie's hand fell on his shoulder and she turned him to face her.

"Wha—" he began but Brannie shoved him against the nearest tree trunk.

Startled and annoyed, Aidan barked, "What did I do now?"

She stood in front of him, hands again on her hips, and staring directly at him.

"Well?" he demanded. "What did I do?"

Her left hand slipped behind his neck and pulled Aidan close.

"Branwen—"

"Quiet," she ordered, her gaze fixed on his mouth.

Aidan knew he could have stopped her. Knew he *should* stop her.

But as his lips neared hers, all he could think about was what it would be like to kiss Branwen the Awful. He had to know. Even though he knew he shouldn't.

Just a kiss, though. That shouldn't be too big a deal. Just one kiss.

He appreciated her tail and warned off Uther and Caswyn. How could she ignore that?

Brannie knew she couldn't. So she decided to try her test. The kiss. If the kiss fell flat . . . then she wouldn't think about Aidan in any other way than as the best friend of her favorite cousin. It was her easiest way of ruling out males—dragon or human—that would be a waste of her time.

A bad kiss usually meant a bad everything else, so why bother?

With that in mind, Brannie pulled a gawking Aidan close until their lips were inches apart. She took a breath and leaned in, pressing her lips to his.

Her first thought was, *Yeah . . . okay. Eh.*

That was . . . until Aidan kissed her back.

He tilted his head a bit and used his tongue to open her mouth. A shock, like getting hit with a lightning bolt from a Northland dragon, went through her. From her lips and down her body until it shot out her fingers and toes.

Aidan's hands, balled into fists at his sides, loosened and came up until he could cup her jaw.

Their kiss deepened, their tongues delving. Brannie pushed her naked body against his chain mail–covered one. Her arms going around his shoulders, her fingers digging into his hair.

That's when he turned them both and pinned Brannie's body against the tree. He was reaching for his leggings, but she beat him to it, shoving them down while she kept up their kiss. Not letting him break away.

She lifted her leg and wrapped it around his waist. With one push he was inside her and they both gasped and smiled at the same time.

Brannie returned her hands to his shoulders, digging her fingers into the back of his neck. She knew that might hurt a bit, but she got the feeling Aidan would like that.

She wasn't wrong.

Aidan hiked her raised leg a little higher and pinned her body to the tree trunk with his weight. Then he pulled his hips back and, with one glorious push, he shoved his cock back in.

Her breath caught and her fingers dug harder, urging him on. He wasted no more time, fucking Brannie hard with long, powerful strokes.

When Brannie had pulled down his leggings, she'd still been kissing him, and hadn't managed to catch sight of his hardened cock. But she didn't need to see it. She could *feel* it. Filling her up completely, hitting a spot deep inside her.

Every nerve inside her came alive, her body now meeting his stroke for stroke. It took little time before she was panting and trembling, her pussy contracting tight around him. She pulled her mouth away from their kiss so she could bite down on his shoulder. She did that to stifle her screams as she came hard, her brain briefly shutting down as everything around her exploded.

She moved his chain mail aside just so she could bite down on his shoulder. The bite was hard, drawing blood. And it was all Aidan needed to send him over the edge, coming hard inside her, his hips jerking, his hands gripping her waist.

She was coming too and that made his release even stronger. If they were attacked right now, he was sure he couldn't fight back. He'd be oblivious even if a sword rammed into his spine.

But Aidan didn't care. Not when something felt this good. It was like her pussy had been built just for his cock, wrapping around him perfectly and holding him tight.

And when her pussy began contracting . . . his eyes crossed and he briefly wondered if he'd lose consciousness.

He didn't, but when they'd both wrung themselves dry, they were still clinging to each other, panting and sweating, even in this cold.

Aidan had no idea how long they stayed like that but Brannie's tap against his shoulder pulled him back to the moment.

"The suns are coming up," she warned, meaning the rest of their camp would be rising at this very moment.

"Right," he muttered, working hard not to growl when he forced himself to pull out of her.

He stepped back and gazed at her.

"No, no," she said with a shake of her head, trying to pretend she wasn't still panting. "We'll have none of that."

"None of what?"

"That look."

"What look?"

"That look on your face that says you're feeling a bit . . . clingy. We needed to get this out of our systems and we did. That's it."

"Is it?"

"Aye. It *is*."

Brannie took a step and nearly crumpled to her knees but Aidan caught her, got her back up, worked even harder not to laugh.

"Not a word," she cautioned.

"Wouldn't think of it."

Tossing her head back, she took a few tentative steps, found her balance, and headed toward the water.

"Need to cool down?" he teased.

Throwing her arm back, she raised two fingers at him.

"Awwww," he said, laughing, "now that was just rude!"

Chapter Twelve

"Why are you smiling?" Caswyn asked Brannie while they were packing up their horses.

"No reason," she replied, dropping her head down. She needed to get hold of herself.

"Don't lie to me. What are you plotting?"

Now Brannie looked at the big dragon in human form. "What?"

"You heard me." His eyes narrowed. "What are you planning?"

Whispering, she replied, "Just your death."

Now Caswyn's eyes grew wide in panic but there was Aidan, pulling his friend away and back toward his own horse.

"We're losing daylight," Aidan announced. "Let's move."

He briefly stopped on the other side of Brannie's horse to glare at her.

"What?" she asked.

"Stop it."

"I didn't do anything. He's being paranoid."

"Is he?" Aidan asked, sounding wonderfully judgmental.

Good-byes were said to her kin, the triplets hugging

Brannie hard before mounting their horses and heading off. Rhona stopped long enough to give her one of her speeches about duty and honor, but when she realized that Brannie had stopped listening halfway through, she went back to her old tactics of hitting her once in the back of the head and ordering, "Don't be stupid!" Then she, the other dragons, and all those wonderful weapons and armor were gone.

They turned the opposite way and began their journey toward the Port Cities. It had been ages since Brannie had been to the port towns, where a growing number of lands and people brought their wares to sell and trade. It was completely logical that Ren would head there to go home.

Which was why Brannie was still hoping that Ren was alive and well. Maybe even heading this way with his mother's army at his side.

For once, Brannie did feel bad for Keita. She'd forgotten how close Keita and Ren had always been. Not as lovers. She wasn't sure, but she didn't think they'd ever been lovers. But as best friends? Maybe even siblings? That they were. That they would always be.

And losing someone you considered a brother or sister had to be hard. Thinking of Izzy being cut down in battle made Brannie sick and they'd been like sisters since they'd met all those years ago.

Even now Brannie missed Izzy. After her morning with Aidan, the first thing Brannie would have done would be to tell Izzy. In detail. And not having her here hurt. Their kinship went beyond the blood and tough times they'd shared during battle. They considered themselves sisters on another level. Their species differences—dragon versus human—meant nothing when it came down to it. Because they understood each other as no one else had ever understood them.

Brannie's brother Celyn didn't even understand her the way Izzy did. And this trip would be ten thousand times more tolerable if only her best friend were here.

"Such sighs," Aidan remarked from beside her, pulling her away from her thoughts. "What makes Branwen the Awful so miserable?"

She gave a little smile. "I'm not miserable. Just missing—"

"The great Izzy?"

Brannie nodded. "This is the kind of mission she loved when there was no war to pull us away. For some, a proper holiday is in the Desolate Caverns. For me and Iz, it was finding shit to get into. A little protection work. A little killing when necessary." She sighed again. "I miss our holidays."

"Wasn't it one of your holidays with Izzy where Éibhear nearly lost a foot?"

Eyes rolling, "Gods, is he still going on about that? We wouldn't have let him be sacrificed. I don't know why he goes on so about it."

"Because he almost lost a *foot*."

"All these years and he's still a big baby."

Keita suddenly pulled back on the reins of her horse and looked around.

Brannie stopped behind her cousin and sighed once more. "You're lost, aren't you?"

"I am not lost. I'm just . . ."

"Lost."

"Orienting myself!"

"This road does lead us to the Port Cities," Aidan pointed out.

"But remember what the priest said. He didn't lose Ren in Port Cities, so I'm just—"

"Lost."

Keita glared at Brannie. "We are not lost, peasant!" She suddenly pointed. "There. We should head that way."

Eyes narrowing, Brannie grabbed Aidan's arm before he could ride off with his Mì-runach brethren who would automatically follow.

"Why?" Brannie asked Keita.

"Why what?"

"Why would Ren turn off that way?"

"Why are you asking me that?"

"Because I'm almost positive you're guessing. And we don't have time for your guesses. So why don't we just go to the Port Cities, then backtrack ten leagues northeast? See what we find?"

"I'd rather follow in Ren's claw-steps, thank you very much."

"That's fine, but you don't know where that is."

"We are five dragons," Keita needlessly reminded her. "I think we can handle a little off-road searching." She pointed at a large dent in a nearby tree. "*And* the mark on that tree. That's from Ren. A message to me."

"You're sure?"

"Are you calling me a liar?"

"Every day, but in this instance, I just want you to be sure. It's not like we have a lot of time here, Keita."

"I am well aware of our time limits. So"—she threw out her arm in a big, sweeping gesture—"can we please go, cousin?"

Brannie glanced at Aidan, but all he did was give a small shrug, which meant he was leaving this decision completely up to her. And since she was the ranking officer, that was probably for the best.

Taking the lead, Brannie steered her horse into the trees and hoped they weren't making a mistake they'd regret later.

* * *

It took Aidan some time to realize that Keita wasn't merely wandering aimlessly. She was actually following the tracks of her friend. More than once, she'd dismount from her horse and study the ground, or nearby trees.

Shocked, Brannie kept looking at him, as if she expected him to tell her, "Don't worry. You're dreaming. Your flighty cousin *isn't* a well-trained spy and tracker."

But she was. And she was damn good.

After three hours of moving through the forest, Keita paused near a small town called Aberthol.

Aidan had passed by this town often when he was on the move with his Mì-runach brethren. But he'd never had the time or need to stop in for the night. It was so far from main roads, Aidan doubted many made Aberthol one of their stops.

So to find evidence that the Zealots had made the town one of their sanctuaries wasn't exactly shocking.

But he'd admit that the sight of the massive fort not even a mile from the town . . . that was a bit of a shock.

And the rows and *rows* of humans who had been "purified," staked out in meticulous lines? That, too, took them all by surprise.

Keita's horse reared back after sniffing the first victim. The decomposing body on its knees, body staked to the ground by a wood spike through its diaphragm and out its spine and directly into the dirt. Its head tipped all the way back, hardened silver covering the sockets where the eyes used to be before they'd been burned out. The mouths frozen open in panic and horror.

That was the Zealots' "purification" process when their victims refused to give up their gods and their beliefs. They poured molten silver into their victims' eyes and allowed them to slowly die under the two suns. It might take hours . . . sometimes days.

Keita expertly got her horse to back up until she was safely hidden in the trees beside the rest of their small party. With a nod, she turned her horse and rode farther away from the fort.

When she finally stopped, the rest of the group surrounded her and Keita's gaze landed on her cousin.

"On Annwyl's land?" Brannie bit out between clenched teeth, her anger great.

"You need to calm down."

"I need to kill them all."

"So many bodies," Caswyn muttered. "How could they kill so many defenseless people?"

Few of the bodies purified appeared to have been warriors. Most appeared to be locals.

Keita took in a breath. "I know this is . . . disturbing."

"It's more than that."

Holding up her hand to her cousin, Keita went on. "But I think Ren . . ." She took a moment, looking off and licking her lips. Attempting to get control of her emotions.

The royal cleared her throat. "I need to know if Ren is in—"

"I'll go," Brannie announced.

"I can't ask—"

"You didn't ask. But I'm not sending you in there. I can get in."

"What if the Eastlander is . . ." Uther paused a moment, worried how to phrase the rest of his sentence. ". . . among the . . . uh . . . purified?"

"They'd know," Aidan explained, "that as an Eastlander he must be a royal. He'd have a place of honor. Either inside the fort or right outside the main gates. I doubt he'd be left among the rows of the dead."

"If he's here. I'll find him," Brannie said.

"I'm going with you," Aidan told her.

"No. I need you to get Keita to the Eastlands if—"

"Caswyn and Uther can get me to the Eastlands if necessary," Keita cut in. "Aidan, go with her. I don't want my cousin in there alone."

"I'll be fine."

"No," Keita said with a determined shake of her head. "*No.*"

"The suns have gone down," Aidan announced, dismounting his horse. "Let's go."

Chapter Thirteen

Letting their horses go with Uther and Caswyn, Brannie and Aidan stayed in the line of trees surrounding the fort and waited.

They waited in the same position for hours. Even when it began to rain and they were soaked to the bone, they waited.

This was why Brannie had sent Keita off with Uther and Caswyn. Not just to keep her safe but because Brannie didn't want to hear her complain the entire time that they needed to "move! Move now!"

As a Protector of the Throne—something that *still* had Brannie's mind spasming every time she thought about it—Keita might have the patience necessary in every assassin, but knowing Ren might be trapped inside that fort, possibly being tortured . . .

No. It was best she was kept out of the middle of this for now. For her own good and the good of everyone else.

The downpour had stopped by the time Brannie saw what she'd expected all along . . . . that this fort was very well protected.

For those unwilling to wait, it probably appeared as if the fort was undefended like many of the temples in the Southlands. But the Zealots weren't like other god worshippers and this was no temple. It was a battle fort. Nothing more or less.

So, as Brannie patiently waited and watched, she finally saw the changing of the guard. Zealots seemed to appear out of shadow and mist to be replaced by comrades who, just as smoothly, disappeared into shadow and mist.

Once she was positive of where the guards were located, she looked at Aidan. He nodded and, still crouching, they began to move through the trees until they were across from the best spot to get inside.

Now it was their turn to move as if part of shadow and mist. A skill Brannie had been trained in when she was still clinging to her father's tail. Her poor father. She'd loved creeping around and sneaking up on him when he was involved in his work, scaring the wits from him. In retrospect, it seemed cruel. Her father was as far from a warrior as one could get. But he'd always been a good sport about it.

"You're like your uncles!" he'd exclaim, picking her up and tossing her high in the air, laughing at her hysterical giggles. "Always trying to find ways to scare the very life from me."

But it was those early years of childish play that had trained her for this.

Aidan was glad Keita had insisted he accompany Brannie into the fort. He would have insisted if she hadn't, but the order was better coming from her. That way Brannie could be annoyed with her cousin rather than him.

His need to go with Brannie wasn't because he feared so greatly for her safety. Not at all. He just didn't want her alone in a Zealot-run fort. He was sure there were priests and priestesses inside who could manage a rampaging dragoness if Brannie were forced to shift. And magick sometimes trumped just being a very large dragon. Especially when the dragon didn't have any magickal skills of her own besides being able to shift.

But two dragons . . . ? Well, that was a bit more of a challenge for anyone.

As the pair stepped away from the tree line, the skies opened up once more and rain poured down on them. They glanced at each other and nodded.

Rain worked in their favor.

But as they began to move forward, lightning struck. That was more of a problem. A good bolt could light up the sky . . . and the land beneath, alerting the guards to their presence.

Brannie paused for maybe a half second before she took off running, keeping low. Perhaps they could outrun the lightning.

Aidan immediately followed after her.

Thunder exploded right over them and Brannie picked up speed. They slammed their backs against the fort wall just as a lightning strike snapped over their heads, lighting up the entire surrounding area.

Letting out a breath, they looked at each other again and, with a nod from Brannie, they split up. He went left, she went right.

The first guard he came to made the mistake of turning his head to muffle his cough. Aidan caught him from behind, wrapping his hand around the guard's mouth and burying his dagger into the side of his neck. He dropped the body and moved to the next one.

Lightning hit at the same time Aidan arrived and the guard saw him. The man opened his mouth to warn his friends, but his words were lost in the thunder and rain. He tried again, but Aidan stopped him by slamming his dagger into his open mouth, pinning the human to the fort wall.

Aidan yanked out his blade and stepped over the body.

His next few attacks went well and he met up with Brannie in under ten minutes.

And yet she still felt the need to complain, "Took you long enough, Mì-runach."

Ignoring her comment, Aidan asked, "Do we storm the front gates, killing everyone in sight? Or sneak in silently, like my worthless brethren?"

Brannie actually thought on that a moment—he'd been kidding!—before she grudgingly replied, "Sneak."

Then she sighed. As if such a suggestion was so beneath her.

Pushing her wet hair off her face, she motioned for him to follow her and then set off. They went halfway around the fort, finally stopping at a small door hidden behind a large bush.

Brannie pushed the door open and got on her knees. She leaned in, looking around before she signaled for him to, again, follow her.

With a deep breath, steeling himself, Aidan waited until Brannie's adorable human ass disappeared inside. Then he went in after her.

The small door led them into a network of underground tunnels. A way in and out for Zealots who might need to escape.

Apparently all the Zealots were *not* ready to die for their precious one god.

When they got to a section of the tunnel that split in several ways, Brannie silently pointed in one direction for Aidan and she took the other. She knew he probably wanted to stick with her, but they were low on time and had a lot of ground to cover. Pretending to be her nursemaid would be a foolish move.

Brannie walked down the long hallway. Above her she

could hear movement, some chanting. She assumed she was close to a center of worship.

The tunnel split off again and, as she briefly debated which way to go, she heard a shout of warning from above. Someone had found the bodies outside.

Another shout from behind her, though, had Brannie quickly moving to the left, her back flat against the stone wall. A few seconds later, Aidan ran by . . . and a squad of armed Zealots ran right after him.

She rolled her eyes. "Idiot."

Brannie knew Aidan the Divine well enough to know—*know!*—that he'd allowed himself to be seen. Why? Probably to protect her. To distract the guards already searching the tunnels and fort for them.

Stepping out of the shadows, she started to follow Aidan but stopped short when she saw a door at the end of the hallway.

She gritted her teeth. Follow Aidan? Go to the door?

"Eh," she said with a wave of her hand. "He'll be fine."

Brannie ran to the door and eased it open to find stone stairs. Closing the door behind her, she made her way down. As she neared the last step, she could hear chains . . . and sobbing.

A dungeon.

Just what she'd been looking for.

Brannie reached the last step and stopped, silently waiting for a guard to pass. Once he did, she moved up behind him and quickly cut his throat.

Footsteps came from behind and Brannie turned, throwing the blade. It slammed into the second guard's head and he fell back. She retrieved the weapon and slid it into the sheath at her side.

Brannie checked for more guards, but didn't see any, so she made her way down to a large open space. In the middle of the room were tables covered in chains, metal cuffs, and blood. Chains also hung from the ceilings. And on each wall Chramnesind's sigil had been burned into the stone.

If the sigils were magickal, Brannie wouldn't know until they destroyed her. But she didn't deal with magicks. She left that to witches and other blessed folk. All warriors could do was hope for the best.

Brannie moved to the far wall and started down the long room. Not every cage had someone in it, but most did. So she studied each carefully in the hope of finding Ren.

She'd just reached the end of the first wall of cages when she heard, "Branwen the Awful?"

It was a female voice, so not Ren. But Brannie spun around, wondering who called to her.

Blinking, she rushed across the floor to the cages on the other side.

"Kachka?" She stopped in front of the cage and gawked at the three Riders inside. "What are you doing here?"

Kachka Shestakova of the Black Bear Riders of the Midnight Mountains of Despair in the Far Reaches of the Steppes of the Outerplains—and yes, that was her *entire* name—had come to the "decadent and corrupt" Southlands with her sister Elina Shestakova. They were true Daughters of the Steppes. Hearty, powerful women who thought men were beneath them, only good for sex and garbage removal. They were warriors and horsewomen known for breeding and raising small but remarkable horses that were great in battle and during long, cross-country rides.

The Daughters of the Steppes were nomads, moving their many tribes around the steppes and, when necessary, raiding Northland and Outerplains towns in search of boys to use for husbands. A term that Annwyl said should be changed to "slaves."

Although the leader of the Daughters of the Steppes, the one they called the Anne Atli, had an alliance with Annwyl, her involvement in the war—and thereby the involvement of her people—had been limited to providing food, water, and horses when necessary. Otherwise, the Daughters of the Steppes had not raised a sword against any of the Zealots as long as they stayed away from their territories.

So, in the end, less of an alliance and more of a truce. The Riders didn't strike the Zealots but they also didn't strike Annwyl's troops.

So why were *these* Daughters of the Steppes fighting for Annwyl in a small squad referred to as "The Scourge of gods"? Because these were the Riders no longer wanted by the tribes for varying reasons. Kachka and Elina had lost their positions because of their mother, a price Elina wore on her face every day with an eye socket that no longer held an eye. Kachka had defended Elina and that had put her outside the tribes as well. Now, both women had found dragons to keep them company. Brannie's brother Celyn had fallen in love with Elina, and Kachka had managed to snag the very handsome Rebel King of the Quintilian Provinces, Gaius Lucius Domitus.

Even Brannie thought that was a coup. Gaius was an exceptionally gorgeous Iron dragon and, coincidentally, also missing an eye.

But even more impressive to Brannie was that Kachka hadn't suddenly given up her life as a warrior once she'd made a king her mate. She hadn't taken her place on a Quintilian throne to give orders behind the safety of a legion of guards. She had left that to Gaius's twin sister, Agrippina, and continued to do what she'd done before. She took her orders from Annwyl or, if necessary, Dagmar. And she still took her squad of Rider Rejects—Gwenvael's nickname for them—around the country, attacking Zealots where and when she could under the cover of darkness, leaving nothing but blood, death, and Zealot remains behind.

But there should be at least seven of the Rider Rejects,

including a male, and she'd never thought that Riders would allow themselves to be taken alive.

"What are we doing here?" Kachka repeated, her elbow resting against the steel bars. She looked over her shoulder. "Yes, Zoya Kolesova, tell Celyn's big-shouldered sister how we got here."

"Still?" the giant Zoya Kolesova asked from the corner of the cage. "Still you blame me for this?"

"Yes!" Nina Chechneva, the actual witch of the group, shouted. "This is your fault, Zoya Kolesova! It will be your fault until the day you die. And on that day, I will wear red, dance on your still burning corpse, *and sing the song of happiness!*"

"Always so dramatic, unclean one," Zoya lashed back.

"Shut up!"

Kachka looked at Brannie and drily asked, "Does that answer your question, Celyn's sister?"

"Not really."

Uther knew as soon as the rain started that Keita would begin to complain. So he found a very large tree with lots of protective leaves and got her situated before going off to find something to feed her. A hungry She-dragon could be annoying *and* dangerous. So he grabbed Caswyn and they went in search of something to feed on. Because it was raining, it was harder than usual to track something down, but they eventually caught a deer, killed it, and dragged it back to the tree where they'd left Keita.

Dropping the deer, Uther turned in a circle. "Where . . . where is she?

"If something happened to her . . ." He threw up his arms. "First Puddles and then Keita? Brannie will tear our bloody heads off!"

Uther looked at the ground, trying to find any tracks or signs of where Keita might have gone.

The heavy rain, however, had turned the ground into mud and the flashes of lightning weren't helping. Sniffing the air was useless, especially since every time he raised his face, his nose filled with water.

Frustrated, they both started walking, still searching the ground, hoping to find something—anything—that would tell them where Keita had gone. They found a few tracks under the bigger trees, where the leaves offered some protection.

"Oh, no," Caswyn said, barely audible above the harsh rain.

"What?" Uther demanded. "What is it?" Uther ran to his side, desperately pushing his wet hair off his face.

"I think she went there."

Uther's gaze followed where Caswyn was pointing. He'd been focused on the ground so hard, he hadn't realized where they were heading.

He gawked at the fort and shook his head. "Brannie is definitely going to kill us."

"They must have been tracking us for weeks, these pathetic fools." Kachka let out a breath. "They waited until we separated. I sent the Khoruzhaya siblings, Marina Aleksandrovna and my cousin Tatyana Shestakova back to Garbhán Isle to protect the weak Northwoman until the Dragon Queen's concubine—"

"I'm gonna warn you now that Uncle Bercelak is *not* going to like that nickname," Brannie called over her shoulder. She was desperately searching for something that would get the cage open. There was no lock for Brannie to simply rip apart. Instead, the cage was welded shut on all sides. She could use her flame but that could put the Riders in danger of burning to death if the metal didn't melt quickly enough.

"—and Annwyl's armies destroy the Zealots."

"Why did you three stay behind?" Brannie asked.

"To find Ren. But we were too late."

Brannie froze and faced Kachka. "What?"

The Rider shrugged. "When they sealed us in here, he was in the cage right next to ours. We talked a bit but he was taken away by three guards. We heard screams . . . then nothing. Later they brought out his head."

Brannie felt sick, but she forced herself past it. "They didn't purify him?"

"Not that we saw."

"Where is the head now?"

Kachka gestured to the cage. "Perhaps you do not see we are still behind bars."

"Oh. Right. Right." Shaking her head, she went back to the torture tables and looked at the weaponry hanging overhead. There had to be some way to get the damn cage open.

"How long ago was this?"

"Two weeks."

Brannie stopped again. "You haven't been out of that cage in two weeks?"

"Do you want to see bucket?"

"No, thank you."

"They hope to starve us."

"They haven't fed you in all that time?"

"No food. No water."

"Shouldn't you be . . . weaker?"

"We are Daughters of Steppes. Some seasons on the plains are very good. Very plentiful. Others? We are lucky if we do not eat the weakest of our tribe."

"Sometimes we do." When Kachka, Nina, and Brannie all stared at Zoya, the giant Rider asked, "What? Only the Mountain Movers of the Lands of Pain in the Far Reaches of the Steppes of the Outerplains have ever eaten their weakest members?"

Nina glared directly at Brannie. "Get me the fuck out of here. I will spend not one more minute with this giant open sore!"

"I have saved your life, Nina Chechneva, the Unclaimed!"

"And I have saved yours, Zoya Kolesova! We owe each other nothing *except disdain and hatred!*"

Calmly Kachka motioned Brannie over with a wave of her hand. When Brannie stood in front of her, Kachka grabbed her throat and yanked her even closer.

"I will say this once to you, Celyn's sister—"

"I have a name," Brannie choked out.

"—get me out of here or burn everything down around me. Because I cannot listen to another moment of this *ridiculous horse shit!*"

Aidan had led the Zealots on a merry chase through the tunnels and eventually out of them but, sadly, he ended up trapped inside their main hall, Zealots surrounding him.

He didn't know if he'd given Brannie enough time to find Ren but there was nothing he could do about that now. He had to get the two of them out of there.

Aidan was reaching for the sword at his side when he heard the screams of other Zealots moments before Uther and Caswyn came charging into the main hall, covered in blood, and in a complete panic.

"What are you doing?" he asked, trying not to laugh.

But it was hard. The Zealots were screaming and running in such a panic that he couldn't help himself.

His laughter died, though, when Caswyn exploded with, "Keita's gone!"

"Gone? Gone where?"

"We have no idea," Uther explained while snapping a Zealot's neck. "We went to get her something to eat and when we came back—"

"You left her?"

"Who knew she'd wander off?"

Aidan yanked his sword out of a Zealot's gut. "Keita doesn't wander anywhere. Don't let her bare feet fool you. That dragoness always has a plan."

He looked around, pointed at a door with his blood-covered sword. "There. The dungeon. Let's get Brannie and get out of here."

"What about Keita?"

"She'll find us when she's done."

Caswyn yanked the spine out of a Zealot's back before asking, wide-eyed, "When she's done doing what?"

"Let's not ask. Let's just get Brannie."

It didn't matter that Keita couldn't find Ren's body. She knew her friend was gone. Dead. And that these people had killed him.

Standing among all those "purified" bodies, Keita closed her fist and raised her face to the sky. Rain poured down and mingled with her tears.

Tears for her friend.

She had more to do, but not before she got revenge for Ren, before she made these Zealots suffer.

And they would suffer. . . .

"Move to the back," Brannie ordered the Riders. "As far back as you can."

Once the three women had gotten in place, Brannie went to the side of the cage and studied a spot she hoped would be easily melted by fire.

She also hoped that she wouldn't burn any of the Riders when she unleashed her flame. Some dragons had amazing control of their flame. It was said the queen could use her flame like a whip. But that was the queen. When Brannie unleashed her flame, she could easily wipe out a small forest. Once she took out half a town. She'd felt really bad about that, too.

She'd warned the Riders of the risk, though, and they didn't seem to care. Of course, they had a thing about dying . . . they weren't afraid to. But she'd never hear the end of it from Celyn if she ended up accidentally killing Elina's sister.

"Ready?" she asked.

"Just go already!" Kachka bellowed.

"All right. All right."

Brannie let out a breath, focused on a spot, and opened her mouth—

"Brannie!"

Growling, she turned to see Aidan and the other two barreling into the dungeon. Aidan quickly came forward, while Caswyn and Uther slammed the double doors shut.

"We have a problem," Aidan told her as soon as he was close enough.

"What did they do now?"

"It's not their fault."

"Don't make excuses for them. Just tell me what's going on."

He swallowed. "Keita disappeared."

Brannie felt a muscle in her neck twitch. "She was captured?"

"No."

She took in a breath. "We need to get them out." Brannie pointed at the bars. "I can try and melt them but—"

"Uther! Caswyn! Cage!"

The two lumbering oxen made their way over to the cage and Brannie tossed keys to Aidan. "Get as many out as you can."

As soon as Aidan began the process, Brannie heard a

horrible wrenching noise and turned in time to see Uther and Caswyn ripping apart the cage with only the help of their human hands.

Even the Riders were impressed. Well, all except Zoya.

"At least these two men have *some* skills."

"Males," Nina corrected.

"What?"

"They're not men. They're males. Dragons. Remember?"

Zoya stepped out of the open cage, eyeing the two males before loudly announcing, "Then I would expect more of them! Such weak dragons! Dragons!" she exclaimed, walking past the shocked—and hurt—pair.

"We could have left you in there, you know," Uther reminded her.

"The great dragon captain would not have allowed that, would you, Branwen the Awful?"

"Well—"

"Exactly!" She pushed past Aidan and, with her bare hands, began prying open doors that, unlike hers, hadn't been melted shut.

Aidan didn't bother to argue with the Rider. He didn't bother to argue with anyone really. Instead, he just made his way over to the other cages and worked with Kachka to release everyone else.

Nina Chechneva didn't help anyone—as was her way—but instead stared at the sigil burned into the wall.

"Did you know that mark keeps you and your friends from shifting to dragon, Branwen the Awful?"

"What? Oh . . . no. I didn't. But I hadn't tried either."

"You do not feel weak?"

"No." She faced the strange and, frankly, unpleasant witch and added, "I'm sure we can still murder anyone in our way and burn the flesh from their bones for a tasty meal. You know, in case you were wondering."

Dark, *dark* eyes studied Brannie but, after facing "Auntie"

Brigida's soulless stare on occasion, Brannie had learned not to show any fear to the magick wielders.

She flashed Nina a smile before giving her a hearty slap on her back. The witch stumbled forward, shocked, and Brannie announced, "But we're all friends here, aren't we, Nina Chechneva?"

"All friends!" Zoya agreed as she hustled the few weakened humans that were let out of their cages. "Some of these humans we may want to kill now. They are too weak to travel."

"No, Zoya Kolesova," Aidan said before Brannie had the chance. "We'll not do that."

"I do not listen to you, penis haver."

"Then I'll say it," Brannie cut in, using her firmest captain voice. "We kill no one. If someone can't travel out of this fort on their own, you can carry them on your strong Kolesova back."

Zoya nodded. "All right."

Aidan rolled his eyes, frustrated his words alone hadn't bent Zoya to his will. But to Zoya Kolesova, a male was a male was a male. It didn't matter if they were dragon or men or giant trolls. If they were male, they simply weren't worth listening to.

And, honestly, Brannie enjoyed that part of Zoya. Her logic was pure, as was her unwillingness to change it.

"Oy!" Caswyn yelled out. "I found another way—"

The double doors Aidan and Uther had closed off burst open and armed Zealots flooded into the room, one of their eyeless priests leading the way.

When both eyes were missing, Brannie knew she was dealing with not only a slavering sycophant of Chramnesind, but a powerful priest. Apparently Chramnesind really liked his followers to slaver.

The weakened humans that had been trapped in these

dungeons for days immediately panicked and moved as quickly as they could behind Branwen and the others.

"Going so soon?" the priest asked. "And we had so many plans for those who follow the Abominations and their whore mother."

Brannie was already moving on the priest when Aidan grabbed her arm and yanked her back. She had no idea why he'd bothered. He'd never stopped her from killing one of the Zealot priests before.

But then she saw it. Easing into the room from the stairs. Smoke.

Brannie's nose twitched and she immediately knew this wasn't some regular fire. The smoke was tainted with . . . something. She could smell it.

Then, the Zealots in the back of their group began to spasm. Eyes—those who had them—rolled back in the Zealots' heads, saliva poured from their mouths, weapons dropped to the floor from paralyzed fingers.

"Keita," Aidan said softly. And it was all she needed to hear.

"Move!" Brannie ordered the others. "*Move!*"

Those too weak were picked up by Zoya, Uther, and Caswyn. Caswyn led the way to a door in the walls he'd found. He pushed it open and went inside, the rest of them following.

Once Brannie stepped in, she turned to close the door firmly behind her, giving her a brief view of what was happening to the Zealots she was leaving behind.

Whatever poisonous smoke Keita had released into this place, it was not merely killing the Zealots. It was torturing them. Giving them the most violent, painful death any of them could imagine.

That's how Brannie knew. She knew that Keita had somehow found out that her longtime friend was dead and that these Zealots were responsible.

Shutting the door, Brannie turned and charged up behind the others. She grabbed two of the slowest humans and began to run with them in her arms.

"Move!" she ordered again. "All of you, *move!*"

It took a little time, but they eventually found their way back to the door that they'd used to get in.

Once Aidan got the humans he was carrying out, he went back to help the others.

He assisted as many as he could until they were far enough away to drop to the ground.

The smoke had nearly caught up to them as they'd made their mad escape. Now, gasping and coughing, Aidan stretched out on the ground with the others under the pouring rain and looked back at the fort.

Most dragons would have burned it down to the ground and been done with it. But not Keita. There was no fire. Just smoke. *Poisonous* smoke.

And that poisonous smoke came out from behind every small window, from behind and under doors, from every crack in the foundation. It came out and curled up into the air.

And with it, he could hear the screams and cries of the suffering and slowly dying Zealots.

It wasn't that Aidan was bothered by the deaths of their sworn enemies. Actually, that didn't bother him at all. What did bother him however . . .

"Did you forget we were in there?" Brannie demanded of her cousin when she walked up to them.

Keita shrugged. "You were taking too long."

Despite his need to cough up whatever was traveling through his lungs, Aidan still managed to jump up and grab hold of Brannie before she could throw herself at Keita.

"Do you ever think of anyone but yourself?" Brannie demanded. "We are here for you and this is how you treat us?"

With an eye roll, Keita walked off and Brannie tried to go after her, but Aidan kept his arms around her waist, holding her back.

"Let it go," he suggested.

"Let it go? She could have killed us, too!"

"She lost Ren," Uther said, helping some of the stronger humans up so they could assist the others. They wouldn't be able to travel with the dragons. The humans would have to rely on each other.

"Yeah," Caswyn tossed in. "How would you feel if it had been Iz?"

Brannie stopped fighting, but she clearly didn't like what they were saying either because she rammed her elbow into Aidan's collarbone, forcing him to release her.

"Ow! That hurt."

"Good."

Uther pointed. "You should talk to her."

Brannie's mouth dropped open at the suggestion. "*Talk* to her?"

"She's your cousin."

"So?"

"If this was Izzy—"

"Shut up!" Brannie closed her eyes and blew out a breath. "I hate all of you," she complained before going after Keita.

Brannie grudgingly followed after her kin.

She felt her logic was sound. Keita had taken a stupid risk doing what she did and, as Cadwaladrs, conversation wasn't necessary.

A good beating, however . . . that was more than warranted. But the "nanny gang" seemed to think Brannie owed

Keita some kind of consideration. And invoking Izzy every time they wanted her to do something. . . .

It was just wrong!

Brannie's relationship with Izzy was different from every other relationship she had. Unlike Brannie and Celyn, Brannie didn't have random, morning fistfights with Izzy. They didn't argue about who Mum and Da loved more. They didn't argue about who was more stupid: Oxen or their brother Fal. They simply enjoyed each other's company, whether sitting in Izzy's tent drinking Uncle Bercelak's ale or in the midst of battle.

Brannie and Keita, on the other hand, had little in common. They were blood relations but that was all.

So what could Brannie possibly say to the royal that would somehow connect them and make this bloody trip at least tolerable?

"I . . ." Brannie began, walking fast to keep up with Keita. "I . . . uh . . . heard that cousin Eugenie is sleeping with Duke Clemens."

Keita got a few more feet before she stopped and, slowly, faced Brannie.

"What?"

Brannie cleared her throat. "Eugenie is sleeping with Duke Clemens."

"He's more than sixty winters. And her mother *hates* humans."

"And he's an old human. Eugenie's mum is said to be beside herself with rage. Uncle Rhys doesn't know how to handle it. His wife is that angry."

"I don't blame her," Keita said, glancing off. "Eugenie's a baby. Not even eighty yet."

"Her brother says she's an old soul."

"She's not an old soul. She's a young soul that likes pissing off her mother. I should know . . ." She shrugged. "I'm the queen of Pissing-Off-Mother Land."

Brannie chuckled but, after a few moments, she asked, "How did you know?" Keita raised her eyebrows. "About Ren."

She held out her hand, revealing a gold medallion and chain in her palm.

"This was his. I found it among the bodies outside the fort."

"So? He could have dropped—"

"It was sewn inside him." She stroked her left side. "I and other Protectors have the same thing. The only way they could have gotten it—"

"Was to cut it out of him."

"And he wouldn't have let that happen unless he was already dead."

"I'm sorry, Keita. I really am. I've always liked Ren so much. We all have."

She closed her palm and placed her fist against her chest. "He fit in well among us. On both sides of the family. Amazing, since he was nothing like any of us."

Keita's head dropped and she stared at the ground. That's when Brannie realized the rain had stopped. It was much quieter now, so they could hear the screams of the dying from the fort more clearly now.

"Look, Branwen . . ." Keita's shoulders slumped a little under her wet cape. "I have to do things. When we get to the Eastlands. And I don't have time to argue—"

"I know what you have to do. Mum told me."

Keita lifted her gaze to Brannie's. "And?"

"I have my orders, cousin. I'm with you on this. My feelings on it don't matter. But I'd prefer you not forget the rest of us exist and kill us in the process. You know . . . *accidentally*."

Keita gave a small smile. "I'll do my best. Oh!" she suddenly exclaimed, looking back in the direction of the fort. "We should really get everyone *away* from there."

Brannie briefly closed her eyes. "You're poisoning the air, aren't you?"

"A little."

With a growl, Brannie ran back toward the others as Keita yelled after her, "It won't last or anything, but . . . you know . . . for now . . . best to err on the side of caution . . . to avoid death."

Chapter Fourteen

Lord Phalet entered the dungeons with his personal guard and assistant Harex. They didn't rush forward, though. Not after word of his guest's antics had reached his long, pointed ears.

But, seeing her sitting on the floor, her back against the wall, head bowed in defeat . . .

Smiling, showing all his fangs, he pointed to the human. "See, Harex? She just needed a little time to cool down and to understand how completely trapped she is."

"Should I greet her properly, my lord?" Harex asked, his own fangs showing, his excitement at the prospect obvious.

"Please."

Harex moved down the hall until he reached her cell. He stepped close to the bars and purred, "Hello, my la— *ahhhhhhhhhhhhhhhhhhhhhhhhhhhhhhhhhhhhhhhhh!*"

Harex's scream of anguish rang out, startling them all.

The crazed female had launched herself from the ground to the bars, reached through, and gripped Harex by the head. Then she began attempting to pull him *through* the bars.

Harex fought back valiantly, but every time he got one arm off his head, she used the other. When she couldn't seem to get his rather large head between the bars, she gripped both of his ears and used her thumbs to dig into his eyes.

"Help him!" Phalet ordered. His guards actually hesitated before following his orders.

By the time they dragged Harex away, both his eyes were gone, his nostrils were torn open, and his throat nearly torn out. And the crazed female had done all that with only her hands.

Still attached to the bars, she screeched and clawed at Harex and the others. Once they were definitely no longer close, she stopped screeching, spit, lowered herself from the bars, and went back to sitting against the wall. Calm as she was before.

A panting, blind, profusely bleeding Harex was taken out of the dungeons but Phalex remained, staring at the woman he'd brought to his hellish kingdom.

He'd had humans here before. Warriors. Peasants. Even kings and queens. Some had died before they arrived, his world their fate after death; and some had fallen into a hell trap when they were still alive.

But this one . . . he'd brought her here specifically for his own purposes. She wasn't cooperating, however.

And, more disturbing, she was completely insane!

"What kind of rulers do these humans have?" he asked one of his guards.

"Do you want us to kill her now, my lord?"

"No. We need her. But"—he gestured vaguely in the woman's direction—"I don't know what to do with her."

"We can break her," his guard suggested. "If you'd allow us to deal with her . . . as a group."

Phalet had wanted to avoid that. It seemed so . . . human. But, sighing, he realized he didn't have much of a choice. They didn't have a lot of time and he needed her . . . flexible.

With a nod, he gave his permission, but added, "Break her, Cursain. Do not kill her."

"Of course not, my lord."

"Then good luck."

With orders given, plans neatly mapped out, and Lord Phalet back in his hall to meet his guests for dinner, Cursain and his fellow guards walked to the prisoner's cell. The door was unlocked and opened and they all silently entered.

As one, they stood and gazed down at her. When they were done . . . she'd beg to do anything for Lord Phalet if it meant the torture would stop.

The woman, hair falling in her face, lifted her head and Cursain had only a moment to see crazed green-gray eyes angrily glaring at him from underneath all that hair before her scream echoed around the walls and she was on him. . . .

Sitting at the head of the dining table, enjoying the screams of the dismembering happening at the other end of his hall while enjoying the casual conversation of the guests enjoying his feast, Lord Phalet was surprised when someone stroked his hair from behind.

He was about to turn when the stroking hand gripped his white strands tightly and yanked his head back. An arm reached over him and a blade slammed into his chest again and again.

His guests screamed and stumbled away from his table, no one bothering to assist him.

Worthless scum!

With the blade buried to the hilt in his chest, his attacker's lips pressed against his ear and whispered, "Come for me, demon, and you'd best bring an entire army."

Then Phalet was flipped out of his chair and dragged across the floor, his neck stomped on, his nose crushed. . . .

Then she was gone.

"Lord Phalet?" one of his worthless guests asked, coming into his blood-smeared view. "Are you all right?"

"Of course I'm not all right, idiot!" He raised his arms. "Get me up!"

He was brought to his feet so he could pull the blade from his chest. He recognized it as Cursain's dagger.

Thankfully that woman didn't know about demon anatomy. His heart wasn't in his chest as a human's was. And that lack of knowledge was the only thing that had kept him alive.

Stumbling and still bleeding profusely, Phalet made his way down to the dungeons along with some of his guests.

He saw the blood first. All over the floor. The walls. The ceiling. The other cells. Arms and legs were scattered everywhere. Many of his guards appeared to have been attacked as they were trying to get to the exit.

But the heads . . . the heads of his guards were in a nice pile in her cell, Cursain's at the top, his eyes and mouth open in horror.

"By the blackest hells, Phalet," one of his guests asked from behind him, "what unholy thing have you brought here?"

Phalet could only shake his head. "I don't know." But if the bitch wanted an army . . . then an army she would have.

Turning to a nearby servant, Phalet bellowed, *"Bring me General Scrilis!"*

Chapter Fifteen

They made it to the Port Cities and found a pub with rooms on the top floor and stables for their horses.

Uther, Caswyn, and the Riders stayed at the pub to drink and listen. See if they could find out anything.

Unlike Dagmar and anyone she hired to spy for her, Aidan's fellow brethren weren't actually *good* at being sneaky—nor, for that matter, were the Riders—but they were known for accidentally finding out information because they were drinking ale at the right place at the right time. Might as well try their luck once again.

Aidan, however, went with Brannie and Keita to the docks to find a boat that would take them to the Eastlands.

At least that's what Aidan thought they were going to do. So he was a little surprised when Keita took a turn down a street that moved them away from the docks and farther into town.

After nearly half an hour, she walked up stairs that led to a front door. She knocked and a servant answered.

Keita merely nodded her head and the servant opened the door fully, allowing Keita, Brannie, and Aidan inside. She had them wait in the hallway. He noticed marble floors, a gorgeous staircase leading to other floors, and expensive furniture.

Someone very wealthy lived here.

The servant returned and with another silent nod, she led them down the hallway to another doorway that opened onto stairs leading deep into the bowels of the building.

After his experience in the fort tunnels, Aidan would have been more than happy to wait somewhere near a speedy exit for Keita to finish her business, but that was never given as an option.

Once downstairs, they were taken through a dark tunnel until they reached a doorway. With a sweep of her hand, the servant gestured to the elaborate knob.

Keita pulled a small scarf from her cleavage and wrapped it around her hand. Then she opened the door.

"Is that doorknob poisoned?" Brannie asked, but the glare she got from her cousin instantly silenced her.

Males sat around a large room filled with books and parchment, and as soon as Keita stepped inside, they all got to their feet.

Keita moved quickly, cutting through all the men to throw herself into the arms of an elf.

"We just heard," the elf told her. "I'm so sorry, Keita."

She nodded against the elf's neck before pulling back. "Gorlas, this is my cousin, Branwen the Awful and Aidan the Divine."

The elf smiled. "Yes. I know Aidan the Divine."

Brannie and Keita stared at him, but Aidan could only shrug. "I'm sorry, but—"

"You don't know me, but we attempted to recruit you a few decades back. You were being sent to the Mì-runach, but we gave you another option."

Now Aidan smirked. "Oh. Yes. That."

"You had a chance to become a Protector of the Throne," Brannie asked, "but you *chose* to become Mi-runach? What for?"

"The queen was very clear—"

"Try again."

He gave a small shrug. "I knew it would piss off my father."

Brannie's eyes crossed. "I will never understand males."

Only Gorlas the elf introduced himself and, before Brannie had a chance to ask about anyone else, the others left. Exiting silently and not through the door they'd come through.

Fascinated—she walked around the room trying to find more exits—Brannie barely listened to the conversation going on around her.

An important conversation to be sure, but it wasn't like Brannie had a word to say about any of it. She was merely Keita's protection. "Get her to the Eastlands" were her only orders now that they were sure Ren was dead.

"The *Dowager,* a lovely sea vessel, will take you to the Empress Ports," Gorlas explained to Keita. "From there you can get transport to the palaces." Gorlas leaned his backside against a large table, arms folded in front of his chest. "You do know she won't be glad to see you without her son?"

"I know," Keita replied. "But by the time I get there, I'll be in full performance mode. Never fear."

"Good. She'll be looking for anything. Anything that will tell her the truth. Her powers, Keita—"

"I know. They rival my mother's."

"They may do more than that. The Empress comes from a long line of powerful She-dragons. She won't be easy to distract. Even for you."

"Understood."

"What do you plan to use?" the elf asked.

It was such an oddly phrased question that Brannie finally looked away from the wall where she was sure there must be some kind of hidden doorway.

"I can't bring anything with me. She'll find it. I'll have to use something local."

"Something she won't recognize?" Gorlas shook his head. "That's impossible."

"Don't worry. I have a plan."

"It'd better be a good one. If you go down"—he motioned to Brannie—"so does your cousin."

Now they were all staring at her.

Brannie took a step back. "I don't plan to go down that easy," she retorted. "So you can all stop looking at me like I'm already dead."

Gorlas gave a small smile and asked Keita about Branwen, "Is she very much like her mother?"

"Mirror images, if you ask me."

"You know my mother?" Brannie asked.

"Yes. She once tried to take my head."

"Did you deserve it?"

"A little." He walked to a small wood box, opened it, and handed Keita several items. A good-sized purse that rattled with much coin, a rolled parchment that Brannie would guess had a map drawn on it, and a small vial with something liquid and red inside.

"Why are you giving me this?" Keita asked, holding up the vial.

"You know why," Gorlas said plainly.

Keita looked down, but eventually nodded. In silence, she walked to a corner, her back to them, and it looked as if she was pulling up her skirts.

Brannie blinked and looked at Aidan, who returned her gaze with one of his own. Eyes wide.

Is she really putting that up her . . . yes. Yes, she is.

Smoothing down her skirts, Keita turned back around.

"Is that to kill yourself?" Brannie asked, stopping everyone in the room.

"Uh . . ."

"If it can do that—kill you, I mean—are you sure you should put it inside your pussy?"

Cringing, lips pressed together tight so he didn't laugh, Aidan began to study the ceiling while Gorlas merely stared at her, his eyes wide. Keita glared.

"Can we discuss this somewhere else, cousin?"

"Because *you* are suddenly shy?"

Keita faced Gorlas again.

"It's a valid question," Brannie insisted, but Keita merely raised her hand to shut her up. Not as if that had ever worked on her before unless they were in the midst of an ambush.

"Thank you, Gorlas," Keita said to the elf.

"Take care of yourself, my dearest Keita," he said, hugging her tight.

"Are you returning to Fenella right away?"

He pulled back, his expression surprised. "You don't know?"

"Know what?"

"Fenella is practically abandoned. The Zealots . . . they attacked the universities, the guilds . . . nothing and no one are safe. Until this war is over . . ."

Keita nodded. "It will be," she promised. "Very soon."

Chapter Sixteen

"You don't really think I'm going to let you kill yourself, do you?" Brannie asked her cousin.

"You'll do what I tell you to do," Keita snapped back, walking quickly through the streets. "But just so we're clear, destroying the perfection that is me is *not* my first choice."

"If I have any say—"

"You don't, cousin."

"Keita—"

The She-dragon stopped so quickly, both Brannie and Aidan almost rammed right into her. She pointed a small but angry-looking finger in their faces.

"You will do as I tell you, Branwen."

Brannie grabbed Keita's finger and twisted it down until she yelped.

"Vile beast!"

"This isn't about who's in charge, cousin," Brannie calmly explained. "Because whether you're a royal and I am a grunt, we are—in the end—both Cadwaladrs. And I'm not about to let you do something that will bring shame upon our kin. So let's just get over to the Eastlands, kill whoever needs to be killed, and then at least attempt to get back home before they kill us all."

Holding her wounded finger against her chest, Keita glowered at Brannie. But it was obvious she had nothing to say back to her. What was there to add? Brannie had the best argument-ender . . . Cadwaladr logic.

But because there was nothing for her to say to her cousin, she focused her rage on Aidan.

"And you," Keita said, stepping closer to Aidan, "I told you to distract her. And fucking her once is not enough of a distraction. And yes!" she barked, glaring at Brannie. "*Everyone* knows you two fucked. But get it together, Aidan! Do your job!"

Stunned, now Aidan had nothing to say. He could only stare in shock and horror at the princess.

What had the evil She-dragon done? If Brannie thought for a moment . . .

But Brannie was bent over at the waist, laughing. Hard.

"You don't believe me?" Keita asked.

Brannie straightened up, her hand against her side. "Do I believe that you ordered Aidan to fuck someone for your own ends?" She wiped at a tear. "Of course I believe that! But do I think he did anything because *you* told him to? The same dragon who turned down the Protectors of the Throne to be Mì-runach just so he could piss off his da?" She now wiped both hands against her eyes to remove the tears. "Thanks for that, Keita. I needed that laugh today. And you know what?" she asked, abruptly changing the subject. "I've never been on a boat. I'm a little worried."

She grabbed Keita by the back of the neck, turned her around, and shoved her. "Now let's go get the rest of this done. I need an ale before the Mì-runach and the Riders finish it all."

Brannie started to follow but Aidan—who'd finally stopped being so stupidly stunned—caught hold of her arm and tugged her back.

"I never—" he began.

G.A. Aiken

She held up her hand. "I wasn't lying to her. If anything, because she told you to do it, I'm sure you went out of your way not to." She stepped back, arms held out from her body. "But look at'cha, weak bastard. Couldn't resist me, could ya?"

Aidan shrugged and admitted the truth. "No. I couldn't. Still can't."

Her smile faded. Her breath hitched.

They stared at each other, the moment lasting for seconds or forever. Aidan didn't know. They would have continued to stand there if Keita hadn't returned to them and stamped her bare foot on the ground.

"Oy!" she barked. "Do you two mind? We have an empire to destroy! *Move your asses!*"

She stormed off and Aidan had to admit, "She is so much like her mother."

Brannie snorted. "You tell her that, mate, at your own risk."

Uther thought he'd be able to get some sleep, but the longer he stayed in that pub bed, the more awake he felt. Only not a normal awake, but an exhausted one.

He finally gave up, deciding an ale might help him sleep, and stumbled down to the first floor.

The pub was busy, all the tables filled with locals. A lot of talk about the war and rumors about recent Zealot attacks, including what had happened at Aberthol. Not surprisingly, everyone in the place was armed, even though most of them seemed like farmers.

Uther spotted Caswyn at a back table with the Riders and made his way over.

"Uther!" Zoya cheered. "Come. Sit, comrade. Barkeep," she called out, "more of this watery ale!"

Many empty bowls cluttered the table, but for once Uther didn't think Caswyn had emptied them. Not the way the Riders were still eating, shoveling food into their mouths.

Brannie had said they'd been starved while at the Zealot fort, but they hadn't really looked deprived. Now, he wasn't so sure. He'd never seen Kachka eat like this before.

"Sit, sit," Zoya insisted.

He did as two serving girls came over. One cleared off the used bowls and the other poured more ale into everyone's tankard.

"Bring food for our comrade, weak female," Zoya told the serving girls, and Uther cringed. He'd always gone out of his way not to irritate serving girls because he didn't want anyone pissing in his food.

"Thank you," he said to the girl before she could do just that.

Kachka finished her bowl of food, dropped the spoon into it, and leaned back. She let out a loud sigh, which she followed up with a loud burp.

"Now I feel better," she said to them.

"Was it very bad in that dungeon?" Caswyn asked.

"Could be worse," she replied, reaching for bread and tearing the loaf in half. "They were scared of Riders, so they sealed us in cage and waited for us to die. But starving is not enough to kill Daughter of Steppes."

"I believe that," Uther said.

Biting off a huge chunk of the bread and chewing, Kachka asked, "Why were you there, Uther the Despicable?"

"Branwen didn't tell you?"

"We had little time for talk. And coming here, all we could think of was eating."

Uther looked at Caswyn. Although no one had said it, he'd gotten the feeling their current assignment wasn't meant to be announced to anyone not in their small group.

True, Kachka Shestakova was close to the human queen and the mate of the Rebel King, but he wasn't in the mood to get yelled at by Brannie and Keita because he opened his mouth when he shouldn't have.

And he was guessing Caswyn felt the same way since he was still living down the "Puddles Incident" as Aidan now called it.

"Just taking care of a few things for the queen," he said. It wasn't a lie.

"I see," the Rider said before she poured him another tankard of ale. He hadn't realized he'd finished the first one.

But he doubted another could hurt. Who knew if those Eastlanders even had ale? This could be his last chance to indulge for a long while.

"Cheers," he said, holding up his tankard. He and Caswyn took a sip of theirs but the Riders drank down their own in seconds and slammed the cups back onto the table, calling for more ale.

"You drink like old men," Kachka taunted Uther and Caswyn. "Come. You can do better than that."

Well . . . of course they could. They were dragons and, more importantly, Mì-runach. They had drinking contests with their brethren constantly and nearly always won. So a few drinks with these females wouldn't matter much, would it?

Vateria, last of the House of Atia Flominia, stood on the ramparts of her home, gazing out over the vast territory surrounding her.

Usually, on a clear day, she could see for miles. But today . . . all she could see were the troops of the Dragon Queen and her human cohorts. And she knew that in time, her cousin and his legions would also be showing up. He, too, would be taking his place for the last assault on the armies of Chramnesind.

"Mother?"

"My son." She looked back at the boy who'd grown into a man. Now, nearly eighteen summers and Benedetto was still perfect. Her three other boys, however, were still more like their father.

When she held her hand out, Benedetto took it and briefly squeezed.

"It's all coming together," he said, now standing beside her, still holding her hand.

"It is."

"And you think it's a good plan?"

"Brilliant," she said plainly. "I never doubt your father's battle plans. Chramnesind chose him for a reason."

Her son glanced off, his thumb rubbing against her forefinger.

"What is it?" she asked. "You know there is only honesty between us."

"I agree this is a good plan, but it depends on everyone acting their part. Doing what we expect of them. What if they don't?"

"That's a risk we take."

"It's a risk I don't want *you* to take."

Surprised, Vateria turned to face her son. "What do you mean?"

"I want you to leave this place, Mother. I want you to escape as soon as you can."

Smiling, she used her free hand to cup her son's beautiful face. "Why would I do that? Leave at our moment of triumph over the House of Gwalchmai fab Gwyar and, in turn, our triumph over Gaius and that cunt Agrippina? Not while I have breath, my son."

"If this was just a battle between the Dragon Queen and the Rebel King, I'd be fine with you staying. But you forget the Mother of Abominations." Benedetto blinked. "Why are you grinning like that?"

"She's gone."

"Who's gone? Annwyl?"

Vateria refocused on what lay around them, listened to

the building of wood fortifications by their enemy to trap them within these walls. "She will no longer be a concern of ours."

"How do you know?"

"I heard from Chramnesind himself. She's been dragged to the pits of hell, where she belongs." Vateria gripped her son's hand tighter, her soul content. "And once the hordes of all the hells are done with that vile bitch, she'll be begging to have her soul ended if it means a stop to the torment."

Benedetto leaned down and kissed his mother's temple. "I love your cruelty, Mother."

"So do I, my beautiful son. So do I."

Chapter Seventeen

With their passage secured for the following day, Aidan returned to the pub with a bickering Brannie and Keita. At this point, they weren't going at each other as hard as they had been doing before. Now they were just bickering like cousins tend to do.

It was annoying but not dangerous. He could deal with annoying.

As soon as Aidan walked into the pub, he spotted Caswyn and Uther sitting at a table with the Riders. He cut through the crowd until he reached them, but he felt his stomach drop when both looked up at him with bloodshot eyes, their bodies hunched over their pints of ale.

"So you're going to the Eastlands to start another war, eh?" Kachka asked.

Eyes wide, Aidan found himself stunned again into silence.

Then it got worse.

Zoya Kolesova slammed her fist onto the table. "We will come with you, comrades! Help you start this war with the evil Empress! *We shall kill them all and bathe in their Eastlander blood!*"

Keita gasped and Brannie put her middle finger to her forehead and pressed hard. He sensed she had a headache now.

"What have you been doing?" Keita demanded of Uther and Caswyn.

"Chatting with our friends," Uther said.

"We told them everything," Caswyn admitted. "And we did it loudly."

Before Aidan could move, Brannie had slammed Uther's head into the table, then moved on to Caswyn. She grabbed him by the throat and lifted him out of his chair, slamming his back against the wall. The full tables beside them cleared out as the humans fled.

She pinned Caswyn's drunk ass to the wall with one hand.

"I should have killed you when we were still on that mountain!"

"Bran—" Aidan began but she silenced him with one raised finger on her free hand. And for once, he didn't think his intervention would help any.

"Do not abuse them so, Branwen the Awful," Kachka said with a small smile. "It was your fault for trusting anything to weak males who cannot hold their watery ale."

"Oy," Uther drunkenly cut in. "We've won contests."

"Contests with other weak males," Kachka replied. "I am unimpressed." She looked back at Branwen. "Being angry at them is like being angry at stubborn cow. Why bother? It will not move faster."

"And that is why you need us," Zoya said, her grin wide. "We will come with you and help you die with honor! Will that not be fun?"

"No," Brannie said. "That will not be fun. I don't plan to die. I plan to live a nice, long happy life destroying others!"

"Caswyn's turning blue," Aidan felt the need to interject.

"Good!"

Rolling his eyes, Aidan finally ordered, "Let him go."

"No."

"Branwen . . . let him *go*."

She did. Right after she threw him into the corner, making sure his head slammed against the wall before he hit the floor.

Brannie faced him. "Happy?"

Laughing, Kachka motioned to the empty chairs. "Come. Sit. Let us discuss our plan."

"There's nothing to discuss," Keita stated. "I can't go to the Eastlands with a bunch of burly Riders coming along with us."

Zoya looked Keita up and down before asking, "Who are you, tiny female?"

Aghast, Keita barked, "I am Princess Keita of the House of—"

Spitting on the floor, Zoya cut in, "Another decadent royal. Who *cares?*"

"Everyone. Everyone cares. Because I'm me. I'm Keita!"

Kachka leaned toward the other Riders. "She is one that gives my sister useless eye patch in many colors."

"Those are *fashion* statements. So your sister doesn't look like a bloody freak at family get-togethers. I'm trying to help her."

"Yes, yes. Very helpful," Kachka said with a dismissive wave. "Now, Branwen and Aidan, you two sit down. Let us talk about our plans."

"Our plans?" Keita slammed her hands on the table. "They are *my* plans, peasant."

"Your plans? To what? Give Empress festive gown for when the rest of us kill her?"

"Now, now, Kachka Shestakova," Zoya interrupted. "Do not be so mean." Reaching her long arm across the table, she patted an astounded Keita on the head with her giant hand. "I am sure you were very helpful, weak and useless female. And do not worry. We will tell everyone how helpful and pretty you are and everyone will believe our lies."

Brannie quickly covered her mouth and looked down at the floor and Aidan forced himself to focus his gaze across the room on something else. Anything to stop the laughter.

But then Uther's big head drunkenly hit the table on its own and that sad *thud* sound was all it took to have them leaning against each other as their laughter shook the entire pub.

Brannie started to drag a still-passed-out Uther up the pub stairs, but Zoya grabbed the dragon in human form and said, "I have him."

Then she picked him up, placed him on her shoulder, and easily carried him up the stairs.

Even in his human form, Uther was excessively large. It usually took three or four human soldiers to carry him anywhere, and there was always complaining and grunting. But Zoya whistled happily.

Still, Brannie wasn't surprised when Keita grabbed her arm and began whispering furiously in her ear.

Finally Brannie couldn't take it and dragged her into her room.

"Stop!" she ordered. "I didn't understand a word you just said and there was much spit."

Disgusted, she took a cloth out of her boot and began to wipe her drenched ear.

"They can't come with us," Keita said. "They just can't!"

"We tried to get them to go away. To go back to Garbhán Isle or at least go to the front, where I'm sure they would eventually die a hearty death. But you heard them. They're determined. And when a Rider female is determined . . ."

Keita sat on the edge of Brannie's bed and pressed the palms of her hands against her eyes.

Brannie immediately sat down next to her and put her arm around her shoulders. "Gods, Keita. Are you crying?"

Keita dropped her hands to her lap, turned her head, and glared at Brannie for a long, *long* moment. "*No.*"

Brannie pulled her arm back. "No need for that tone, cousin."

"The Empress won't question that I've come to her court with armed guards. But she'll definitely question that I've come there with armed guards and Riders."

"There are only three. It's not like you're bringing a whole tribe with you."

"It won't matter when just one Rider can cause problems. We'll have to get rid of them."

Brannie blew out a breath and firmly stated, "You are not poisoning Celyn's sister-by-mating. I'll never hear the end of it."

"Have you ever tried to poison a Daughter of the Steppes?" Keita asked. "It's nearly impossible."

"But you've tried."

"Of course I've tried! Why do you ask such stupid questions when we're desperate?"

Her bedroom door opened and Aidan walked in. "I've got Caswyn to bed," he announced before dropping into a nearby chair. "And then I had to escort Zoya back to her room from Uther's. I don't know what she was planning but . . . I know I don't want to think about it."

Brannie chuckled but Keita was focused on her current issue.

Leaning forward and resting her elbows on her knees, Keita asked Aidan, "What should we do about the Riders?"

"Well, poisoning is out. That never works on Daughters of the Steppes."

"Again," Brannie repeated, "killing the sister of my brother's mate is *not* an acceptable suggestion."

"I think we should bring them with us."

Keita straightened. "You do? And how do we explain their presence to the Empress?"

Aidan shrugged and smiled. "Tell the truth. They attached themselves to us and we couldn't get rid of them. The Eastlanders know all about our Riders and they have their own, led by some human named Batu . . . or something. They trade with them. Plus, your cousin is mated with Kachka's sister. Her insisting on also protecting you because she doesn't trust the males to do it is a story any monarch would believe about the Cadwaladrs *and* the Daughters of the Steppes."

He yawned and used both hands to scratch his head. "Besides, it wouldn't hurt to have the backup of two raging warriors and a disturbingly evil witch."

"She *is* evil, isn't she?" Brannie asked. "It's *not* just my imagination."

"No. It's not."

Standing, Keita began to pace for a minute or two. Then she stopped, nodded her head. "You're right, Aidan. This might work to our advantage. We'll bring them."

She smiled at them both, then left.

Brannie smirked at Aidan. "She actually thinks she had some say in that shit."

"She's a royal. Of *course* she thought she had some say."

Now yawning herself, Brannie fell back on her bed. She was exhausted. Perhaps too exhausted to even take off her boots.

She felt the bed dip and looked to her right. Aidan had stretched out beside her.

"Before you complain about me being here . . . I need your protection."

Brannie grinned. "From Zoya?"

"I'm the only one not too drunk to speak. And now that she's been fed, I'm sure she has"—he shuddered—"other needs."

"Doesn't she have, I don't know, ten thousand husbands?"

"Close."

"Where's the loyalty?"

"Apparently their husbands are supposed to understand that when they're away from the tribe to do battle, they will get their needs met by others."

Brannie snorted. "My mother never did that to me da and she was off in battle all the time."

"They're dragons. Completely different."

"And they have hands!" When Aidan frowned at the statement, she added, "You know." Then she moved her hand to just above her crotch and moved it around a bit.

When he understood, he laughed.

"Excellent point, Captain. They have hands."

"And Elena better not do that to my brother."

"The brother who you say is a big baby?"

"He *is* a big baby. That's why I'm saying it. He couldn't handle something like that. She'd break his heart. Even worse, my mother would snap her neck. As you know, she absolutely adores her baby boy."

Aidan suddenly rolled onto his side, his mouth pressed against her chain mail–covered shoulder.

"Comfortable?" she asked.

"I'll be more comfortable when this war is over and I can enjoy *my* bed in my cave."

"You have a bed in your cave?"

"Don't you?"

"I don't have a cave."

"You don't have a cave?"

"Never had time to get one. I went from my father's castle right into army training. And after that, I was always with my unit or with Izzy at Garbhán Isle or her house. I always had a place to stay."

"Where do you keep all your things?"

"What things?"

"Your hoard."

"Who needs a hoard? I have kin."

"Must be nice," he murmured, moving in closer.

"You have kin, too."

"Horrible, horrible kin."

Smiling, she could feel herself beginning to slowly doze off. "They are horrible. But you have them. And you like your youngest sister well enough."

"I do."

Brannie was seconds from falling asleep when she felt it. A kiss against her temple.

She immediately snapped awake.

Raising herself on her elbow so she could look down on Aidan, she snapped, "What was that?"

His gold eyes fluttered open and he yawned. "What was what?"

"That kiss you just gave me."

"I guess it was . . . a *kiss*. But based on the way you're staring at me, perhaps it was more a form of pure evil."

Brannie sat up again. "Look, we're friends, right?"

Aidan rolled to his back and propped himself up on both his elbows. "Are we?"

"Of course we are."

"You hate me."

"No, I do not hate you. I hate Caswyn. He killed Puddles." She brushed her hair off her face. "Besides, if I hated you, the last thing I would have done was fuck you."

"Then what's the problem?"

She glanced back at him. "We're friends."

"Friends that fuck."

"Yes!" she replied, gleeful he understood. "Friends that fuck. Exactly." She patted his knee. "And we should keep it like that."

"As opposed to . . . what? Exactly."

"As opposed to loving kisses as we snuggle."

Aidan studied Brannie carefully. It wasn't like he'd branded her with his Claiming mark. He hadn't even realized he'd kissed her. He was half-asleep at the time.

But she was obviously serious. And greatly concerned. He just didn't know why.

He had no intention of Claiming anyone. Possibly ever.

His parents' mating hadn't been anything that made him believe love was never-ending. He knew better.

But great sex? Now that was something worth indulging in as often as possible. And he'd only had a small taste of Branwen the Awful. He definitely wanted more, and was happy to give her what she wanted if it meant things could keep going as they were.

"Oh, right." Aidan nodded. "No out-of-bounds kissing."

"Exactly. We're friends who fuck. Not Claimed mates."

"I'm fine with that."

"But we need to make sure that it's clear at all times."

"I already agreed to no out-of-bounds kissing."

"You can't keep that up," Brannie argued, her hand gesturing around her face. "We both know I'm irresistible."

"You and Keita really are blood relations, aren't you?"

She jumped off the bed, began pacing. "I'm just trying to do what's best for both of us. Because when this is all over, assuming we both survive, we'll be going our separate ways. And I don't want you sobbing over it."

Insulted, "I don't sob." She gave him an exasperated glare,

but he argued, "I don't! I saw my own brother eyeless . . . didn't sob then."

"You hate your brother!"

"You're right," he easily admitted. "I do. But you met him—he's a prat."

She paced a little more before stopping and pointing at him. "I've got it. No sex as dragons."

Aidan gazed at her. When she only gazed back, he finally asked, "What?"

"No sex as dragons," she said proudly, as if she'd discovered something brilliant. "We only fuck as human."

"And your reasoning?"

"I'm saving it."

"Too late for your virginity then?"

She glowered. "I'm saving it for the dragon I Claim."

"Actually, he's supposed to Claim you."

"Och! So old-fashioned. We're in modern times now. I can Claim who I want. And when I do, he'll get me as dragon. In my true form."

"What if he's human?"

"What?"

"It's possible. Your best friend is human. Princess Morfyd mated with a human. Your male royal cousins all mated with humans. What if it turns out a human is your true love? Then you'll never have sex as a dragoness again. That would be so sad."

She dropped her hands on her hips, sucked air between her teeth before asking, "Do you or do you not want to keep this friends-fucking thing going?"

In answer, Aidan pushed himself off the bed and moved in front of her. He grabbed the bottom of her chain mail shirt and lifted it.

"Arms," he ordered. She raised them and he pulled the shirt completely off.

"What are you doing?"

"Keeping the friends-fucking thing going." He untied the material that bound her breasts. "Is that all right with you?"

"You still need to agree."

"Yes. I agree. No fucking as dragons. I totally understand it," he added as he unwound the cloth from her body and tossed it on the shirt. "Like prostitutes that won't kiss their clients."

"Are you calling me a whore?"

Smoothing his hands down her waist, he stopped. "No. Do you want me to? I've known a few She-dragons who like that sort of—"

"No. I don't want you to."

"Oh. All right. But what about dirty . . . and naughty?"

"Yeah, that's all right."

Grinning, he leaned in and kissed her neck. He stopped briefly so Brannie could get his shirt off, then he was back. Kissing her neck, her shoulder.

He inhaled her scent before moving down to her breasts. He sucked on one nipple, then the other.

Brannie's hand pressed against the top of his head and he happily took the hint, dropping to his knees before her. He gripped the top of her chain mail leggings and pulled them down. She lifted each leg as he tugged them off. He removed her boots last before pressing his face against her pussy.

He took another breath in, slipping his hands around her hips and gripping her ass. He pulled her in close and began to kiss her stomach, making his way down . . .

The door abruptly opened and Zoya Kolesova walked in, shocking them both. But when she saw Aidan on his knees, her smile dropped.

"Oh. You have Aidan."

He pulled back a bit, clearing his throat. "Um . . . do you need something, Zoya?"

"Well . . ." She glanced at Brannie, then Aidan, then back

to Brannie. "You will not be long with him, yes? I can be next?"

Brannie's entire body got stiff and her hand took firm hold of the hair at the back of his head. She clearly had no intention of letting him go—which he truly appreciated!

Between clenched teeth, Brannie snarled, "Get. Out."

Zoya pointed an accusing finger. "You Southlanders do not know how to share with others!"

"*Kachka!*" Brannie bellowed.

"Zoya Kolesova!" Kachka yelled from her room across the hall. "Whatever you are doing—*stop it!*"

"Selfish She-dragon," Zoya snapped before storming out and slamming the door behind her.

Stunned, Aidan looked up at Brannie and asked, "Does she really think I have no say in any of this?"

"Penis-havers have no say. Those are her words, by the way, and she's said them . . . often."

"Well, don't let the fact that I'm on my knees confuse you, Captain," Aidan teased. "I'm in complete control."

She grinned and shoved him to his back. "That won't be for long."

Chapter Eighteen

Keita knew the second she was no longer alone in the tiny pub bedroom. She opened her eyes and saw the human standing over her in the dark, a blade out.

She took in a breath, willing to blast this man—and perhaps the entire pub—into oblivion. But before she could unleash her flame, big hands came from behind the man and grabbed him, slamming him into the wall beside the door.

"You try to kill such a small female with such a big knife?" Zoya Kolesova pinned him there with her left hand. "Weak men like you disgust me."

She rammed the flat of her hand against the man's chest once, and Keita heard bones breaking.

Keita grinned. Perhaps Aidan was right about having these Riders with them on their journey.

The bed was small, so they were wrapped around each other, but Brannie didn't mind. She'd woken up in worse positions over the years.

But it wasn't being curled up with Aidan the Divine that

had dragged her from a solid after-sex sleep. It was the scent of humans she didn't recognize.

She opened her eyes and Aidan was already staring at her. They'd fallen asleep with their arms around each other, their legs intertwined, and his cock still inside her. Both of them too tired to even bother separating.

Now they were both reaching for their weapons when the door was kicked open. A hard *bang* was heard from one of the other rooms just as Brannie got to her knees, a short sword in hand.

Two men stormed in, their faces hidden behind hooded robes. A blade flashed, coming down at Brannie. She blocked it but before she could tear out the man's heart, another blade slammed into him from behind.

Blood hit her in the face and the man coughed up more before he was pushed off the sword and to the floor.

Aidan had already disemboweled the other one, but she wasn't sure it had happened before that man's throat was cut from behind.

"We must move," Kachka ordered, walking out of the room now that her work was done.

Brannie quickly grabbed her clothes, armor, and weapons off the floor and started for the door. "I have to check on Keita."

"She is fine!" Zoya announced from the hallway. With her arms around the She-dragon's human waist, she carried Keita like a child's doll. "I will take her out. We must go."

"I can walk, peasant," Keita complained.

"You are too weak to fight. Look at her!" she ordered, holding Keita out. Her cousin's arms hung limply at her sides, red hair still mussed from bed, lips pursed. If she suddenly set Zoya on fire, Brannie would not be surprised.

Quickly putting her clothes on in the middle of the hallway, Brannie asked, "Who are these men? More Zealots?"

"I tried to look," Keita replied, "but the giantess wouldn't give me any time."

"She's protecting you," she reminded her cousin. "Be nice."

Aidan, now dressed, crouched beside one of the men. He pulled the hood back and yanked down the cloth that covered the man's face.

Frowning, Aidan shook his head at Brannie. "They're not Zealots."

Surprised by that, Brannie quickly pulled on her chain mail shirt and stepped back into the bedroom, close to the other male. She also pulled back the hood and removed the black cloth around his face.

Aidan was right. These men weren't Zealots.

"They could have been hired by them," she suggested. "Keita said Salebiri had been hiring troops. That's why he needed the gold."

"Either way," Keita said. "They came for me, trying to stop me if they thought I could get the Empress's armies on our side."

"Do not worry about danger, tiny female," Zoya told her, pulling poor Keita in close and holding her against her ample chest. "I will protect you."

Then they were both gone.

"It will not be long before Keita kills her," Aidan said with a sigh.

"I know. I know." Brannie stood, took a moment to get her boots on, then grabbed all her weapons, putting her "stick" into a small holder on her belt.

Brannie went out into the hallway, with Aidan behind her. A hung-over Caswyn and Uther were trying their best to appear intimidating, even though they looked more like they were about to pass out.

She was heading over to ask them how they were when Nina Chechneva rushed back up the stairs.

"There are more men outside," she warned. "I think they wait for us."

"Do it," Kachka ordered, and Nina ran back down.

"What's she going to do?"

"Take their souls."

And Kachka said it so matter-of-factly that Brannie didn't really think about it until Aidan asked, "Pardon?"

"That is what Nina Chechneva does. She takes the souls of men and uses them to increase her power. We let her as long as she does not betray us. If she betrays us, then we let Zoya Kolesova tear her arms off."

Aidan nodded at that. "So you have all formed a nice . . . bond, I see."

"No. We loathe her and she loathes us, but we work well together to defeat the Zealots."

"Okay, then," Brannie said with a smile, refusing to ask any more. Because she honestly didn't want to know.

By the time they made it outside, Nina Chechneva was nearly done devouring the last soul.

Her slim body was covered in dark light and she seemed to be in the throes of passion, her head thrown back, gasps rising from her throat, her body undulating.

It was disturbing to watch; Aidan couldn't imagine how horrible it was to go through it. To be the one whose soul she was taking.

And what happened to those souls? Were they trapped inside her? Did they merely disappear, never moving on to the next level? Never seeing their ancestors on the other side?

Again, Aidan didn't know and he didn't think he wanted to. Strange things could sometimes give him nightmares and he'd rather sleep well.

Keita walked past the bodies, studying each one carefully before facing Brannie.

"I don't know them."

"But they're here for you. For us."

She put her hands on her hips and again looked at those sent to kill them all. "We need a new boat. Another way to get to the Eastlands."

Aidan understood. Everything they'd already planned was suspect now. Someone wanted to stop Keita from making this trip.

"You need boat," Zoya said. "We get boat." She patted Keita's head. "Do not worry, tiny weak female. The Daughters of the Steppes will protect you."

The Riders began hauling the bodies to an alley so they wouldn't be found for a while, and Brannie immediately moved to her cousin's side.

"Keita—"

Keita raised her hand. "No, no. I have seen the benefit of having the Riders around. And I have no intention of killing any of them . . . until we're done. If we survive, *then* I'll kill them all."

"Not Kachka," Brannie reminded her, giving her cousin a short hug. "I'll never hear the end of it from Celyn."

"Fair enough."

Chapter Nineteen

To protect Keita, only the Riders went to the Port City docks to find a boat that could take them to the Eastlands. The rest of them stayed well inside the city in a back alley, all of them surrounding Keita's tiny human form.

She was very tense the entire time, pacing and constantly scratching the back of her neck. The She-dragon wanted to know who was trying to stop her trip if it wasn't the Zealots. Who was willing to kill the entire party just to stop her?

Since Aidan didn't know who was on Keita's vast list of connections, he couldn't help. All he could do was stand guard with Brannie and his Mì-runach brethren until Kachka returned to them.

"Zoya found boat," she told them, motioning the group out of the alley.

They moved quickly, aware the two suns were beginning to dawn in the sky.

Reaching the dock, they hastened past the fishermen heading to their own boats and the merchants and fishmongers who were already setting up their stalls for the day.

"There," Kachka said, pointing at a Northland-type ship docked in the harbor. It was bigger than Aidan expected, round shields lining the outside of the boat for, Aidan guessed, easy access during a fight.

They stopped by a load of crates that would be placed on another boat heading out. Zoya stood on the dock between the boat and the crates. She studied the area closely before she motioned for them all to come forward.

Walking quickly but not running, they headed toward the boat. But as Aidan was about to pass a still-watchful Zoya, she caught hold of his arm to halt him.

"What?" he asked.

She motioned behind him, her confused gaze focused in the same direction.

Aidan looked over his shoulder, expecting to see more of the robed assassins coming for Keita but . . . no. That was not what had Zoya's attention.

It was Branwen. She still stood by the crates.

Surprised, Aidan rushed back to her side. "Come on," he urged. "We have to move."

"You know, I was thinking . . ."

She was thinking? Now? When they were trying to avoid those trying to kill them?

"Why don't I stay here? Take care of those pesky assassins?"

Pesky?

"That way we can be sure that you guys . . . you know . . . get away. Safely and all."

"What are you talking about?"

Keita appeared at his side, Kachka behind her.

"What's going on?" Keita asked.

"I was thinking I should stay here," Brannie said, her gaze seemingly locked on the ground.

"Take care of those *pesky* assassins," Aidan added, frowning at Keita.

"If we get on the boat and get out of here," Keita reasoned, "we won't have to worry about anyone. So let's go."

Brannie lifted her head, looked at all of them, then said, "I'm . . . I'm not leaving my troops. I'm going back to the front."

Keita threw up her hands. "Are we actually here again?"

"We're here again," Brannie insisted. "I'm not leaving my . . . my men . . . for anyone. Including you, cousin. So there!"

Keita let out a disgusted sound from the back of her throat. "I don't have time for this centaur shit. Kachka, grab her and let's go."

Without question, Kachka reached out and grabbed Brannie's arm . . . and that's when everything went particularly strange.

"No, no, no, no, *nooooo!*" Brannie abruptly screeched, yanking her arm away from a stunned Kachka. "*None of you are getting me on that fucking death trap!*"

"Branwen!" Keita barked.

"I'll die here, thank you! Here on land! You can go out there"—she waved her hands wildly in front of her—"and die on the open seas! I'm staying right here! *Right here until the end of time!*"

Mouths open, Aidan and Keita looked at each other, the princess's eyes as wide as his own, he was sure.

Kachka leaned forward and told them calmly, "Could be wrong, dragons, but I think mighty warrior . . . terrified of ocean."

Branwen couldn't think straight. She just knew—*knew!*—she wasn't getting on that death trap and allowing it to drag her out into the middle of an angry ocean where they might or might *not* get to the other side.

No. No! *Never!*

His hands raised, Aidan tried that soft voice thing he did

when he was trying to calm something out of control. Like a horse. Or a stampeding elk. Or Annwyl.

But Brannie knew. She was *not* crazed! She knew exactly what was going on and she wasn't about to let anyone convince her otherwise! Even Aidan!

"Bran—"

"Nooooo!" she screamed in his face. "I'm not listening! I'm never listening! *I will not allow any of you to drag me to my death!*"

Aidan backed up. "All right," he said to Keita. "I'm out."

"Typical male," Keita complained with a sigh. "Completely useless!"

Then Brannie's tiny cousin swung her fist and . . . that was the last thing Brannie remembered.

Aidan watched the back of Branwen's head collide with the wood crate before her body slipped to the ground.

And all that from one punch.

From *Keita*.

Now he and Kachka Shestakova gawked at the dragoness as she brushed one hand against another.

"Do you mean that?" Keita asked when she realized they were staring, her punching hand gesturing to a still knocked-out Branwen. "The first thing my father ever taught me was how to handle a male who didn't understand the word *no*. And in the end, the difference between a persistent male and a crazed Branwen is negligible." She smiled and motioned to the ship. "Now . . . shall we?"

The entrances to different hells were not elaborate or complex. Annwyl found out she could easily enter one without even meaning to.

She'd walked into at least five different ones so far and

G.A. Aiken

in the process had nearly frozen to death, burned to death, been eaten by flies, chased by snakes, and attacked by screeching harpies. Thankfully getting back to the hell she started in was not hard, either. She just had to turn around.

Who knew she'd started off in the "nicer" hell?

Well, at least the most tolerable. It seemed almost like a normal world for demons. There were houses and towns and roaming animals. But everything was tainted. And because Annwyl wasn't, they would go for her. So she avoided the towns, the houses, and stayed off the main roads.

Despite her exhaustion, Annwyl just wanted to get out. She wanted to return to her troops, her kin.

At some point she had hit some kind of wasteland, characterized by dirt and rocks and a red, overcast sky.

Deciding to take a break, she dropped down by a deformed tree, her back against its lumpy trunk. She closed her eyes and tried to relax, but the branches of the tree kept trying to grab her. So she caught hold of the closest branch and pulled and pulled until she tore the branch off. Blood poured from the wood like sap and the tree made a strange mewling sound before the branches withdrew and left Annwyl alone.

"You fit in here quite well," she heard.

Annwyl opened her eyes and looked at the brown-skinned warrior woman standing in front of her. At some point, the woman's throat had been cut and her arm was nearly hacked off at the shoulder, but she didn't seem dead. Not like everyone else Annwyl had seen who was not a demon.

"Do I know you?"

"We've . . . met before. But you weren't at your best. I doubt you remember. But you know a friend of mine."

"Do you know the way out of here?" Annwyl was in no mood for chitchat.

"Sadly, not for you. It took me ages to find you as it is. So you'll have to find your own way out. I have no power here."

"That's unfortunate."

"I'm sure it is. But you need to be careful. Die here and you're staying. There's nothing anyone can do about it."

"I assumed."

"And the ruling lord of this hell . . . you didn't kill him. He's coming for you."

"Figures." Annwyl stood up, brushing red dirt off her leggings. "Anything else?"

"You do know you're not talking to yourself, don't you?"

"Of course I'm talking to myself."

"Annwyl, I'm a god. I'm Eir."

"Riiiiight. Sure you are. You're a god. I'm a completely rational human being right now. How could it be anything else?"

"But you've spoken to gods before. Mingxia, for instance—"

"That's my point. If you were real, you'd be Mingxia. I don't know you."

"Annwyl—"

"No, no. I don't want to argue with myself. I'm sure once I get out of here, I'll be much less crazy."

Annwyl's delusion smiled at her. "There's nothing wrong with a little crazy, Annwyl the Bloody. Never forget that. Hold on to that. It may save your life."

"That's really sweet. But we both know I'm *way* more than a little crazy."

Chapter Twenty

Since Gwenvael had been off to war with his brothers, Dagmar had been waking up every morning surrounded by her five dogs. They didn't replace Gwenvael, but they helped with the loneliness.

As someone who'd spent her entire life in the Northlands mostly alone—and enjoying every second of that solitude—missing someone as much as she missed Gwenvael was not an easy thing. But the dragon had a way of digging his claws into a being's heart and making himself quite comfortable there. She should hate him for doing that to her . . . making her care. But it was too late now. Not only did she care about him, she cared about his siblings, the mates of his siblings—including the human queen of these lands—the people who lived in these territories and, of course, her own children. Var, Arlais, and Gwenvael's Five. Her youngest daughters.

And she did truly adore them. That didn't mean, however, she felt comfortable waking up with the youngest of the Five sitting on her bed, silently gazing at her.

"Thora?" Dagmar raised herself up on her elbow, quickly noticing her very brave, very *large* dogs were huddled in a corner of the room, watching but not really helping. They hadn't even let out a little bark so that Dagmar would know she was no longer alone. "Is everything all right?"

Her youngest nodded that beautiful, golden head. Eyes bright gold like her daddy's. Gwenvael's Five were mirror images of him, the eldest of the Five now fourteen and this little one just turning eight.

"Do you need something?" Dagmar tried again.

Thora had one of the puppies from the kennel stretched out in front of her. She played with the puppy, handling it with care. Something Dagmar was very glad to see about her youngest child, who rarely spoke.

"I don't need anything, Mummy. I just have to keep you busy for a little while."

Sighing, Dagmar fell back on the bed. "What are your sisters up to now?"

"Nothing. We just don't want you facing her. We know how you are. And she's in a . . . mood."

Dagmar studied her daughter before asking, "You don't want me facing who?"

Gold eyes lifted to meet Dagmar's and Thora said softly, "Auntie Brigida." She chewed her lip for a bit before adding, "She's here to see Arlais."

Arlais walked into the kitchens, pausing as soon as she stepped inside. She glanced back at the armed female guard that followed her around. Her mother said she'd put this female on Arlais to protect her from being kidnapped. But Arlais knew better. Her mother just didn't like her "sneaking around."

That's what her mother had called it! "Sneaking around." Like Arlais was a barn cat!

Arlais didn't sneak anywhere. She walked. With purpose. Anywhere she bloody wanted to go.

Gods! She couldn't wait for her father to get back so he

could keep the great Dagmar Reinholdt busy. Arlais was tired of being that woman's focus. Amazing since Dagmar had an entire kingdom to deal with, but somehow . . .

"Let my dog outside and then wait in the hall for me," she ordered, but the guard simply stared at her. Petting the wonderful, furry beast pressed against her side that she'd raised from a pup, she added the warning, "Don't make me unhinge my jaw."

Glaring, the guard snarled, "Don't try and run."

Arlais smiled. "Wouldn't dream."

Once her nosy protection was gone with her pet, Arlais walked over to the main cook and took the bowl of fruit she offered her.

"Here to see me?" she asked the robed figure in a shadowed corner. "I'm honored."

Arlais placed the bowl on the big worktable, pulled a chair out, and dropped into it. Popping several of the finger-sized pieces of fruit into her mouth, she said, "Well, greetings, Great-Great-Great-Great-Great-Great-Great-, plus ten or minus a few thousand Greats, Auntie Brigida. What brings you here to grace us with that face?"

Holding on to her big stick, the She-dragon in human form stepped out of the shadows, one leg dragging uselessly behind her.

Without saying anything, she looked over at the servants.

Arlais asked the small group of humans, "Could you lot leave us for a bit?"

The servants walked to a separate exit that would take them outside. That way they could get fresh eggs and milk from the chickens and cows being guarded in the fields and nearby barns.

When they were alone, Arlais put her feet up on the table and popped more fruit into her mouth. "So what do you want?"

"I wanted to talk to you about your future."

"My future? What about my future?"

Brigida moved closer to the table, but she didn't sit. Instead she simply leaned against it.

The old witch looked tired. Exhausted. Like just breathing was taking a lot out of her. But no one could live forever. Perhaps it was simply her time to die.

"Do you want to stay here, Arlais? Trapped with those who do not understand who and what you are? Living this life that means so little? All these royals and what can they offer you? Not much from what I've seen. You may have your father's attitude, girl, but you've been gifted with your mum's face. That won't do much for you down the line."

"But you can offer me more?"

"I can offer you anything. Because you can get anything . . . when you have power."

"And what's the price I'll have to pay for all that delicious power?"

"Come with me. Find out."

Arlais nodded her head and was about to reply when a giggle slipped out. She didn't mean for that to happen but she simply couldn't keep it in.

"I'm sorry," she said around more laughter. "But . . . do you honestly expect me to give all this up"—she swirled her finger in the air—"so I can go and live in some slimy cave with *you*? Listening to you pontificate about magicks and power and making me read a bunch of boring, dusty old *books*?" She pointed at herself. "Do I look like my brother to you? Then again, you'll never pry him away from my mother's very dull skirts. But I'm not about to walk away from anything so you can have a surrogate hatchling of your own."

Arlais swung her legs off the table, stood, and began walking around. She liked to move when she spoke. She didn't really know how to sit quietly for hours.

"I have big plans for the House of Gwalchmai fab

Gwyar," she announced. "And those plans don't involve boring books, ridiculous witch rituals, long-winded lists"— she said, thinking of her mother—"and they definitely don't involve . . . *you*."

Arlais gazed directly into her great-aunt's eyes. She found that milky one kind of fascinating and could stare at it for an age, just so she could see what it would do at any given time.

"Personally," Arlais went on, "I don't believe life and the obtaining of power has to involve so much sacrifice. And look at you, dear auntie . . . you have clearly sacrificed so much for the life you lead. That body. That face." Arlais shuddered. "I may have my mother's face but at least no one looks away from me in horror. Besides, who needs to be beautiful when you're a royal? When the whole world is open to you simply because your grandmother is queen. And why would I risk losing any of that merely to be the daughter you never had?"

Reaching a spot near her aunt, Arlais rested her ass against the table, crossing her arms over her chest. "I wouldn't risk losing any of that. I haven't *not* killed my mother for this long so I can give it up to follow you into a dank cave for the next few centuries.

"Of course," she added, walking around her aunt and picking up the bowl of fruit, "you can always try to go after the Five but my daddy and uncles will tear your cave down around your ears, and I don't even want to think what my mother would do to you. She can be really mean when she's angry," she mock-whispered.

Arlais pushed the kitchen door open but stopped before she walked out, looking back at her aunt. "Keep in mind one other thing, auntie dear. As long as you're on our side— the right side—you have nothing to worry about from me. But cross me . . . and I'll show you how much I truly am like my mother."

Arlais smiled and waved. "Lovely seeing you, auntie dear. When this nasty war is over, we must have tea!"

Brigida had just passed the tower behind the human queen's castle when a voice behind her pointed out, "I thought my grandmother made it clear no one was to be opening doorways and moving around mystically until this war was over."

Brigida stopped walking and looked over her shoulder, but no one was there.

"Well?" the voice pushed and when Brigida looked forward she found Unnvar Reinholdt standing before her. He'd been calling himself by his mother's name for a few years now. Although why anyone would want the name of a Northland warlord rather than the House name of a royal, Brigida had no idea.

"I do as I like, boy," she told him. "I don't answer to you or anyone."

"It seems reckless," he said, not even looking at her because his focus was on some parchments he held in his hands. His shoulder-length gold hair was pulled off his face and tied by a leather thong at the back of his neck. He wore black chain mail that must have been made for him by one of the better blacksmiths, and stood well over six feet. "I can honestly say I'm not sure the family would help should the Zealots manage to take you."

"You seem highly concerned."

"Only about how it would look to the other kingdoms." He glanced down at her. He didn't have the gold eyes of his father, but the shrewd, mistrusting gray eyes of his mother. "I'm sure you understand."

"Don't you worry. No Zealots can touch me, even if they try." She grinned. "And none of them are brave enough to try."

"Fine," he said, focusing again on his papers. "Just be mindful."

Brigida nodded and walked away from the boy. She was hungry and she'd seen some elk near one of the lakes.

"Did you and my sister have a nice talk?"

Brigida stopped again, looked back at the boy . . . but he wasn't there.

She swung around and he stood in front of her again.

"Ain't you wily."

It had taken Brigida centuries to learn to do what the boy did so easily at eighteen. She'd learned it to terrify others. He did it to irritate. To let others know he was ahead of them.

The little prick.

"My sister," the boy prompted.

"Don't worry. She has no interest in what I have to offer. I'm sure she'll figure out that mistake soon enough."

"A mistake? Really?" He smirked at her before refocusing on his fancy parchments. "My sister is many things, but she always knows a good offer when she hears one. She could haggle the horns from the head of Rhydderch Hael himself . . . if she so wanted. She walked away from what you had to offer because she knows as well as I do that what you propose is hollow. Empty. You should know that vapid doesn't mean stupid."

Brigida decided to cut through it. Her stomach was grumbling. "What do you want, boy?"

"Stay away from my kin. My sisters, specifically."

"Or what?" She leaned into the boy, lowered her voice to a whisper. "What are you going to do to me?"

The boy lifted those cold gray eyes and Brigida looked deep. Deeper than she'd looked before. And she saw it then. Behind all that coldness, locked deep inside the boy, was the kind of hidden rage Brigida had only seen once, maybe twice in her life. A rage the boy controlled with sheer will and reason. Just like his mum.

The only difference was that Dagmar Reinholdt had no mystical powers built into her bones, ready to be called up whenever needed. But this boy . . . he didn't need spells. He didn't need rituals. He didn't need gods. It was all inside him, held at bay because he felt like it.

But unleashed . . .

Brigida took two painful steps back, away from the boy and his hidden depths.

There went that smirk again and the boy said, "I'm glad to see we understand each other, dear aunt."

"Boy."

Brigida moved away from the royal as fast as she could, dragging her nearly dead leg behind her. Now she knew! Now she was sure.

She couldn't count on any of them to do what needed to be done. To hold this Clan together. It was down to her. Like always.

Her plans immediately changed as she considered the research she'd have to do. The spells she'd have to locate. She knew she was short on time, but now she knew . . . she had no choice. No choice at all.

Var walked into the middle of a typical morning fight as his mother and Arlais squared off across the dining table. The servants, so used to it all, ignored the pair completely as they began to place food down so that everyone else could eat while the pair squabbled.

Even their dogs got in on it. His mother's dogs barking at Arlais's dog. Arlais's dog snapping back.

It was . . . ridiculous. But, like the servants, Var had gotten used to it.

"What's going on?" Frederick asked, coming from the back halls behind Var.

Var opened his mouth to explain but all he could do was roll his eyes and sigh. "I'll fill you in later. Is Uncle Bram up?"

"I think the question is whether Bram got any sleep. Rhiannon sent for him. He's been at Devenallt Mountain since last night. Final plans being locked in, I guess."

"What do they expect from a peacemaker?"

Bram the Merciful was known for his truce-making skills as far north as the Ice Lands and as far south as the deserts. He'd even negotiated the original plans for the Empress's favorite son to travel from the Eastlands to Devenallt Mountain, where he'd met and befriended a very young Keita.

Var adored his great-uncle, could spend hours talking to him about philosophy and reason and knowledge. But he held no delusions about the dragon. His mate, Ghleanna, handled the battles and the wars that destroyed many a nation and Bram handled the clean-up and the eventual truces when the destroyed nations begged for mercy. Made sense because that was what he loved to do.

What *didn't* Bram the Merciful love doing? Dealing with Var's grandfather and grandmother, if he could help it. Bercelak the Great seemed to take great pleasure in tormenting his brother-by-mating.

"Just admit it!" Arlais screamed at her mother. "Just admit you don't trust me!"

"*Of course I don't trust you!*" his mother barked back.

Frederick chuckled but Var didn't understand why his sister wouldn't simply tell their mother the truth. She'd turned Brigida down. Even if the old She-dragon hadn't told him, Var would have known that. His sister would never trust Brigida and, more important, she wasn't about to go live in a cave. With anyone. For any reason.

But instead of simply telling their mother that, she decided to torment her instead.

Honestly, the pair of them.

"By the way," Frederick said, as he removed the spectacles on his face and quickly cleaned the glasses on a bit of cloth. "Your off-putting aunt Brigida was in the book tower a few minutes ago and—"

Var grabbed his cousin's arm, cutting off his next words. "What do you mean she was in the tower? Doing what?"

Putting his spectacles back on, Frederick shrugged. "I don't know. She went into the stacks and then she was gone."

"Which stacks? Which books was she looking at?"

Frederick closed his eyes and Var knew his cousin was going through the titles in his head. He only had to read or see something once and the Northlander could remember every detail. It was quite a remarkable gift and one that Var and his mother used to their benefit whenever necessary.

After a few seconds, Frederick opened his eyes and looked at Var. "Ancient spells."

"Fuuuuuuck." Var pulled his cousin toward the back hallway.

"Where are we going?"

"To find out what that old witch is up to."

"Should we tell your mother what's going on?"

Var glanced back at his mother and sister. They'd started throwing loaves of bread at each other while still yelling.

He pushed his cousin ahead of him. "I'm going to say no."

Chapter Twenty-One

Aidan stroked Brannie's back, cringing each time she heaved again into the ocean water. And after each heave, she said the same thing to him: "I hate you. I hate you for doing this to me. I hate you. I hate you."

Then she'd heave again.

"Still?" Caswyn asked, sitting down across from Aidan and Brannie. When Aidan only nodded, "How could there be anything left but blood and her internal organs?"

Aidan honestly didn't know. Even drunk, Branwen had never vomited so much in front of him.

Continuing to rub her back, Aidan noticed that she'd finally stopped vomiting. He leaned over the edge of the ship, trying to see how she was holding up, but her arms hung down, fingertips coasting across the waves.

He caught her before she slipped completely into the water and dragged her back into the boat.

"She passed out?" Caswyn took out a cloth from the top of his boot and poured fresh water from the canteen in his travel bag onto it, handing it to Aidan.

Using the wet cloth, Aidan wiped Brannie's face and neck.

Aidan had never seen Brannie like this before and he didn't really know how to handle it.

He pulled her into his lap, her head against his chest, and stroked her hair.

"You think she'll be all right?"

"I'm sure she'll be fine!" Keita crowed happily.

She walked past them and stood by Caswyn, staring out at the ocean. "Isn't this delightful?" she asked them. "Such a beautiful day. And that fresh sea air."

"Your *cousin,*" Aidan felt the need to remind Keita, "has been vomiting since she woke up after being hit by you."

Keita faced him. "And?"

"Do you not care?"

"Of course I care. I love little Brannie."

"Little?" Caswyn muttered.

"Look at her, Keita," Aidan ordered. "Look at what's happened to your cousin."

"Why do you keep pointing out she's my cousin? I *know* she's my cousin."

"And yet you don't seem to care."

"I care, I care. But so she has a little boat sickness . . ."

"A *little* boat sickness?"

"It's not that big a deal. And, when you think about it, not actually surprising."

Aidan let out a breath. "*Why* isn't that surprising, Keita?"

"You know."

"No. I don't know."

She shrugged her shoulders, raised her hands. "About her father . . ."

"What about her father?"

"He was once kidnapped by Sea Dragons."

Caswyn blinked hard and stared up at Keita in shock. Uther, who'd been asleep against the hull, with his back to everyone, rolled over, his mouth open.

Aidan took a moment to calm himself. When he felt certain he wouldn't yell, he said, "Her father was kidnapped by Sea Dragons and you didn't say anything?"

"Why would I? She's not Bram. She wasn't even there. She wasn't even hatched then. Bram and Ghleanna weren't even mated. So what does it matter?"

"You don't really understand . . . emotions, do you?" Uther asked.

"What does that mean?"

"For the first few decades of Branwen's life," Aidan reminded the princess, "she was raised by her father. Her mother was off in battle. You don't think his fear of being kidnapped by Fins for a second time didn't—"

"Third," she cut in.

"What?"

"If I recall the story correctly, he was already kidnapped a second time, but that second time he was *with* Ghleanna."

"*Both her parents were taken by Fins?*"

"I don't know why you're yelling at me."

"Because you're an idiot!"

"Well, that's a tad unfair. It happened to them, not to her. I doubt they ever mentioned it."

"A mated couple gets kid—"

"They weren't mated."

"What?"

"They weren't mated when they were taken. They did, however, fall in love while they were there. Now isn't that nice?"

"So of course her parents would never talk about the time they fell in love . . . to their offspring. While trapped *underwater* with the Fins."

"I hear sarcasm," Keita snapped.

"Because I was being sarcastic!"

"If she was so concerned, she should have said something."

"She probably didn't know."

"How could she not know?"

"When was the last time *any* Cadwaladr had to travel by ocean? Or take a boat anywhere?"

"Um . . ."

Aidan shook his head and looked up at the sky as Uther suddenly stated, "Branwen probably didn't realize how she felt. She picked up the fear from her father, but she buried it under layers of Cadwaladr bravado and denial until she was faced with the actual reality of getting on a boat and going out on the ocean. *Then* she had to face her true fear and it overwhelmed her."

Shocked, the three of them gawked at Uther.

"I know," the dragon said confidently. "Emotions. They can torment you."

Not knowing what to say to Uther, Aidan focused back on Keita. "You should have said something and you *know* you should have said something, but you didn't because you didn't want anything to get between you and us going to the Eastlands."

"Oh, so what?" Keita asked. "It's a beautiful day, we're already on the boat, on our way to the Eastlands, and look at this . . ." She pointed at Brannie who'd suddenly sat up and, struggling a bit, got to her feet.

"Look at my beautiful cousin," Keita said, her grin wide. "Bravely facing her fear!"

The boat pitched and Brannie stumbled into Keita. But always a warrior, Brannie slammed a foot against the hull behind Keita and grabbed her cousin by the arms, keeping them both safely on the boat.

The boat righted and Keita smiled up at her much bigger cousin, but her expression changed just as quickly to panic and she tried to pull away.

But Brannie's grip tightened on Keita's arms, holding her steady while she vomited on her again and again and . . . aye . . . a third time.

Mortified, Keita stood there, covered in dragon bile—
which meant it was like lava—while Brannie stumbled back
to Aidan's side and sat down beside him.

"Heard everything?" he softly asked Branwen.

"Every gods-damn word," she growled out.

Brannie didn't know how long she'd slept after vomiting
all over Keita, but the arguing woke her up as it had before.

She was still sitting on the floor of the boat, her legs
bent, her knees under her chin. Seabirds and crows circled
overhead, fighting each other, more aggressive than she'd
ever seen them. The sky was overcast and forbidding even
though she sensed it should still be light out.

"What's going on?" she asked, shocked at how hoarse
her voice was, how raw her throat. It hurt even to swallow.

"Well?" Uther barked. "Are you going to tell her?"

Brannie focused on Keita. "I see I need to vomit on you
again. And I will."

"It wasn't *me*." Keita pointed at the Riders. "It was her."

Kachka and Nina moved back, leaving Zoya Kolesova to
stand alone.

"I thought I helped," she lazily said with a shrug.

Uther spread his arms out, motioning to the surrounding
empty seas. "Does it look like you're helping?"

"I will not get yelled at by weak male!"

"Fine!" Keita snapped. "I'll yell at you!"

"What is wrong?" Brannie demanded even while her
stomach roiled.

Keita faced her. "My plan was simple. Take a boat to the
Eastlands, kill the Empress and all of her kin. See? Extremely simple."

And stupid, but Brannie wasn't going to add that at the
moment. "So? We're on a boat, headed to the Eastlands. I
don't see the problem."

"Thank you, large-shouldered one!"

"Really?" Brannie snapped at Zoya. "Throwing boulders from that glass cave?"

"What you need to know," Keita continued, "is that there are several ways to get to the Eastlands. There is a mystic doorway, which we cannot use because of the Zealots. Sailing northeast across the seas, which takes one around the Rock of the Blue Birds. This trip requires several weeks—"

"See?" Zoya interrupted. "I—"

Keita held up her hand and, to Brannie's shock, Zoya stopped speaking.

"Several weeks that I had already built into our schedule, assuming that by the time we got there, the war in Outerplains would be over—one way or another—and I could do what I need to do before the news arrived in the Eastlands about Ren."

"So the problem . . . ?" Brannie asked.

"Most ship captains who trade with the Eastlanders will tell you they will *only* go that way, despite the storm issues. It's the northeast way or no way. But Zoya managed to find the one captain who goes the southeast way."

"It is faster!" Zoya interjected. "We get there in two, three days tops."

"Do you want to know *how* we get there in two or three days?" Keita asked gently.

Brannie thought a moment and finally answered honestly, "No. Not really."

"We'll get there in two or three days," Keita said anyway, "*if* we survive. That's a big if."

"I thought I helped," Zoya said with another shrug.

"Well, you didn't!" Keita barked. "This is bad."

"We are Riders," Zoya explained. "You are dragon. We will be fine."

"I don't understand," Brannie said, gratefully taking the

canteen of fresh water that Aidan handed her. "What kind
of ship captain would take such a dangerous route?"

"What kind, you ask?" Keita stepped back, her arm sweeping wide toward the front of the boat. "A Northlander!"

Covered in furs, the captain stood on the deck of his
boat, laughing into the rising storm winds and telling his
men that, "*If all goes well, we will die with honor among the
sea gods, my friends!*"

The dragons and Riders turned their attention back to
Zoya, who shrugged once more and said again, "I thought I
helped."

Aidan sat down next to Brannie and offered her dried
meat. She waved it away with a distinct look of disgust on
her face.

"While I am stuck on this death trap," she said, her voice
nothing more than a rough growl, "I am not eating anything."

"At least keep drinking water." His canteen was beside
her and he picked it up and handed it to her.

She took several large gulps of the water before putting
the stopper back.

"I'm sorry," she said softly.

Aidan blinked. "For what?"

"For being afraid to stand up because I'm afraid I'll fall
into the water and never come up again. For being afraid to
eat because I'm afraid I'll vomit . . . everywhere. For being
afraid to even look in the water because I'm afraid of what
will look back."

"It'll be you," he said simply.

"What?"

"If you look in the water, you'll mostly see yourself looking back. Water's reflective."

"Yes, you're right." She gave a little laugh. "Silly me."

"If it makes you feel better, the closer we get to the storm area Keita is so concerned about, the less we'll see of the Fins."

"Have there been Fins?" Brannie asked.

"None. But it's probably best they don't know there's a boat of dragons making its way across their ocean."

Brannie looked down. "Excellent point."

Aidan moved closer to her, their shoulders touching, but Brannie immediately leaned away.

"I don't *need* that, Aidan."

"What if I do?"

She thought a moment. "Fair enough."

Brannie leaned against him and Aidan put his arm over her shoulder, pulling her even closer.

"We'll get through this," he told her. "I'm sure it won't be that bad anyway. You know how Keita can exaggerate."

"You think?"

Aidan rested his temple against Brannie's head, closed his eyes. "Of course. She's overdramatic."

"Really?" Brannie asked. "Is that overdramatic, too?"

Aidan opened his eyes and saw the wall of water heading right toward them.

Kachka watched the wall of water bearing down on them.

"This cannot end well!" she yelled over the roar of the ocean.

It was what they had to get through, though. Not just the wall of water heading straight for them, but the violent storms behind that water. They'd need to deal with all that if they hoped to make it through the night.

The Northland men yelled orders to each other as they

prepared themselves and their boat to fight what was before them.

Nina Chechneva held up a rope. "We can tie ourselves to the mast!" she yelled.

"Then we can go down with boat," Kachka replied. "Good idea."

"It is better than nothing, Kachka Shestakova!"

"If we die here," Zoya Kolesova screamed into the wind, "we die with honor!"

"*Shut up!*" Kachka and Nina yelled at her.

Nina looked behind Kachka, then spun in a circle. "The dragons!"

"What of them?"

"They are gone!"

Kachka now did her own turn and Nina was right. "They left us!"

"I told you we cannot trust the dragons!"

Debating whether to slap Nina—some days she truly deserved a good slap—a gold tail dropped behind Zoya and wrapped around her waist. The tail yanked her up and out of the boat.

Angry, Nina yelled, "*What about—*"

A brown tail snatched up Nina, carrying her away. A few seconds later, a black tail wrapped around Kachka and she was yanked from the doomed boat.

The black tail lifted her up and over, placing her on Branwen's back.

"*Hold on!*" Branwen screamed at her.

Kachka grabbed hold of Brannie's chain mail and flattened herself against her back.

Brannie girded her loins and dove headfirst into the nightmare ahead.

She'd rather take on legions and legions of Zealots than fight nature itself. With soldiers and warriors, Brannie had a chance. She could watch their eyes and guess their next move. She could see how they ran toward her and find the weak spot that would take them down. Even a quick shoulder move would give her enough information to block a sword to the gut before cutting off a leg or ripping out a spleen.

But nature had no warnings. It had no weak spots. It had no move that told Brannie what she could do to stop it or wear it down. All she could do was dive and dodge and pray. She didn't pray during battle but she prayed now. She had to.

Following behind Keita, Brannie and the others went up high until they were able to go over the wall of water; their claws skimming the top for what felt like a mile or so until the wall crashed down. Most likely taking out the North-landers' boat in the process.

But the wall of water was only part of their problem.

As the group flew, nature threw everything else it had at them. Rain came down on them in sheets of never-ending water. Thunder crashed around them, seemingly shaking the entire world. Lightning bolts came directly at them as if thrown with great aim.

The only thing that helped them? Their past battles with Lightning dragons. They'd all been trained to face Lightnings. Even Keita, who'd been forced to escape the Olgeirsson Horde a few decades back.

But again, Brannie could watch a Lightning and from the turn of a head, the slash of a tail, or even the raise of a brow, she could tell where their bolts might hit. The same didn't apply when nature had its way. All Brannie could do now was wait until the last second and hope she moved fast enough.

* * *

It was like flying through a Mì-runach gauntlet, but instead of dodging the fists and tails of his brethren, Aidan was dodging lightning bolts and tornadoes of water.

Zoya held on to his chain mail shirt and laughed into the wind. The woman obviously didn't fear death, but Aidan did. He had much more living to do; he didn't want to die just because he couldn't avoid a sudden cyclone that sent him spinning wildly up into the air and then farther out into the ocean.

By the time Aidan righted himself—Zoya miraculously still clinging to him—he'd lost sight of the others.

He pushed his way back to where he thought he'd come from, although he was only guessing. He'd spun like a top from those winds and had no idea where the battle-fuck he truly was.

Something slammed at him from the side and he saw brown scales pushing into him, attempting to lead him back.

Uther.

Aidan took his friend's direction and forced his way through the rain and . . . and . . .

Good gods! Was that sleet? Why was he facing sleet?

Several lightning bolts flashed past him. Aidan felt like they were specifically aimed at him until he saw black scales tumbling down. Caswyn, another black dragon, was on his left, keeping as close an eye on Keita as he could.

So the black dragon freefalling?

"*Hold tight, Zoya!*" he yelled at his charge and dove after Branwen.

He zigged and zagged past more bolts crashing down around him, the thunder exploding over his head, nearly shaking him off course. But Aidan kept at it. He kept Brannie in his sights until he was near her.

She'd been hit by one of the lightning bolts, the scales on her back, under her right wing, smoking from the impact.

Aidan aimed down, slammed his wings against his body,

pushing through the winds that were coming up—which seemed especially strange—and maneuvering himself until he was beside Brannie.

"*Don't let go!*" he ordered Zoya before he reached out and grabbed Brannie's forearms. But her body was still spinning with great force and now Aidan was spinning with her—and heading straight to the ground below.

Keita turned to one side, then the other, barely avoiding the bolts of lightning clearly aiming right for her.

She dove down and flipped to her right, missing the geyser of water that had risen up out of nowhere.

For the first time in Keita's life, she worried that she'd never get out of something. How could she when she couldn't use her greatest assets to protect herself? She couldn't talk to lightning bolts or fuck tornadoes. Nature couldn't be enticed, seduced, or destroyed. All Keita could do was dive and roll and avoid.

But when she glanced back, hoping to see her cousin flying right behind her—calling her all kinds of horrible things because Keita had gotten her into all this—she quickly figured out she was alone.

She faced forward again with every intention of turning completely around and going back for everyone, but bright light suddenly hit Keita in the face. So bright she had to close her eyes and turn her head. A powerful screeching filling the air—and then she was falling.

Keita was falling and she had no idea how to stop.

Didn't matter, though. The ground took care of all that for her. . . .

Chapter Twenty-Two

The armor and chain mail were made specifically for him by Sulien the Smithy.

And the queen herself helped him into that armor, not allowing any of his siblings or squires to assist. That was their way, any time he was going off to war. But this time felt different. This time, Rhiannon feared—truly feared—she'd never see him again.

So Rhiannon took her time, placing each piece onto his dragon body with care.

The two suns were rising and soon Bercelak the Great would be flying out with his war-loving siblings and cousins to face the Zealots in the Outerplains.

With his armor in place, Rhiannon cut the length off his black-and-gray hair until it reached his shoulders, then plaited several war braids, entwining her own white hair into a few of them for luck.

They didn't speak during all of this. There was nothing to say.

When their longtime ritual was complete, they stood at the exit to their chamber, Rhiannon's white claw clasped in Bercelak's black one. They gazed into each other's eyes for several long minutes until Rhiannon finally said, "Kill all of them. Leave nothing for even the crows to dine upon."

Bercelak stepped close, his tail entwining with hers while their snouts brushed against each other.

Then he was gone. Out of their chamber and through the throne room. His siblings joined him, with Ghleanna on his right and Addolgar, his left. The rest trailing right behind.

He didn't look back at her. She didn't want him to.

Instead Rhiannon sat on her throne and the Mì-runach immediately surrounded her. They would not leave her side until Bercelak returned.

Not surprisingly, no others of her court approached her the entire day.

At first Annwyl thought the noise she heard was in her head. Just something else to torment her. But the more north she traveled, the louder the sound became.

After ten minutes of walking, she found it. A giant animal, not quite as big as Fearghus and his brothers in their dragon form but ten times bigger than her. It was on its side, crying out.

She started to walk away. The thing had black eyes; big horns on its head, elbows, and knees; enormous claws; and spikes running down its tail. The flesh of something once human still caught on several of the tips. It also had extremely large fangs that didn't fit completely in its mouth. This was not something she wanted to get too close to if it suddenly decided to get up or attack her. It was a demon animal of some kind and she still intended to get out of this hell alive.

But it kept screaming and something inside her couldn't walk away. She didn't know what was wrong with her, but she simply couldn't do it.

So Annwyl turned around and went back. She moved in

close and reached her hand out to pet its belly. The fur was hard, a few individual hairs sticking into her hand like splinters. But she ignored that and kept petting.

"Shhh," she said. "It's okay." She studied the claws, looking for something that could be causing the animal pain, but they looked clean. Nothing between the pads either. She then checked its belly, chest, and groin. Still nothing.

"Come on, big boy. You're fine. Nothing to cry about."

Annwyl heard footsteps behind her and she turned to see a group of armed demons.

"Move!" one of them ordered. "It's ours. We feast tonight."

"He's not even fighting. Fuck off."

"Move or we'll take you down with it."

"Find something else to eat, demon."

"It'll eat you, human."

Annwyl shrugged. "Probably."

"Just move."

"I can't. I heard his pitiful cries and I . . . I just can't." She petted his stomach again. "He may be dying anyway. I can't find any wounds. He's clearly in distress. Maybe he's just old. Why would you want to kill and eat something that's old?"

The lead demon shook his head and the entire group began to back up. "It's not old. It's a baby." He pointed behind Annwyl. "And you should run."

Which was what the rest of them did. They ran.

But Annwyl couldn't bring herself to move. Even as the ground shook beneath her feet and what she could only guess was the mother of the crying animal leaned her head around him and focused on Annwyl.

Annwyl stepped back, her gaze moving up to see the back of the mother as it towered over her offspring.

Then she moved to the side and saw more of the animals. This was a herd . . . that had come when they heard the youngest of their number crying for help. That's what had drawn Annwyl. Just as her own children's calls would pull her to them.

Of course, if Annwyl found some strange, armed woman standing over them . . . petting their stomachs . . . no. That would not end well. So probably not for her either.

The mother let out a threatening snort-snarl that had Annwyl quickly moving away. Then she nudged at her off-spring until he got up. When he was on his feet, she pushed him toward the others of her herd before returning her gaze to Annwyl.

All Annwyl could think to do was raise her hands to show she meant no harm. "Sorry," she said. "Just trying to help. Meant no offence."

The mother leaned in close and sniffed Annwyl from head to foot and back again. Then she nudged her with her snout, sending Annwyl flying back about a hundred feet.

Annwyl hit the ground hard, but she didn't complain. She saw that those fangs were *much* bigger than the babe's. So the fact the mother didn't bite her head off . . .

Annwyl pushed herself up until she was standing again and nodded at the She-beast.

"Thank you," she called out. "For not killing me."

Turning, Annwyl started back the way she'd come, but the beast made a noise and she glanced back, half-afraid she'd find it charging her. But it was moving its head to the side.

She changed direction and went where the She-beast indicated. Maybe this was the way out. Or just another entrance to another hell. Annwyl didn't know. But why not try? It wasn't like she had many choices at this point.

First there were only a few of them, watching her. But then more were drawn here from the other hells toward this place where they could look down from a high vantage point and watch what she did. Where she went. They'd all sensed her here, in this place. She was alive while they were all dead. It wasn't fair and something they would not stand for.

She was always supposed to end up here, they all knew it, but it never occurred to them she'd end up here still alive . . . and vulnerable.

She headed away from the herd of corpse-eater cattle and they began to follow.

Because they'd waited long enough, lost in their brutal hells. And it was now her time to know suffering. To know true pain and horror.

Now she was here, and they could settle it.

Settle it and end it. For eternity.

Chapter Twenty-Three

Aidan woke up on his back, coughing dirt, sand, and water out of his lungs.

When the coughing subsided, he let out a breath, relieved he was alive. Until he remembered that he'd had Zoya Kolesova on his back.

Moving fast, he rolled out of the crater his body had created when it landed and turned back to look down into it.

Half-covered in dirt and sand was poor Zoya Kolesova, on her back, her arms and legs bent. Probably similar to the position she'd been in when they'd landed.

But Aidan lurched back when Zoya suddenly coughed, a plume of sand exploding from her mouth.

Shocked, Aidan leaned into the crater again and called out, "Zoya?"

The Rider coughed again . . . and sat up, shaking her head in an attempt to remove the dirt and sand from her eyes.

"How . . . I don't . . ." Aidan was beyond words at this point.

"I am Zoya Kolesova of the Mountain Movers of the Lands of Pain in the Far Reaches of the Steppes of the Outerplains," she announced. "And sometimes, when you move mountains, the mountains, they fall on you. If you cannot survive a few thousand pounds falling on you . . . what kind of weak Mountain Mover are you?"

"Uh . . . excellent point?"

"Of course it is." She stood. "Now get me from this pit."

Aidan reached down and grabbed Zoya's arm, lifting her to level ground. Once she was safe, he concentrated on helping the others. He had to walk a bit across the beach until he reached them and the craters in the sand where each of the dragons had landed.

Caswyn and Uther were already awake and alert, doing their best to get their bulk up. The Riders were all alive, including Kachka.

Branwen, though, was still buried in the dirt, not moving. Keita knelt beside her.

Aidan arrived quickly at her side, standing opposite Keita.

The lightning bolt had torn open a spot underneath her right wing. It wasn't bleeding, though, because the heat from the lightning had cauterized the wound.

He knelt beside her and pushed her hair off her brow. "Brannie? Brannie, can you hear me?"

She growled in response, her front claws digging into the sand, but her eyes remained closed and she didn't get up.

"Aidan?" Keita said softly.

He looked at the princess and she was staring up. He followed her gaze and saw the women standing on the cliffs looking down at them. There were many of them and they didn't seem disturbed that there were five dragons on their beach.

These women were all Eastlanders. If they knew dragons, they only knew Eastland dragons, which were very different from Aidan's kind. So, at the very least, they should be reacting to that. But they weren't.

"Who are they?"

"Warrior witches," Keita replied. "Like the Kyvich and the Nolwenn."

"What are they called?"

"Heaven's Destroyers."

Aidan admitted, "Their name suggests we might have an issue with them."

Keita snorted. "If they wanted to kill us, Mì-runach . . . we'd be wet, sticky spots in the sand by now."

"That information does not make me feel better."

"I'll handle them," Keita said, "and you, Aidan, take care of my cousin."

Keita shifted to human and stood, her long red hair covering her naked body. She motioned to the witches and walked away from Branwen.

Aidan snapped his claws at Uther and Caswyn and pointed at Keita. The two males shifted to human—their Rhona-provided chain mail shifting with them—and rushed after her to keep her safe.

Taking Brannie's claw in his own, Aidan held it and watched the witches make their way down to the beach. Armed with swords and bows and arrows, the witches also carried staffs made from bamboo, each individually adorned with jewels and gold chains and items from nature, like large feathers from predatory birds and fangs from jungle cats. They used those staffs like they were walking sticks but Aidan knew better.

A witch with shoulder-length black hair that had gray and red strands peppered throughout, light brown skin, and catlike brown eyes stepped in front of the other witches and smiled at the royal.

"Princess Keita."

"Lady Meihui. It's delightful to see you again."

"And you, Princess." Meihui took Keita's hand and held it, her smile for Keita alone.

Uther, eyes wide, glanced back at Aidan but he shook his head, indicating Uther should let it go. Aidan was not about to fall down this gopher hole over Keita's past.

"So what brings you back to our shores, Princess?" Meihui asked, still holding Keita's hand.

"I'm here to see the Empress, but the boat we took decided to pass through the Trail of Storms."

Meihui snorted a laugh. "Let me guess . . . Northlanders?"

"What do you think?"

"Well, of course, we don't mind you here, Princess, or your entourage . . . but we are concerned with"—using her staff, Meihui pointed at the Riders—"*them*."

Before Kachka could stop her, Zoya stepped forward, hands slapping her chest. "Have something to say to me, decadent Eastlander? Come and talk to Zoya!"

Meihui sighed and released Keita's hand. "See what I mean? Barbarians."

"They're part of my protection."

The witch blinked. "Riders? Part of *your* protection? That's . . . unusual."

Keita stepped closer to Meihui and said low but quickly, "They've attached themselves to me and now I can't really shake them. Can we just . . . overlook them? They've committed to me and I will make sure they cause you no problems."

"Now, Keita, we know what your commitments are worth," Meihui purred back.

"Come, come. That was decades ago. And it wasn't my fault."

"Still blaming Gwenvael then?"

"When it's necessary." Keita turned and gestured to the others. "Uther the Despicable. Caswyn the Butcher."

"I do love Southland dragon names."

"Aidan the Divine. And my cousin, Branwen the Awf—"

"Branwen?" Meihui suddenly asked, her back straightening, her gaze going immediately to Brannie. "Your *cousin* is Branwen the Awful?"

Keita glanced at Aidan, unsure where this was going. "Uh . . . aye. She's my cousin."

Meihui looked at the other witches and, as one, they pushed past Keita and descended on Branwen, surrounding her and Aidan.

Meihui leaned over Branwen's wound, studied it. "This is deep."

"Should we have her shift?" one of the witches asked their leader.

"No. That might kill her." She leaned in. "We need a poultice." She snapped her fingers and half the witches took off running.

"You need to move back so we can work," Meihui said to Aidan.

"I'm not leav—"

Without even looking at him, Meihui waved her staff and it was as if someone grabbed him by the forearms and dragged him back several hundred feet.

Shocked, Aidan could only stare at the witches as they worked on Branwen. There weren't a lot of human witches who could move his dragon form around like a leaf on the wind, and he wasn't sure he wanted these women caring for a wounded Brannie. But it wasn't like he had much choice.

Aidan shifted to human and went to Keita's side. "Are you sure they can be trusted?" he asked the princess.

"She'll be fine. Meihui and I are very old friends."

"So I noticed."

"My, my, we are judgey, aren't we?"

"I'm not judging. Just wondering if Ragnar knows exactly what he's gotten himself into."

Keita let Uther place the cape he wore around her shoulders

since any clothes she had in her travel bag were still soaking wet.

Wrapping the cape around her body, she told Aidan, "I can assure you, there's nothing that Ragnar the Cunning does not know about me. And he accepts me despite it all."

"Then you should make him your mate," Uther said while also watching the witches take care of Brannie. "After all this time and twelve bloody hatchlings, it's the least you can do."

Aidan cringed, watching Keita slowly—so slowly—take a few steps forward and then turn so she faced Uther directly. Glaring up at him with those dark eyes.

Uther, oblivious as always, stared back. "What? What did I say?"

Keita was shown to a room in the Heaven's Destroyers' temple. She found parts of her old wardrobe tucked away in a wood chest.

She lifted a purple dress in front of her and smiled at her reflection in the tall mirror at the far end of the bedroom.

"I can't believe you still have my clothes," she said.

"How do you always know when I'm in the room?" Meihui asked from the doorway.

"Your scent." She glanced back at her. "Lemon."

"I work the grove every day. It calms me."

"Really?" Keita stepped into the dress. "So all those rumors about you and your coven attacking the Darkest Night temples?"

Meihui sat on the bed, her arms stretched out behind her, long legs crossed at the ankles. "That's none of your concern, Keita."

"No, of course not." She pulled the sleeves of the dress up her arms. "But I am curious. As always."

"Your curiosity has always gotten you into trouble."

"Very true." She walked over to Meihui and turned. "Tie me up?"

Meihui stood and proceeded to lace up the back of Keita's dress.

"I hear you have a mate now."

"Something like that."

"Do you like him?"

"I do . . . which is surprising. I never thought I would."

"All done."

Keita turned and smiled at her old friend.

Brushing Keita's hair off her forehead, Meihui asked, "Why are you really here, Keita the Viper?"

"To see the Empress."

Meihui leaned in close. "I truly hope I don't have to kill you, my friend."

"Me?" Laughing a little, Keita kissed Meihui on the cheek, then lifted her skirt and twirled a few times. "I forgot how much I used to love this dress!"

Brannie woke up human . . . but that was strange because she didn't remember shifting to human.

She was stomach down on a bed with Aidan asleep in a chair beside her. Snoring.

"Not very royal."

Gritting her teeth, Brannie took her time turning over and sitting up. She remembered well when that lightning bolt had hit her in the back and she was just grateful to be alive. She wasn't about to risk her progress by jumping up and running around the room.

When she was sitting and comfortable, she got to her feet, again, taking her time. When the room was no longer spinning, she made her way over to a tall mirror on the other side. Brannie turned and tried to see her back. In her human form, the wound went from her shoulder to the back of her calf.

"If you're wondering," Aidan said from his chair, "your wing is fine."

She had been wondering, and hearing that information . . . She closed her eyes and let out the breath she didn't realize she'd been holding.

"Good. How long have I been out?"

"A day." Aidan frowned, looked over his shoulder at the darkness outside. "Okay, maybe two. Barely."

"How is everyone else?" she asked, heading back to the bed and carefully stretching out.

"The same. Fine. Mostly sleeping in, though."

Brannie lay down on her back but it hurt; so she rolled over onto her stomach, using her elbows to raise her chest up a bit.

"Did I shift?" she asked.

"No," he said on a yawn, stretching in the chair. "The witches shifted you to human after they took care of your wound while you were still dragon."

"What witches?"

"Human warrior witches. Heaven's Destroyers. We're at their temple."

"Never heard of them."

"Your cousin seems to know the leader quite well."

It was something in Aidan's voice and, after a few seconds, Brannie caught on. "Oh. Yeah." She shrugged. "Well, the one thing Ragnar must know is that Keita loves him, because she's never stayed with anyone too long. *Everyone* bores her eventually."

Brannie leaned her head down and dug her fingers into her hair, massaging her scalp for a bit.

"Can I admit something to you?" she asked Aidan.

"You're just relieved to be off that bloody boat?"

"By the gods, Aidan," she gasped out, "you have *no* idea."

The room door slid open and a woman stepped in. She was beautiful and tall and definitely in charge.

"You're awake," she announced.

"Branwen, this is Lady Meihui. Lady Meihui, Branwen the Awful of the Cadwaladr Clan, captain of the First and Fifteenth Companies."

Brannie smirked at him. "You're such a royal."

"I know. It's a flaw."

"No introductions are needed for us," the witch said, moving into the room. "We all know Branwen the Awful." When Brannie cringed, she added, "Don't worry. You didn't kill anyone we know."

"Well, that's a relief. Always a bit awkward when you have . . . but you don't know it until you're face to face."

"We've just heard a lot about you."

That surprised Brannie. "You have? About me?"

"Of course. You're the great Branwen the Awful."

"I am?" She heard Aidan chuckle. "Shut up."

"I didn't say anything!"

Meihui leaned over Brannie and studied her back. Fingers prodded the wound.

"It's healing very nicely, Captain."

"Brannie's fine. Everybody calls me Brannie."

"All right, Brannie. You'll need to stay another day. Maybe two before you can head inland to Emperor's City."

Brannie looked at Aidan. "Do we have time for that?"

"We'll make time."

"Is there a rush?" Meihui asked.

Aidan gave his most charming smile. "Not at all. Captain Branwen just hates to dawdle. Military logic."

"Of course." Meihui moved back to the door. "I'll be sending up some medicinal tea. It tastes awful, but drink all of it anyway. It'll help the healing."

"All right."

"And your Riders . . . we put them out in the stables because they annoyed me."

Meihui walked out, closing the sliding door behind her.

Brannie and Aidan were silent for a long moment until Aidan noted, "At least the Riders like horses."

Laughing, Brannie buried her face into her pillow.

Chapter Twenty-Four

The torrential rains started that night. Aidan went out on the terrace outside Brannie's room and watched the rain fall for an hour while she slept.

He would forever be grateful to the warrior witches for helping Branwen. When trapped in that storm, he hadn't known if any of them would survive, but Branwen . . .

She'd been right. He was falling for her fast. And he didn't mean to. It wasn't like he was one of those dragons looking for a mate. It had always been the last thing he wanted.

But Branwen . . .

"What are you doing up?" she asked from the bed. Still on her stomach . . . still naked. Her wound still healing.

"Can't sleep."

"Come here."

He did. Afraid if he didn't, she'd get up again and hamper the healing.

Aidan eased onto the bed and stretched out on his back. He put one arm behind his head and gazed up at the ceiling, waiting for Brannie to go back to sleep.

Her hand reached out and gripped his chain mail shirt. She began tugging, but when that didn't work, she yanked.

"What are you doing?" he finally asked.

"Closer," she commanded, her eyes closed, half her head buried deep into the pillow.

Aidan moved over until he was able to reach out to Brannie and gently move her so her head was resting on his shoulder and her arm was over his chest.

"I thought you didn't want any cuddling?" he asked even as he stroked his fingers against her waist with the hand currently trapped under her body.

"No cuddling while dragon," she said into his shoulder. "We're not dragon. So we're fine. We can cuddle away."

Aidan chuckled and tucked in even more.

"Are you sure we're okay with time?" Brannie asked, although she seemed half-asleep.

"By Keita's original time line, we're still supposed to be on that boat. Not even close to Eastland shores. So we have time for you to heal properly."

"Okay. Where is everyone else?"

"No idea."

Brannie lifted her head a bit and stared at him. "You haven't checked on everyone?"

"I'm sure they're fine."

"Even Uther and Caswyn? Seriously?"

"I'm not leaving you."

"I'm not dying." She thought a moment. "I wasn't even dying before. I was just wounded and in a lot of pain. But the witches helped with that. Now you need to go and keep the peace."

"Keita can take care of it. She knows the Eastlanders better than I do."

"But—"

"I'm not leaving, so shut up."

"Fine. But if those witches strip Caswyn and Uther of their scales, that's going to be on you."

* * *

Keita eased the door closed and began tiptoeing away when a hand was slapped over her mouth, an arm went around her waist, and she was carried down the hall and into another bedroom.

When she was finally released, she spun around and began slapping. Caswyn immediately put his arms up to block the blows.

"What is wrong with you, lizard?" Keita demanded.

"I didn't want those witches to know we were talking," he whispered, stepping back to the door and pressing his ear against it.

"What are you doing?"

"Listening for spies."

Keita rubbed her eyes with the palms of her hands before reminding the big idiot, "I *am* a spy."

"Yeah, but you're on our side—so I don't care." He listened a few seconds more. "All right. I don't hear anything."

That's when the door swung open hard and Uther rushed in, closing the door behind him and using his body to block it.

"Those witches are putting poison in our food!" he whispered desperately. "They're going to kill us all!"

"Told you!" Caswyn stated from the floor, where he'd landed on his big ass. "We have to get you out of here."

"I need you both to calm down."

Keita seriously thought about going back to her cousin's bedroom and dragging Aidan out.

A few minutes ago, when she'd seen him and Brannie cuddled together, asleep, she'd decided to leave them alone, assuming there was no situation she couldn't handle at least until the morning. But she'd forgotten about Caswyn and Uther. Helpful dragons, to be sure, but not what Keita would call smart. She instantly missed the days she'd spent with Ren and Gwenvael, the three of them starting trouble wherever they landed. But her brother and Ren had been smart, Ren able to talk them out of any trouble and Gwenvael able to seduce anyone who could help them.

It had been the best time of Keita's life before meeting Ragnar. But now she had to deal with her easily distracted cousin, two dragons who, Keita was sure, couldn't count to five, three Riders who never listened to anyone but themselves, and Aidan.

And what good was he when he was always so busy mooning over Branwen?

Even more irritating? Brannie still didn't seem to understand. She was completely oblivious to how that dragon felt about her. And that was foolish. Not a lot of dragon males would be comfortable with a female who could outmatch him in any type of warrior situation.

There simply were not a lot of Bram the Mercifuls running around, on the lookout for Ghleanna the Decimators! So her cousin needed to snatch up this chance before it was too late!

"I understand your concerns," she told the two idiots, "but I can assure you we are safe here. I know these witches very well and—"

Keita stopped talking when the two males began to giggle.

"What?" she asked.

"Yeah," Uther said, "we can tell you know the witches *very* well. Especially that Lady Meihui."

Then they both leered.

Disgusted, Keita dropped her head and pressed her hands to her eyes again. She even added some shoulder shakes in for good measure.

Both males bolted to her side and crouched a bit.

"Are you okay?" one of them asked.

"We were only teasing you," the other said.

They were both close to her now, so Keita reached up, grabbed them both by the hair, yanked them one way, then slammed them back together so their giant heads collided.

"*Owwww!*"

"*Mad cow!*"

"Now listen up," she ordered both dragons. "You will do as *I* tell you. Understand? I don't care that you're Mì-runach. I don't care that I have no military rank. You know nothing of the Eastlands and you can only manage to get us killed. So you'll keep your mouths shut and do as I tell you. Understand?"

"But they're trying to poison us!" Uther insisted.

"And you think that because . . . ?"

"I went by the kitchens and the witches were putting red stuff in the food."

"A red powder?" Keita asked.

"Aye."

"And then a yellow powder?"

Uther frowned. "Aye."

"That's *seasoning,* nincompoop."

"Are you sure?"

"I'm the one who'd know, don't you think?"

"You mean because you're a murdering poisoner?"

"Yes, Uther. Because of that." Keita walked to the door. "Now you two will keep your mouths shut, your eyes open, and you will follow my lead . . . or I will get *very* angry. And you lads don't want to see me angry, now do you?"

Keita grinned when both males shook their heads. "Good! I'll let you know when dinner's ready!" she trilled, but then she dropped her voice and her brow. "And you two bitches better eat whatever those witches put in front of you or I'll show you the real difference between Eastland seasonings and poison."

* * *

The princess walked out, slamming the door behind her.

Uther looked at Caswyn. "Any idea how long before Brannie's better?"

"No. No idea."

"It better be soon," Uther said. "Because that royal is *mean*."

"I know!" Caswyn agreed. "She is *so* mean."

Caswyn's big shoulders hitched a little and Uther immediately put his arm around his friend's shoulders.

"It'll be okay."

"But why did she have to be *so* mean?" Caswyn asked, sniffling. "I mean . . . I'm a nice dragon!"

"And sensitive."

"*Very* sensitive!"

Laughing so hard they could barely speak, Keita and Meihui sat on the floor of Meihui's private quarters. As the current leader of the coven, she had privacy the other sisters did not.

"You should have seen their faces," Keita choked out.

"I saw them at dinner." Meihui pounded her fist on the floor. "They looked terrified!"

"Because they were!"

Meihui fell back on the floor, laughing up at the ceiling. "The really big one looked like he was about to cry."

"Oh, that was my fault," Keita happily admitted.

"I bet it was." Meihui sat up. Keita was pouring two chalices of wine. "I was going to say you haven't changed. But you have, haven't you?"

"Depends who you talk to."

Meihui took the chalice from Keita and, clearing the laughter from her throat, asked, "So, Princess, why are you really here?"

Keita shrugged, sipped her wine. "I'm just—"

"Keita, please. It's me. And your mother is in for the fight of her life. You'd never leave . . . unless you had to." Meihui held her hand up, halting whatever the next set of lies Keita was going to try to tell her. "And don't try to convince me that you're running from your mother. You two may squabble like cats in a bag, but you're still Rhiannon the White's daughter."

"I could have betrayed her."

"Could have. Didn't. But if you did . . . she'd have your head before you could even think to run." Meihui smiled. "So stop trying to bullshit me, old friend."

Keita let out a breath, placed her chalice on the floor. "I'm here to ask for the Empress's help."

Unable to stop herself, Meihui laughed. "Have you lost your mind? That female won't help you."

"She adores me! Besides, I can be very persuasive."

"Even with your talents . . . forget it. I mean, if the Emperor were still alive, maybe. But since his death . . ." She shrugged. "She makes your mother seem like one of the nuns of the Peace and Love Temple."

"I at least have to try."

"And if she says no, then what?"

"Well—"

"Forget I asked," Meihui quickly cut in. If Keita became too honest, Meihui would have to make decisions she'd prefer not to have to make.

"No matter what you do, Keita, there are some things you have to know about."

"And what are those?"

"The Empress has been in an ongoing battle with Batu of the Dark Mountain Tribes. Batu has been raiding towns

and cities that the Empress considers her own. It's gotten
ugly."

"That's why you were worried about Kachka and the
others."

"There may be much infighting among the tribes of all
the Steppes, no matter where they're located—even on different continents—but in the end, they are loyal to the horse
gods and each other and the rest of us are decadent, weak
imperialists who deserve whatever we get."

"All that may be true but I don't see what it has to do
with me and the Empress."

"Because while the Empress has been in an ongoing war
with the Riders . . . she's been negotiating with her brother
to stop another."

Keita sat up, her back straight. "Lord Xing?"

"He began making his move once the Emperor died. But
the negotiations for a truce have been going on for months.
Honestly, I don't know what's taking so long. I thought she
would have just had him killed by now. In truth, I thought
maybe that was why you were here."

Keita rested her back against the bedframe behind her
and raised her knees, placing her arms on them. The chalice dangled from her right hand and her shrewd eyes were
locked on the far wall.

Meihui knew she was one of the few who ever saw the
other side of Keita. The side that wasn't a flighty, vacuous
royal. A side many should fear.

"Do you feel he's stalling?" Keita asked.

"Not that I'm aware. But he must have something she
wants. I do know there are rumors that he has made alliances
with other lords. Some say he's raised an army. A big one."

"Some say?"

"If he's done it, he's done it quietly."

Keita nodded but didn't say anything. Meihui knew why.
She was plotting.

And woe to anyone who got in Keita the Viper's way when she was plotting.

Talwyn was poring over maps with her brother, father, and uncles when one of the Abominations, a young man with fangs he'd been born with, stepped in and announced, "Dragons heading this way."

"That's your grandfather," Fearghus said. He stood straight and looked at his daughter. "You go."

Talwyn shrugged. "All right." She didn't mind. She adored her grandfather. "But why me?"

Her father and uncles just stared at her, so she didn't push further. She simply walked out to the nearby grassland and waited; Talan showed up a few minutes later.

The ground shook as their grandfather, Bercelak, and a cadre of Cadwaladr kin landed hard.

Shifting to human, his gorgeous armor and weapons shifting with him, Bercelak strode forward, reached down, and lifted Talwyn up into his arms, giving her a quick but strong hug.

When he placed her on the ground, Talan threw his arms open and moved toward their grandfather, but Bercelak stopped him by slamming his hand against Talan's forehead.

"But, Grandfather—"

"No."

Laughing, Talan stepped back. "As always, it's good to see you too, Grandfather."

"Where is everyone?" Bercelak asked Talwyn.

"In Izzy's tent."

"Show me."

She led him, Ghleanna, Rhys, and Addolgar to the tent while the rest of the Cadwaladrs went to set up their camp or check on their own troops. Bercelak's sons immediately stepped back from the table and the elder Cadwaladrs took their places.

With a shake of his head, Bercelak swiped his hand across the map, knocking all the miniatures off the table and onto the floor. "Wrong." He glanced at his sons. "As usual."

"Glad to see you too, Dad," Briec muttered.

"We start our assault tomorrow," Bercelak announced.

"Why?" Fearghus asked.

"Because I said so." He looked at Ghleanna. "Start off with aerial first. Our dragons attack with stones from the sky and the humans can use catapults against the walls. Let's get them moving."

"Get them moving?" Briec asked. "What do you mean get them moving? Get who moving?"

"The Zealots. You know I'm not much for waiting. They wanted me here"—he glanced at his kin—"they wanted *us* here. Let's find out why."

"If you know they want you here, why are you here?" Fearghus asked.

"Don't you know me yet, boy?"

"I know you, Daddy," Gwenvael said, putting his arms around his father's chest, and gently resting his head on his father's shoulder. "And I love you despite that."

"I could have thrown his egg over the side of that mountain," Bercelak said as everyone attempted to hide their laughter at his expense. "But I never did. So stupid."

Chapter Twenty-Five

Brannie woke up to the face of fear and terror. She tried to move as far away as possible, but she was trapped between that face and Aidan's big body on the other side of her.

"What are you doing?" she finally asked.

"Are you feeling better? Can we leave now? I want to leave now."

Not knowing how to answer any of that, she jabbed the body next to her.

"What?"

"You deal with him."

Aidan raised his head and rested his chin on Brannie's shoulder. "What's wrong, Uther?"

"We want out. The witches are trying to poison us—"

"You sure that's just not seasoning you're looking at?"

"—we think the Riders are dead somewhere—"

"Or just relegated to the stables."

"—and Keita is meaner than we ever thought. We want to go."

"We have to wait until Brannie's better."

"She looks better." Uther suddenly leaned in close. So close, if it had been Aidan, she'd assume he was trying to kiss her. "*Tell him you're better!*"

The door opened behind Uther and several of the witches walked in. One came over to the bed. She held a large bucket of steaming water.

"We thought you'd like a bath," she said to Brannie while staring at Uther.

"That sounds lovely."

The witch pointed at Uther with her elbow. "Is he bothering you?"

"No," Uther said.

"Yes," Aidan said.

The witch pulled one hand away from the bucket and flicked it.

Fascinated, Brannie watched a panicked Uther slide backward out the door and into the hallway.

"That was wrong!" he yelled, but he didn't come back into the room.

Smiling, the witch joined her sisters and together they filled up the metal tub. Oil was added to the water and the smell was so delicious that Brannie didn't even wait for the witches to leave before she made her way to the tub and lowered herself in.

She closed her eyes and relaxed her head back against the tub rim. It suddenly occurred to her it was morning, the suns' light filtering into the room through slats in the wood ceiling. The pain in her back had lessened to the point of being nonexistent and even the itching of healing skin was no longer present. But her human skin was definitely scarred. She reached back and could feel the difference between recently damaged and undamaged.

Not that Brannie cared, but this particular scar was big, still stretching from her shoulder to the back of her calf on her right side.

Of course, it could have been worse. That scar could be at the front instead. That would be unpleasant.

Deciding not to worry about any of that, she closed her eyes again and let out a happy sigh . . . until the water around her sloshed, splashing her in the face.

Lifting her head and opening her eyes, she watched Aidan getting comfortable opposite her in the tub.

"What are you doing?"

"Why shouldn't I bathe, too?" he asked.

"You can . . . when I'm done."

"I'm not the great Captain Branwen the Awful. Those witches aren't going to set up a bath for me. They're just going to chuck me out of the room like they did poor Uther."

Brannie snorted a laugh, unable to help herself.

"Don't look at me that way," she told Aidan. "I didn't mean to laugh. It's just . . ."

Aidan smiled. "I know. And it was a little funny." He studied her. "How's your back?"

"Better than I expected."

"Good."

"Were you worried?"

"You got a lightning bolt to the back, Branwen. Of course I was worried."

Brannie shook her head. "I have to admit . . . it hurt like a bitch. And worse than anything you can get from a Lightning, that's for sure. I mean, their bolts hurt, but . . . the real thing?" She shuddered. "Don't need to go through that again. Ever."

"Let me see."

Brannie turned, pulling her knees up under her chin, her arms around her legs, her head bent forward. Aidan's fingers brushed against the back of her neck, moving her wet hair out of the way.

"Humans," he murmured. "I don't know how they survive anything with such frail bodies."

His fingers moved down the edges of the wound.

"So," he said, and she could feel him getting closer even though the water barely moved, "here's the question."

"Uh-huh."

"Would you go through that again . . . if it meant you didn't have to go near a boat?"

"Absolutely."

He laughed against her neck and Brannie dropped her head back, trying to see him. But then his lips were against hers. She automatically opened her mouth and their tongues met.

Aidan dug his hands into her hair and his urgency . . .

Brannie went up on her knees and turned completely around, throwing her arms around his shoulders.

"Shut up!" Brannie told him.

"I didn't say anything!" he replied, laughing.

"You were about to. I could see it in your eyes."

"You should be resting."

"I find fucking restful."

Aidan smirked. "Not the way I do it."

Now determined, Brannie slapped her hand against his chest, shoved him back into the water, and launched herself at him.

Laughing, Aidan grabbed Brannie's hips and tried to push her back, but she was unwilling to give up the territory she'd already taken.

Plus, she was slippery, the water and oils making it hard to keep his grip on her.

"Can we not discuss this?" he asked.

"No. We can't." She pinned him against the tub wall and leaned in. "Just take it. Take it like a dragon!"

Aidan snorted and they both started laughing, Brannie dropping onto him.

"You're ridiculous," she complained against his neck.

"Why is everything always my fault?"

"Because it is."

She began to nibble at the skin beneath his ear.

"Branwen—"

"Stop talking."

"Make me."

She kissed him, and it did shut him up.

Aidan slipped his fingers into Branwen's hair and pulled her closer, wanting to explore every crevice of her mouth. Wanting to know what every part of her felt like.

Her hands pressed against his chest, eased down his skin and under the water. She gripped his cock, held it tight. She really didn't have to squeeze, though. Just her touch had him hard. Knowing she wanted him had him hard.

Brannie settled her knees on either side of his thighs and lowered her body. She held onto his cock until it entered her pussy. She moved her hands to his shoulders and dropped down hard. He gasped into her mouth, fingers gripping her wet hips again, holding her tight against him.

Her muscles squeezed him, her arms now around her neck, her lips locked against his.

They kissed and Brannie squeezed until Aidan knew he couldn't take any more. He wrapped his arms around her waist and pulled out of their kiss enough so that he could ask, "Am I hurting your back?"

She shook her head and leaned in for another kiss.

"Good," he whispered against her lips before he slipped his tongue into her mouth and drove into her hard from below.

Brannie released the grip she had on his neck and caught the rim of the tub with both hands, holding on, letting Aidan fuck her.

She didn't speak but she groaned and occasionally gave

the most adorable squeak when he thrust up, her head resting on his shoulder.

After a few minutes, he pressed his hand against the side of her neck and pushed her back until she released her hold on the tub. He bent her back a bit more, then leaned forward and licked the space between her breasts before sucking a nipple into his mouth.

Brannie growled and her fingers gripped his hair, pressing him to her breast. He continued to suck and tease even while he hammered into her.

With one hand still twisted in his hair, Brannie grabbed his shoulder with the other and dug her fingers into the skin. She had no real nails, always keeping them short for battle, but her grasp was brutal. Painful. Ruthless.

He loved it.

Especially when she came. Her entire body clenched and Aidan's eyes crossed from the pain and pleasure. The way she clamped down on him, biting her lip to stop from crying out.

He watched her. Amazed at how beautiful she looked coming like that. So beautiful, he came right behind her, unable to control himself.

And it was all because of her. All because of Branwen the Awful.

When Branwen could see and hear again, when she was no longer lost in fucking Aidan the Divine, she collapsed against him, her head landing on his shoulder.

They held on to each other, both breathing hard, waiting for the tremors racking their bodies to stop.

And, when they did, she said, "Shut up."

"Again, Branwen," he laughed, "*I didn't say anything!*"

* * *

Bram the Merciful closed his eyes and dropped back into the chair.

"Are you sure?" he asked the two sitting across from him.

Var raised an eyebrow. "Of *course* I'm sure," he said with an arrogance Bram usually only heard from Var's mother. "Do you think I'd bother telling you Brigida was rooting through our library of books if I wasn't sure?"

"What could she be looking for?"

"An ancient book of dragon spells," Frederick explained again.

"I don't mean what did she take? What was she looking for *within* the book?"

"That we don't know," Frederick admitted. "I couldn't read it—"

"—and I hadn't gotten to it yet to fully know what's inside," Var finished.

"And now you know why I told you, Unnvar, to deal with the dragon books first."

"They're boring."

"Not everything can be entertaining, and now we don't know what Brigida the Most Foul is up to."

"That's hardly my fault."

"You didn't help."

"So what do we do *now?*" Frederick asked, always one to stop a possible dispute with reason.

"I've already taken care of that," Var said simply. Too simply.

It was the strangest thing. The boy had such intense arrogance. Not about his beauty—and, like his father, he was beautiful—nor about his intelligence. He just accepted them as part of who he was. But when it came to his certainty that he was making the best decisions for all involved . . . that's where Var's arrogance outshone his mother's *and* father's. He didn't ask questions about his decisions, he simply announced that he'd made one and everyone else had best keep up.

But the boy was only eighteen. He didn't seem to grasp that he had much more to learn.

Bram shot an exasperated glance at Frederick, who also looked worried about Var's pronouncement.

"And what, exactly, does that mean?"

Now focused on whatever papers he had in front of him, Var didn't even bother to look up at Bram when he replied, "That I've taken care of it."

"I need specifics."

After writing something down—and still not looking up—Var motioned to the doorway with his quill.

Before Bram could blink, she suddenly swept into the doorway naked. Arlais ran in after, pushing past all those Mì-runach who had accompanied her, and placed a robe around her grandmother's shoulders.

"Think of the servants!" Arlais snapped at her before flouncing out.

"I do know how hard it is for them to see so much perfection," Rhiannon agreed until she realized her granddaughter was gone. "Stay outside," she ordered her Mì-runach guards.

"But, my lady—" one began.

Rhiannon kicked the door shut with her foot. "I adore my Mì-runach," she admitted, "but now that Bercelak is gone, they don't give me a moment without seeing their needy, eager faces."

She pushed her white hair off her cheeks and the strain he saw on her face told Bram the weight she now carried on her shoulders. A weight she usually managed with no effort, no strain. But that was because Bercelak was always at her side, lightening everything around her by being so impossibly angry and barely controllable.

With that support gone, Rhiannon didn't bother to hide her true self. A side Bram was sure her grandson had never seen.

"So," Rhiannon asked flatly, "why am I here?"

Bram glared at Var. "You sent for your grandmother before speaking to me first?"

Var sighed and wrote something on the parchment in front of him. "I hear tone, Uncle."

"I'm waiting," Rhiannon pushed.

Var could hear Bram's tone but he couldn't hear his grandmother's? Foolish boy!

"Nothing, my queen," Bram tried. "You have much bigger concerns than—"

"Brigida took one of the books out of our library," Var cut in, still scribbling away. "A book on dragon magicks. I hadn't had a chance to go through that book myself so we have no idea what she wanted with it, but my concern is that she only went for it *after* Arlais turned down her offer to be her apprentice. I strongly suggest we move on her quickly. I understand she's family, so my recommendation is we just put her somewhere safe until we figure out exactly what she's up to. I'm assuming you can handle that, Grandmother, since the twins and Rhi are currently at the front?"

With a flourish, he signed the bottom of the paper he was working on and finally—grudgingly—looked away from his work and up at his grandmother. That's when Var blinked and leaned back a bit in his chair.

It was, for Var, a reaction that suggested immense shock.

"Is there an issue, Grandmother?" he asked.

"You want us to magickally bind and *bury* an elder of the Cadwaladr Clan?" Rhiannon asked, her voice calm.

Extremely calm.

"As I said, I know she's family and has been useful in the past," Var explained, "so I'd never suggest we kill her."

"Then what are you suggesting?"

"That we get and maintain control of her. She's a danger."

"She's a witch."

"And your point?"

Bram gave a small jerk of his head at Frederick and the boy, a survivor like his aunt Dagmar, immediately moved out of his chair and to the back of the room.

Bram followed. He'd been working with Rhiannon for centuries. He knew her almost as well as he knew Ghleanna. And he knew the dangers of both. Sadly, his grandnephew had not bothered to learn those dangers yet. Nor had he learned when to listen to Bram.

"There was once a royal," Rhiannon told her grandson, "who attempted to control witches. He marked them so they'd be easy to spot. Your aunt Morfyd, because she didn't want the humans she tended to know she was dragon and be frightened of her, stood while a *human* marked her as a witch on her face."

"I . . . I wasn't suggesting—"

"Do you know what happened to that monarch?" Rhiannon asked. "Your aunt Annwyl killed him and took his head. His name was Lorcan and he was her brother. She never mentions him," she continued. "With reason. Of course, if Annwyl hadn't killed him . . . I would have. I'd called Keita back to do just that once I saw what he'd done to my daughter."

"Grandmother, I—"

Rhiannon twitched her fore- and middle fingers and the heavy wood table Var was still sitting at slid hard across the room and slammed into the far wall.

She took a few steps until she stood in front of her still-sitting grandson.

"So I'm sure you'll understand," she went on, "if I'm concerned that you want to bind and trap a witch for being a witch."

"That's not what I said."

"I will not allow you, Unnvar, to travel down a path made up of those Annwyl has already killed. Not my grandson. Now, if Brigida does something that concerns *me,* then I will handle it. *Witches* will handle it. Not you, with the backing of legions. Do we understand each other?"

"We do."

"Good." She turned and started toward the door. "In future, you may want to discuss these sorts of concerns with your uncle Bram first. He's very good at knowing how to handle situations before they ever have to come to me. The mark of a good representative of a queen, wouldn't you say?" She opened the door and looked back at Var. "And you, my good lad, still have a bit more to learn."

After the queen walked out, slamming the door behind her, Bram and Frederick went across the room, picked up the table and carried it back until it was in front of Var again. They then pulled their chairs out and sat down.

Var, eyes downcast, said, "That was a bit of a miscalculation on my part."

Bram and Frederick exchanged surprised glances. The boy wasn't one for admitting when he'd screwed up. It wasn't in his nature. He might be thinking it, but he rarely admitted it.

"It was," Bram agreed. "But you care about your kin. Nothing wrong with that."

"So what do I need to do next time?"

"Make sure there's not a next time."

"Do you know what your mother does?" Frederick asked. "She learns from others' mistakes. But she especially learns from her own. Master that, and I'm sure you'll keep your head."

Frowning deeply, Var turned to gape at his human cousin, his mouth open.

"What?" Frederick asked. "We all know how Annwyl is about witches and her kin. Especially kin that are witches. You cross that line, Var, and she'll take your head right off."

Bram laughed and his grandnephew now looked at him with his mouth open.

"Oh, Var, you have to know that your cousin is right."

Chapter Twenty-Six

They didn't bother to leave the room and no one visited. Not even Uther and Caswyn. Food was left at the door for them along with a jade jar of salve with handwritten directions explaining how it was to be used on Brannie's back.

Somehow, that particular process led to Branwen being held upside down with Aidan's cock in her mouth.

She didn't mind, though. No. Not at all.

Because Aidan was not one of those stingy bastards who expected to receive but wasn't much in the way of giving. For every time she had the Mì-runach's cock in her mouth, she would soon find herself with her legs over his shoulders and his head bobbing between her thighs.

All of that was amazing too, but there was just something about Aidan being buried deep inside her, fucking her hard. Or sometimes fucking her slow and easy. It didn't really matter which, it all just felt . . . perfect.

Brannie didn't know what was happening. She should have been done with Aidan the Divine a while ago. After their first time.

She might go back a time or two with some blokes, but only if she was bored and had nothing better to do that day. But staying locked in a room all this time with the same being who wasn't Izzy, telling her the most delicious gossip about whom Dagmar was blackmailing or which cousin was fucking which royal whose father was none too happy? That simply didn't happen to Brannie.

Even worse, Brannie couldn't dismiss what was happening because they were mostly fucking and had no time for words. They did have time. They talked. Then they'd fuck. Then they'd talk some more.

And she was really starting to hate him for making her like him so much.

Naked, their backs against the floor, their legs on the bed; they gazed up at the ceiling.

"Why," Aidan had to ask, "would your parents have so many offspring?"

"That's nothing. My aunt Maelona . . . she has eighteen."

"Offspring?"

"Aye."

"Why would she . . . why would anyone . . . I don't understand."

"She's very happy. Her mate and my cousins adore her. Of course, she did move as far away from her siblings as she could manage. But I think that had a lot to do with her mate. He didn't really get along with me uncles."

"I can see that. I don't get along with your uncles."

"Not many do."

"Tell me . . ."

"Hmm?"

"Do you remember all your kin's names?"

"Oh, no. I barely remember your name."

"That's lovely."

"Just being honest."

Aidan thought a moment. "They must take that sort of thing personally, though."

"Oh, they do. But I learned from my uncle Bercelak, who pretends he remembers everyone's name . . . but he doesn't. You see, he just does the same thing to everyone. He points to someone and says, 'You. Come here!'"

"That's how he's always talked to me. And Éibhear."

"I said everyone. Except his daughters. Never his daughters. Never Auntie Rhiannon or Dagmar, but I think that has a lot to do with fear."

"No one ever said your uncle was stupid."

"True. Anyway, there's a look to all the Cadwaladr that makes them easy to spot. So when I see someone I'm sure is a cousin and they greet me warmly, with a big hug, I reply, 'Hey, you!'"

Aidan looked away from the ceiling so he could gaze at Brannie. "'Hey, you'?"

She shrugged. "It works. I just make sure to do it with a smile. I've learned from Rhiannon that you can get away with almost anything as long as you smile while doing it."

"That really only works for females. When a male smiles like that . . . he just looks sadistic."

"You might have a point. No one in the universe likes it when Uncle Bercelak smiles."

Aidan returned his gaze to the ceiling. "Do you think Keita will want to leave tomorrow?"

"No. She won't. But we will."

Surprised by that answer, Aidan pulled his legs off the bed and rolled to his side, resting on his elbow. He looked down at Brannie, whose focus was still on the ceiling.

"*We'll* be leaving?"

"Uh-huh."

"And you know this . . . how?"

"I've been part of a military Clan since hatching. All

me aunts, uncles, cousins, siblings . . . almost all of them in the military. And my father, the peacemaker . . . ? Well, you can't have peace without war and you can't make truces and alliances without understanding war. I spent the first years of my life attached to his tail while he plotted and planned with the brilliant elders of the Southlands. So, I'll admit it's a guess." She finally looked at him. "But I'd be shocked if I was wrong."

"But we still have tonight."

"No one would be foolish enough to enter these territories at night. All the warrior witches I've known are like cats. They look for prey when the suns go down. I doubt the Destroyers are any different. We'll be safe until the morning."

"Good." Aidan moved into a crouch, reaching down to grab Brannie under the arms and lifting her up as he stood.

He tossed her over his shoulder and Brannie laughed, slapping at his ass.

"What are you doing?" she asked.

"Looking for somewhere we haven't already fucked." He turned in a complete circle. "I don't see anything. Everything in this room has been defiled."

"We haven't used the bed . . . except to sleep."

"You're right!" He pulled her off his shoulder and casually tossed her onto the bed. Branwen bounced once and flipped onto the floor.

"Brannie!" Horrified, Aidan scrambled over the bed to the other side. Brannie was curled into a ball, laughing so hard, she could barely breathe.

"Are you all right?"

But she was laughing too hard to even answer.

"By the gods, female." He reached down and pulled her onto the bed. "You are ridiculous."

He checked to make sure nothing was broken or, at the very least, knocked out of an important socket. But he should have known better. This was Branwen the Awful. She'd survived a mountain crumbling around her with barely a scratch and a lightning bolt to the back. So surviving a flip off a bed . . . ?

Aidan sat on the mattress and waited for Brannie to stop laughing, which she did eventually. But then she became fascinated with the actual bed.

"What are you doing?" he finally asked when he got tired of watching her crawl around the bed and press her hands into it.

"Wondering why it's so bouncy. None of our beds at home are bouncy. You'd think Annwyl would have bouncy beds."

"Seriously?"

She stopped, gazed at him. "What?"

"We're both here, naked, on our last night of what may be freedom or possibly our lives . . . and you're worried about a bouncy bed?"

Brannie nodded. "Yes."

Aidan grabbed Brannie's arm and pulled her close. "Kiss me, Brannie."

"All right, but if we make it back home alive . . . I want you to get me a bouncy bed."

Aidan stared at her for so long, she thought maybe she'd crossed a line. Not about suggesting that they might not get back to the Southlands alive, but by suggesting they'd still be involved somehow. Enough, anyway, to insist on a gift.

Uncomfortable, she asked, "Why are you staring?"

He never answered, but he kissed her. A sweet kiss that confused her even more.

"What is happening?" she asked when he pulled back.

"I like you, Branwen."

She smiled and replied, "Awwwww, Aidan . . . I like me, too."

Rolling his eyes, Aidan pushed her back on the bed and settled between her thighs.

"Why do I bother?" he asked her.

And, laughing, Brannie admitted, "I have *no* idea!"

Chapter Twenty-Seven

Meihui was meditating. She got up early, hours before the two suns rose, to meditate. It healed her mind and body and helped her maintain the strength she'd built over the centuries. Although she was born to human parents—farmers—she'd been sent to Heaven's Destroyers before she'd reached her thirteenth year. That had been about fifteen hundred years ago, give or take a few stray years she might have forgotten. And in that time, she'd honed her skills until they were absolutely razor-sharp.

So what she heard moving outside her temple wasn't footsteps. It was breathing. Very controlled breathing by very controlled killers.

Brazen ones if they were trying to sneak into a Heaven's Destroyers' temple.

No. These killers wouldn't be here for one of her sisters or for Meihui. They were here for Keita.

Reaching under her bed, she pulled out her seax, a fighting knife, given to her by her training mistress a long time ago, and quickly slipped out of her room. She knew she didn't have to warn her sisters. They were already aware of what was happening. But Keita and her friends . . .

Meihui ran up the stairs to the guest rooms and to

Keita's door. She eased inside and went straight to the bed, but before she could shake Keita awake, a blade was pressed to her throat.

"Come to kill me, old friend?"

Meihui smiled. "No, you idiot. I'm here to rescue the damsel."

The blade pulled away from her throat and Meihui faced her friend. "And you, my dearest Keita . . . better run."

Brannie's mother used to warn her that sometimes good sex could be a distraction. She used to roll her eyes at her mother's speech and then beg her to stop talking because it was so embarrassing having this conversation with her mum.

But when she felt the air around her move, Brannie had to grudgingly admit her mother was right. Because she should have realized something was wrong long before her attackers were in the room.

Brannie jerked back and the head of an ax landed on her pillow. She struck out with her fist, knocking her assailant back.

By the time she got to her feet, Aidan was up as well. He grabbed his weapon and tossed her the special weapon Rhona had given her. It quickly extended into a spear and Brannie blocked another blow from her attacker.

It was a male, dressed all in black with no armor or chain mail.

She twisted her spear in an attempt to get the blade from him, but he moved with her weapon and kept his grip. He struck again. Fast. Brannie blocked the strike with her forearm, shortened her spear to fit in the small room, and drove it up through his chin and into his head.

She yanked it out, turned, and cut the throat of the man behind her.

Aidan had three bodies at his feet and was moving across the room to grab their things.

"Get Keita and the others," she ordered him.

He tossed her chain mail to her. "What are you going to do?"

Brannie quickly tugged on the leggings and carried the rest to the balcony. A small group of witches were surrounded by at least twenty of the killers dressed in black.

Without answering Aidan, she jumped over the railing and landed in the middle of the fight.

"Help my friends," she told the witches. "Including the Riders."

"And you, Captain?" one of the witches asked.

Brannie lowered her head and the spear in her hand thickened, extended to twice its length with a pointed blade on each end.

She swung the weapon, cutting across several throats.

The killers attacked and the witches ran, leaving Brannie on her own.

Aidan kicked open the doors to his friends' rooms.

"*Move!*" he bellowed.

And they did, jumping from their beds and grabbing their weapons and travel bags.

They were both already dressed, having dropped on their beds fully clothed.

They came out of their rooms, weapons raised. They were awake and alert. Ready for battle. Just as they'd been trained.

"Keita."

They went down the hall to Keita's room but it was empty. There were, however, a number of assassin bodies littering her floor.

"Outside," Aidan barked, and they moved.

They passed enemies along the way and executed them

quickly and cleanly. Not wasting time with anything fancy or fun.

When they arrived on the first floor, they went out the front door—and froze on the top step.

Mouths open, Aidan and his brothers watched the legion of fighters marching toward them from the beach.

"Did you call them here?" he asked the witch closest to him.

"We did not."

"Find the Riders!" he barked at Uther and Caswyn before running into the temple and toward the back.

The blade sliced into her arm. The blood began to drip down her skin.

Bending her elbow, Brannie swiped her wounded arm against her attacker's face, temporarily blinding him with her blood.

With her other arm, she rammed her blade into his belly, and shoved him away with her shoulder.

Someone ran up behind her and she turned at the waist and took his head.

"Branwen!" Aidan came sliding out the back door. "Soldiers. Lots of them."

Brannie stepped over the bodies of those she'd just killed and, finally managing to get her chain mail shirt on, she called out to one of the witches pummeling an assassin, "Where's my cousin?"

"With Meihui." She pointed to the other side of the building.

With a grateful nod, Brannie grabbed her travel bag and ran, slinging the strap over her shoulders as she did, Aidan right behind her.

They'd just cleared the other side of the building when a

black horse charged past them. The only reason Brannie didn't get run down was that Aidan grabbed her by her chain mail shirt and yanked her back.

"Keita!" Brannie yelled. But her cousin was charging off into the woods.

"Here." Meihui arrived with another horse for her, with Kachka right behind her. "Go."

Brannie turned to Aidan.

"Go," he said.

"But—"

"We'll keep them off your back. Go. Now."

Brannie didn't have time for grand good-byes. She just had to keep moving.

Grabbing the reins of the white-and-brown horse, she mounted him, and took off after her cousin.

Aidan faced Meihui. "We have to—"

He jerked back but it was Meihui's quick reflexes that saved Aidan from the black-clothed attacker who'd snuck up behind them.

She blocked his strike with her forearm, and one of her sisters snatched the weapon from his hand while the others stabbed at him with their seax.

Meihui motioned to a sister who came out the back. She held up the attacker's weapon. "Find out if there are any others still alive. I'll be in the front."

She headed back into the temple. "Watch these," she said offhandedly, moving quickly, Kachka following them both.

"Watch what?"

"These weapons. The edges have been dipped in poison."

* * *

Uther cringed watching Zoya taunt the legion that marched toward them.

"Come!" she yelled out. "You want to challenge Zoya? Come challenge Zoya!"

Aidan returned to the front of the temple with Meihui and Kachka.

"What is she doing?" he asked.

Aidan shrugged. "I really don't know. But she's been doing it for a while." He glanced at the others. "Where's Brannie and Keita?"

"Gone. We need to keep the attackers off their backs until they get some distance between—"

Meihui stepped close to Aidan. "Those are the Empress's legions."

"So?"

"A mix of dragons and humans. You'll be outnumbered and you no longer have Branwen the Awful clearing the way for you."

"Suggestions?"

"Act like they're welcome. Like you were just attacked and they're saving you."

"We were just attacked."

"Act like you were just attacked by someone other than those sent by the Empress."

"Are you so sure they *were* sent by the Empress?"

Meihui smiled. "No, but the way Keita went running for a horse as soon as she checked one . . ."

"What about Keita?" Uther asked. Their queen had asked them to protect her. As far as he was concerned, they had just failed.

Aidan nodded at Meihui and she went to her sisters to organize them before the Empress's army arrived right at her door.

"Keita left on purpose, but she's got Brannie with her," Aidan told Uther.

"So we're just going to let them go?"

"We have no choice. All we can do now is keep playing the game and hope Keita has a plan."

Caswyn snorted. "If Keita's anything like her mother . . . she'll always have a plan."

Chapter Twenty-Eight

They rode hard throughout the day, stopping only a few minutes at a time by streams and lakes so that their horses could get a break.

By the time the suns were beginning to go down, they'd arrived at a large, dark forest. And that's where Keita stopped.

Brannie dismounted her horse and rested against it. "What are we doing here?"

Keita also dismounted. "We're going in."

"Why?"

"Because I said—what's wrong with you?" Keita abruptly asked.

"I'm exhausted."

"That's what you get for fucking all night."

"He was there and I had needs."

"Liar," Keita accused, grabbing her horse's reins. "You like him."

"He's me friend. Of course I like him."

"'He's me friend,'" Keita mocked.

"Don't make me slap you." Brannie followed her into the forest. "Do you have any idea what you're doing?"

"Can't you just trust me to know what I'm doing?"

"No."

"Cow."

"Do you even know where we are?"

"Stop snapping at me because you're worried about Aidan."

"I am not!"

"Such a liar. And a bad one at that!"

They walked on in the growing darkness, neither speaking, until Brannie realized she heard no birds in the trees. No sounds of animals scuttling away.

Branwen stopped, blew out a quick burst of air through her teeth. Keita froze, her gaze moving.

Stroking her horse's neck to keep him calm, Brannie also looked for signs of what was in these woods. It was the scent she recognized first. Human men.

She was reaching for her weapon, tucked innocuously into her boot, when the sword pressed against her throat.

Shocked, Keita gawked at Brannie. Not that she blamed her cousin for being so surprised. Brannie couldn't remember the last time she'd let a gods-damned human sneak up on her.

To protect her cousin, Brannie was about to make a move anyway, but somehow she ended up facedown on the ground, vomiting and praying for sweet death.

"Branwen!"

Keita yanked herself away from the Eastland Rider who gripped her arm and ran to her cousin's side. She turned her over.

"Fuck," she growled, grabbing the hem of her dress and tearing off a bit to quickly clean Brannie's face.

She leaned in close, lifted her cousin's eyelids, opened her mouth, checked her nostrils.

Keita was just checking her fingers when she noticed

there was blood on her wrist. She pulled up her chain mail shirt, tugging out her arm until she found the wound.

She sniffed, recognized the scent, but refused to panic. If she panicked, Brannie would die.

Looking around, Keita stood. One of the men stepped toward her but she pointed at a smarter-looking fellow and ordered, "I need the pallavi root. Now. Find it."

"Uhhh . . ."

"Was I unclear? *Move!*"

Startled into action, the man began to search the ground for what she needed. She also grabbed some other ingredients and began to shred and tear until the man handed her a small root.

She used her thumbnail to shred several pieces off, and mixed it with the other materials in the palm of her hand.

Snapping her fingers, Keita ordered, "Ale. Now."

Someone handed her a canteen of ale and she added several drops to the mix in her hand. She cupped her hands and brought them close to her mouth. She used a bit of her flame to activate her little poultice. Done, she spread the concoction on Brannie's wound and then placed a small bit under her cousin's tongue.

She stood. "You," she barked at one of the bigger men. "Get her on her horse and let's move. I need to get her to a shaman or witch. Now."

Fed up, the leader of the team stepped forward and pointed his finger at her. "You don't seem to under—"

Keita grabbed him by the hair, yanking his head to the side and forcing him to bend at the waist.

"You do what I tell you," she growled, "or I will kill *all of you!*"

* * *

Batu the Iron Hearted relaxed in his tent, surrounded by his pillows and concubines, while a musician played songs to keep him calm.

As leader of the Dark Mountain Tribes, he would always get the best of what his people had. But as the ruler of the strongest and most brutal tribes on the Steppes, a leader not afraid to take that which the Empress believed belonged to her, he could really enjoy his time in this world.

This evening, he was planning a good night, knowing he had some new concubines to break in.

So the last thing he wanted to deal with was one of his men running into his tent and babbling about some royal they'd found in the Hidden Woods, near their tribal lands.

"What are you going on about?" Batu demanded.

"We have a royal and—"

"So? Put her in chains and I'll go to see her tomorrow."

"She's demanding to see you now."

Batu grabbed the soft hand rubbing his chest and pushed it away.

"She . . . what?" Slowly Batu stood, his entire body shaking in rage. "*What?*" he bellowed, his concubines scrambling to a far corner. The musician joined them.

"Great Leader," the soldier groveled, dropping to his knees. "I only bring the message from the royal. She is—"

"*Where is she?*"

"With Bolormaa, Great Leader."

Batu stormed across his tent, stepping on the soldier's back as he did so. He went outside and walked toward Bolormaa's tent, which was not far from his. She was the best shamaness in his tribe so he kept her close in case he needed her after a battle.

When he flipped the tent flap back, Bolormaa and her

assistants were busy working on a large woman with black hair and the look of a Southlander from the west.

"Are you Batu?" a small, red-haired woman asked. She also looked like a Southlander . . . and acted like a royal.

"I—"

"Good," she snapped, grabbing his arm and yanking him outside.

"Lady Keita," she said by way of introduction. "That's my cousin in there. She's been poisoned and your shaman is helping me. Once I know she's stable, I'll be by to talk."

"Uh—"

She was gone. Back into the tent.

Angry, Batu began to follow, but he stopped. Something about that female . . .

Deciding to be smart rather than angry, Batu motioned to one of the soldiers.

"Keep your eye on her and bring her to me when she's done."

He returned to his tent but sent the concubines and musician away. He then sent for Nergüi the Knowing. If anyone would know who this royal was, it was Nergüi.

Armed warriors were located behind them and in front of them. Some were human. Others were dragons in human form.

The general and his soldiers had been polite and friendly to Aidan and his brothers. But they did question the presence of the Riders. It wasn't until Aidan convinced them that they were from the Outerplains and not associated with the Eastland Riders that the Empress's soldiers backed off.

With great charm, the general offered the services of his army to escort them to the Empress as "favored guests."

Aidan, of course, agreed for all of them, knowing that he

didn't want this army out searching for Brannie and Keita. They needed time to make it out. Wherever "out" might be.

It was really the best Aidan could do at the moment.

But Aidan was no fool.

Meihui might have sent them off with a smile, but she'd also brushed her hand against Aidan's when he was walking away and he took it as the warning it was meant to be.

Because on the surface this all might appear normal. A royal caravan.

But they were actually pampered prisoners and all of them knew it.

As they moved through the countryside, Aidan did marvel at the surrounding lands. The Southlands near Garbhán Isle had always been his favorite, but the Empress's territory rivaled his home.

Behind them loomed snow-capped mountains. The home of many dragons that refused to spend much time among humans.

The road they took led them through thick, multicolored forests. Trees of red, gold, and vibrant green. Along the way, they went through smaller forests with vast plains mixed in. And those plains had grass so green they seemed to be painted.

By the next morning, they reached massive gold gates connected to massive gold walls that surrounded the Empress's palace and lands. They waited while the gates were pulled open, allowing their entourage to pass through and into the Empress's true domain.

The first thing that greeted them were flowers. Rows and rows of all kinds of beautiful flowers in a variety of stunning colors.

The road that passed by these flowers was wide enough for a small army to come through without going near the Empress's garden, and Aidan wasn't exactly surprised. The dragoness clearly loved her flowers.

As they approached, Aidan could see the palace he'd heard so much about over the years. It, too, was made completely of gold and he could see Eastland dragons circling the top tiers of the palace, as well as open terraces where a large number of Eastland dragons were sitting around, chatting, and enjoying the morning suns.

"Now what?" Uther muttered next to him.

"What are you talking about?"

"Now that we're here . . . what are we going to do?"

"Oh." Aidan shrugged. "I don't know."

"What do you mean you don't know?"

"I don't know."

"Well," Uther said, throwing up his hands, "this is just *great!*"

Chapter Twenty-Nine

The screaming filled the castle walls, but Vateria didn't mind. She knew it was leading to better, more important things.

Besides, the sound reminded her of the old days when her father ruled the Quintilian Provinces. She missed those days, when she had slaves and the complete run of her father's home. But those days were gone and she was here . . . doing needlepoint.

It still galled her this was her life now, but not for much longer.

Soon, she'd rule more than just what her father had had. She'd rule more than what anyone had.

But first, a few things needed to happen.

Outside, in the territory surrounding her current home, the Abominations and their armies had built fortifications that prevented any of them from leaving and anyone from getting in.

They believed they were trapping Vateria and her people in this place and that they would launch one final attack.

A good plan . . . if Vateria was anyone else. But she had the backing of Chramnesind and even now, he was giving her a mighty weapon.

More screaming filled the entire castle and Vateria smiled, allowing the sound to wash over her while she continued her needlepoint.

"My lady?" a priestess interrupted, standing beside Vateria's chair in the Main Hall. This one gazed at Vateria out of empty eye sockets. Her god had never asked Vateria to make such a sacrifice. Instead of taking from her, he'd continued to give and give and give, which only told her what she already knew. She was more important than any of these little witches who had to prove their loyalty. Vateria didn't have to prove anything to Chramnesind. He already knew what she wanted and what she was willing to give to get it.

"What is it?" Vateria asked, still working. Much easier than looking into that scarred face.

"Things below are getting . . . complicated."

"And?"

"We're afraid he'll die."

Vateria snorted. "Our god will not allow him to die. Keep going."

"But the pain—"

"Is not my concern. Nor yours. Keep going."

"But—"

Vateria lowered the needlepoint into her lap and gestured with her hand toward the stone walls in the Main Hall. "As you bicker with me over this, our enemies are completing *their* plans to destroy us. We don't have time for you to be concerned."

"I understand what you're saying, but I must insist—"

"Insist? With me?" Vateria frowned, confused. "*Really?*"

"It's just—"

"Yes, yes, I know. He's suffering and you're afraid he'll die and our plans will be ruined. But I assure you . . . he won't die. So keep going. This isn't a punishment. This is a gift from our god. Embrace it."

The priestess sighed. "Yes, my lady." She started to return to the others when another long, pained scream rang out. The woman faltered and she stood there a moment, unsure what to do next, before she came to the realization there was nothing to do but follow Vateria's orders.

Vateria already knew how much it annoyed the priests and priestesses that "Ageltrude"—the human wife of Salebiri whom they all still believed Vateria to be—had so much control and power here. Especially when it was obvious she hadn't sacrificed a damn thing. But none of them bothered to challenge her, which was disappointing. Vateria used to adore putting others in their place when she'd ruled by her father's side, but she expected all that to happen again once this war was over and she was reigning supreme.

And to be honest, she could barely wait. Because none of these beings, dragon or human, knew what true suffering was. But Vateria would be more than happy to teach them.

She'd teach them all.

Chapter Thirty

Keita walked into the tribal leader's tent, briefly turning to slap off the hands trying to stop her.

"Go away!" she snapped at one of the soldiers.

"But—" one tried to argue.

Waving her hands, she shooed them from the tent and turned to face the sleeping Batu the Iron Hearted.

Stepping over pillows, silk bedding, and naked female asses, Keita stopped by the man's side.

She tapped at him with the side of her foot. When that didn't wake him, she yelled, "*Oy!*"

Batu's head jerked up, his black-and-blond braids covering his face and beard. "What . . . what's happening?"

"We need to talk. Mind getting rid of your whores?"

Keita walked over to a small table that had a chalice and a decanter. She sniffed the liquid inside the decanter, decided it smelled tolerable, and poured herself a chalice-full.

Sipping what turned out to be a very nice wine, Keita watched Batu get to his feet. He wasn't as tall as she expected, but he was frighteningly broad. Although she had a few cousins who were weirdly wide like that.

"Everyone out!" he bellowed, standing in the middle of

all those silk pillows. It was sort of ridiculous, but the way everyone ran for their lives . . .

Glaring at Keita, he pointed his finger. "And you—"

"Look," she cut in, "normally, I'd let you swagger all over the place. Let you beat your chest and be very manly before I use my skills to turn you into my puppet."

"I am puppet for no woman."

"Then I would have killed you." She smiled. "Because that's what I do and I do it well. But I'm not doing that because I am very short on time. I mean, things changed when I realized who exactly was trying to kill me. And it isn't the Empress, which is surprising because I was absolutely going to kill her."

Batu leaned in. "Go away, crazed female."

"Batu—"

"Great Leader."

Keita laughed and patted his shoulder. "Yeah, right. Anyway, Batu, I've decided that we can work together. Get what we both want."

"I want nothing from you. I don't even want to kidnap you for ransom. I want you to go away."

"That is not going to happen when I have a great opportunity for you."

"I do not want your opportunity."

"Of course you do."

"I do not."

"Why are you arguing with me? You know I'm right."

"I know I want you to go away."

Keita rolled her eyes. "Now you sound like my mother."

"Even your mother does not want you."

Laughing, Keita slung her arm around Batu. "You are *so* adorable. I think we'll work well together."

"Why? Why will you not go? Most flee from me. In terror."

"Isn't it *the best* when people flee from you in terror?

I know, I've always loved it. And that's how I got my name Keita the Viper! But I do try not to abuse my ability to terrorize others. That seems wrong . . . somehow." She stepped away from him. "Now, why don't you get dressed and meet me in Bolormaa's tent. My cousin should be waking up soon."

Keita started to walk out but stopped, and kissed Batu on the cheek.

"You and I are going to be *such* good friends."

Batu put on his clothes and his weapons and walked out of his tent just as Nergüi the Knowing was about to walk in.

The older tribesman bowed before Batu. "Great Leader—"

"Stop bowing and just tell me what you found out. I have to go meet that crazed bitch in Bolormaa's tent and I need something to help me manage her."

"I've found a long list of many Lady Keitas, but without a family name or—"

"Wait." Batu thought a moment. "She said her name was Keita the . . . the . . . Viper. Yes! Keita the Viper. Does that help you?"

Nergüi stepped back. "Are you sure, Great—"

"Of course, I am sure. Why?"

"Then she is no lady, Great Leader. She is a She-dragon."

"So? We've had dealings with the dragons before, Nergüi."

"We have had dealings with dragons from *our* lands. She is not an Eastland dragon . . . and Keita the Viper is not her entire name."

"Her entire name?"

"Her entire name, Great Leader, is Keita the Red Viper Dragon of Despair and Death. She has destroyed whole towns. She has eaten people. She is a princess and the daughter of

Rhiannon the White, the Dragon Queen. And if Rhiannon is her mother, Great Leader—"

"Then," Batu finished for Nergüi, "she is a Southland dragon."

"Yes. And that means this entire region is in great danger."

The steps leading up to the palace seemed never-ending.

Why all the steps? Was it because the Eastland dragons thought that humans would just give up halfway and they'd never have to see them?

It made sense, when Aidan analyzed it. That's why Rhiannon's throne was in the highest mountain in the Southland area. So that she and her predecessors never had to deal with random visits from humans.

"I'm tired," Caswyn complained.

"Keep walking. We're almost there."

"Come, dragons!" Zoya Kolesova cheered as she jogged by them. "You are not so weak you cannot get up little stairs, are you?"

"Can we beat her to death?" Caswyn asked, watching Zoya easily reach the top without any real effort.

"Yes," Kachka and Nina said together as they passed Aidan and his brothers.

When Aidan finally reached the last step, Zoya had her hands on her hips and was looking up at the palace.

"So much decadence," she observed. "I never thought I'd know others more decadent than Southlanders, but I was wrong. Look at all this! Their people starve while they live in gold house."

Trying not to pant, Aidan reminded Zoya, "We don't know that their people are starving, Zoya. And shut up."

The Empress's army had stayed at the bottom of the stairs, but the general was waiting for them.

"The Empress and her court are expecting you," he said with a sweeping arm.

A loud gong sounded somewhere and the tall, gold doors were pushed open by burly servants.

"Such imperialist scum!" Zoya cheered. "I cannot wait to meet them!"

"I told you we should have cut her throat so she could not speak," Nina grumbled.

Aidan scratched his head and took a second to get his breath back. That's when he realized that no one was moving and they were all staring at him.

"What?" he asked.

"Well," Uther said, pointing to the open palace doors, "go on."

"Wait . . . you want *me* to go in first? Why? I'm not in charge."

"With Keita *and* Branwen gone, of course you are in charge, dragon," Kachka explained. "You cannot send Zoya. She will call them all imperialist, decadent scum."

"I will!" Zoya said proudly.

"I cannot do it," Kachka went on, "because I will also call them imperialist, decadent scum. Nina is just disturbing and untrustworthy."

"It is true," Nina replied blandly. "But I like that about myself."

"And these two"—Kachka gestured to Uther and Caswyn with a jerk of her head—"are idiots."

"She's right," Uther agreed. "We are idiots. You go."

Growling, but knowing they were all right, Aidan walked in first, and the rest of them followed.

But he had barely stepped inside before he had to stop, gawking at the beauty and, as Zoya had accused, the decadence.

So much decadence.

He didn't know *anyone* lived this way, dragons or otherwise.

The entire building was made out of gold and copper. The throne at the very end of the main hall was made out of gold and covered in massive jewels. He had expected the palace to be large, but he'd never known how large it would be. Big enough that dragons Éibhear's size could be in their natural form and not smash their heads on the ceilings. And based on the design of those ceilings, the other floors were strong enough that dragons could stand without worrying they'd crash through and kill whomever was beneath.

"So much . . . everything," he whispered.

"You'd lose your soul here, dragon," Kachka said, patting him on the back. "And those who lose their souls, I and my comrades eventually come to kill." She winked at him and pushed him forward. "Go now, Aidan the Divine. And introduce us to this Empress of decadence."

The counterattack from the Zealots started before dawn.

They sent human fodder to ride directly toward them, screaming out their assault and easily picked off by the archers while Zealots on foot snuck in and cut the throats of still-sleeping soldiers.

But they didn't have the upper hand for long; those on guard duty sent up an alarm as soon as they realized what was going on.

Her mother's army pushed the Zealots out of their camp and prepared for another assault.

"This is it," Talwyn said to her brother.

"I know. Is everyone ready?"

"As ready as they'll ever be. The Sovereign Army is standing by in the west fields. The Lightning Army is lying in wait in what's left of the forests. We've got dragon armies in the mountains. And our legions everywhere else. They're never getting out of here," Talwyn said of the trapped Zealots in Salebiri's enclosure.

"Don't get cocky, sister. They still have Chramnesind on their side."

Her brother was right. And so far their multiple gods hadn't bothered to help them at all.

The pair walked through the camp, while soldiers ran past them and officers called out orders.

They stopped when they saw Morfyd hugging Uncle Brastias good-bye.

She pointed at the twins. "You two . . . don't be so reckless. Understand?"

Talan and Talwyn nodded as a mystical doorway suddenly opened by their aunt.

"Rhi!" she called out. "Come on!"

The doorway had been opened by Rhiannon, pulling all the witches to her so they could do their part in a place safe from the Zealot priests and priestesses.

Rhi ran out of a nearby tent with her travel bag and robe flopping behind. She was completely frazzled by the attack and worried for the lives of her kin. Talwyn, however, was glad she wouldn't have to worry about protecting her younger cousin during the fight.

Rhi stopped to hug her father, her uncles, her great-uncles, her great-aunts, etc., while Morfyd waited . . . and waited . . . and waited. When the tears began, Talwyn moved closer to Morfyd.

Rhi stopped to hug Talan, sobbing on his shoulder and making him promise "not to die . . . *ever!*" before she came to Talwyn and hugged her.

Her cousin didn't want to let go. She didn't want to leave them all. But she needed to be someplace safe, away from here. Away from the Zealots. Talwyn knew this even if Rhi didn't.

Talwyn pushed her away. "Go. Grandmother's waiting."

"Yes. Of course. Oh!" She started back toward her tent. "I forgot my—"

Talwyn grabbed her cousin by the back of her dress and tossed her into the open doorway.

"Talwyn!" her kin gasped, shocked. But if she didn't do it, no one would.

Thank you, Morfyd mouthed at her before she followed Rhi inside and disappeared, the doorway slamming shut behind them.

Her kin watched her, still appalled by her behavior.

"Gods know someone had to," she told them before walking off, Talan right behind her. Laughing.

"I feel like shit," Brannie moaned.

"Worse than when you were on the boat?" she heard Keita ask from . . . somewhere.

Where were they anyway?

"Mention that boat again . . . and I will kill you."

Someone put their arm around Brannie's back and helped her sit up.

"I think you'll live," Keita said.

"I don't believe you. I think I'm dying."

"You *were* dying. You feeling like shit, cousin, means you're getting better."

"Why are you still talking, Keita? Stop talking."

"Isn't she delightful, Bolormaa?" Keita asked another female in the tent.

"I wish you would stop talking, too."

"Och! All of you are so ungrateful."

Sitting up with her knees raised, her elbows resting on them so she could cradle her head in her hands, Brannie accused, "You poisoned me, didn't you?"

"Don't flatter yourself! You're not worthy of my poisoning skills. You took a blade to the arm from one of those

310 *G.A. Aiken*

assassins. They used poison on the edges. In fact, cousin, you're lucky that I am as talented a poisoner as I am. Isn't that right, Bolormaa? Tell her! Tell her how *I* saved her life."

"Yes," the shamaness said to Brannie. "Your cousin is such great murderer that she was able to save your life from death."

"Really?" Keita snapped. "You couldn't find a nicer way to say that?"

"No. I could not." She took Brannie's hand and wrapped it around a cool cup. "This is clean water. Drink. It will help."

Realizing how thirsty she was, Brannie began to down the water, but Bolormaa stopped her and made her sip instead. It took longer, but once she was done, Brannie couldn't believe how much better she felt. Worlds better.

"Where are we?" she asked Keita.

"With the Tribes of the Dark Mountain."

Brannie gawked at Keita. "Were we captured?"

"Well . . . they *think* they captured us. But I actually found them."

"Why would you do that? Why are you *trying* to kill me?"

"Och!" Keita again gasped, her arms flung in the air. "You are always so dramatic!"

Brannie glanced at the old woman tending her but Bolormaa could only shrug.

"You don't understand, Brannie," Keita went on. "I have a brilliant plan!"

"Oh, gods, not one of your brilliant plans."

"You need to trust me."

"But I don't trust you. At all!"

"Of course you do. Besides, this new plan will mean I won't have to kill the Empress and her kin! That's a good thing, right? You didn't want me to kill them, right?"

Bolormaa placed a cool cloth against Brannie's forehead. "Just block her out. You will sleep better when you block her out."

The tent flap was pulled back and a large man and several soldiers stormed in. They were armed and ready.

Although Brannie still had on her chain mail leggings, her shirt and boots were lying across the tent with her travel bag. Of course, she could shift to dragon but she might hurt Bolormaa and, as far as she could tell, the shamaness had helped her. So that would have to be a last ditch option.

She pressed the cloth against her head and made a quick scan of the room, looking for something she could turn into a weapon while letting her cousin do what she did so well.

Annoy people.

"Batu!" Keita cheered, throwing her arms around the big man with braided hair and a large, long beard. "I'm so glad you're here! Brannie just woke up. Branwen, this is Batu the Iron Hearted. Batu, this is Brannie."

Brannie eyed Batu—the brutal leader of these tribes—and he eyed her back.

"You," he said, turning his attention to Keita, "did not tell me everything."

"What didn't I tell you?"

"You are not human."

"Oh, gods no!" Keita laughed. "Wouldn't that be horrible? Yuck!"

"Keita!" Brannie barked.

She dismissed Brannie with a wave. "Ignore her. She's very sensitive to the needs of humans."

"She looks like man."

"Fuck you," Brannie snapped back.

"Now, now. Everyone be calm. It's important we get this moving."

"Get what moving?" Batu demanded. "You need to leave, She-dragon."

"Why would you throw me out when I can give you what you want?"

"What? What can you give me?"

Keita's grin was ridiculously wide. "An alliance . . . with the Empress."

Frowning, Batu stared at Keita. Then he turned to Brannie. They both exploded into hysterical laughter at the same time.

Keita crossed her arms over her chest and tapped one bare foot.

"And what, exactly, do you two think is so funny?"

"*You!*" they laughingly yelled out at the same time.

Aidan moved deeper into the palace's first floor.

The ceilings were so high and the room itself so big, that he was really tempted to call out to see if his voice echoed.

Gods, he didn't want to be here. He didn't want to be doing this. He wanted to be with Brannie. He wanted to know she was safe. What if he never saw her again?

A small group of Eastland dragons in their human form stood in a circle across the hall. They were whispering and seemed concerned about something. Probably palace politics, which Aidan assumed were just like court politics.

Now standing in the middle of the hall, Aidan looked around and wondered what he should do next. Keep standing here? Find a room for everyone? Melt one of the gold dragon statues with his flame?

Aidan almost smiled at his ridiculous thoughts but then someone slammed into his back, which seemed rather on purpose since there was no one else in the entire giant room other than his small group and the small group of Eastland dragons.

"Sorry," the She-dragon in human form muttered, her focus locked on the Eastland dragons, which was probably why she'd walked into him. She was dressed in worn clothes and boots, a longbow slung over her shoulder along with a quiver of arrows. She was tall and lean; her black-and-dark red hair was in a loose, rather messy braid that nearly reached her feet.

She stopped and looked directly at the Eastland dragons.

"What are you all doing here?" she called out.

"We've come to see the Empress," one of the dragons volunteered. "We have a very important mess—"

She waved her hand at the group and turned from them, effectively dismissing them in mid-request. She looked next at Aidan.

"And who are you?"

"I'm Aidan the Divine."

"A Southlander. Does the Empress know you're here?"

"Well—"

She rolled her eyes and started walking. "Just come on. Don't dawdle!"

Aidan began to follow. He had no idea who this female was but she seemed to be in charge. Maybe she was. Maybe she *was* the Empress despite the fact that she seemed way too young. But the Empress was a very powerful shamaness, with abilities similar to Rhiannon's. Maybe she had a way of staying young.

Aidan shook his head. Now he was overthinking and coming to ridiculous conclusions like Brannie.

"Wait!" the Eastland dragon called out. "We must speak to the—"

"Shut up!" the female snarled back.

She led Aidan and the others behind several extremely large gold statues of big cats and into a marble hallway.

"Keep up!" she ordered.

Aidan followed her down several long hallways until they reached a wooden door. Soldiers in elaborate gold armor stood outside and they immediately jumped to attention when they saw her. One opened his mouth to say something but she held up a finger and snapped, "Quiet!"

She pushed the door open and motioned Aidan and the others in.

"Move! Hustle!"

Aidan, Uther, and Caswyn quickly walked in as ordered. But the Riders strolled in a little more slowly, taking their sweet-ass-Rider time.

"Do you not understand the word *move?*" the She-dragon asked.

"We understand," Kachka replied, "we just ignore."

"Barbarians," she muttered before slamming the door and walking across the small room—small compared to the rest of the palace anyway—to another door, which she opened.

She gestured with a crook of her finger. "Come on." She walked in.

Aidan again followed her, but stopped as soon as he stepped into the room. There were five more Eastland dragons in the room. Two males and three females. But it was the one wearing a gold dress and intricate gold nail guards on the pinky and ring fingers of both hands and sitting in a plain wood chair who simply had to be the Empress.

Her long black hair was pulled into a large bun at the back of her head and covered in decorative pieces of gold shaped into flowers. Dark brown eyes looked Aidan over and bare feet stuck out from under that gold dress, reminding him of Keita.

Unlike Keita, however, the Empress appeared worried, the fingers not wearing pointed nail guards rubbing her forehead, her elbow resting on the arm of the chair.

"Who is this?" the Empress asked, gesturing to Aidan with her free hand.

"Southland dragons and some barbarian women," said the She-dragon who'd escorted them into the room. "I thought you'd want to see them right away."

"Why would I want to see them right away?"

"They're Southlanders."

"What? You think all Southlanders know each other?" She looked Aidan and the others over. "As if my Keita would be involved with any of this riffraff."

One of the Eastland males sighed and added for Aidan's benefit, "No offense."

Slapping her hand against the arm of the chair, the Empress sat up straight and snarled, "I don't care if I offend them! I don't care if I offend the entire universe!" She pointed at the male who'd spoken. "My baby is still gone and I'm tired of going back and forth with those idiots!"

"We'll get him back."

"And," another female reminded her, "he's not your only baby."

Leaning forward, the Empress snarled, "He's the only one that *matters*."

"*Ma!*" several of the Eastland dragons yelled at the Empress.

"Do you want me to *lie* to all of you?"

"It'd be a nice change of pace," one of them complained.

The Empress waved her hand at her own offspring and focused again on Aidan.

"So, Southlander, who are you?"

"Uh . . . I'm Aidan the Divine of the House of Foulkes de Chuid Fennah. Third son of Jarlath and Gormlaith—"

Holding up her hand, the Empress cut him off. She took a moment to look him over completely before asking, "*You're* a Southlander royal?"

Aidan glanced down at himself. "Cut me some slack. It's been a rough few days."

* * *

"You are foolish She-dragon if you think you can make me and your Empress friends."

"I didn't say friends, Batu. You and I are friends."

"No, we are not."

"I'm talking about an alliance between you and the Empress. And that's more important for your needs."

"The Empress hates my people. She has no respect for the tribes that made this country what it is. Why would she want alliance now?"

"Because she needs one now."

Brannie took the chain mail shirt and boots that Bolormaa handed to her. "Keita, just get to it. I'm running out of patience."

Batu pointed at Brannie. "Her I like."

Keita's eyes narrowed on the tribal leader, but Brannie snapped her fingers to catch her cousin's attention before she got into one of her moods.

"Fine," Keita said. "It came to me when I saw who was trying to kill me. I'd always assumed it was the Empress—"

"Because everyone wants you dead?"

"*No*, Batu. Everyone loves me. I'm Keita."

Brannie pulled on her shirt and asked Keita, "If it wasn't the Empress, who was it?"

"I think it was her brother."

Batu straightened. "Lord Xing? What does he want with you?"

"He wants me dead—"

"I want you dead."

"Perhaps"—Keita sneered at Batu—"but not for the same reasons I'm sure."

Brannie pulled her boots on. "What reasons could he have?"

"I think he was afraid I'd find out the truth and get that information to the Empress."

Tucking her wonderful new weapon back into her boot—
Batu had no idea how dangerous her "stick" was—Brannie
paused and looked at her cousin. "What truth?"

"That Xing has already made an alliance . . . with
Salebiri."

Chapter Thirty-One

The Empress's head tilted to the side. "How do you *lose* a princess, Mì-runach?"

There had been introductions and a brief update on what had happened in the last few days, but Aidan was still holding much back. He had to. His goal at the moment was the same as it had been hours ago . . . to keep the Empress off Brannie's and Keita's back.

"It's complicated," he replied.

"Is it?" she asked, not looking terribly convinced.

"My lady, she ran."

"From you? What did you do to her?" She pointed an accusing finger at Kachka and the others. "Was it these unclean Riders?"

"No. She ran from you. From your army."

"Keita would never run from me. I adore her more than my own children . . . except for Ren."

"Really, Ma?" asked her eldest daughter, Fang, the archer they'd originally met. "*Really?*"

Everyone in the room except the Southlanders and the Riders were kin. Along with Empress Xinyi, there were her two sons, eldest Zhi and third oldest Kang; and her three daughters: second oldest Fang, fourth oldest Ju, and youngest daughter Lei. Ren was the baby of the group. They were all members of the Chosen Dynasty, the royal family of the Eastlands for the last three thousand years.

Aidan had expected all the pomp and circumstance he'd seen in the main hall to continue with the family, but it didn't.

Fang liked to hunt down her own meat apparently.

Zhi enjoyed reading and was seriously considering becoming a monk in the service of one of the Eastland gods.

Lei had on a dress but it was covered in dirt and leaves and she was currently resting on the floor, her legs up against a wall.

Kang and Ju were warriors, in gold-and-black chain mail, armed to the teeth, and more than ready for any of the Southlanders to test their strength and speed.

In a lot of ways, they reminded him of Rhiannon and her offspring, but he wasn't about to say that. He really didn't know if they would consider it an insult or not.

"Stop complaining, Fang," her mother said. "I'm waiting for an answer from this cretin."

Wanting to see how the Empress would react, Aidan replied, "Assassins have come after Keita twice, my lady. Once in the Southlands near the docks. And then again at the Heaven's Destroyers Temple."

She pulled back a bit. "I would *never* attack Keita anywhere, at any time, but especially at the Destroyers Temple. Everyone allowed entry into that sacred space is considered protected. To attack the inhabitants is to risk the wrath of the gods."

"Unless your god is Chramnesind."

"Who?"

Fang's eyes crossed. "Ma. The Zealots."

"Oh, yes. Yes. Of course." The Empress let out what Aidan assumed was supposed to be a sad sigh. "Such a tragedy what's been happening over in the Southlands with those horrid people. Although I am surprised that dear, sweet Rhiannon has bothered to involve herself with those she has always referred to as 'two-legged cattle.' You see, your queen has never truly understood the connection my people have with the humans of this land."

"You mean because they worship you?"

The Empress smiled. "Yes."

"What my mother means—"

"He knows what I mean, Fang. Don't you, Aidan the Divine?"

"I do. But, of course, times have changed, haven't they, Your Majesty?"

"Oh, they have. At least for the Southlanders. Not much change here. Not in . . . two thousand years or so? Sadly, Rhiannon can't really say the same. It has been fascinating to watch, though."

"I'm sure it has. Of course, change comes to all eventually," Aidan replied, keeping his voice carefully modulated. "The question is, are you ready to face it when it does?"

"Unless you can control that change. Harness it for your own benefit. Some have quite a talent for that."

Enjoying this dangerous discussion much more than he should, Aidan began to reply, but Fang quickly cut him off.

"I'm so worried about Keita," she said, drawing her mother's attention back to her.

"Yeah," Kang suddenly said, chewing on a piece of fruit. "Makes you wonder if this has something to do with—"

Brutal glares from both mother and daughter ended the prince's words abruptly. Grabbing another piece of fruit, he moved to a corner and kept his head down.

His reaction was telling.

Especially when the Empress looked at Aidan with a sad expression he knew was forced and said, "Poor Keita. Running off like that. All alone. Defenseless. You must feel horrible about her being unprotected, Mì-runach. Since it was your job to ensure her safety."

Aidan was going to lie, to say how he feared for her and felt lost after failing his queen but . . .

"She's not unprotected," a new voice blurted out. "She's got her cousin Brannie with her."

Aidan looked at Caswyn and his friend immediately realized his mistake.

"I'm not supposed to talk, right?" Caswyn asked.

"Right."

The Empress pushed herself out of her chair. "Cousin Brannie? *Cousin?* Do you mean Branwen the Awful of the Cadwaladr Clan? Daughter of Ghleanna the Decimator also of the Cadwaladr Clan? *That* Cousin Brannie?"

Aidan cleared his throat. "My lady—"

"You have let loose a Cadwaladr in *my* territory?"

"I . . . I wouldn't worry. Brannie's quite . . . uh . . . nice?"

"Oh, well, if she's anything like her mother, I'm sure she's a fucking delight!"

"*Ma,*" Fang said, shocked.

"Oh, shut up, Fang!"

The Empress began to pace around her lone wood chair. "A Cadwaladr, roaming our lands, and she thinks we tried to kill her cousin."

"It wasn't one of us," Zhi noted, pausing to pointedly look at each of his siblings. "But Uncle Xing . . . ? That sounds more like him, don't you think?"

"But why would Xing try to kill Keita?" the Empress asked. "What would be the purpose? As much as I adore her, she has no true effect on my throne."

"You know how Keita is," Fang said. "She can find out anything. Maybe she knows something we don't. Maybe Xing didn't want her to give us the information."

The Empress stopped behind her chair, placed her hands

on the back, and leaned in. "Well, Aidan the Divine? Is that true? Did Keita know something she needed to tell us?"

Aidan was caught off guard. He'd never imagined he'd have to talk to the Empress himself. He'd assumed that Keita would do the talking and they would all just stand behind her looking tough.

So what was he going to say? Was he going to tell the Empress her youngest son—her "baby"—was dead? Was he also going to tell her that Keita was going to poison them to ensure they didn't strike back because Ren had died on Southland territory? Was he going to tell them any of that?

Absolutely not!

He shrugged and did what he used to do when his mother asked him questions he knew better than to answer—he lied.

"I don't know anything, Your Highness."

The Empress studied Aidan for several long—and terrifying—seconds before she smiled and said, "Of course, of course. Why would she tell any of you anything?"

She moved around her chair and walked toward them. "I'm sure all of you are exhausted after your hard travels. Perhaps a bit of rest and fresh food? Does that sound acceptable?"

"More than acceptable, Your Highness," Aidan replied, relieved she seemed to be taking his statement as fact.

She stood in front of them now, her forefinger touching her bottom lip. "Now let's see if I've got this right. You're Aidan, you're Uther and you're . . . Caswyn?"

Caswyn nodded. "Yes, my lady."

"Excellent." She smiled, then, like a snake, struck, her hand reaching out and wrapping around Caswyn's throat, eyes rolling back in her head, her body leaning in as she used her magicks to look into Caswyn's mind so she could find the true story.

She didn't bother with Aidan because she knew he'd

fight to keep her out. But Caswyn, who wasn't good at keeping his mouth shut in the first place . . .

Gasping, the Empress released Caswyn and stumbled back. Fang and Zhi caught her before she could hit the floor and placed her in her chair.

"Ma? What is it?"

"He's been lying," she whispered desperately. "He's been lying. He's been lying. He's been lying."

"Ma," Fang begged. "Stop. What did you see?"

"Xing. He's been lying. He doesn't have my son." With tears spilling down her face, the Empress announced, "My Ren . . . my Ren is dead."

"You don't know you're right," Brannie argued with her cousin.

"But I'm sure I'm not wrong."

Brannie shook her head. "Wait . . . what?"

They followed Batu to his war tent. Generals and lower-level tribal leaders waited within, and the one he called Nergüi the Knowing came a few seconds later. Batu updated them all on what Keita believed, but from what Brannie could tell, her cousin had no hard evidence. How could she move on any of this without hard evidence?

"Wait," Brannie cut in when the tribal leaders, all male, began to debate what they should do next. "Before we make any move, we should think about what we're doing. There's no guarantee that any of this is correct."

"Who is this big-shouldered woman," one of the tribal leaders demanded, "that she believes she can speak among men?"

Brannie, with her head still pounding, her cousin smirking, and some human male attempting to look down on her despite the fact she towered over him, snarled, "I am Branwen the Awful. Captain of the First and Fifteenth Companies of the Dragon Queen's Armies. Daughter of Ghleanna the Decimator and Bram the Merciful. And best friends forever with Iseabail the Dangerous. That's who I am. And who the battle-fuck are you?"

Keita eased up behind Brannie and whispered in her ear, "Nicely handled, cousin. Now we can watch the poor fucks completely lose their shit when they realize there are *two* Southland dragons here."

The tribal leader, after looking at all the others, finally asked, "You are Branwen the Awful? *The* Branwen the Awful?"

"I . . . I guess so." Brannie only knew of one Branwen the Awful.

Suddenly each tribal leader and general dropped to one knee, one fist against the heart, head bowed.

"It is an honor, Captain," one of them said with great reverence.

Batu, who would bow to no one, put his hand on Branwen's shoulder and finally smiled. "I knew I liked *you* for a reason."

Disgusted, Keita threw up her hands. "You do know that she is no one?" When Brannie snarled at the insult, Keita added, "Other than the cousin I *love*."

They all tried to stop her. Even Aidan, who knew better than to get involved. But the Empress was not to be stopped. She was not to be soothed. She was not to be calmed down.

"Ma, please," Zhi begged. "We're supposed to be negotiating with them. Let's talk to Xing's ambassadors first. Let's find out the truth before you do anything rash."

Without answering, the Empress stormed back into the palace's main hall and across the giant room to the small group of Eastlanders who still waited for her.

Aidan understood who they were now. They represented

Xing and were trying to negotiate for the Empress's kingdom by using her favorite son. She had been making them wait as a tactic, to pretend she wouldn't give up everything for Ren of the Chosen.

But Ren of the Chosen was dead. And the Empress's tenuous hold on her royal rage had snapped with the loss of her offspring.

The Empress swung her arm away from her body and lifted her fist. A blade shot out from under the long-sleeved gold dress she wore, and she rammed the hidden weapon into the belly of the dragon who had tried to talk to Fang not so long ago.

Shocked, the dragon gaped at her. "But . . . Your Majesty . . . Lord Xing and his army—"

She yanked the blade out with such venom that his intestines splattered across her dress and the floor.

The other dragons tried to run, but she stabbed one in the spine, another in the chest, and cut off the last one's head. She might not be a warrior but, like Rhiannon, the Empress had her skills.

Breathing heavily, she walked away from the delegation as their human bodies shifted back to dragons in death. It was strange seeing a giant catlike head with antlers roll across the main hall. Aidan didn't really know how to interpret that.

"Ma," Fang said on a loud sigh. "You shouldn't have done this. Not until we talked to them."

"And what about Xing's army?" Kachka whispered to Aidan.

"Talk? About what?" the Empress demanded of her daughter, her pain so great, Aidan was sure the entire region could feel it. "They killed him! They killed my baby!"

What was there to say to that? Nothing. Until Caswyn's head jerked up, his eyes focusing on the ceiling.

"What?" Aidan asked.

"Wait for it." He held up one finger. "Wait for it . . . *now!*"

Aidan grabbed Kachka and Nina, pulled them in close, and charged to one side. Uther grabbed Zoya, because he was a very brave dragon. Zhi caught hold of his mother around the waist and dove out of the way with his siblings as the first giant lava ball came through the gold wall and exploded in the middle of the floor.

They were just picking themselves up when arrows poured through the hole the lava ball had left. Several landed in Aidan's back but the chain mail kept them from piercing his spine.

He pushed Kachka and Nina away and shifted to his dragon form, shaking the arrows off.

"Mì-runach!" he bellowed. "*With me!*"

But before they could burst out of the palace and kill all in their way until they were cut down by their enemies to die with honor, Ju moved in front of them.

"Wait! We can use you and your friends, Southlander," she told Aidan, "but not if you are all going to be idiots about it."

Aidan didn't think he was being an idiot about it until the Riders ran out the doors and right into the battle, Zoya screaming, "*Who wants to be first to die before I meet my ancestors?*"

Aidan shrugged. "Okay, you may have a point. . . ."

"I think Xing is going to strike *now,*" Keita said. And she sounded so confident that Brannie almost took her at her word, but she was her mother's daughter. She still had to ask the question.

"Why do you think that?"

"Because the time is right. In fact, the time is perfect."

Not really liking the sound of that at all because it was

just so vague, Brannie sort of growled in the back of her throat. A reaction that Izzy would understand immediately. Sadly Keita didn't understand much about Brannie and she didn't seem too interested in finding out.

"Look, I think I was to be the first. A message to Xinyi to tell her how far they'd go."

"But you weren't the first, Keita. Ren was the first, which was stupid. They should have held him for ransom." Brannie motioned to Batu. "Wouldn't you have held the Empress's son for ransom?"

"I would have held dragon over mother's head, sending her pieces of him, until I got what I wanted and then I would kill him in front of her eyes, so I could see her suffering." He shrugged. "That is how we do it."

"That was a lovely story, Great Leader. Thank you." Brannie turned back to her cousin, widening her eyes to suggest to her kin they might want to burn the tribal territories to the ground, but Keita was gazing past Brannie.

"Keita? Are you okay?"

"It was . . ." She took in a breath. "You were right, Brannie! You were right, we have to go!"

"Go? Go where?"

Keita turned to Batu with sudden urgency. "You need to go to the Empress's palace. *Now*."

"To do what? Fight for decadent imperialist dog?"

"Fight *with* the imperialist dog."

"You must be mad."

"Hardly. Trust me. You want free rein to raid the rich and plentiful cities outside the Empress's domain? You'll do this, Batu the Iron Hearted."

"And what will you be doing while my people fight *with* imperialist Empress?"

Keita grinned. "Something completely insane." She motioned to Brannie. "Come on, cousin! You're with me."

She lifted her skirts and ran out of the tent, expecting Brannie to follow right behind her.

Batu and the other tribal leaders watched her, waiting for Brannie to make her move.

"She's my cousin," Brannie said, by way of explanation. "And I promised me mum to take care of her. No matter what."

"Your mother, Branwen the Awful, is very cruel to you," Batu said sadly.

"*Branwen!*" Keita bellowed through the tent flap. "*Move your fat ass!*"

Brannie briefly closed her eyes and let out a long breath. Batu came over to her side and put his arm around her shoulders.

"Do not worry, mighty Branwen. Crazed female like her . . . she can only live so long. Then you will be free."

Annwyl stopped walking and stared. The herd of demon animals stared back. And that's when she knew.

"I've been walking in circles." Her head dropped and she let out a shuddering breath. "I'm never getting out of here."

Something sniffed her and Annwyl lifted her gaze to see the baby animal she'd petted earlier. He pressed his slimy— and quite honestly disgusting—snout against her. Like he was trying to comfort her. It was very sweet and, while the mother watched her attentively from a distance, Annwyl stroked her hand down his snout.

She kept doing it too, because it soothed her. It calmed the voices she'd been hearing in her head while she was wandering around here, seemingly unable to block them out. Petting her new friend seemed to help for a little while.

That was until she heard *that* voice. Right behind her and taunting, just as always. Because some things would never change.

"I heard you turned into a whore," the voice said. "Just like your mother."

Annwyl closed her eyes and pressed her fists against her temples. "No. I don't hear you. I don't hear you. I don't hear you. You're in my head. You're in my head."

The voice spoke again, laughing at her. "Stop being a dumb little twat. Turn around and face me! Face *us*."

Annwyl did turn around. Taking her time, keeping her eyes closed at first. Afraid of the game her cruel mind was playing on her.

Gritting her teeth, she opened her eyes and lifted her head. And there he stood.

Gray-green eyes. Light brown hair with blond streaks. And his throat open where it had been cut the day he'd died.

"No. Not you," she begged her mind. "Anyone but you."

The image of her father smiled. "I've been waiting a long time to see you again. Although I can't say it's just been me." He gestured behind him to the hundreds of men Annwyl had cut down over the years. "We've *all* been waiting for you."

Chapter Thirty-Two

Short on time, Brannie and Keita didn't bother with horses. They simply shifted to dragon and flew to Lord Xing's palace.

Brannie took the lead, landing hard in the middle of the courtyard, swinging her halberd as soon as her claws touched the ground. She struck several guards and went for more, using her weapon to hack and slash her way through those protecting the palace.

Keita landed behind other guards and quickly, expertly, cut their throats before they even knew she was there.

Guards inside the palace attempted to close the door but Brannie rammed her shoulder against it, forcing them back.

"Mistress Yeow!" Keita greeted the She-dragon scrambling across the main hall in an attempt to get away. "I strongly suggest you take your offspring and leave this place. And pray to your gods that the Empress does not hold against you what your mate has done."

"This is my home," the She-dragon said, although Brannie could hear the fear in her voice. "I will not leave."

"Then my cousin will hack you into pieces."

No. She wouldn't. But it was fine for Mistress Yeow to believe that if it made her leave.

"Do you want your offspring to witness that, Mistress? Do you want the same thing to happen to them?"

Horrified, Mistress Yeow ran up the large stairs toward the rooms of her offspring, Brannie assumed.

"Great," Brannie snapped at her cousin. "Now you're making me out to be a baby killer?"

"Oh, they're hardly babies! Now, come on!"

Keita shifted to human and ran down a corridor, snatching up a silk robe from several hung on a wooden stand.

Brannie shifted and followed her. They reached a door and went down a long set of stairs to the dungeon.

Unlike the dungeon at the Zealot fort, there was only one captive, trapped in a gold cage, with a rune-covered gold torc around his neck.

"Ren!"

Ren of the Chosen jumped to his feet and broke into a smile so wide and beautiful it nearly blinded Brannie with its joy.

"Keita!"

The pair hugged through the gold bars.

"You're alive!"

"You thought I was dead?"

"I found your sigil chain at a Zealots fort and the Riders said that you had been there with them—"

"Gods, so much Zoya." Ren suddenly pulled back from Keita, staring down into her face. "You came east to kill my family, didn't you?"

"I thought you were dead!"

"That's your excuse?"

"You would have done the same if the situation were reversed."

"I wouldn't have to. Your mother adores me." He looked at Brannie. "And how did you get here?"

Brannie stretched her neck, trying to loosen the tight muscles. "How do you think?"

"Oh, ignore her. She's been so difficult lately." Keita moved back from the bars. "We need to get him out," she said to Brannie.

"Why haven't you gotten yourself out?" Brannie had to ask.

Ren pointed at the gold torc. "This is magickal. It's kept me in human form and my magickal skills quite weak. I've been trapped like this for ages."

Brannie looked over the cage door. "You best step back."

Ren and Keita moved to the back of the cage. Not because they were in danger from her flame but so that pair could whisper through the bars while Brannie shifted to dragon again. Unleashing her flame on the lock, she pulled with both claws, tearing the door open once she'd softened the gold.

With the door open, Brannie realized that Ren and Keita weren't talking, they were arguing.

"You sent Batu to my mother's house?" Only an Eastland royal dragon would call the Empress's Palace *my mother's house.* "What were you thinking?"

"There will be an alliance."

"He hates my mother!"

"Would you leave it to me? Now, let's go. We have a war to end!"

Keita flounced off toward the exit and Ren turned to Brannie. "Has she been like this the entire time?"

"The entire time!" Brannie rubbed her forehead. "To be honest, I really thought all of us would be dead by now."

"Oh, don't worry. There's still time for that to happen. Especially when Keita's involved."

Annwyl backed away from the false image of her father, and the faces of all the men she'd killed in her life. Their heads were back on, but she recognized them. They could be real. Those men she'd killed. She clearly remembered condemning many of them to whatever hell would have them.

But her father . . . her father had to be false. How could he be anything else?

She hadn't killed her father. She'd never been brave enough. Someone else had done her the favor. But then her brother had taken over and things didn't get better. Not for her.

Actually, not for anyone.

"What are we doing, Da?" an angry voice demanded from behind her and Annwyl recognized that voice, too. Without even looking, she recognized that voice. "You said—"

"Shut up, boy! Me and the great Annwyl the Bloody are talking. Don't you see that?"

And that's when Annwyl knew. She wasn't being haunted by those she'd killed. It wasn't her brain torturing her with her past.

How did she know that now? Because never in a million years would Annwyl the Bloody allow her brain to torture her over her idiot *brother*.

Because if anyone had deserved to die, it had been her brother, Lorcan the Butcher. When she'd taken his head, he'd earned every second of his pain in that world and this one.

Standing behind her, glowering, Lorcan reached for Annwyl but she slapped his hand away. That did what it had always done. Pissed him off. So he grabbed at her again.

Annwyl caught his grasping hand and twisted, turning her body at the same time. She dropped him to the ground and twisted his entire arm until she heard something break and her brother began screaming.

They were dead, but they could feel pain. That made sense since it was hell.

Releasing her brother's hand, she faced her father.

"What do you want?"

"Is that how you talk to me? Your father? Your king?"

"*Dead* king. I'm queen now. I rule."

"Not very well. From what I hear."

"Who have you been talking to? Men I've already killed? I doubt they'd be fans."

"You even killed your own brother—*and would you shut up, Lorcan!*"

His rage getting hold of him, Lorcan stopped screaming in pain and struggled to his feet, cradling his broken arm.

"You always take her side!" Lorcan accused.

Father and daughter rolled their eyes, having heard this particular argument since the day Annwyl had been brought to her father's house all those years ago.

"You always say that," Annwyl finally told her brother, "but he hates us equally."

Her father nodded. "I really do. Of course," he added, "at least you aren't a whore for a dragon, Lorcan."

"That's because the She-dragons I know wouldn't want anything to do with him."

Her father turned those gray-green eyes on her. "You think this is funny? You don't think I'm disgusted by you?"

"No, I just don't care. And I do think it's funny."

"I don't understand how you could do what you've done."

"What I've done?" Annwyl asked her father. "You mean fuck a dragon? He was the best thing that ever happened to me. Speaking of which . . . you do know that you're a grandfather, don't you?" She smirked. "I'd love for you to meet the twins. Especially Talwyn. She'd *adore* you."

Annwyl had to laugh at that, knowing her daughter as

well as she did. But it seemed to her father as if she was laughing at *him*. Something he could never abide.

Her father grabbed her by the neck of her chain mail shirt and yanked her close. Like he used to when she was a child.

"You betrayed me," he snarled at her. "You betrayed our name. You betrayed our blood."

Fighting her rage, Annwyl told her father, "Get your hands off me."

"*You had one job!*" her father bellowed in her face. "*To use that pussy for something useful!*"

Rage began to move through Annwyl. The way it used to. But back then . . . she'd had no outlet. She'd been too afraid to challenge the man who ruled the Southlands. So she'd curl her hands into fists and dig her nails into her palms until blood dripped onto the floor. She'd had no voice then. No power.

"I was not put here by the gods to whore *for you!*" she screamed in her father's face.

Without even hesitating, her father shoved her away and swung, just like he used to do all the time when she angered him . . . but this time Annwyl caught his fist and held it; the pair stared into each other's eyes. Their mutual rage growing and growing until—

"Oh. Excellent. You have her."

Annwyl looked to her left and saw the demon lord she'd tried to kill sitting on something that those with bad eyesight might call a horse.

And behind him was his personal army of demons. It was not a big army. Not like Annwyl's. But they were demons, which meant they were probably much deadlier than any army she'd ever faced before. Even dragons.

The men who had come with her father began to panic,

trying to back away, but the demon lord raised his clawed hand to soothe them.

"No, no. No need to fear. We're not here for any of you." He pointed one claw at Annwyl. "We're here for her."

Her father, never a man to back down, replied, "When I'm done with her."

"I need her alive, human. I know this is hard for you to hear, but she has great work to do."

Shocked by that, Annwyl dropped her father's hand and faced the demon lord and his army.

"Great work? For *you?*"

"Absolutely. Even now, Chramnesind is about to unleash his Zealots on your armies and the armies that have joined your cause. They will be wiped out. And that's when you will return."

"Why would I return?"

"To bring this world to yours. All of it under my rule."

"And why would you need me to do that?"

"I cannot leave this world of my own volition. But you can bring me and my army to yours." The demon lord dismounted from his horse and walked toward Annwyl. "And once there, Annwyl the Bloody, you will give me your children. The other Abominations will follow your unholy twins and your unholy twins will follow you." He slid his hand behind the back of her neck, the claws scraping her skin. "Now, this may be where you're thinking of sacrificing yourself in an attempt to save your children but that would be foolish. Because I can spend an eternity"—he yanked her close, his lips nearly touching hers—"a gods-damn *eternity,* making you pay for such a mistake. So choose wisely, one-time queen."

He smiled at her and, waiting a heartbeat or two, asked, "So . . . what is your choice?"

But Annwyl couldn't answer him. Everything had turned

red around her. Not just the sky and the dirt . . . but everything. And she could no longer hear anything except . . . rushing waves? Right in her ears.

All Annwyl knew was that the demon lord wanted to use her children. *Her* children. And Annwyl . . . she couldn't . . . she wouldn't . . . she . . . she . . .

He saw it coming. Knew his daughter better than he knew himself, and he saw it coming. As soon as that idiot mentioned her unholy children she just started . . . screaming.

Like she used to do when she got into it with her brother. She'd scream and attack him and take him down to the floor even though she wasn't even eight yet. She'd hurt him, too. But she was only a child then. A child with no skill and no strength.

But now?

Annwyl wrapped herself around the struggling Lord Phalet, her screams completely drowning out his. She dug her hands into his scalp and pressed her thumbs into his eyes.

Lord Phalet spun, trying to get her off, but Annwyl held on tight, unwilling to let go.

Then he screamed for help. "Get her off me! *Get her off me!*"

Several of his soldiers ran to aid him, grabbing Annwyl around the waist and pulling her one way while two other soldiers pulled Lord Phalet the other. Annwyl still didn't let go.

The soldiers tried harder; Phalet's screams getting more desperate.

Finally they pried her off, but her thumbs were covered in the remains of Phalet's eyes.

The demon lord dropped to his hands and knees, spitting and screaming and bleeding everywhere.

But they still didn't know his daughter. She wasn't done. She wouldn't be done until Lord Phalet was dead.

She fought off the soldiers holding her and managed to get a sword from one of them. As soon as she yanked that weapon free, several of the men she'd already killed once made a crazed run for it. Away. They ran away.

Annwyl swung the blade and took one demon's head and then the leg of another.

She ran back to Lord Phalet and tackled him to the ground. She sat on him and buried her sword deep into his chest. But he wasn't dead. The demons around here didn't have their hearts in the same place humans did. Annwyl seemed to understand that now.

She kept him pinned to the ground with the sword and then pulled his dagger from his belt. She cut off his fine clothing and then began on his skin. Cutting, then tearing off whole sheets. Then she went for the muscle, ripping into that. First with the dagger, then her bare hands.

She dug and she dug, until she finally grabbed something and yanked it out.

Annwyl held Lord Phalet's beating heart in her hand and got up.

Phalet was still alive, blindly staring up at her as she held the heart in front of him as if he could still see it.

And Annwyl was *still* screaming.

With that rage she'd had since she was a very little girl, Annwyl ripped Phalet's heart apart until there was nothing but tiny pieces, littering the ground around her feet.

Then she leaned down, staring into Phalet's face and screamed and screamed until he was gone.

Taking deep breaths, Annwyl stood straight, wiping her

bloody hands on her chain mail leggings. When she faced the remaining dead who'd come for her . . . they ran.

None would face her again. Not now. Not ever again.

Even his idiot son ran. Pathetic boy that he always was.

He stood, however, and watched his daughter for a little longer. Their gazes locked and he saw the hatred he'd always seen in those eyes.

"Such a disappointment," he told her one more time, before turning his back on her and walking away.

The baby demon animal came and stood next to Annwyl, brushing his snout against her.

The army was still behind her but no one said anything to her or tried to grab her. It seemed Lord Phalet's plan was his and his alone. But unlike the dead she'd faced, the demons weren't walking away.

They would take her back, she guessed. To that dungeon. Until whoever was replacing Phalet decided what to do with his live victim.

Still, seeing her father walking away from her . . .

Annwyl reached over and patted the baby's side. "Hungry?" she asked him. "Would you like a chewy corpse?"

They looked at each other, and the baby's sizable tongue swiped from one side of its massive mouth to the other.

Smiling, Annwyl coaxed, "Go on, baby. Go eat."

He took off, running down her father, tearing into him with his giant baby fangs.

Annwyl turned around and faced Phalet's army. They were still staring at her.

Letting out a breath, she asked, "So . . . what now?"

As one, the demon soldiers slammed the blunt ends of their spears into the ground, dropped to one knee, and bowed their heads.

Eyes wide, Annwyl looked at the mother demon animal standing beside some of the soldiers. They stared at each other a moment before Annwyl looked back at soldiers, opened her mouth, and said, "Huh . . ."

Because, honestly, she really didn't know what else to say.

Chapter Thirty-Three

The Empress's generals were impressive. Moving quickly as soon as the threat came into view, they rallied the troops and began to fight back immediately.

But the Empress was still undone by the loss of her youngest son, and her remaining offspring were having a hard time getting her to face her brother. Not in a one-on-one fight, but at the head of her troops in a show of fearlessness.

Her sobbing, though, made that impossible.

"Ma," Fang tried again while Aidan and his brothers secured the windows and doors of the palace's war room. "You have to stop this. Ren would want you to fight."

"My Ren is gone! He's gone! Why would I want to go on?"

"Because you have other offspring. And, of course, an empire to run."

"Eh."

Fang threw up her hands and walked away.

It was amazing, really, the way the entire family ignored the sound of rocks and lava balls ramming into their home; the crash of swords and shields. Instead, they all focused on their mother and trying to talk her into doing something. Anything.

As for Aidan and his brethren, they did what they always did. They protected the royals. It was what they were trained for. If Keita were here, and she still wanted to poison the entire family, that would be up to her. But Aidan wasn't about to carry out anything like that.

"Ma, please." Lei tried.

"My Ren!" the Empress suddenly burst out before throwing herself onto a large metal table, sobbing hysterically.

The Empress's offspring huddled together, whispering. Aidan moved from window to window, looking outside to see if any of the enemy troops were getting close. He'd prefer to move the Empress to a more secure location but until she calmed down a bit that would probably not be possible.

Aidan glanced over and saw that the offspring were watching him. He had to admit . . . he didn't like it.

He especially didn't like it when Ju grabbed his arm and yanked him out of the room.

"You work with Rhiannon the White, don't you?" Ju asked Aidan.

"It's been my honor to protect, Her Maj—"

"Right, right. Whatever you say. Now we need you to use some of that skill on our mother."

But Aidan didn't know the Empress. He didn't know anything about her.

"We need her to get up and face her brother."

"But . . . as her children, wouldn't it be easier for you to—"

"She never listens to anyone but Ren. But he's dead, so . . ."

Surprised that Ren's *sister* was taking his death so casually, Aidan didn't really put up a fight when Ju shoved him back into the room and over to her mother.

The Empress had been placed back in a chair, but she

was still sobbing, wiping her eyes with a cloth clutched in her hand.

The others watched Aidan expectantly. As if they hoped for some miracle from him!

His gaze flicked to each of them, wondering what he should do next. He had no fucking idea. But he also had nothing to lose at this point. So he borrowed knowledge he'd learned from Keita on the art of pissing someone off.

Aidan crouched beside the chair and took the Empress's hand, being careful not to let the tips of those nail guards nick his human flesh. He'd heard rumors she had poison on them and, true or false, he didn't want to take any risks.

"My lady, I know you are devastated by the loss of your son—"

"My perfect, amazing son."

Clearing his throat, "Yes, your perfect, amazing son. And I have to say, I find it distasteful that even though your perfect, amazing son lost his precious life in a Zealot fort outside of Aberthol in the Southlands, your brother had the nerve, the audacity to lie to you and say that he held your perfect, amazing son captive all this time. You built your hopes on that. That he would return Ren of the Chosen to you . . . when he knew he never would. That's a lie I know I could never forgive."

Still gripping the cloth, the Empress slowly turned her head, her gaze locked on Aidan's face.

And then she just stared at him. For what felt like hours. She stared and didn't speak.

Aidan didn't know if he was simply afraid to break eye contact with her or if he was unable to. Was she holding him in some sort of thrall?

He wondered if he would die right now, her gaze was so hard. So angry.

"Xing," she finally bit out.

"My lady—"

The Empress threw back her head and screamed to the ceiling, "*XINGGGGGGG!*"

Aidan fell back, her offspring scattered, and Uther and Caswyn grabbed Aidan's arms and yanked him across the room.

The Empress stood, her entire body shaking with rage, her fists balled up, her beautiful face terrifying as her lips twisted and her jaw clenched.

Gold light circled her, starting from the ground up, moving around and through her. The Empress shifted and Aidan gawked, fascinated. She had gold scales and black-and-gold fur that reached from her head, down her spine to the tip of her tail. No obvious claws, but fur-covered, striped paws. No horns, but antlers. Long whiskers that reached out from her nose. A nose. Not a snout like every other dragon Aidan had ever seen but a nose, because she had a face like a striped jungle cat.

Any other time, Aidan wouldn't even think of being afraid of such a docile-appearing animal. He wasn't even sure he'd consider her a dragon of any kind.

But then he looked into her eyes and they were no longer brown. They were fire.

Without wings—she had none—the Empress's body shot up, going through the ceiling above them, leaving a gaping hole. Aidan moved forward until he stood under it and saw that the Empress had gone through the entire building until she'd reached the outside.

"What did you do?" Ju demanded.

"What you told me to do!"

Now pissed at him—because of course they were—the Empress's offspring shifted and took off after their mother.

Uther and Caswyn stood beside him, all three of them gazing up into the sky.

"They look like big cats," Caswyn announced.

"And?"

"Just noting."

"Do you want to look like a big cat?" Uther asked.

"Sometimes," Caswyn replied. "Who doesn't want to look like a big cat?"

Disgusted by the entire conversation, Aidan walked away.

"Oh, what?" Caswyn demanded. "You've never wanted to look like a big cat?"

Kachka didn't have to fight dragons. There were humans in Xing's army that kept her and her comrades quite occupied. And they kept coming. Xing's army of humans. But the Empress had her own army of humans as well, so the Riders didn't fight alone.

It was strange, though. Something in the air. Something . . . off.

Using the spear she'd taken from a dead soldier, Kachka impaled one soldier and with her sword, cut another soldier nearly in half. She was about to run into a small group of soldiers moving toward Zoya when the ground rumbled and she heard an explosion come from the palace.

She spun and looked up, watching in acute surprise as gold light and flames shot into the sky.

"What the fuck is that?" Kachka asked Nina in their own language.

"That is rage, comrade. Rage and a mother's pain."

"The Empress."

"*Xingggggggg!*" the Empress screamed out, her body turning circles in the air, leaving a trail of fire and gold light behind her. "*Brother! What have you done?*"

"I'm here to take what's mine!" the insignificant male shot back.

"I would have given you all this, brother. I never wanted it. But my son—"

"You can still give it to me, sister. Give me the throne and I'll return your precious Ren to you, alive and well."

"You lie! He's dead!"

"He isn't. I have him. I will return him to you!"

"*Liar!*"

"We've seen the truth, Uncle," one of the Empress's off-spring said, floating behind their mother. Kachka honestly couldn't tell them apart . . . but she could only tell the Southland dragons apart by their scale color. And more than once, she'd confused her own iron-colored mate with his twin sister when they were both in their dragon form. When she'd played with his sister's tail . . . by the horse gods, *that* had been awkward for a few days after. "We know our brother's dead."

"My perfect, amazing Ren!" the Empress cried out in pain.

Of course, it would have been a much more devastating moment if her children hadn't rolled their eyes.

Frustrated, Lord Xing snapped, "All right, one more time, sister. *He's fine!* He's at my palace!"

"No," the Empress insisted. "He was killed at some Zealot's fort. He's dead! My baby is dead!"

"We saw his head," Kachka finally yelled up to both royals. "The Zealots walked right by our cage with it."

Xing stared down at her. "You saw, barbarian, what my soldiers wanted you to see. Ren was taken but that head was not his. We wanted the Southlanders to believe he was dead, so they would send Keita. Her, I had every intention of killing so that you would know how serious I am."

"You lie," the Empress snarled. "You lie, brother, and I will *never forgive you!*"

"Don't then. Don't forgive me. It'll make it easier to lay waste to all you hold dear. To bring it down around you and

augh while you burn. I tried to save you, sister, but now I
see I cannot."

"Comrade," Zoya said from behind Kachka, "we may
have problem."

"You think you can defeat me?" the Empress asked Xing.

"I am no longer alone, sister. And I will not only rule
here, I will rule the Southlands. I will rule everything."

"Oh, brother," the Empress sighed. "You truly will believe
anything."

Trying to keep her attention on the fight between siblings,
Kachka still glanced behind Zoya to see what she was talking about.

"By the darkest horse gods."

Zoya nodded. "There are many."

And they were riding over the hills in the distance, their
small but powerful horses confidently charging right into
the battle.

"It's Batu and all his horse riders," Nina said, coming
close.

Now speaking in their language, Kachka noted, "But
they are not fighting with Xing's legions . . . they're killing
them."

As the siblings began to circle one another, Aidan and his
brothers moved forward to assist the Empress. But Kang
grabbed Aidan's arm and held him back.

"You do not want to get into the middle of this," Zhi
warned.

Xing raised his sword and, screaming, charged his sister.
He shot forward even without wings, as if the Eastland
dragons could manipulate the very air around them. But his
sister was equally quick, slapping him hard with her paw as
she moved aside.

Now that she had her paw raised, Aidan could see her

claws, which had been hidden behind fur until unleashed. And her claws had torn a large hole through her brother's armor and into his flesh.

Crying out, Xing spun away from her and his sister went after him. He had armor and weapons. She had her claws and a mother's rage.

She grabbed her brother and yanked him up with her as she lifted her body higher. She turned with him, then threw him down.

Xing couldn't catch himself as he fell, landing hard in front of the palace.

The Empress landed next to him and circled around him, snarling.

He tried to pull himself back up, but she went up on her hind legs and, with her front paws, wrote flame-covered runes in the air.

The runes flew into her brother, sending his dragon body skittering into the Empress's beautiful flowers.

"My son," the Empress growled at him. "You took my *son!*"

She began to chant in an ancient language, one so old and dark that even Aidan, with his lack of magicks, had to back away, and the Empress's offspring and his mates moved with him.

Magicks swirled around her, through her, until they exploded out of her in a blinding light, ramming into her screaming brother.

He flipped over and over through the flowers, leaving nothing but burned ground behind.

Aidan thought the power would send Xing off the Empress's territory completely but she clenched her paw and Xing abruptly stopped. He tried to scramble to his feet, but was held in place by her clenched paw as the Empress pulled back the other.

Xing began screaming and in horror, Aidan watched the

scales on Xing's back tear open, his spine following, slowly ripped from his body until his screams finally ended and his body stopped moving.

The fighting ground to a halt and everyone fell silent, while the Empress dropped to her knees, her rage waning.

That's when Aidan caught sight of the Eastland Riders for the first time.

"That's Batu," Ju said from behind Aidan. "Batu the Iron Hearted. Leader of the Eastland Riders."

"What's he doing here?"

"I really don't know."

Batu moved away from his troops and into the garden, stopping to stare down at Xing's body before looking at the Empress.

They watched the Empress, all of them too fascinated and terrified to move.

"Batu the Iron Hearted," the Empress said, her gaze cutting over to the Eastland leader. "Here to fight for my brother?"

"No." He pointed toward the palace. "I'm here to fight for her. Branwen the Awful."

The Empress looked up at her palace.

Brannie and Keita stood on the palace roof in their dragon forms and on Brannie's back was a human Ren.

Aidan felt relief flood his bones at the sight of Brannie and he had to fight his urge to fly to her and take her in his arms. A gesture he knew she would not appreciate.

Ren waved and smiled at his mother. "Ma . . . I'm okay!"

"Ren?" The Empress pressed her paw to her chest. "Ren . . . is that you?"

Brannie took to the air and quickly landed next to the Empress.

Ren jumped down from her back and walked toward his mother, barely glancing over at his uncle's body.

"I see you've been busy, Ma."

"I thought you were . . ."

The Empress shifted to human and threw herself into her son's arms.

"My beautiful, handsome son!" she cheered, hugging him tight. "My baby!"

"Ma. I'm okay. I'm really okay."

Pulling back, one arm still around her son, the Empress grabbed his jaw with the other hand, and squeezed until his lips protruded.

"Look at this face," the Empress ordered. "Look at this beautiful, gorgeous face!"

Ren's siblings rolled their eyes and exchanged annoyed glances. It didn't make Aidan appreciate his kin any more, but it did make him grateful he never had to spend any time with them. Ever.

Sadly he didn't think Ren could say the same thing.

Branwen shifted to human and turned away from the sight of Ren reuniting with his kin. She didn't begrudge him that, knowing he'd been through much because of his uncle. But she also knew her own kin were about to go into battle with the Zealots. She wanted to be fighting by their side.

She wanted her own reunion.

"You all right?" Aidan asked, stroking his hand under her chin.

"I got poisoned, but I'm all right now."

Aidan and his two brethren immediately looked at Keita and the red She-dragon gasped in outrage.

"*I* didn't do it! It was on one of the blades of the assassins who attacked us."

"You sure?" Uther asked.

"I'm positive. Tell him, Branwen."

"It wasn't her fault," Branwen admitted. "But I understand why you'd think it was."

"Ungrateful," Keita hissed. "All of you are ungrateful!"

The Empress chanted a spell over the gold torc around her son's neck and it fell off, allowing the Eastland dragon to shift to his natural form.

"Thank you so much, my dear Keita," the Empress greeted Brannie's now-human cousin. "I can't tell you how much what you've done means to me."

"I know he's your favorite."

"He absolutely is."

"We're right *here*," Fang reminded her mother.

"I'm just glad I could help," Keita said so demurely that Brannie had to look at Aidan to make sure she wasn't imagining it all.

She wasn't.

"Reuniting mother and son." Keita pressed her hand to her chest, right over her heart and her voice hitched a bit as she spoke. "You have no idea how much it means to me, Empress."

Good gods, was Keita the Viper crying? What was happening?

"I can never repay you, my child, for bringing my most important and best loved child back to me."

Ren at least cringed a bit at his mother's words, while his siblings glared at him behind her back.

"No repayment necessary. Ensuring the continued happiness of the Chosen Dynasty is enough."

Aidan pressed his mouth against Brannie's ear and whispered, "Wait for it."

Keita gave a sweet smile and added, "But if I *were* to ask for a favor . . ."

"Boom," he added before pulling away. Brannie's snort causing Ren's siblings to suddenly look at her.

"Anything, my dearest Keita. Just tell me."

"Fight by my mother's side against the Zealots in the Southlands."

"And why would I do that?"

"Uh-oh," Brannie muttered.

"Why would you do it?" Keita asked, her voice no longer demure. "Because your beautiful, gorgeous son is back—alive and well. And that, Your Majesty, is due to *me*."

"And your cousin, yes?"

"Her cousin is mighty," Batu added. "Very helpful in this. More helpful than decadent royal."

"You and I," Keita said, her finger swinging wildly between her and Batu. "*No longer friends!*"

The Empress faced Brannie. "Well, Lady Branwen—"

"It's just Captain, Your Majesty."

"Captain Branwen. I remember when your dear mother was a captain. I wonder how long before we call you general as we call her."

"Oh, puleese." Keita sneered.

"And for bringing my son back to me, dear, *dear* Captain Branwen, ask me for anything you may want. Jewels, gold, a fancy palace with a view here in the Eastlands. Ask and you shall receive."

Branwen really didn't know how to answer. Because she didn't know what was going on.

Aidan pressed his hand against her back and she knew he was trying to tell her something but, again, she still didn't know what was going on.

"Uh . . . well . . ."

"Her?" Keita demanded, stepping between the Empress and Brannie. "You're giving *her* what she wants?"

"Why not me?" Brannie asked. "I'm affable."

"Oh, shut up."

"Well, let me ask you this, my dearest Keita," the Empress said, curling a lock of Keita's red hair around her finger. "Did you come here to find and release my son? Or did you come here to poison my entire family because you thought Ren was dead and you wanted to make sure we didn't attack your mother from the sea?"

"What does that have to do with anything?"

Ren flinched and rubbed his forehead, his siblings smirking behind him.

"That's what I thought," the Empress replied flatly, dropping Keita's hair and walking around her. "Now, Branwen . . . you were saying?"

Again, the pressure from Aidan's hand at her back.

"Uh . . . Your Majesty, I speak for the entire Cadwaladr Clan when I ask that you allow your troops to fight by our side against the Zealots and that you personally assist my queen in whatever magickal endeavors she may be undertaking."

The Empress framed her hands around Brannie's face and Brannie was proud—because she didn't flinch. "For what you've done for my precious son, I will do this"— she looked at Keita, although her hands were still around Brannie's face—"for *you*, Branwen the Awful."

"All of you are *so* ungrateful," Keita accused, heading back to the palace.

"I wouldn't go far, Keita," the Empress warned.

"And why is that?"

"Because something is happening." The Empress removed her hands from Brannie's face, closed her eyes, and took in a breath. "I hear your mother on the wind. She calls to me."

Keita walked back toward them. "My mother wouldn't do that unless . . ."

"Unless the final battle has begun," Branwen finished for her.

"Lord General!" the Empress called out.

An Eastland dragon came to the Empress, dropping down on one knee, head bowed. "Prepare my army. I'll be sending us all to the Southlands. I'll be opening a doorway within a quarter hour. Will you be ready?"

"Of course, Your Majesty."

"Good." The Empress looked over at the Eastland Riders. "And you, Batu the Iron Hearted? Will you fight with us?"

"We will, decadent royal. We'll do it for Branwen the Awful."

"Our friendship is *so* over," Keita growled at the Rider.

Batu grinned. That was probably exactly what he'd wanted to hear.

And Branwen was just glad to know that she wouldn't have to travel by sea again.

"You will need us, decadent She-dragon." Batu glanced around at the remains of Lord Xing's army. "But what of your brother's men and dragons?"

"Well, I'm not wasting my magickal skills to bring riffraff with us." She gave a wave of her hand before walking off; tossing over her shoulder, "So kill them all."

Chapter Thirty-Four

Talwyn blocked the blade with her shield and speared the wielder through his chest.

She'd lost her sword hours ago and since had been using weapons she'd picked up off the dead.

The grasslands were no longer green but red from the blood spilled. But still, the Zealots kept coming. They wouldn't let their enemies move closer to Salebiri's castle. Even if it meant sacrificing themselves.

But a challenge had been sent. Written on the flesh of a Zealot that they'd catapulted through the damaged main hall roof and now, they waited for the answer.

"Talwyn!" her brother called out, two fingers pointing at his eyes and then off in the distance. "To the hills!"

The Zealot priests and priestesses were moving into place.

"Get Grandfather!" she ordered her brother. She speared another Zealot and moved to get her father and uncles prepared. But in the fields behind her there was a flash and then the sound of racing horses and armed men.

"*Izzy!*" Talwyn roared. "*Behind us!*"

Her cousin climbed onto the back of the nearest dragon and stood on her shoulders.

"I see Riders!" she yelled back to Talwyn, which was strange, because the Daughters of the Steppes had said they would allow Northlanders through their territory but they wouldn't take part in this battle. "And gold armor!"

"On Riders?"

"No! Two separate armies and . . ."

"And what? What do you see?"

"Brannie! *It's Brannie!*"

Izzy jumped off one dragon's shoulders and onto the back of Éibhear, who quickly took to the air.

Brannie led the charge on horseback, motioning with her hammer to where the Riders should attack and where the Empress's army should mount a defense.

Once her commands were given, she charged forward toward the main battle near Salebiri's castle. But something caused her war horse to flip, head over tail, crashing hard into the ground.

Brannie rolled free and back onto her feet before the horse could crush her. She ran, ducking under a swinging sword and flipping over a jabbing spear.

Zealots ran toward her and she changed her hammer to a halberd. She'd only impaled one of the Zealots on the end when Éibhear slammed down onto the rest.

"Izzy!"

"Bran!"

Izzy jumped off Éibhear's giant shoulders, but he caught her with his tail and safely lowered her to the ground.

"I wish you wouldn't do that," he grumbled but Izzy ignored him, throwing herself at Brannie.

"I thought you were dead!" Izzy yelled into Brannie's neck as the pair hugged.

"Not yet," Brannie said, holding her best friend tighter. "Definitely not yet."

* * *

Aidan landed behind Brannie and Izzy, but before he could say anything, his best friend was squeezing the life from him.

"Can't breathe."

"Stop complaining." Éibhear finally pushed him away. "We all thought you lot were dead until Ghleanna got here. But then we heard you were with Keita, so . . . you know . . . we thought you were still dead . . . eventually."

"That's lovely to hear."

"You've been with Keita all this time?"

"Uh-huh."

"I'm sorry, old friend."

"Your sister's mean," Caswyn complained, stalking past Éibhear and Aidan with Uther behind him. "Really, *really* mean."

Dagmar stood on the top step and stared into the court-yard. She closed her eyes; breathed in, breathed out, and fought a nearly overwhelming desire to panic about what she knew was happening hundreds of leagues away in the Outerplains.

"Mum?"

Forcing a smile, she glanced back at her son, but he wasn't fooled.

"I'm all right," she insisted.

Var walked up to her and took her hand. "Maybe I should have gone. I'm sure I could have helped."

"If they don't succeed, I'll need you here. We'll need to get the children out before the Zealots come."

"That's disappointing."

"What is?"

"I was hoping more for a Northland way of handling things."

Dagmar, who no longer thought about panic, had to fight hard not to laugh. "Unnvar—"

"We'd kill the children. The servants. Ourselves. The dogs. The horses. The squirrels in the trees."

"Var, stop it," Dagmar ordered around her chuckles.

"I was actually looking forward to cutting Arlais's throat myself since we both know she'd put up a fight."

Laughing out loud despite herself, Dagmar leaned against her son, but she immediately stopped when Arlais suddenly ran out the castle doors.

She opened her mouth to announce something, but her eyes abruptly narrowed and she glared at her mother and brother.

"You two are talking about me," she accused.

"Is there a reason you're out here?" Dagmar asked.

She pointed to the middle of the courtyard and a mystical doorway suddenly opened. A moment later Keita and Ren of the Chosen tumbled out. A living, breathing Ren of the Chosen.

Arlais squealed and ran to her favorite aunt while Var leaned in to her and whispered, "And now, Mum, we have a fighting chance. . . ."

The witches met in Rhiannon's sacred space, including the Empress, whose power Rhiannon desperately needed if they hoped to make this work.

The queen, the Empress, Morfyd, Nina, Rhi, and Brigida, all in their natural forms, stood in a circle. And while the others began to chant, Rhiannon walked inside the circle they created, tossing the ashes from the sacrifices she'd made, creating a circle within a circle.

Once she was done, she stood between her daughter and

granddaughter, everyone linking claws and paws and hands. Then they began the summoning.

The Zealots retreated back toward the castle and Brannie finally returned to her troops. When Aidan, Caswyn, and Uther tagged along, Izzy immediately noticed and raised an eyebrow.

"Don't you have a war to fight, General?" Brannie snapped. "Legions to command?"

"Mmm-hmm," Izzy replied in that annoying, high-pitched way.

After that, they all waited in silence until Duke Salebiri finally appeared, riding into the middle of the battleground with a company of soldiers behind him. He dismounted from his horse and turned in a circle. "You sent me a challenge, queen's whore," he called out. "And now you hide?"

The ground shook as Bercelak landed hard in front of Salebiri.

"Hide?" Bercelak asked. "From a human? That day will never happen."

"Well, well, well," Salebiri taunted. "The great Bercelak the . . ."

"Great," Bercelak finished for him. "It sounded better in your head, didn't it?"

Brannie and the Cadwaladrs laughed—they couldn't help it. But that only enraged Salebiri.

The duke stepped back and spread his arms out.

And he began to change. He went from human into something . . . unholy. Unclean.

He grew in size. Bigger than Bercelak. Maybe bigger than Éibhear. His skin turned gray, his handsome features stretched and pulled until Brannie could no longer see the man he was.

And then there were the tentacles.

They spilled and spun out from his body. So many of them.

One side of each tentacle had multiple spikes to grab and tear.

Eyes wide, Bercelak looked at Ghleanna and mouthed, *What the fuck?*

But Brannie's mum had no answer for her brother. None of them did. They'd never seen anything like it.

Brannie prayed they'd never see anything like it again.

"Look what my god has given me!" the duke cried out from the fang-covered hole that was once his mouth. "Look at me and weep! *For I will destroy all of you!*"

One tentacle pointed at Bercelak. "And I will begin with you, Bercelak the Great!"

Brannie's uncle pulled his broadsword from the sheath strapped to his back, and clasped it in both claws.

"Come for me, Duke. Let's see what your god has given you."

A tentacle lashed out, slapping at Bercelak.

Using his sword, he blocked it, but another came from the other side, catching Bercelak on the neck. When it pulled away, it tore out some of his scales, his blood splashing on the ground.

Several more lashed out, but Bercelak cut them down and rolled under a few others.

Brannie was impressed. Her uncle was no longer the young dragon who'd gone up against the Lightning dragons and brought them to heel. But he fought like he had nothing to lose, when they all knew he had everything to lose.

Then something horrifying happened.

The men that the duke had ridden out with began to shake and twitch and they, like he, began to change. All that had happened to the duke happened to them. Now, instead of one tentacle thing, there were hundreds.

For the first time Brannie had ever seen, Bercelak backed away, but only until he stood by his sons.

Fearghus motioned to his kin.

The Cadwaladrs would fight. They would fight and they would kill until their ancestors called them home.

Fearghus then looked out at the other armies. None of them were backing down either. This would all end here. Now.

Rhiannon and the others pulled and pulled, using all their skills and energy to drag Chramnesind from his world into theirs.

He appeared in the circle, the smell of dirt and shit invading Rhiannon's precious sacred space and her nostrils.

The eyeless god roared in rage, trying to force his way out of the protective circle.

"*You will pay for this!*" he swore. "*All of you heartless bitches will pay!*"

"Will they?"

Rhiannon looked over her shoulder. A brown-skinned warrior woman stood behind Rhiannon and the others. And standing next to the woman was a giant wolf. A few feet to the left was another woman warrior. This one an Eastlander.

All of that was strange enough, but on the opposite side of the circle stood a man with violet eyes and black hair so long it pooled at his feet.

Rhiannon motioned to Xinyi and the Empress frowned and mouthed, *What?*

Rhiannon jerked her head again and Xinyi finally looked over her shoulder. When she turned back around, her eyes were wide.

With a nod, the two rulers moved at the same time. Rhiannon opened her left claw and Xinyi opened her right paw. Then, they both yanked those they still held in the opposite direction, pulling the other witches out of the way and breaking the circle.

But before Chramnesind could flee, the giant wolf crashed into the stunned god, taking him down to the ground. The two females pulled out their weapons and began stabbing and hacking at the god, chopping him into pieces as he screamed and cursed and attempted to fight them off.

"You should have listened to us, old friend," the male said, watching the assault impassively. "You should have backed off long ago. But you didn't."

"You can't do this to me! You can't do this to me!"

"You did this to yourself. And because of you," the male went on, "a doorway from hell has been opened that should never have been. For that affront alone, you must pay. And pay you will."

The male never raised his voice. Never showed any anger. He simply waited until the females finished hacking Chramnesind into pieces. Then he crouched beside the still-breathing remains and softly said, "Your time here is done, old friend."

Chramnesind cursed them all and, as he did, the male backed away. Far away. Then he shifted and Rhiannon, lying on the ground with the other witches, knew this was Rhydderch Hael, the father of all dragons.

When the god pulled in a large breath, Rhiannon grabbed her granddaughter, pulling her close and protecting her with her body while Morfyd sent Nina Chechneva out of the sacred space completely.

The god unleashed his flame, and it filled every corner, leaving nothing untouched.

When the flames stopped, the gods were gone . . . including Chramnesind.

* * *

Weapons were drawn and Ghleanna, Bradana, Addolgar, and Rhys moved up until they stood beside their brother.

"Come for us all, Cadwaladrs!" Salebiri yelled out. *"Come!"*

Bercelak took a step . . . but then he froze. He looked down at the ground, then around.

"Uh-oh," Gwenvael muttered next to Fearghus. "Dad's gone 'round the bend."

"No," Éibhear said, also staring down at his feet. "Something's coming."

"Something big," Briec added.

"Shit," Fearghus sighed. "Now what?"

Gaius Lucius Domitus made his way to their side, his recently arrived mate, Kachka, on his back. "Do you feel that?" he asked. "Coming from underneath."

"From out there." Kachka pointed with her sword from Gaius's back. "Something is coming from out there."

"Uh," Gwenvael asked, "are the Northlanders running?"

It was true, the Lightning dragons were exiting the forest as fast as they could run or fly.

"Ragnar Olgeirsson is running? That can't be good."

And Fearghus knew he was right when he saw the first one come over the hill and then he, too, wanted to run. He wanted to run for his life.

"By the gods, Salebiri," Fearghus accused. "What have you done?"

Blinking at Fearghus, Salebiri slowly turned his odd body around and watched the demon thing that came over the hill. First one, then two. Then more. Many, many more.

Salebiri stumbled back, his army moving with him. None of them seemed to care that they were moving right into their enemy.

"Those things are not with him," Briec guessed.

And Briec was right. Salebiri was terrified by what was coming over the hill. Giant animals with tusks and horns and black eyes. Something not of this world but clearly coughed up from one of the hells. And running behind them until they veered toward Salebiri's castle was an army of demons, weapons brandished, horrifying battle cries polluting the air.

"Daddy?"

Fearghus heard his daughter's voice and looked over at her. She pointed and he followed the direction of her hand . . . and his breath caught in his throat, his knees went weak.

"Holy. Shit."

Annwyl sat on one of the animals as she would a horse, holding on to it by the fur at its neck. The animals moved slowly, waiting until she'd passed them and was now in the lead. Blood covered her face and chain mail. Bruises seemed to cover the rest of her.

She appeared calm, but Fearghus knew better. He knew his mate better than he knew himself sometimes. And while she appeared calm, her eyes told a different story. A long, painful, angry story.

Bercelak looked at Fearghus over his shoulder and, with a small nod, Fearghus told his father to move back. They all needed to move back. Now.

Salebiri pointed one of his tentacles at the queen. "*Annwyl!*"

Annwyl gazed down at Salebiri, her head turning first one way, then another.

The sight of him, like that, seemed to trigger something in her that many had not seen in years. Her unrestrained rage. A rage with no questions. No concerns. No doubts.

"Kill it," Annwyl said, her voice carrying on the wind. Then she bellowed, "*Kill them allllllllll!*"

The demon things suddenly charged down the hill right toward them.

"*Fucking move!*" Fearghus ordered, using his tail to grab hold of both his children as his wings took him to the sky.

Their human armies made a crazed run for it, charging off to opposite sides.

But Salebiri didn't move fast enough. He didn't move at all. Instead, he pointed at the Zealot priests and priestesses nearby and yelled, "Call to him! Call to him now!"

The Zealots did as ordered, raising their voices to their god . . . but he did not come. He did not appear. Chramnesind did not give his loyal followers the power they begged for to fight off this new attack.

With no sign of help, Salebiri tried to build a defense with the twisted warriors he still had, but it was too late. Annwyl's demon animals had closed the gap. Roaring—the animals *and* Annwyl—battered Salebiri's men, taking them down and tearing into them.

Tentacles flew into the air as they were ripped off. Claws tore into gray flesh. The screams of the Zealots rang out but nothing could or would help them. Not when Annwyl was like this. Not when she had no intention of stopping.

Fearghus landed on a safe hill so they could watch the carnage from a distance. He placed his children on the ground and they moved in front of him.

"Well," Talwyn said, "Mum's back."

Talan nodded. "And she's brought hell with her."

"Now you two can see why I love that woman."

The twins looked up at him, their faces matching images of consternation.

And their expressions didn't change when he smiled. . . .

Chapter Thirty-Five

The corpse-eaters feasted on the bodies of the Zealots—some, tragically, not fully dead yet—and Annwyl made her way to Salebiri's castle.

By the time she stood at the doors, she knew she was no longer alone. She walked inside and Vateria stood in the middle of her Main Hall, waiting.

"So," Vateria said, "it's you and I, Blood Queen."

Annwyl shook her head. "I have no issues with you. Now that I think about it . . ." Annwyl glanced off for a moment before finishing, "I barely fucking know you."

"Then what do you want?"

The roof of the castle was abruptly torn away, stones and wood raining down.

Annwyl didn't even bother to move. She was still close to the door if she had to make a run for it.

From above, Gaius Domitus looked down at Vateria.

"My sister sends greetings, cousin."

Cadwaladrs in human form came in behind Annwyl. Other dragon kin leaned in from above with Gaius.

Vateria shrugged. "Do your worst. My children are dead. I have nothing left to lose."

"The demons killed your children?" Annwyl had made

it clear to them that sort of behavior would not be tolerated, but she did see the bodies of the young behind Vateria.

"No," Vateria replied. "*I* killed my children. So they would not be captured by the likes of you."

Blinking hard in shock, Annwyl muttered, "*Wow.*"

"So come, Gaius. Come, Blood Queen. Do your worst to me."

Annwyl was ready to do just that after what Vateria had done to her own children, but then she heard it. The telltale *bang-drag, bang-drag, bang-drag.*

Moving slowly from behind them, panting with exertion, Brigida entered the castle, and the Cadwaladrs parted without waiting for her to ask.

And Annwyl did the same.

The old She-dragon, in her human form, made her way over to Vateria until she was only a few feet away. She raised her free hand and flicked it in their direction.

"Out. All of you."

And they all left. Again, without question. Even Gaius.

They walked away from the castle, back to the armies, where they waited.

When they heard the first scream coming from the castle, they moved farther away.

No one wanted to know what Brigida was doing. What Vateria was going through.

Once again, not even Gaius, who hated his cousin with every fiber of his being.

As orders were given to the various armies and the preparations began for the long trips home, eventually they all seemed to forget about Vateria and whatever horror she was going through.

For all she had done, maybe she deserved the suffering.

But then, after a few hours, Annwyl went back to the castle. There were no guards, no soldiers, no servants left here. Just a lump under a tapestry.

Annwyl went over and pulled the material back. She cringed and stepped away, her fist pressing against her nose to block out the smell of an already-decomposing corpse. A *human* corpse that did not change back to dragon in death, which Annwyl had never heard of before.

But it was the face . . . or what was left of it that disturbed Annwyl the most. Such horror, such unbelievable terror on that rotting face. Frozen that way in death.

"Gods, Vateria," Annwyl whispered, "what the hells did she do to you?"

Benedetto stayed hidden in the woods, tears streaming down his face. When the final battle had turned, his mother had smuggled him out through the tunnels but she had stayed behind, knowing that the Abominations wouldn't stop until they'd tracked her down.

He didn't know if his brothers had gotten out. Something told him they hadn't. That she'd also used the younger boys to protect him.

But now what was he to do? He had no one and nowhere to go.

Benedetto's head snapped up when he heard someone coming through the trees toward him. He started to jump up, but a gravelly, rough voice said, "Don't bother. I know you're there, boy."

He sat back down. Good. He'd been caught. Now they could kill him and it would be over.

She came out of the trees, covered head to toe in a gray robe, her face hidden. But he saw her walking stick, saw the power that emanated from it. He was doomed.

She stopped in front of him and he could smell the flame that was buried under human skin. A She-dragon.

"You're her boy, ain't'cha?"

"I am."

"And proud, too."

"I'll always be proud of my mother. Now just kill me and get it over with."

"I could kill ya, but looking at you, such a strong, young boy with so much untapped power . . . I think I got a better plan now."

"Plan for what?"

"To get me an apprentice."

Confused, Benedetto asked, "But . . . why? I mean, you're with the Abominations, aren't you?"

"They're kin."

"Then why? Why would you want *me* as an apprentice?"

"Well . . . I guess I feel I owe your mum a bit. For me new life."

"New life?"

She pulled back the hood of her robe and Benedetto gasped at the beautiful face staring at him. With one big blue eye and long, soft white hair falling onto smooth cheeks. Only her one milky-gray eye suggested a harder life than Benedetto had ever experienced.

He didn't understand. From the voice, he'd thought the She-dragon would be ancient. But her face . . . her hands . . . everything *but* her voice was young.

"Come, boy. Let's get you safe."

Not knowing what else to do, he stood and together they walked away from the war and the life Benedetto had once had.

"What's your name, boy?" the She-dragon asked.

"Benedetto. Benedetto Salebiri."

"Well, I'm your new mistress, Benedetto. I will teach you what I know."

"All right."

They walked on and, finally, when she still had not killed him or led him into a group of armed Abominations scouring the hills for any survivors—simply toying with him as his mother would have anyone else—he asked, "And your name, Mistress?"

"Name's Brigida. Brigida the Most Foul." She tossed her walking stick to him and picked up her speed, nearly skipping to wherever she was leading him. "And we'll be close, you and I, Benedetto. And true power will be all ours."

Chapter Thirty-Six

Brannie and Izzy sat on one of the hills looking down at what was left of the battleground.

They were silent for a very long time, gazing at their soldiers killing any Zealots still left. Annwyl didn't want any captives. She just wanted the Zealots wiped out.

A few had probably escaped but Brannie doubted the power of the cult would return. Who would want to be part of a defeated, eyeless cult?

Suddenly Izzy looked at her and asked, "Who gets trapped under a mountain?"

Brannie laughed. "It just went down."

"I can't believe you didn't fly away. You must have been distracted." Izzy smirked. "Was it Aidan distracting you?"

"Nope. It was Caswyn. He ate me horse."

Izzy gasped. "Not Puddles!"

"My Puddles. I should have killed the idiot when I had the chance, because now it'll just seem wrong after all we've been through together."

"I'm sure I could get his Mì-runach brethren to beat him up for you."

"Don't bother. It won't bring back Puddles."

Izzy put her arm around Brannie's shoulders. "Don't worry. We'll get you a new horse. It won't be Puddles, but you'll learn to love your next one, too."

"I know you're right."

Izzy rested her head on Brannie's shoulder and quietly admitted, "I'm so glad you're not dead."

"Me too."

"And I'm glad you're back."

"Iz, you have no idea. Keita's insane."

"Oh, that I know."

"There you are." Éibhear dropped down next to Izzy and handed her a leather bag with dried meat. "Eat. Both of you."

Brannie was just reaching for the bag when Aidan sat down next to her, Uther next to him, and Caswyn next to Uther.

"You all right?" Aidan asked.

"I'm fine." That's when she felt Izzy jab her in the ribs with her elbow.

Brannie snatched the bag of dried meat from her friend and barked, "Stop it."

Izzy leaned forward and for a second of panic, Brannie was afraid her best friend was about to say something that would embarrass her in front of Aidan.

Thankfully she didn't.

"Caswyn! You *ate* Puddles?"

"Awww," Éibhear said, also leaning forward to look at his friend. "Not good ol' Puddles!"

Caswyn balled his hands into fists and screamed out, "*He was dying anywayyyyyyy!*"

Annwyl heard a scream and turned around, looking up at the hills in the distance.

"So," she asked Fearghus, continuing on with their conversation, "Brannie was gone, too?"

"Aye. We thought she'd been killed when the mountains went down."

"Tough like her mother, that one."

"Very true." She heard him take a breath. "Annwyl . . . we have an issue."

She faced her mate. "The Salebiri castle, right? I say we raze it to the bloody ground, salt the earth, and cover it with rocks. I don't want anyone coming here to worship."

"I'm not talking about the castle."

"Oh, then what?"

Fearghus gestured to the left. "You can't keep your demon army."

"But they said I was their queen."

"Annwyl—"

"Oh, come on! Why can't I have a demon army? I killed their leader. Apparently that's all it takes."

"They belong in hell. They'll be happier in hell. *I'll* be happier with them in hell."

Annwyl looked at Fearghus's kin huddled by a tree, closely watching the demons.

"What do you lot think?"

"Send them back!" they all yelled at her.

"Well, no need to bark at me." She again looked at Fearghus. "Fine. I'll send them back."

"Thank you. Now what about the cattle? The ones the demons call the corpse-eaters?"

"But look at the bang-up job they've done cleaning up for us," Annwyl argued. "Usually we have to burn all these bodies, which is an awful mess and smell. But look . . . they're halfway done and they're just calmly grazing."

"Annwyl . . . you'll have to send them back, too. And that includes the baby."

"But we've bonded!" she argued. "And the mother likes me."

"But you'd never separate a mother from her baby, so we all know that you'll want to keep both."

"I like his mother."

"*No*. You'll have to send your demons back to hell."

"You're all being unreasonable, but I'll do it."

"You can wait til they're finished grazing, though," one of Rhy's daughters said, causing everyone to stare at her. "You lot won't be the one who has to burn bodies. Me and the grunts will. So let them finish."

"Lazy," Ghleanna complained before walking away, the rest of the Cadwaladrs going off to get their work done.

When they were alone, Fearghus gazed down at Annwyl and said, "You went to one of the hells and you came back with an army. That's impressive."

Annwyl shrugged. "He wanted our children, and he was planning to use me to do it. You know how that sort of thing makes me."

"Insane with rage?"

"Exactly." Annwyl stepped closer and whispered to Fearghus, "My father and brother were down there."

"What? You saw them?"

"They came for me. To hurt me."

"What happened?"

"Broke me brother's arm, didn't I? And when I dealt with the demon lord, he ran away like the big wanker he always was."

"And your father?"

"I let the baby eat him since he was basically a corpse anyway."

Fearghus started laughing. "You *what?*"

"He apparently was quite disappointed that I fuck a dragon and felt the need to tell me that, which was rude."

Still laughing, he put his arm around her waist and pulled her in close. "Annwyl the Bloody, you never fail to amaze me."

"I did tell him that he should get to know his grandchildren and that Talwyn, especially, would adore meeting him."

Fearghus dropped his head back and laughed loud, some of the soldiers stopping their work to see what the dragon known as Fearghus the Destroyer could be laughing about.

Ghleanna the Decimator was now the rank of major general of Her Majesty's Dragon Army. She had been promoted to the position three years ago and was put in charge of the Fifth Battalion.

It hadn't been easy getting this rank. She'd worked her ass off for it. And although some tried to accuse the Cadwaladrs of nepotism, giving their own an easy time of it, everyone eventually learned there was no free ride for any of them. In fact, Cadwaladrs were brutally hard on their own kin during training because they cared more if one of their own died in battle. They felt they'd failed to prepare them.

Which was why Ghleanna had always worried about her Branwen more than some of her other offspring. She'd been afraid the brutal training would change who she was. Would take away that spark that made Branwen Brannie.

But eventually Ghleanna had realized she had nothing to worry about.

Standing by a tree, she watched her daughter talking to her cousin-by-mating and best friend Izzy, telling some story about drunk Caswyn, Uther, and the Riders. And Branwen didn't simply talk . . . she acted it all out as well.

"So, of course, I shoved him into the wall," Brannie said, throwing out her arms to demonstrate the force she'd used. "I mean, why wouldn't I? He ate Puddles."

"Still can't believe he did that."

"I still can't believe those two idiots told the Riders

everything! Then we had Riders with us! Not that I minded. I mean, you can't beat having Kachka at your side."

"I know! She's bloody amazing in a fight!"

"But, of course, Keita is complaining. *Constantly!* And I'm worried she's going to poison everybody. Like *no one's* safe!" she announced, her arms going wide.

Ghleanna laughed, as always entertained by her youngest daughter.

Brannie turned, saw her mother, and ran to her, throwing her arms around her and hugging her tight. None of that "we're on a battlefield, we're in charge, we *must* be stoic until in private" stuff for her Brannie. She showed love where and when she wanted and didn't care who saw. Of course, the only one really bothered by that was Bercelak but Ghleanna also knew that Brannie was his favorite niece.

Ghleanna pushed her daughter back and took her hands in her own. "I want to tell you that you did an amazing job, Brannie. I know you didn't want to do any of this, but I'm really glad you did."

"I'm glad I did it, too. I think any of my sisters or cousins would have killed Keita right from the start."

"Did you hear?" Izzy asked, slinging her arm over Bran's shoulder.

"Shut up, Izzy," Brannie warned, which made Ghleanna want to hear whatever was going on immediately.

"Our Branwen has a gentleman suitor." Izzy frowned, looked off, and changed it to, "Gentle-*dragon* suitor."

Brannie rolled her eyes but so did Ghleanna.

"That's nothing new," Ghleanna told her niece. "*Every-one* knows Aidan likes my Branwen. And he's liked her for *ages* now."

Brannie pulled away from her mother. "That's not true!"

"*Branwen.*"

And that was all Ghleanna said before walking away, leaving her daughter standing there, annoyed and frustrated.

* * *

"What was that tone?" Brannie asked Izzy.

"I think that was your mother's version of 'duh.'"

Brannie stepped close to Izzy and pointed her finger right in her face. "Listen to me and listen to me good. Aidan and I are not—"

"Blah, blah, blah, blah, blah!" Izzy covered her ears with her hands. "I'm not listening! I'm not listening! I'm not listening!" And she kept chanting that over and over while running away.

Brannie put her hands to her forehead and rubbed.

"You all right?" Aidan asked as he came to stand by her.

"Everyone I know is insane."

"Are you just figuring that out?"

"Oh, shut up!"

"Fair enough. Here." He held a bottle in front of her. "Ragnar gave me a bottle of—"

"Ale!" She grabbed the bottle from his hand. "Thank the gods!"

Brannie walked off, but realized Aidan wasn't behind her.

"Well, come on then!"

"Am I allowed to come with *my* ale?"

"Oh, shut up and get your ass over here!"

Aidan found a nice, quiet cove outside of a nearby bay. He'd hoped to find a quiet cave but, of course, all the local mountains had been brought down by the Zealots and the hills were simply too small. Even when he and Brannie were human.

But the cove worked for them both. No one had anything fresh to eat—the armies had been at the front for months and months—but he did find more dried beef and some flat bread for them to eat while they enjoyed the Northlanders' ale.

"So what's wrong?" he asked when they were settled and Brannie had enjoyed a few sips—or gulps—of the ale.

"Nothing."

"Really? Nothing? You're gritting your teeth."

"I'm not gritting my teeth."

He pressed his finger against her jaw.

"All right, fine! I'm gritting my teeth."

Aidan laughed. "And I ask again, what's wrong?"

"I hate when everyone acts like things are written in stone. How about leaving things to me? Letting me handle things?"

"Brannie . . . you are in charge of *two* dragon companies with the nicknames Destruction and On Pain of Death. In what world are you not handling anything?"

"Why do you always have to be so bloody rational?"

"Are you aware of whom I associate with? Do you honestly not understand what I deal with on a *daily* basis?"

Brannie began to giggle.

"I love my brethren, would die for any one of them, but I have no delusions about their incredibly high level of idiocy. If it wasn't for me and a few other Mì-runach who like to think things through . . . we'd all be dead."

Laughing harder, Brannie nodded. "Fine. I get it. We all do what we must. That's why Keita's still alive and I didn't stab her in the face."

"I was amazed about that," he admitted. "Several times I thought she was definitely dead."

"It crossed my mind more times than I could ever admit to my kin."

She took another swig of ale before handing it back to Aidan.

"Let's stay here tonight," she suggested, looking at him. "You and me. Fucking."

Aidan smiled. "I will always enjoy your subtlety."

"I'm a Cadwaladr. That *was* subtle."

He raised the bottle. "Then here's to a night of fucking."

Brannie crawled into his lap, placing her knees on either side of his hips. She took the ale. "And drinking." She took one more swig and handed it back to him.

Watching her, Aidan took a drink. When he lowered the bottle, Brannie put her arms around his shoulders and leaned in. She kissed him, long and deep, and Aidan immediately dropped the bottle so he could put his arms around her.

He pulled her in tight, automatically lifting his hips. They were both still dressed and yet he was already trying to fuck her. To be inside her.

Their kiss got deeper, more intense. Her hands moved to his hair. He gripped her waist. They began panting, clinging to each other.

That's when Brannie jerked back, her breath harsh.

"What?" he asked, almost barking at her. He didn't want to stop.

"This is it. Tonight."

"This is what?"

"The end of it. You and me. This is our last night."

"Gods, are we dying?" He began to panic. "Did you have a vision?"

"No!" She briefly closed her eyes, tried to calm down her breathing. "What I mean is this will be our last night of fucking. All right?"

"Uh . . . well . . . if you're sure."

"I'm sure. I'm positive!" Now she sounded like she was trying to convince herself. "All right?"

Aidan couldn't help but feel that Brannie was forcing herself to do this. Forcing herself to break off what they had because she didn't want to deal with how she truly felt.

He knew he could fight her on this. Spend all night trying to get her to see reason, but he also knew that would never work. Not with Brannie. He'd just have to wait it out. Let her figure it out for herself.

But until she did . . . they had tonight.

And they had ale.

"All right." He grabbed the bottle again, lifted it. "To our last night."

She let out a relieved breath and smiled. "To our last night."

Gaius Lucius Domitus found a quiet spot away from all the camp activity and sat down, his back against a tree stump.

He opened his mind and, finally, after months of no contact for the safety of everyone, he called to his sister.

Agrippina.

Gaius?

He smiled at just hearing her voice in his head.

It's done, sister.

She's . . .

It's done.

Aggie was quiet and he knew she was dealing with the realization that the She-dragon who'd held her hostage for politics and tortured her for amusement was now dead. Dead and suffering in whatever hell she'd ended up in.

Will you be home soon? Aggie finally asked.

Back to Garbhán Isle first, then home. But if you want, you can meet me at Queen Annwyl's—

No, thank you, she immediately cut in. *I'll just wait until you get home.*

All right.

And I assume you're bringing that Rider with you?

Gaius laughed. *You know my mate adores you.*

She calls me the weak one!

With affection!

Oh, shut up and go to sleep.

I am tired. I'll talk to you when we arrive back in the Southlands.

All right. And Gaius . . . ?

Uh-huh.

I love you, brother.

And I love you, sister. Forever and always.

The two suns rose and Brannie instantly woke up. And, as soon as she did, she wished she didn't have to.

She'd had too much to drink, that was for sure, but it didn't matter, she'd had a great time. And now it was *over*. Done. She could walk away from Aidan and not look back. They'd just be good friends from now on with no regrets.

Pleased with that, she started to get up. She knew she'd have to get her troops moving. Bercelak wanted them heading back to Garbhán Isle in the next few hours and she wasn't about to be the one to get on the wrong side of her cranky uncle.

But when she tried to get up, she realized Aidan's arm was around her, holding her tight.

Laughing a little, she reached down to pull his arm away. But instead of human flesh . . . she felt scales under her talons.

Brannie froze, eyes wide. Especially when she realized that Aidan wasn't just holding her . . . he was inside her. And his tail was entangled with her own.

"That mother—"

"—*fucker!*"

Aidan snapped awake, his arm reaching out for his sword, assuming he was under attack.

And he was . . . from Brannie.

"*We had a deal!*" she screamed at him.

"What?"

"*You lying, son of a—*"

Aidan grabbed her forearms to stop her from tearing his scales off and . . . and . . .

Oh, shit.

Aidan looked down at himself. He was dragon. Brannie was dragon.

And his cock was still wet.

Brannie swung at him, but Aidan rolled away and to his feet. They squared off against each other on either side of the cove.

"You tricked me!" she accused.

"Excuse me?"

"You heard me! You got me drunk and you tricked me! But that doesn't mean anything! That means *nothing!*"

"I tricked you? *I* got you drunk? Because suddenly I'm a human male and naturally do horrible things to females?"

Aidan used his tail to grab the bottle of Northlander ale. He held it in front of Brannie and flipped it over. Half the bottle—the remainder—poured out.

"And what's that supposed to mean?" she asked.

"I've seen you put away three bottles of Rider ale that left you *almost* comatose. But half a bottle of Northlander ale that we *shared?* You might as well be drinking water."

"Your point?"

"You weren't drunk. We both knew what we were doing last night. We both *remember* every second of it. And since we're putting it out there—"

"Don't you dare say it."

"—I'm in love with you. There. *Said it.* Now what? Now what are you going to do, *Captain?*"

The fireball hit Aidan right in the face and a lesser dragon would have been knocked back for miles, but his bastard brothers used to throw fireballs at him as entertainment from the time he could crawl.

But when the flames subsided, Brannie had flown off, leaving Aidan alone by the bay.

Head bowed, he took a moment to calm down. He wasn't about to chase after her. Capture her. Chain her up. Demand she listen.

No, no. That's how *other* dragons did things. Aidan was not like other dragons. He'd always known that long before Rhiannon the White had said as much to him upon their first meeting.

But he'd be damned if he'd let Branwen the Awful just storm out of his life!

If that crazy She-dragon thought it was over, she was very, *very* wrong.

Chapter Thirty-Seven

Bram the Merciful stood on the top step and watched as Ghleanna dropped to the ground. She pulled in her wings, shifted to human, and walked toward him. Right behind her landed Brannie, and Bram let out a breath he'd been keeping in far too long.

Mother and daughter walked toward him, but Brannie was walking faster and Bram quickly realized his lovely daughter was pissed beyond all rational thought.

"Brannie?" he said as she walked past.

She stopped, came back, kissed Bram on the cheek, and then disappeared into the castle.

Ghleanna smirked as she walked up to him and hugged him tight.

"What's happening?"

Laughing, she said, "You don't want to know. I'll just say . . . stay out of your daughter's way for a bit."

Celyn walked into the bedroom he shared with Elina Shestakova and stopped to stare at his baby sister's feet sticking straight up in the air on the other side of the bed.

He was sure it was her feet not only because of the size but because of the scar from where Celyn once bit her during a family brawl.

He moved farther into the room and found his sister was bent so that her head and most of her torso were under the bed.

Celyn placed his travel bag and sword in a corner, faced the bed, and took off running. When he was near the bed, he jumped, arms and legs spread wide, so that he landed hard on the mattress.

"*Motherfucker!*" his sister screamed out, the lower half of her body rolling forward so that her legs slammed into the floor.

Celyn laughed, even when his sister scrambled onto the bed and began pummeling him with her fists.

As he used his arms to protect his face, Elina and Kachka walked into the room, speaking to each other in their native language. Elina grabbed her bow and a quiver of arrows and left. Probably to do some hunting with Kachka.

"What, Kachka?" Celyn called out. "You can't say hello?"

Kachka stopped in the doorway. "You are busy getting slapped like whore by own sister. Did not want to disturb."

Elina closed the door, leaving Celyn alone with his baby sister and, by then, Brannie had worn herself out.

She stopped swinging her arms and dropped next to him, the pair gazing up at the ceiling.

"Feel better?" Celyn asked.

"What made you think something was wrong?"

"You only go upside down when you've had a bad day. The last time I saw you like that, you were pissed because Mum wouldn't let you start your Dragonwarrior training. So what's wrong now? Keita?"

"No. We found a way to work together." Brannie turned

her head to look at him. "Did you know she was a Protector of the Throne?"

"*Everyone* knows she's a Protector of the Throne. I've told you myself that she was a Protector of the Throne, but you would just giggle and say, 'Go on!' After a while, I stopped trying to convince you." He bumped her shoulder with his own. "Now tell me. What's bothering you? It's not a male, is it?" He frowned in disgust. "Please tell me it's not a human man."

"Gods, give me some credit!"

"But it *is* a male?"

"It's nothing."

"It's not Caswyn, is it?"

Brannie snorted. "No. It's not Caswyn."

"Don't give me that tone. You're the one who's always liked them big and stupid. Just tell me if you need me to beat someone up."

"No." Brannie scratched her head. "Probably not." She let out a breath. "We'll see."

Aidan easily found his baby sister by searching in the rafters of the queen's stables. She was curled into a corner, doing her best to stay as hidden as possible.

"Have you been living up here since I left?" he asked when he'd finally tracked her down.

Orla rubbed her nose with the back of her hand, smudging dirt across her lower cheek. "I like it up here."

Aidan sat down on one of the wood beams across from his sister. "Where's our mother?"

"I don't know. I haven't seen her in—"

"Years?"

"Months. I don't think she's missed me, though."

"I hear there's going to be celebrations tonight in the Main Hall. Are you coming?"

Before Aidan could even finish that question, his sister's face was curling into an expression of utter disgust at even the suggestion.

"That's fine," he said quickly. "You don't have to come."

"Good." She had her legs pulled close. Her arms around her calves, her chin resting on her knees. "I'm glad you're alive."

"Me too."

"Still . . . something's wrong. What is it?"

"Nothing."

"Liar."

"I am."

"Aidan?"

"Hmm?"

"With the war over . . . will we have to go back?"

"You mean to Stone Castle?"

Stone Castle was the home of the House of Foulkes de chuid Fennah, where Aidan's kin had lived for centuries. The castle itself was built from the mountain face. But then the Zealots had launched an attack and Aidan's mother, sisters, and one brother had fled to Garbhán Isle. His father, as far as Aidan knew, was still living among the dwarves deep inside the Western Mountains. And his brother Ainmire, who'd joined with the Zealots, even going so far as to remove his eyes . . .

Well, Aidan wasn't exactly sure, but chances were great he was long dead.

"Don't worry, little sister," Aidan promised, "the queen currently owes me a great debt. So even if our mother wants you to go back with her, I'll make sure you don't leave Garbhán Isle unless you absolutely want to."

His sister's smile was small but brilliant because she used it so rarely.

"Thank you, Aidan."

Aidan reached out and grabbed his sister's hand. "Anything for you."

Gwenvael walked up the castle stairs with his five youngest offspring hanging from him like monkeys. They'd met him out in the courtyard and he knew that no one had told them he'd arrived. They had simply known.

Laughing, the six of them made their way into the hall but stopped when a loaf of bread flew past Gwenvael's head. Although, for once, it hadn't been directed at him.

"Daddy!" Arlais called out when she spotted him. "Thank the gods!" She rushed over to him and said, "Now that you're back, you can get control of this woman."

"You mean your mother?"

"It's not like *I* had a choice in the matter."

"I did," Dagmar said, still sitting at the dining table, working on a stack of papers and attempting to enjoy her breakfast. "And yet I foolishly allowed you to live."

"Oh!" Arlais snarled. "You are a horrid mother!"

"You're right. I am a horrid mother. But now that your aunt Keita is back, you can feel free to head off to the Northlands with her and forget you ever knew me."

"What? You don't think I will?"

"I'm *hoping* you will."

"*Fine! That's what I'll do!*"

"*Well,*" Dagmar suddenly bellowed back, "*there's the door! Don't let it hit you in your snobby ass!*"

Lifting her skirts, Arlais stormed out the double doors. Grabbing her stack of papers, Dagmar stormed from the Main Hall.

"I am so glad to be home!" Gwenvael announced to his giggling daughters.

A few seconds later, Var walked into the Main Hall from the back hallway. But as soon as he saw his father, he stopped, sighed, and stared.

Gwenvael threw his arms wide, a daughter still attached to each one, and cheered, "Son!"

Cringing, Var turned around and followed after his mother.

Gwenvael looked down at his grinning daughters. "So glad."

Talaith was looking at a bolt of cloth for new dresses for her daughters. Dagmar was planning a party and she knew both her girls would want to dance and look beautiful.

Although the thought that *Dagmar* was planning a party shocked Talaith. That Northlander was usually the last one to enjoy a party. But then she'd found out the Eastlander royals were still in town and it suddenly made sense. Dagmar was nothing if not a politician.

"You weren't even around to greet me, little witch!" Talaith heard from behind her.

She turned and gazed up into the violet eyes of the dragon she would love until she was called home to her ancestors. And with complete love and adoration she barked back, "When did I become the royal greeter of Garbhán Isle?"

"You're my mate, woman! You should have been waiting for me with bated breath."

"I have more important things to do than tend to your needs."

"Such as?"

"*Anything* is more important than your needs!"

"Peasant!"

"Arrogant bastard!"

He smiled at her. "I'm glad I'm home."

Talaith ran into his arms.

"I'm glad you're home, too," she whispered against his neck.

Rhiannon was sitting on her throne, bored out of her mind because she was being forced—literally *forced*—to be a gods-damn royal when her Mì-runach suddenly swarmed around her.

"Ooooh!" she giggled. "Activity!"

She watched royal dragons rush out of the chamber or attempt to hide in small caverns. Everyone seemed to be panicking and she had to admit, she was enjoying it all immensely.

Then Bercelak stomped into the chamber. His scales were damaged and his glower was so bad that it would terrorize the bravest dragon.

He came right to her, and even her Mì-runach moved out of the way once they realized it was Bercelak the Great and not some assassin.

Without a word, he put a metal cuff around her neck, took hold of the chain, and dragged Rhiannon from her throne and to their bedchamber.

After watching a laughing Rhiannon the White dragged from her own throne by a half-mad dragon, Xinyi looked at her son and asked, "Why are we here again?"

"Shhhh," Ren said, leaning in close. "Ma. Be nice."

"It was a valid question. I mean, what did I just see?"

"Love."

Xinyi curled her lip in disgust. "Gods, these peasants."

"Rhiannon is a queen."

"Fine. Barbarians then. When are we leaving?"

"After the party."

"Must we go?"

"Yes. Now be nice."

Trying not to act disgusted by dragons who insisted on living in caves when they had gold to buy very nice palaces, Xinyi forced a smile at some Southland lord or other nodding at her in greeting and glanced around the chamber until she saw who was sitting behind her.

Blinking in surprise, Xinyi asked, "What are you lot doing here?"

Her eldest daughter frowned, and her siblings walked away, making obvious sounds of annoyance.

"We've *been* here," Fang reminded her.

"Have you? Doing what?"

"Fighting in the battle with your army. Helping to save the world from a mad god. Remember?"

"No. But that was *very* nice of you." She reached back and patted her daughter's paw with her own. "Aren't you a good . . . uhhhh . . ."

"Daughter?" Fang asked with a sneer.

"I know you're my daughter. I remember! Usually."

After Fang stalked off, Ren whispered to his mother, "You know you're going to hell, don't you, Ma?"

Giggling, Xinyi admitted, "From what I've heard about Annwyl's time there, it's not that bad."

Arlais spun once. "What do you think?"

"Perfect!" Keita crowed about the dress she'd picked out for Arlais. "Gods, I'm good. I don't know why anyone in the universe bothers to question my decision-making."

"Because they're all idiots."

"You are so my favorite. Now"—Keita grabbed a few things off her dresser and headed toward the bedroom door—"come with me. The feast will be starting soon but there is someone you just have to meet."

"Och! It's not another simpering *boy,* is it?"

"As if I'd ever waste your or my time."

Arlais followed her aunt out of the bedroom and down into the Main Hall. The servants had already put the food out and guests were starting to arrive.

Keita stopped at one of the tables and held up a teal-colored eye patch.

Letting out a very long, pained breath, Elina Shestakova looked away from the Riders she was speaking to and said, "Go away, demon female."

"I told you!" Batu the tribal leader said, slamming his fist on the table. "I told all you females that Keita the Viper is demon. But no one listens."

"Because you are penis-haver," Zoya told him.

"Anyway," Keita interrupted, her focus still on Elina, "don't you want to look pretty for my cousin?"

Elina shook her head. "No."

Keita swung the eye patch and said in a singsong voice, "It will look divine on you."

"Why will you not go away?"

"Why do you Rider types always ask me that? All of you should feel blessed by my presence."

Knowing this argument could go on for hours, Arlais snatched the eye patch from Keita, tore off the boring black one that Elina insisted on wearing every day, and quickly tied the new one into place.

"There," Arlais said to the shocked group. "Now wear it, barbarian, and feel honored that my aunt even bothers to waste her time with you and your obvious lack of style!"

With that, Arlais grabbed Keita's hand and dragged her toward the back hallway.

"I so adore you, my dearest niece," Keita laughed.

"Well, she's being so unreasonable! And I am done with unreasonable women!" she yelled as they passed her mother's study, where Dagmar was still working before the feast.

Once they were outside, Keita took the lead and led Arlais down to one of the smaller lakes. As they approached, Arlais could see Ren of the Chosen talking to a man that she didn't recognize.

Arlais stopped, pulling her aunt up short. "This is my mother's plan, isn't it?"

Keita turned, blinking in surprise. "What?"

"You brought me down here to talk to me about going to the Northlands with you and Ragnar and you're hoping Ren's charm will loosen me up. Well, just so you know, it won't. And she just wants to get rid of me because I'm not a sycophant like her needy son!"

"Are you done?" Keita asked.

"Actually, I can go on for quite a while."

"Don't." Keita pulled her along until they reached Ren and the man. But that's when Arlais realized this wasn't a man. It was an elf.

"Arlais, this is Gorlas. An old and very important friend of mine. Gorlas, this is my niece, the one I told you about."

"Princess," the elf greeted. "I've heard many interesting things about you."

"Interesting?" Arlais asked her aunt. "You told him *interesting* things about me? Seriously?"

"You *want* interesting, my dear," Gorlas explained. "Good things and bad things don't really hold my attention. Because everyone is good or bad. But interesting . . . ?"

Arlais crossed her arms over her chest and studied the two dragons and one elf who wanted to talk to her about how interesting she was.

"What is this about?"

"About your future," Keita said.

"Does it require me to live in a cave?"

"No."

"Do I need to read a lot of boring, *boring* books?"

"Just recipe books."

"I don't cook, Auntie. That's what I have a staff for."

Keita smirked. "Neither do I, Niece."

Arlais stared at Keita and the others, confused. But then she remembered the rumors and whispers Arlais had always heard about her favorite aunt. About how Keita the Viper ruthlessly protected her mother's throne with a poisonous skill that few, if any, among their kin had.

"Ohhhh. *Recipe* book." Arlais grinned and winked at her aunt. "That does sound interesting."

"Would you mind talking to me for a little while, Princess?" Gorlas asked.

"Not at all. But my mother . . ."

"I'll take care of her," Keita offered, and they all gazed at her silently, eyes wide.

"I meant," Keita growled out between clenched teeth, "I'll keep her busy."

"Ohhhhhhh," they all said together.

"Rude!" Keita sniped, heading back to the castle. "Just rude!"

Izzy and Rhi were nearly done putting flowers in Brannie's hair as she sat in her chair and seethed.

"I'm not going," she said again.

"You are going," Izzy replied. "Or I will drag you there myself."

"I don't want to go."

"You're being unreasonable!"

"I am not!"

"He loves you," Rhi said. "What's wrong with that?"

"Everything! And shut up."

Rhi gasped. "But I'm the nice one."

"She's right," Talwyn said from her spot stretched out on the bed. "I'd be fine with you being unhappy."

Talan sat on the floor, his back against the bed's footboard and a book in his lap. "And I could go either way."

"I hate all of you."

"No, you don't." Izzy pulled Brannie out of the chair and looked her over. "Beautiful. Now go tell poor Aidan you love him, too."

"I will not. He tricked me."

"Aidan doesn't trick anybody. He may have smooth-talked you into dragon sex but that would be about it."

"I thought you were on my side!"

"Of course I'm on your side, idiot. And I want you to be happy. Aidan makes you happy."

"I can be happy without him."

"But why would you want to be?"

Surprised that the question came from Talan, they all looked at him.

"I mean, wouldn't you want to be with someone who makes you happy?" he went on. "Why would anyone want to be with someone who doesn't make them happy?" He blinked up at Brannie. "Do *you* want to be with someone who doesn't—"

"Oh, shut up!" Brannie stormed out of the room, slamming the door behind her.

"Gods," Talwyn said with a shake of her head. "Is it me or does love sound *miserable?*"

"It's you," Izzy replied.

Brannie was halfway down the stairs when Aidan suddenly walked up, blocking her way.

She tried to step around him, but he stepped with her. She went the other way, and so did he.

"You going to talk to me now?" he asked.

"No."

Brannie stepped again and so did Aidan.

"Are you going to move?" she asked.

"Are you going to talk to me?"

Brannie was seconds from exploding at Aidan when Celyn went by them. Her brother glanced at them as he passed, then he looked a little harder, his eyes narrowing on Aidan before he was all the way down the stairs and joining the others in the Main Hall, where the feast had already started.

That's when Brannie smiled.

Aidan saw that smile and was about to make a run for it when Brannie took his hand.

"Come with me," she purred, leading him to the hall.

Musicians began to play and Gwenvael and Keita were, as always, the first to start dancing, brother and sister swinging each other around the floor.

Brannie led Aidan into the middle of the room and faced him.

He knew Brannie loved to dance and maybe if they danced, she'd give him a chance. That was all he wanted. Just a chance.

Still smiling, she raised her hands to his face, cupping his jaw in her hands. Then she leaned in and kissed him. Right there in front of everybody.

When she pulled back, she didn't smile . . . she leered.

"Good luck," she said before walking across the hall and out the front doors.

Aidan looked after her, wondering what she was talking about. And, as he watched, Celyn suddenly stood in front of him . . . staring. Then Addolgar. Then Rhys the Hammer. Then Fearghus. Briec. Even Éibhear, his best friend.

Then Gwenvael, of all dragons, stopped dancing and came over, crossing his arms over his chest and glowering at Aidan.

Gwenvael. The one whose entire family referred to him as Gwenvael the Whore.

And then . . . there it was. There *he* was.

Bercelak the Great, glaring down at Aidan like an angry mountain.

But before the angriest dragon Aidan had ever known could rip out his throat, Bram the Merciful stepped in front of all of them and roared, "*What have you done to my baby?*"

Izzy paced in front of Brannie, ranting. "That was, by far, the *meanest* thing you've ever done!"

"If he wants me, he'll have to fight for me."

"That's not a fight. That's a slaughter!"

"Are you saying I'm not worth dying for?"

"Branwen, *no one* is worth that!"

Branwen looked away from her best friend. "I don't want to discuss it anymore."

"Oh, we're discussing."

"Oh, no, we're not."

"Yes. We are."

"No. We're not."

"You go in there and fix this, Branwen. Right *now*."

"Nope."

They both growled and looked away from each other.

Standing there, seething, and trying not to worry about crying at Aidan's funeral procession, Brannie noticed Caswyn coming across the courtyard leading a big war horse by his reins.

Brannie's mouth dropped open and, needing an outlet for her panic and anger, she ran down the steps and over to him.

"If you eat him—" she began.

Caswyn immediately raised his hands, palms out, like he was trying to ward her off.

"It's not for me! It's not for me!"

"No one is eating him!" she snapped, yanking the reins from him and pulling the horse toward her.

"No, no. He's not for eating. He's for you. I bought him for you."

"What?"

"Sam the horse dealer was in town. Aidan says that most of the Cadwaladrs get their horses from him."

"He's expensive."

"I have some gold," he said, looking a bit insulted. "Anyway, I picked another one, but Aidan said you'd like this one. Even though he's cranky and scarred and considering how many times he's bitten me in the back of the head . . . mean, but Aidan said this was more your type of horse. He's strong, I know that. And if you bond with him, Sam says he'll be loyal to you to the end. And I promise not to eat him if he gets killed in battle." He glanced off. "That will *not* happen again, I can assure you."

Caswyn shrugged. "Anyway, this is just a little something to say I'm sorry about . . . Puddles."

"But you didn't think you did anything wrong."

"No, but . . . I want to stay friends with you, and Aidan said this would be a good way to start."

"Aidan just came up to you and—"

"No. I went to him. I was thinking armor or a new weapon. You know, something like that. But he said, 'You ate her horse. Get her a bloody horse.' Once he said it, it made sense. And he knew just the kind of horse to get you . . . which is apparently big and mean."

"Oh, gods!" Brannie gasped. "I've killed him."

Caswyn's eyes grew wide. "*What?*"

Brannie didn't answer; she just ran back into the hall, but her male kin and Aidan were gone.

Imagining them burying the poor bastard alive in a grave, Brannie stood in the middle of the floor, turning in circles, looking for any sign.

That's when she caught sight of her mother. With a disapproving shake of her head, Ghleanna jerked her thumb toward the back hallway and Brannie took off running.

She bolted through the back door but slid to a stop when she saw Aidan standing by her father's book tower, gazing up at the sky.

Worried he was internally bleeding and would drop dead at any second, she charged over to him, stopping right in front of him.

"I'm so sorry. I'm so sorry. I'm so sorry."

He peered at her. "You tried to get me killed."

She opened her mouth to absolutely deny it but all that came out was, "Sort of."

"Seems a little harsh for telling you I love you."

"Izzy says it was the meanest thing I've ever done."

"If it were anyone else . . . it would have been."

Brannie took a step back. "What does that mean?" She looked him over. "And why aren't you destroyed? You should be lying in a pool of your own sick right now."

"Branwen, don't you know me yet? I deal with unreasonable dragons all day, *every* day."

"So?"

"So your kin wasn't exactly a challenge. The only one I really had to worry about was your father. And by the gods was he pissed."

"He was?"

"You're his baby. He adores you like the suns."

"So what did you say?"

"That I loved you and I was willing to do anything to

make you happy and make you my mate." Aidan shrugged. "That was all he needed to hear."

Brannie fought hard not to smile. Not ready to give in just yet.

"And the rest of them?"

"I just gave them some gold."

"*What?*"

Aidan laughed. "I'm kidding. Your father reasoned with them and they went off with the Riders to get more of that vile ale they insist on burying."

"My father was able to reason with Uncle Bercelak?"

"Oh, gods no. He actually growled at him. It was rather uncomfortable. But then Keita stepped in."

"And said?"

"Who else would love such a large-boned She-dragon?"

"That cow! And stop laughing!"

Aidan slipped his arm around Brannie's waist and pulled her in close. "Don't be mad at her. She was trying to help."

"By insulting me?"

"I know it's hard to believe but yes. I mean, I'm still alive, aren't I?"

"Excellent point." She wrapped her arms around his shoulders. "I'm *really* sorry. I was just—"

"Panicking?"

"Aye."

"You're not used to panicking."

"Oh, no. I panic all the time. Just not in battle . . . or with males." She took a deep breath and admitted, "But I've never been in love before, so . . . that could have something to do with it."

Aidan nodded but he made sure not to smile. He didn't want her to think he was laughing at her. He wasn't.

He was ecstatic. Branwen the Awful loved him. She loved him.

"You're smiling," she told him.

"Sorry. Didn't mean to."

"It's all right. I'm over the hard part. But you know it's not going to be easy for you."

"As long as you don't hit me with any more fireballs—"

"No, no. I mean . . . it won't be easy. My father's easy, of course, but the rest of my kin . . . are . . . uh . . . they're . . . uh . . ."

Brannie was staring at something over Aidan's shoulder so, without letting her go, he looked and his mouth dropped open.

Together they watched Annwyl the Bloody ride by on the back of one of the demon animals that had appeared at their last battle.

"Isn't that one of those corpse-eater things that she was supposed to send back to hell?" Aidan asked.

"Uh . . . yeah. The baby, I think. Oh . . . and look . . . there's the mother."

"Should we tell Fearghus?"

Brannie shook her head. "No. I'm sure he'll find out . . . when they eat something appalling . . . and dead."

Annwyl smiled and waved at them and they both waved back.

As they did, Brannie asked, "Are you sure about this?"

"Are you kidding? So much more interesting than my own kin."

Brannie rested her head on his shoulder and sighed out, "Well, if you're sure."

Not wanting to push his luck, Aidan kept quiet, deciding to just enjoy the wonder of this amazing night.

Yet he still wasn't surprised when Brannie suddenly barked, "Oh, shut up!"

Aidan laughed. "But I didn't say anything!"

402   *G.A. Aiken*

* * *

Rhiannon and Bercelak walked down a private, human-sized corridor of Devenallt Mountain. Moving slow, taking her time, Rhiannon rested her head against Bercelak's shoulder and held his hand.

"Lovely night," she said.

"Too many royals. And Gwenvael kept trying to hug me."

Rhiannon chuckled and moved aside to allow a robed She-dragon carrying several books to pass as they stepped into an even tighter passageway.

The pair had just gone past another entrance to one of the libraries they had inside the mountain when Rhiannon stopped walking, pulling Bercelak up short.

He looked down at her, frowning in concern when she suddenly shuddered. Rhiannon recognized the energy coming from that other female. "You all right, luv?"

Rhiannon released Bercelak's hand and quickly walked back to the passageway turn. She could see the robed She-dragon still striding along in no particular rush.

"Brigida?" Rhiannon called out and the She-dragon stopped and, slowly, turned to look back at them.

Rhiannon let out a sharp gasp and Bercelak's "Holy shit," echoed through the chamber.

The now-young Brigida grinned at them but before Rhiannon could stop her, she opened a doorway and was gone.

"I don't understand," Bercelak blurted out. "How could she . . . how did she . . . ?"

"Do you know the worst part of what that treacherous, psychotic bitch has done?" Rhiannon asked her mate, her hands curling into fists, her entire body shaking with barely contained rage. "That I now have to go back and tell that boy he was *right!*"

What had she been thinking? Using the "Ride of the Valkyries" as a ringtone? Because that shit waking a person up at six in the morning was just cruel. Really cruel.

And, as always, she'd done it to herself.

Charlie Taylor-MacKilligan slapped her hand against the end table next to the bed, blindly searching for her damn phone. When she touched it, she was relieved. She had no plan to actually get out of bed anytime soon. Not as hungover as she currently was. But she really wanted that damn ringtone to stop.

Somehow, without even lifting her head from the pillow she had her face buried in, or opening her eyes, Charlie managed to touch the right thing on her phone screen so that she actually answered it.

"What?" she growled.

"Get out," was the reply. "Get out now."

Hangover forgotten, Charlie was halfway across the room when they kicked the door open. She turned and ran toward the open sliding glass doors that led to the balcony. She'd just made it outside when something hot rammed into her shoulder, tearing past flesh and muscle and burrowing into bone. The power of it sent her flipping headfirst over the railing.

"What do you think?" the jackal shifter asked.

Sitting in a club chair in his Milan, Italy, hotel suite, Berg Dunn gazed at the man holding up a black jacket.

"What do I think about what?" Berg asked.

"The jacket. For my show tonight."

Berg shrugged. "I don't know."

"You must have an opinion."

"I don't. I happily have no opinion on what a grown man who is not me should wear."

The jackal sighed. "You're useless."

"I have one job. Keeping your crazed fans from tracking you down and stripping the flesh from your bones. That's it. That's all I'm supposed to do. I, at no time, said that I would ever help you with your fashion sense."

Rolling his eyes, the jackal laid the jacket on the bed and then stared at it. Like he expected it to tell him something. To actually speak to him.

Berg wanted to complain about this ridiculous job, but how could he when it was the best one he'd had in years? Following a very rich, very polite jackal around so that he could play piano for screaming fans in foreign countries was the coolest gig ever.

First class everything. Jets. Food. Women. Not that Berg took advantage of the women thing too often. He knew most were just trying to use him to get to Cooper Jean-Louis Parker. Coop was the one out there every night, banging away at those Steinway pianos, doing things with his fingers that even Berg found fascinating, and wooing all those lovely females with his handsome jackal looks.

Berg was just the guy to get through so they could get to the musical genius. And, unlike some of his friends, being used by beautiful women wasn't one of his favorite things.

It was a tolerable thing, but not his favorite.

"I can't decide," the jackal finally admitted.

"I know how hard it is to pick between one black jacket and *another* black jacket. Which will your black turtleneck go with?"

"It's not just *another* black jacket, peasant. It's the difference between pure black and charcoal black."

"We have a train to catch," Berg reminded Coop. "So could you speed this—"

Both shifters jumped, their gazes locked on the balcony outside the room, visible through doors open to let the fresh morning air in.

Another crazed female fan trying to make her way into Coop's room? Some of these women, all of them full-humans, were willing to try any type of craziness for just a *chance* at ending up in the "maestro's" bed.

With a sigh, Berg pushed himself out of the club chair and headed across the large room toward the sliding glass doors. It looked like he'd have to break another poor woman's heart.

But he stopped when he saw her. A brown-skinned woman, completely naked. Which, in and of itself, was not unusual. The women who tried to sneak into Coop's room—no matter the country they might be in—were often naked.

What stopped Berg in his tracks was that *this* woman had blood coming from her shoulder. The blood from a gun wound.

Berg motioned Coop back. "Get in the bathroom," he ordered.

"Oh, come on. I want to see what's—"

"I don't care what you want. Get in the—"

The men stopped arguing when they saw him. A man in black military tactical wear, armed with a rifle, handgun,

and several blades. He zipped down a line and landed on the
railing of their balcony.

Berg placed his hand on the gun holstered at his side and
stepped in front of Coop.

"Get in the bathroom, Coop," he ordered, his voice low.

"We have to help her."

"Do what I tell you and I will."

The man in black dropped onto the balcony and grabbed
the unconscious woman by her arm, rolling her limp body
over.

"Now, Coop. Go."

Berg moved forward with his weapon drawn from its
holster. The man pulled his sidearm and pressed the barrel
against the woman's head.

Berg aimed his .45 and barked, "Hey!"

The man looked up, bringing his gun with him. Gazes
locked, fingers resting on triggers. Each man sizing the
other up. And that was when the woman moved. Fast. So
fast, Berg knew she wasn't completely human, which immediately changed everything.

The woman grabbed her attacker's gun hand by the wrist
and held it to the side so he couldn't finish the job on her.
She used her free hand to pummel the man's face repeatedly.

Blood poured down his lips from his shattered nose; his
eyes now dazed.

Still holding the man's wrist, she got to her feet.

She was tall. Maybe five-ten or five-eleven. With broad,
powerful shoulders and arms and especially legs. Like a
much-too-tall gymnast.

She gripped her attacker by the throat with one hand and,
without much effort, lifted him up and over the balcony railing. She released him then and unleashed the biggest claws
Berg had ever seen from her right hand.

Turning away from the man, she swiped at the zip line

that held him aloft and Berg cringed a little at the man's desperate screams as he fell to the ground below.

That's when she saw Berg. Her claws—coming from surprisingly small hands—were still unleashed. Her gaze narrowed on him and her shoulders hunched just a bit. She was readying herself for an attack. To kill the man who could out her as a shifter, he guessed. Not having had time to process that he was one, too. Plus, he had a gun, which wouldn't help his cause any.

"It's okay," Berg said quickly, re-holstering his weapon. "It's okay. I'm not going to hurt you."

"Yeah," Coop said from behind him. "We just want to help."

Berg let out a frustrated breath. "I thought I told you to get into the bathroom."

"I wanted to see what's going on."

Coop moved to Berg's side. "We're shifters, too," he said, using that goddamn charming smile. Like this was the time for any of that!

But this one rolled her eyes in silent exasperation and came fully into the room. She walked right by Berg and Coop and to the bedroom door.

"Wait," Berg called out. When she turned to face him, one brow raised in question, he reminded her, "You're naked."

He went to his already packed travel bag and pulled out a black T-shirt.

"Here," he said, handing it to her.

She pulled the shirt on and he saw that he'd given her one of his favorite band shirts from a Fishbone concert he'd seen years ago with his parents and siblings.

"Your shoulder," Berg prompted, deciding not to obsess over the shirt. Especially when she looked so cute in it.

She shook her head at his prompt and again started toward the door. But a crash from the suite living room had

Berg grabbing the woman's arm with one hand and shoving Coop across the bedroom and into the bathroom with the other.

Berg faced the intruder, pulling the woman in behind his body.

Two gunshots hit Berg in the lower chest—the man had pulled the trigger without actually seeing all of Berg, but expecting a more normal-sized human.

Which meant af few things to Berg. That he was dealing with a full-human. An expertly trained full-human. An ex-soldier probably.

An ex-soldier with a kill order.

Because if he was trying to kidnap the woman, he'd make damn sure he knew who or what was on the other end before he pulled that trigger. But he didn't know. He didn't check because he didn't care. Everyone in the room had to die.

And knowing that—*understanding* that—did nothing but piss Berg off.

Who just ran around trying to kill a naked, unarmed woman? his analytical side wanted to know.

The grizzly side of him, though, didn't care about all that. All it knew was that it had been shot. And shooting a grizzly but not killing it immediately . . . always an exceptionally bad move.

The snarl snaked out of Berg's throat and the muscles between his shoulders grew into a healthy grizzly hump. He barely managed to keep from shifting completely, but his grizzly bear rage exploded and his roar rattled the windows. The bathroom door behind him slammed shut, the jackal having the sense to *now* go into hiding.

The intruder quickly backed up, knowing something wasn't right, but not fully understanding, which was why he didn't run.

He should have run.

With a step, Berg was right in front of him, grabbing the gun from his hand and spinning the man around so that he had him by the throat. He did this because two more men in tactical gear were coming into the suite from the front door.

Using the man's weapon, Berg shot each man twice in the chest. They both had on body armor so he wasn't worried he'd killed them.

With both attackers down, Berg re-focused on the man he held captive. He spun him around because he wanted to ask him a few questions about what the hell was going on. He was calmer now. He could be rational.

But when the man again faced him, Berg felt a little twinge in his side. He slowly looked down . . . and found a combat blade sticking out.

First he'd been shot. Now stabbed.

His grizzly rage soared once again, and as the intruder— quickly recognizing his error—attempted to fight his way out of Berg's grasp, desperately begging for his life, Berg grabbed either side of his attacker's face and squeezed with both hands . . . until the man's head popped like a zit.

It was the blood and bone hitting him in the face that snapped Berg back into the moment, and he gazed down at his brain-covered hands.

"Oh, shit," he muttered. "Shit, shit, shit."

The other intruders, ignoring the pain from the shots, scrambled up and out of the suite. As far away from Berg as they could get.

Someone touched his arm and he half-turned to see the woman. She raised her hands and rewarded him with a soft smile.